THE SOCIALITE'S GUIDE TO DEATH AND DATING

ALSO AVAILABLE BY S. K. GOLDEN

The Pinnacle Hotel Mysteries

The Socialite's Guide to Murder

THE SOCIALITE'S GUIDE TO DEATH AND DATING

A PINNACLE HOTEL MYSTERY

S. K. Golden

CROOKED LANE

NEW YORK

Published in the United States by Crooked Lane Books, an imprint of The Quick Brown Fox & Company LLC.

Crooked Lane Books and its logo are trademarks of The Quick Brown Fox & Company LLC.

Library of Congress Catalog-in-Publication data available upon request.

ISBN (hardcover): 978-1-63910-485-7
ISBN (ebook): 978-1-63910-486-4

Cover illustration by Kashira Sarode
Cover typography by Jerry Todd

Printed in the United States.

www.crookedlanebooks.com

Crooked Lane Books
34 West 27th St., 10th Floor
New York, NY 10001

First Edition: October 2023

10 9 8 7 6 5 4 3 2 1

To my children: Samuel, Avery, Eloise,
Madeline, and Margaret.

There are just so many of you. Maybe one day
I'll have enough books that you'll each get your
own. But for now, you'll have to share this one.

CHAPTER 1

It isn't everyday a young woman wearing Little Red Riding Hood's cloak saunters into a busy kitchen, so why did none of the chefs stop what they were doing and look at me? With a huff, I slid off my hood and whistled.

Chef Marco, without looking away from the stove, managed to wag his massive eyebrows at me anyway. "No," he said.

"What do you mean, *no*? Please!" I stuck out my bottom lip. Nothing. "I'm sorry that more guests than we expected are showing up, but isn't that a good thing?"

Chef Marco did not look my way, but his tall white hat tilted to the side.

I batted my eyelashes, my fingers twisting around the hem of my red cloak. "It means more money for the mayor's campaign, after all. And everyone is so enjoying your food because you're simply the best chef in all of New York! Please?"

He picked up a pan only to drop it down on the same burner. "You told me. You said—you *promised*—Mr. Rockefeller would be here! And yet, he is not here."

"Right." I nodded. "Sure. We are all very disappointed that he's not here. But. Okay? But! The mayor is here. Hmm? The mayor? He's pretty good too."

"He has to be here," Marco said. "It's *his* fundraiser. What about your father? Will he at least be here?"

I answered, "He is supposed to be," because that was true. Did I know where Daddy was currently? No. But did I ever? Also no.

Daddy was the owner of the Pinnacle Hotel. But that didn't mean he stayed here often. He visited a few times a year, popped in to play golf with Manhattan politicians and New York City businessmen, and then left just as quickly.

"Why this?" Chef Marco waved a knife at my torso. "Why the red? What are you wearing?"

I looked down at my outfit. A white vest and black matador pants, covered by an exquisite red cloak that latched with a silver leaf brooch at the base of my throat. "It's a fancy dress party, Chef Marco. I'm Little Red Riding Hood!" I gave him a spin. "What do you think?"

"I think you're too skinny," he snapped. "I will—*fine*—I will make the extra plates. But you must promise to eat one yourself."

With a grin, I replied, "Promise. Thank you ever so."

He raised his knife-wielding hand up in the air. "Get out of here. Go! I have work to do!"

Skipping, I left the kitchen, heading for the service door that led to the Silver Room. I was working. Working meant taking the route every other employee took. Did I miss the descent from the top of the grand staircase into the party? Yes. A lot. But this was good too. Less glamorous, and no one was bothering to take a picture of me, but I found myself wishing I had a camera.

Mac and Poppy were in the hallway, fighting over a wolf head.

"It won't stay on like that," Poppy whisper-yelled.

"It was choking me!" Mac whisper-yelled back. "Is that what you want? Are you trying to kill me?"

"Oh, you are so dramatic! Just put on your costume like an adult!"

My giggling pulled the siblings apart.

Mac, frowning, snatched the wolf head out of Poppy's hands. She gasped. I laughed again.

"That's my project, mind you!" Poppy smacked her brother in the arm. "I need it back. I have to turn it in for a grade at my art school so I can graduate and become successful and move out of your tiny little apartment that smells like wet pants."

"You're welcome to move out at any time," Mac said. "Really. I'll help you pack." He smiled at me. "It doesn't really smell like wet pants, Ev. Cross my heart. You'll love it."

Mac was around my height—meaning, tall—with the broad shoulders, muscled arms, and tanned skin of someone who had spent a lot of time hauling luggage outside until a few weeks ago. Now, he was both my assistant and steady beau, and he'd helped me plan and organize this Halloween-themed fundraiser for the mayor's reelection campaign. His thick brown hair was slicked back and out of his soft gray eyes. Stubble covered his strong, square jaw and made the pronounced dip of his upper lip even more noticeable. I wondered if the butterflies that filled my stomach at the sight of him would ever go away. Or if I even wanted them to. He wore a blue sweater over a black, collared shirt, his dark-wash jeans rolled at the ankles to show off his new shoes, perfectly polished. He set the wolf head carefully on the top of his head, leaving the part that clipped under his chin undone.

We'd been planning for weeks for me to visit his apartment, but I still hadn't quite worked up the nerve. It was all the way in Yonkers, and really he could just as easily stay with me as I could with him.

Except it wasn't the same thing at all, and I knew that and I was working on it. I was!

Poppy fixed the silver leaf broach around my neck and straightened out the fabric of my red cloak. She gave a nod when she was satisfied with my looks. "I traded with Florence for the turndown service on the top floor so I could take Presley out."

"Oh, thank you ever so," I said. "That's so thoughtful." Presley is my perfect little Pomeranian mix who is normally with me everywhere I go, but I had to leave him in my penthouse suite for the evening since I was working.

"She ain't doing it to be thoughtful," Mac said. "It's all for tips."

She stuck her tongue out. "Not only tips! It's for cuddle time with Presley too. Be careful with my project, Malcolm! I'll see you later, and don't be confused—that's a threat! "

Mac offered me his arm, and I took it. "Did you get Marco settled down?"

"As settled as I could."

He pushed open the door, and we snuck inside the busy Silver Room. Adults in costumes ranging from a Night-Out-at-the-Opera to vampires to a white sheet with holes cut out for eyes filled the space and vied for time at the mayor's ear. The mayor was dressed like a politician and was pulling off the too-tight-tie look with practiced ease.

"Marco was disappointed Rockefeller didn't make it," I said.

The tables were set with large but respectable floral arrangements—silver, of course, this being the Silver Room after all. A dance floor was open before a small, raised stage that held a grand piano and a podium. Everything was lit by the shimmering chandeliers running down the middle of the high vaulted ceiling.

I hopped up on my tiptoes, but with all the different outfits it was impossible to tell for certain if he was here.

Mac kissed my cheek, the snout of the papier mâché wolf head wrinkling my hood. "Sorry, Ev," he said. "No word from your old man yet."

Sighing, I nodded. I don't know why I bothered looking.

"I'm gonna go in the kitchen and help with expediting." Mac squeezed my hand. "Holler if you need me."

I recognized my new personal care physician, Dr. Smith, among the guests. He was easy to spot as he was dressed like a doctor, in a white jacket with a stethoscope around his neck. At least his ensemble hid his ugly tie, though his unsightly thick-soled shoes were easy to see. He'd been living at the Pinnacle for the last month and a half, and I was sure to invite him, but I was never sure he'd show up.

Introverted was a nice way of describing Dr. Smith.

Crotchety was more accurate.

He was speaking with a couple. The woman had luscious, dark curly hair and stylish red wing-tipped glasses, and was heavily pregnant. Her costume was nothing extraordinary: simple, gauze angel wings strapped over her bare, tawny shoulders. The man at her side had to be twenty years her senior. He wore an expensive suit tailored to his large form. His salt-and-pepper hair was trimmed short. And his gold Rolex watch on his thick, hairy wrist glinted in the light when he exchanged an empty glass for a full one, his fair cheeks already red from the wine.

He wasn't wearing a costume. Party pooper.

"Hello, Dr. Smith," I greeted, extending a hand. "Are you having a good time?"

He shook it, though he frowned when we touched. "Miss Murphy. Have you met Judge Baker? And his lovely wife, Elena."

"Oh!" I shook the judge's hand but brought Elena into a quick hug, kissing her on each cheek. "I didn't recognize you, Judge Baker." I hadn't seen him since his first wife died some years ago, and his hair had been more pepper than salt back then. "How are you doing? How are your boys?"

Judge Baker's sons from his first marriage were both in college. Harvard, to be exact, and could not be much younger than the second wife at his side now.

"They're both doing well," Judge Baker said. "Gordon is at the top of his class. On track to be valedictorian."

I grinned. "Takes after his father, does he?"

He bowed his head. "And your father? How is he?"

"Daddy is excellent, thank you ever so. And how are you, Mrs. Baker? You're positively glowing!"

She held her stomach with both hands, her massive diamond ring sparkling. "I'm so ready to have this little one here with us."

Dr. Smith snorted. "Should be shortly."

"From your lips to God's ears," she said, rubbing her stomach. She grimaced. "It's . . . very uncomfortable, Dr. Smith."

"Hmm. Are you in pain, Mrs. Baker?"

She swallowed hard. "A little. Every few minutes. Not so bad that I think the baby is coming, but enough that I . . ." She closed her dark eyes. "I'm sorry. I don't want to be a bother."

"It's not a bother at all," Judge Baker said. "You made it out here. You shook hands. Go home and get some rest." He kissed her temple. "If anything interesting happens, I'll tell you all about it when I get home."

I reached for the pendant of Saint Anthony I wore as a necklace, its familiar, cold metal soothing. The last thing I was fit to handle was a woman giving birth in the middle of the Silver Room. The *mayor* was here! "Mrs. Baker, you're much more important than this stuffy party. Please excuse me for saying that—I am the one who planned it. If you're at all uncomfortable, I can call a car service for you."

She smiled at me, but her lashes were wet. "You don't mind? That would be most appreciated."

I clapped my hands. "It's settled then. I'll go and call for it myself."

Dr. Smith adjusted his ugly tie. He always wore ugly ties. It was almost as if he challenged himself every day to find the ugliest tie imaginable. This one was brown, like the inside of a used diaper, and covered in what looked to be liberal use of mustard. I wished he'd button up his white coat all the way so I wouldn't have to witness it. "I'll go with you, Mrs. Baker. I can give you an exam in the comfort of your home and make sure it's the usual late trimester discomfort."

"You're a good friend, Doc," Judge Baker said, offering the doctor his hand. "Thanks."

Dr. Smith shook it, the line between his eyebrows increasing drastically. "Nothing to it. Nothing at all."

"If you want to follow me," I said, "there's a back door to the kitchens. That way you won't have to climb up the steps."

"Wonderful. Thank you."

Elena Baker kissed her husband goodbye and then took Dr. Smith's elbow. I led the two of them through the crowded party, to the kitchen, and into the lobby. I waved down Mr. Burrows and told him to order a car, post haste, and put it on my account. Mr. Burrows pushed up his thick glasses with the back of his hand, stuttered some sort of reply, and ran out from behind the mail desk to get the car ordered. I did not see what Poppy saw in him, that much I was sure, but the two of them had been going steady for a while now, and it didn't seem like she was in a hurry to end it.

Once the doctor and Mrs. Baker were on their way, I turned back toward the kitchens, but I never made it.

Mac swept me up in his arms and tugged me into a dark corner of the hallway. His wolf head was suspiciously missing.

I giggled. "What are you doing?"

"Nothing yet." Then he kissed me. "Now I'm gonna convince you to ditch this place."

"What?"

He set me on my feet. "Come home with me."

"I am home."

"To my home." Mac took my face in his hands and kissed my forehead. "Let's go to Yonkers. Come on. Let's do it. I'll be with you the whole way."

"But—" I pulled away from him to search his expression, to look for teasing. He was serious! "But I'm working!"

He shrugged a shoulder. "You planned the party. Party's almost over. Come on. Let's sneak away. I know you want to go, Evelyn. You said you would do it before the year is out."

"Yes. But it's only October!"

He kissed me again, wrapping his arms around my waist and holding me close. When he let me go, I was breathless.

"I promised Chef Marco I would eat," I tried. It hadn't been a *pinkie* promise, and everyone knows the only promise you can't break is a pinkie promise, but Mac didn't need all the details.

"I've got food in the refrigerator," he said.

"Where is your hat?"

"It's not a hat." Mac reached for the brooch around my neck, unclipping it and letting the hood fall on the floor. He picked it up, the red fabric draped over his forearms. "It's a travesty, that's what it is. Come on. What do you say?" He held out a hand. "Let's have an adventure. A perfectly safe adventure," he added.

Maybe he was right. Daddy hadn't made it and probably wouldn't make it. I'd gotten Chef Marco to make all the extra plates. The mayor had already given his speech. What was there left for me to do?

"I guess I . . ." I took his hand. "Yes. Okay. Let's do it."

CHAPTER 2

"Oh, I don't know, Mac," I said, pulse thrumming in my veins for reasons beyond being outside the Pinnacle's walls. We were still in its shadow, and he kept me boxed inside it, his strong, warm hands on my waist. He'd dropped my cloak off at the mail desk with a befuddled Mr. Burrows and zero explanation. "What about Presley?"

The air felt crisp, and even though it was dark outside, leaves shone brightly in yellows, oranges, and reds, illuminated by street lamps. Menacing smiles were carved into the pumpkins in the window of the Pinnacle's candy shop. I waved goodbye as the candles inside their carcasses flickered.

"We'll call the front desk. Chuck is working all night with Poppy. They'll take care of the ankle biter."

I swatted his chest, but my fingers got distracted by the soft, bluish-gray fabric of his sweater. The same color as his eyes. Toying my bottom lip between my teeth, I looked up at him under my lashes. "And you won't stay with me here, lover?"

He groaned and pressed his forehead to mine. Mac took a deep breath, and I rather got the impression he was breathing me in. He kissed me softly, lips barely parting. And then he pulled back much too quick, a wet kiss on my forehead my only consolation prize.

"Nope! Come on, Ev. You've got a world to conquer. And it starts with Yonkers."

With his fingers laced through mine, Mac pulled me alongside him. His long legs meant long strides, but I was close to his height and was practically born in heels, so keeping up with him wasn't difficult. He grinned down at me and wrapped an arm around my back, his hand finding purchase on my waist again. "I'm chuffed. Wish I'd picked up the flat a bit and ran for some groceries, but it'll be hunky-dory with the lights off, Ev." He winked and my face flushed.

"Malcolm," I whispered, "I haven't got a change of clothes!"

"Why would you need clothes?"

I shot him an exasperated look under the streetlights. "Where are we going, anyway? Surely you don't mean to walk to Yonkers."

"Of course not." He chuckled. "The Pinnacle's parking garage is around the corner. I'm going to drive your Rolls. Make up for that—you know—hospital business a few weeks ago."

I did know. His first time driving my Rolls-Royce had landed us both in the hospital, though it was hardly his fault. "But what about my makeup? Or a toothbrush?"

"Evie, baby." He stopped walking long enough to pull me into another heart-stopping kiss. "I promise. You won't be thinking about brushing your teeth once we make it to my apartment." He held my hand in his and placed it over his heart. I was surprised to find I could feel it pounding beneath my palm. At this point in our relationship, having been a steady item for a month—six weeks, to be exact, not that I'm counting every day that goes by with a little heart in my calendar—I worried he'd grow bored of me. Used to me. But the prospect of me in his apartment had him as flustered as my leaving the Pinnacle had me.

But I'd do anything for Mac.

Maybe he felt the same, though the very idea was foreign. I wasn't the sort of person that anyone stuck around long enough to feel that way about.

I nodded. "All right. Let's go get the Rolls." A wicked grin tugged at my mouth. "I trust you not to crash it for a second time."

He huffed, a smile on his face, nonetheless. "Come on then. No more stalling. The garage is after this left."

I've lived in the Pinnacle all my life. I used to come and go often, nowadays not as much. But even in my childhood, traveling to and from with Mom, or later with Nanny, I'd never been inside the garage. I was always dropped off and picked up on the steps of the hotel itself.

It was seven floors, not counting the empty roof, with no walls, only cars lined up to the edge of each floor. I stopped and stared at it, at the neon sign that spelled out "PARKING" in bright red letters along its side, at the metal stairs that curved around each floor.

"We aren't walking up those things, are we?" I asked Mac, unable to keep the shake out of my voice and hands. "They're likely to crumble in a good gust of wind!"

He made a rude noise with his lips and tongue. "We'll use the ramps inside," he said. "But those things aren't going anywhere. You think your dad wants a lawsuit from employees on his hands?"

My attention was stuck on the old, rickety staircase. "I suppose," I said. Daddy did hate to be tied up in court. But better safe than sorry. "Ramps inside, I think. But Mac—I don't have the keys!"

"No, the valet here has them." He smiled at me like I was a lost child. I didn't like it one bit and rolled back my shoulders so I might stand at my full height and remind him how grown I was. "Come on." He kissed my cheek. "We're almost there. Don't quit on me now."

He tugged me by the hand to the small booth outside the parking garage's entrance, shaded by a large umbrella striped in white and blue. Cars trickled in and out of the entrance, not quite a steady stream, but enough to make me wary of being run over. A Pinnacle employee, wearing the same uniform all the bellhops and lift boys wore—long sleeves, long slacks, green with gold buttons on the jacket, unshined black shoes—watched us before his eyes lit with recognition. "Cooper!" He greeted. "Miss Murphy! You two eloping?"

My cheeks burned and my heart skipped a beat. It was embarrassing to have a stranger describe your most precious dream out loud like that in front of your face. But I smiled at him all the same and hoped he didn't realize how well he knew me when I didn't even know his name.

"Ah, not quite," Mac said. "Taking the missus to Yonkers for a nightcap. You got the keys?"

Mrs. Evelyn Elizabeth Grace Cooper had a certain ring to it. Would Mac buy me a ring on his own, or would I be able to pick it out and help pay for it? There was always Mom's wedding ring, tucked away in a safe at the bank. Perhaps Daddy would let me use that when Mac and I exchanged our vows in front of a priest?

Mac would have to convert. Or we could find a priest who might look the other way if there was a hefty donation that followed the ceremony.

"Silver Cloud Rolls-Royce," the valet said, tossing Mac the keys. "Third floor. Can't miss it."

Mac dangled the keys in front of my face. "See? Easy as pie." He set his empty hand on the small of my back and started walking, his soft but insistent press making me leave the safety of the valet's podium and venture into the strange structure filled with parked cars.

"It's rather beautiful," I said. "In its own way."

Mac laughed as we walked up a sloped ramp. "That's one of the things I love about you, Ev. You can see beauty in a garage."

I tossed my hair over my shoulder. "Beauty always recognizes beauty."

He kissed my hand and kept walking. Some of the cars were in better shape than others, some more expensive. Each one backed into a little square and off, with no driver or passenger in sight.

"Only valets come in here?" I asked as we ascended, walking up the twisting ramps of concrete only cars normally drove on. One passed by us on its way down, a valet in green in the driver's seat, and Mac waved. "Or do people park their cars themselves?"

"Oh no—there'd be chaos," Mac said. "The valets on duty get to pick the spots. They keep track with little tickets. Here, see?" He held up the keys again, and I noticed a laminated keychain I hadn't seen before, with a number written in pen in the center: 321. "You get a forever spot because you're you."

I gave a little skip in acknowledgment.

"But if we let all the guests park their cars, valets would never be able to find them again. There'd be accidents. More than we got now, anyway. Scott let me in because he knows us. Granted, if you were some filly, he'd have got the car himself."

"Do you speak from experience, Malcolm?" I asked, giving him a look from the corner of my eye. "You take a lot of other girls here to this parking garage?"

"Evelyn, baby, I've never dated another girl with her own car before. You're the first filly I've ever taken into this beautiful garage."

We made it to the third level, two more valets driving customers' cars passing us on our hike, and I spotted my Silver Cloud-Rolls Royce towards the entrance, the number 321 painted in white on the asphalt underneath its trunk. The car was shining and undented, like the accident had never happened. "Let's keep it that way." I bopped him on the nose.

Mac pretended to bite my finger, and I giggled. He pushed me up against the passenger side of my car, his nose on my neck. "Of course," he whispered, "nobody says we gotta hurry outta here."

I relaxed into Mac's embrace, wrapping my arms around his back. "Lover, I might be the kind of girl you can talk into going to Yonkers, but I'm most certainly not the kind of girl who is up for a romp in the back seat of a car."

He kissed my neck. "Who said back seat?" He leaned back to grin at me. "Who said car at all?"

"Malcolm Cooper! You're a terrible influence."

He nuzzled my hair before dipping his face to my shoulder, his nose grazing my cheek and the underside of my jaw. I giggled again at the tickling sensation. I glanced around us for the first time. Maybe there was something to his plan. We were all alone, and we'd hear a car approaching. The night was young and so are we.

Except . . .

A . . . shadow? In a driver's seat about four cars away. From a nearby pillar? But it was round, collapsed onto the steering wheel. And appeared much more solid than any shadow had the right.

"Is that a person?"

"No," Mac said without looking. "Valets aren't gonna be hanging around up here."

I pushed his chest to give myself more space to stretch my neck. There was a human-shaped something in the driver's side of the cherry-red Cadillac Coup de Ville four spots away from us.

"Mac," I said, removing myself from his arms with some difficulty. He even pinched my rear once I'd disengaged. "Something is wrong!"

He raked his fingers through his hair, wisps of his fallen pompadour brushing his eyelashes. Long and luscious, it was unfair for a man to have natural lashes like that. "All right. Let's go check out."

I tugged my vest down into its proper place, unsure of when exactly it'd been tugged askew. "Thank you."

"But it's nothing," he said, "and we're hopping in this car and going to Yonkers right after."

I cleared my throat. Yonkers. He had to live all the way in *Yonkers*. "Fine."

"Fine."

"I'll lead the way, shall I?"

He grinned. "Yes, you shall."

Mac had the annoying habit of being almost always right. So, if he thought the person-sized shadow in the Cadillac was nothing, it was probably nothing. But my nose wrinkled at the sight of it anyway, and I was compelled toward the driver's door, my shoes clacking against the rough concrete of the garage. My nose has a terrible habit of wrinkling whenever I'm deep in thought. I'm aware of it, and it does nothing for my appearance—only adds to the number of wrinkles I'll have to deal with as I age—but I cannot stop myself from wrinkling my nose.

It stayed wrinkled until I opened the door and cast light inside the Cadillac, revealing a dead body.

CHAPTER 3

Judge Baker stared up at me with open, unseeing eyes. His bulky body had collapsed on top of the steering wheel, and his complexion was a ghostly white. His arms hung at his sides, his massive hands open on the seat by his legs. A needle hung out of his inner elbow, empty of whatever substance had once been inside it.

"Oh, for Pete's sake!" Mac yipped at my side, startling me. I took in a deep breath, having gone quite some time without air. He backed away from the car and into the one behind us. "Evelyn!" he said, his tone accusing. "Seriously?"

I pointed at myself.

"You had to find a judge dead from a heroin overdose the first time I try to take you out of the Pinnacle for the night!"

I set a fist on my hip. "I didn't do this on purpose, Mac! Judge Baker is dead! And I sent his pregnant wife home from the party with Dr. Smith!" My standoffish posture collapsed, and I frowned down at the dead man. Poor man. Dead in his car, and only weeks away from being a father again. Weeks away from another election. Was he on the ballot? Were judges on ballots? I was pretty sure you had to vote for judges at some point in the process, but not sure enough to place a bet. I made the sign of the cross and hoped his soul would soon find peace.

"Bloody hell," Mac said. "I'll have to go get the police. You think the chief is still in the Silver Room?"

I shook my head, full attention on Judge Baker. I kneeled on the concrete to get a better look. I had read about drugs in the detective novels or splashed across the newspapers, but I hadn't seen anyone use them before. *"Heroin,"* Mac had said, and seemed so sure of it. Craning my neck to get a closer look, there were no other marks on the inside of the judge's arm. Wouldn't there be scars from drug use? The papers mentioned that marks were left behind from using needles.

Mac was speaking, though I couldn't hear the words he was saying. The speaking stopped, and in its place were footfalls as he ran away, presumably to get help. A judge was dead. And while he hadn't died in the Pinnacle Hotel, the garage was Pinnacle property. The Silver Room was filled with politicians and political figures, from the chief of police to the man of the hour running for his second term as mayor.

Daddy was supposed to be here.

If he made it, this would not be a well-received welcome-home present.

Judge Baker didn't seem like a drug user to me, but alas, I am sheltered. Perhaps I simply didn't know enough about it to be able to notice its use in my midst. I leaned over him, nose wrinkled. Sometimes, in the Christie novels, people were poisoned. Cyanide, she'd written, often smells like almonds. Maybe this wasn't heroin at all, but a clever ruse. Face hovering over his, his dead eyes staring at me, I took a deep breath.

There was the pungent, sharp smell of alcohol, the mustiness of sandalwood from high-end cologne, the ash from a cigar, and the garlic from appetizers, but there was no scent of almonds.

"Miss?" a man asked, and I jumped clear out of my skin. The judge's arm was warm against my own, and when the needle clattered onto the concrete I groaned.

"Miss Murphy?" The valet from earlier approached me with his hands up. "What's happening? Mac ran out of here like a bat out of hell, screaming for me to phone the police."

I plucked the needle off the ground and held it at eye level. It, too, did not smell like almonds. "Judge Baker is dead," I said, which seemed like a massive oversimplification. I set the needle by his stiff, open hand. "Please inform Mr. Sharpe."

★ ★ ★

Police cars arrived with sirens blazing. I was both surprised and relieved to see Detective Hodgson step out of the passenger side of an unmarked, four-door sedan. He was a handsome older man with rich brown skin and the natural gravitas that made him the authority figure in whatever room he entered.

He adjusted his fedora on his head as he approached, the same dark gray color as his well-pressed suit. His shoes were black and recently shined, though his face was unshaven and clearly hadn't seen a razor in the better part of a week.

He visibly sighed when he saw me standing by the dead man.

"Miss Murphy," he greeted, his deep voice ringing out with quiet disappointment.

I had helped him solve a murder only a few weeks ago! The least he could do was smile when he saw me. I tried to smile at him, but I was far too shaken up by my discovery to pull it off with any amount of convincing grace. "Detective Hodgson. You weren't at the party."

"Why would he be?" another man asked. I turned my attention away from the familiar, unhappy face and toward an unfamiliar, deeply unhappy face. The man coming up behind Hodgson had driven him to the crime scene. He had to be a detective too, as he wore a suit, though his wasn't as neatly pressed or as finely tailored as Hodgson's. His shoes were dark but hadn't been shined in some time. His facial hair, though, was nowhere to be seen; his squared jaw impeccably clean; his dull beige skin taking on an unnatural sheen in the light of the garage. His hair was a soft blond, cut short. His eyes were green and looked me up and down in a way that soured the back of my throat.

I forced another fake smile. "I invited him. But you never RSVPed, Detective."

Hodgson's answering shrug was almost too casual. "Didn't want to go."

"Then you decline the invitation," I said. Goodness. Men! There are *rules* to a polite society.

"Ma'am," the new detective said, "I believe there are more important matters at hand. Would you please step away from the crime scene?"

"Oh, of course. I'm sorry." I walked toward them and positioned myself near the trunk of the judge's Cadillac. I barely had to stand on my tiptoes to observe them observing the body. "One note," I said. "The heroin needle was in his arm when I arrived."

Hodgson stood straight up, knocking the back of his head against the roof of the car, his hat folding over his face. He righted it with a wince. "What?"

"The heroin needle," I repeated, the familiar heat of shame creeping up the back of my neck. "It was in his arm and then, when I was looking over Judge Baker, the valet started me, and my arm bumped into his arm, and the needle fell to the ground."

The detective stared at me over Hodgson's shoulder, his eyes alight with something similar to fury. "And then you *touched* the needle?"

I twisted my fingers in front of my waist. "Is that bad?"

"Bad?" he scoffed. "Are you serious right now? Who *is* this broad?"

"I'm Evelyn Elizabeth Grace Murphy," I greeted, forcing myself to extend a hand. Neither detective shook it. I resisted the urge to grab onto the fabric of my vest.

Hodgson held the bridge of his nose between his forefinger and thumb. "McJimsey. This is the daughter of the Pinnacle's owner. She fancies herself a detective."

My cheeks burned. "I did recently help solve a murder case, Detective."

He opened his eyes and pierced me with his stare. Tired. Annoyed. Disappointed. He knew me well enough to be disappointed in me. My stomach churned, and I gave in to the urge to tug on my vest. "So you should know why it's a problem that you touched the needle."

I nodded. My eyelids itched, and I blinked to scratch away the feeling. "My fingerprints."

"Your fingerprints." Detective McJimsey nodded. "What were you doing so close to the body, anyway?"

"I was trying to smell almonds."

"Almonds?" McJimsey repeated. He scratched his jaw. "Why? What? Almonds?"

"Cyanide smells like almonds," I said. "But not everyone can smell it. You should have the coroner test for cyanide in his system."

McJimsey shook his head. But Hodgson kept looking at me. He waved a hand at the Cadillac. "Why would we do that? He's got a heroin needle next to him, Miss Murphy." He sounded like one of my tutors trying to get me to understand geometry, or Daddy asking my advice about the markets, to see what I knew. What I understood.

If this was a test, it was one I could pass. "It seems to me that a man of his position, with a young wife due to have his third child any day now, leaving a party in which he was a respected guest, filled with members from his social circle—that it's an odd time to try heroin for the first time. Is all."

"First time?" Hodgson asked. "What makes you say that?"

"There were no marks on his arm to indicate previous injection sites."

Hodgson nodded. "Good," he said. "But we won't know what the judge was injected with until we get results back from the lab. And I have my doubts they'll find *cyanide*."

I did not stick my tongue out, but I did think about it in great detail.

"Look, kid," McJimsey said, though he couldn't have been too much older than me. "Sometimes junkies shoot up between their toes. On their feet. On their stomachs. Places people wouldn't see. Maybe he used his arm this time because he was in the parking lot. And maybe he shot up for all the reasons you listed. Stressed out having a kid with a much younger wife. Running for reelection. Stuck in a stuffy room filled with stuffy suits."

His insult dried my tears faster than any handkerchief. "I beg your pardon," I said. "The Silver Room is hardly stuffy. I planned the party myself." Sure, I had used the exact descriptor earlier when Mrs. Baker was unwell. But it's my hotel and my party. I'm allowed to be insulting.

"You did?" McJimsey's thin lips twitched. "You'd know when the judge left then, wouldn't you?"

"I planned the party," I said. "I didn't man the door. Why?"

He pulled a notebook out of his coat. "You're the first one on the scene. Pretty dark garage, not easy to see inside all these cars.

Yet, you make the discovery. You tamper with the crime scene. Your fingerprints will be on the murder weapon."

I glared at him. "I don't care for what you're insinuating, Detective."

Hodgson set his hand on McJimsey's shoulder, but the younger detective sidestepped away from him to get closer to me. Close enough I could smell his aftershave. It was musky, but cheap, with undertones of rubbing alcohol. He was a few inches taller than me, but I'm tall for a woman, so he didn't have to bend far to get close to my face. Close enough to kiss, if he were someone else. I wished Mac would hurry back from wherever he was.

"Where do you live, Miss Murphy?" His features were striking. The green of his eyes a pleasing contrast to the pallor of his skin tone, his square jaw chiseled, and his roman nose defined. But his clothes were old and made for someone else. Even his cufflinks were simple clips. Cheap things.

A broke, good-looking detective accusing me of murder.

It was one of the funniest things that had ever happened to me. I smiled, a real smile, for the first time since the police arrived. "Why?" I looked up at him under my lashes. He wanted to play? Fine. I'd be exactly the person he expected. The ditzy, easy, inge-nue. The mask was as comfortable as a favorite pair of high-heeled shoes. "Plan on taking me home, Detective?"

He tapped his pen against his empty notebook. "What were you doing in the garage, Miss Murphy?"

"My car is right there," I said, glancing at the Rolls. "It's nice, isn't it? I bought it for a previous boyfriend but got to keep it when we broke up."

"You go through a lot of boyfriends, Miss Murphy?"

"I do all right for myself." I giggled. "Are you single, Detective?"

He sighed and looked over at Hodgson. Hodgson, for his part, was ignoring us, studying the dead judge in the front seat. "I'm gonna ask you one more time, Miss Murphy. What were you doing in the garage?"

"Mac and I—that's my current beau," I said, winking, "we were going to take the Rolls for a spin."

"A spin, eh?"

"Mm-hmm. To Yonkers."

"A spin to Yonkers?"

I twirled my hair around my finger. "That's where his apartment is."

Something knocked. A weird sound to hear in the middle of a parking garage, it caught me off guard, and I stepped even closer to McJimsey. For his part, he didn't push me away. He glanced at Hodgson, who was creeping toward us, a worried look on his face.

"The trunk," Hodgson said. "Has anyone looked in the trunk yet?"

I shook my head. "You two were the first ones near the car. Since I got here, I mean. Mac took off to call for help. He didn't look around." Where was Mac, anyway?

"Right." Hodgson settled a hand on the gun at his hip. "Officer," he called to the nearest uniformed cop, "we need to pop this trunk. Now."

The cop used some sort of tool to jimmy the lock, but didn't open it himself. He backed away and Hodgson took his place, hand still on his gun. McJimsey moved me behind him, one arm out, and turned so I couldn't get closer to the trunk than I was. Still, I hopped up on my tiptoes and watched.

Hodgson opened the trunk.

A woman sat up.

CHAPTER 4

She was a thin thing, all angular bones, with long, brown hair hanging in strings around her pale face. Her wild eyes took in the scene—the two detectives before her, the uniformed officers all around, the police cars with their lights still flashing inside the garage—before her attention landed on me.

And then she screamed.

Sounds of terror reverberated in my ears and made my teeth ache. The noise stopped. Her wild eyes rolled back in her head and she fainted, disappearing once more into the trunk of the dead man's car.

I touched my chest, heart buzzing beneath my hand. "Gracious," I gasped, feeling like I'd just finished a tennis lesson. "What was that about?"

McJimsey spun on his heel until we were nose to nose. "You tell me. She saw you and she screamed in fear. Why?"

Why did she scream when she saw me? She was obviously confused by the place she found herself in, but it was when she noticed me that she screamed so loud and so hard she fainted.

"McJimsey," Hodgson warned, "take a step back."

The detective whipped away from me to turn his glare on Hodgson. "Don't protect her. She needs to answer for what is going on."

I held up my empty hands. "I told you everything already. You can ask Malcolm Cooper. He was with me the whole night. I don't know why that woman screamed when she saw me, but I know that you're wasting time. You should be getting her to the nearest hospital."

"You're right," McJimsey said. I sighed with relief and flashed Hodgson a small smile. But McJimsey reached around his back and pulled out a jangling pair of cuffs. "Don't make me use these, Miss Murphy. Sit in my car, and we'll finish talking later. At the precinct."

I laughed. "You cannot be serious."

"Trust me, Miss Murphy, I am not the kind of man who jokes." He jerked his thumb at the unmarked sedan he'd driven up in. Beige and foreign. Cheap, like everything about him. "As a kindness to my partner here, who seems to like you, I won't cuff you. As long as you go now and you go quietly. If it were up to me? I'd gag you as well as bind you if I could."

"What the *hell*?" That was Mac's voice, and the sound of it filled me with both relief and terror. He was going to witness me being berated and detained by the police, and there was nothing I could do to stop it. He thundered past the police blockade, the flashing lights throwing his face into red shadow, illuminating the fury in his expression. He grabbed the detective's lapels and shoved him away from me. "What did you say to her, you piece of—"

"Hey!" Hodgson shouted, shoving himself between the two men. "Enough, Cooper! Enough!" He put both hands on Mac, his hat high up on his head. "That man you're grabbing is a cop! You wanna get arrested for assault on an officer? How would that look with immigration, huh?"

Mac tore his attention away from McJimsey. He was breathing hard, but he stopped pushing against Hodgson.

I reached for him, our pinkies intertwining. "Where were you, Mac?"

He swallowed, his chest heaving. "I wanted . . . I was look-ing for Mr. Sharpe. To tell him what happened. But he'd gone to Broadway already."

I pressed my lips together. Mr. Sharpe was the Pinnacle's man-ager. It was no wonder Mac wanted to let him know, personally, what was going on. It was also no wonder that Mr. Sharpe had gone to Broadway. Henry Fox—*the* Henry Fox, movie star and my best friend—was headlining a play, and he and Mr. Sharpe had been quite inseparable of late.

McJimsey straightened his lapels. "A judge is dead. And that dame knows more than she's telling. She's coming with us to the precinct."

Hodgson caught my eye and jerked his chin in the direction of the sedan. I followed after him, on shaking legs. This was infinitely worse than going to Yonkers. I should've listened to Mac and never checked out the Cadillac. He'd been right. Again. How annoying. Though, that shadow was *something*, so I'd been right too. No good deed, and all that.

"Get in the back seat." Hodgson kept his voice low. "Don't put up a fight, and answer his questions. You'll be back in your hotel room in an hour, two tops."

Two hours in a police precinct? Two hours without Mac, with-out Presley? Away from home? I swallowed and it clicked in my throat. My palms tingled, and pain shot up both of my arms, shivers down my back. "Will you be with me?"

Hodgson paused with his fingers under the silver handle.

"I don't have my dog, and it doesn't seem like you'll allow Mac to stay by my side." I toyed with the pendant of Saint Anthony around my neck. Air was hard to come by, thin and shallow around me. "I get these attacks of anxiety when I leave the Pinnacle, and it's worse when I'm alone, Detective. With people I don't trust, I mean."

"I remember." Hodgson opened the back door. "I promise, Miss Murphy. It'll be all right. Get in the car now."

I sat down in the back seat, images of the thousands of people who'd sat on it before me passing unwanted in my mind. The dirty, the guilty, the innocent. Germs everywhere, and on my new white vest too. I tried not to lean against the back seat. McJimsey was barking orders at the uniformed officers, though I couldn't hear what they were saying.

Mac stood in front of the chaos surrounding the open trunk, blocking my view of the men in a hurry to help the fainted woman. Crying wouldn't help anything, and it certainly wouldn't be a comfort to my boyfriend to see me losing it in the back seat of a detective's car. I blinked away the tears and held up my pinkie. *I'll be fine. I promise.*

He held up his pinkie and then crossed it over his heart.

His mouth moved over the words *I love you.* I sniffed and mouthed them back. Told myself it was only a visit to the police precinct. If I could handle a Broadway opening with photographers calling my name and taking pictures and asking if I was carrying Henry's illegitimate child, I could speak to Detective McJimsey in a police station.

I did wish Presley was with me, in his little purse. Licking my face and keeping me calm and being the most adorable dog that ever existed.

Oh, Presley! I slapped my cheek. "Presley!" I yelled, hoping Mac could hear me. "Presley! Don't forget Presley!"

He nodded and gave me a thumbs-up. But his eyes were shining. The guilt and sadness in his expression tore up my insides. This wasn't his fault. I wanted to go to his apartment. I've wanted to since we first started dating. It wasn't his fault that Judge Baker was dead in the front seat of his car. It wasn't his fault that I saw the shadow of the corpse and went snooping. It wasn't his fault that I'm the same person I've always been.

This was my fault, and mine alone.

Oh, and whoever had killed Judge Baker. Because he *had been* murdered. There simply was no way he'd overdosed on heroin in the Pinnacle's garage, with a woman in his trunk. No, someone wanted him dead. And they'd ruined his life while they were at it.

Hodgson had promised me that everything would be okay, not that he would be with me the entire time, but he stuck close to my side, even pulling out my chair in a dingy room.

An interrogation room. I'd always wondered what one looked like. In my wildest dreams, I never would have thought it could be this drab. Peeling green paint covered the walls. The cold metal chair dug into my middle back. The harsh lighting illuminated the scratch marks on the tabletop, no doubt left behind by visitors in chains, pleading their case. At least I wasn't in handcuffs.

Detective Hodgson didn't speak to me. Hadn't spoken the entire ride to the precinct. Had barely even looked at me until he pulled the chair back and watched me sit, his eyes meeting mine for a brief moment.

I was not alone. And though it was obvious Hodgson still didn't consider me a friend, I knew I could trust him. It would have to be enough. I closed my eyes and took a deep breath, focusing on my feelings. My analyst, Dr. Sanders, had taught me how to do this—to find the feeling inside my body, identify it, and give it a name. Sometimes a thing lost its power when you called it out for what it was. My neck ached and my blood was warm. *Annoyed.* I was annoyed. But there was something else. My fingers and toes were numb. My stomach was a fist. *Fear.* That feeling was fear. I was annoyed and I was afraid.

The door to the interrogation room swung open, and I released my inward reflection to focus on what was happening. Detective

McJimsey sat down across from me, a tight smile on his face. Hodgson was at his side, watching the other detective. Two against one, I just didn't know which was the team of one and which was the team of two.

"Miss Murphy," McJimsey said, flipping open his notebook. "There are some questions I need you to answer in regards to your whereabouts earlier tonight."

The ache in my neck shot up to my brain so fast I got dizzy in my chair. My whereabouts? Again? We'd already had this discussion.

"I also need a complete history of your relationship with Judge Baker."

I tried to speak, but McJimsey kept going. "And. I need your complete schedule of the day. Down to the minute details of everything you did and saw. *If* you have an alibi, and *if* it checks out, you'll be able to go home. Shouldn't take more than a day or two."

I focused on steadying my breath. This idiot. Wasting time when a real killer was out there somewhere, getting away with it. Like the man who'd killed my mother all those years ago, slipping off into the night, never to be found. A ghost haunting my memories. I see her lying there alone. Her mouth open, blood on her lips as red as her lipstick.

My beautiful mother.

And Judge Baker, dead before his child would even get to know him.

"Miss Murphy, do you understand me?"

I forced myself to sit in the most correct posture I could, considering the unforgiving metal chair they'd given me. "Yes, I understand."

"Good. Now, let's begin. What—"

I held up my hand. "I'm know you have many questions for me. Thank you for that helpful rundown, detailing what it is you're looking for from me. I have questions for you too. And I was looking forward to having a discussion with you, Detective. But now I cannot."

His tongue darted out to stroke the corner of his lip. "Why not?"

"I'm being detained for a day or two, you said. Does that mean you consider me a viable suspect in this matter?"

He nodded once, sharply.

"I'm certain you wouldn't be speaking to me now without confirming my identity. My father is one of the most influential men in the entire world. He advised me long ago what to do in this exact scenario. I cannot answer any questions without legal counsel present. I must request my attorney. Thank you, Detectives." I folded my hands on the table and smiled politely at both of them. Dismissing them, some might say.

But the conversation was over, and they had no reason to stare at me any longer.

Hodgson tapped his wrist against the table's edge. His watch clanged in the unusual quiet of the room. It was a nice one too. A good working man's watch that went well with his tailored suits. McJimsey breathed through his nose, nostrils flaring with every inhale. But Hodgson was doing his damnedest not to grin.

"Who is your attorney, Miss Murphy?" Hodgson asked. "I'll call him for you."

"Lefkowitz," I said. "Mr. Louis Lefkowitz."

McJimsey scoffed. "The attorney general? You want him to call the attorney general for you?"

I hummed. "It is rather late, and I'm sure he's very busy in these last few days leading up to the election. How about Mr. Ferretti?"

Hodgson scratched his brow. "Which one? There's four of those Ferrettis, ain't there?"

I nodded. "They're all great options, but let's go with Ferretti Jr., as he is Daddy's most consistent golf buddy."

Hodgson stood up with a groan. "I'll be right back," he said and left the room. He *left* the *room*. I watched in stunned disbelief as the interrogation door closed, with Hodgson on one side of it and me and McJimsey on the other. He hadn't promised not to leave, but he had promised everything would be all right. And leaving me alone with a strange man in a locked room that I could not escape from was hardly my definition of *all right*.

CHAPTER 5

The chair creaked when McJimsey leaned back with his hands behind his head. Unbothered, relaxed, or at least trying to give off that impression. "You think you're cute," he said.

He was neither unbothered nor relaxed.

Good.

I should have been snooping around my boyfriend's apartment right now while he scooped us some peanut butter and smothered it over apple slices and teased me that I'd never find his most prized possession, no matter how good I was at finding things.

Instead, I was here, in the dreariest room I'd ever had the misfortune of visiting.

"No," I said, "I know I am."

He smiled, slowly, revealing teeth that were a little bit crooked, a little bit yellow. This detective was too green to start earning a profit in his career, at least not as much as Hodgson seemed to have. Or they had different priorities with their dough. Hodgson too pride in his clothes, but maybe not his appearance. Whereas it was the opposite for McJimsey, whose facial hair and hygiene were the epitome of masculine fastidiousness, but whose clothing was worn, old, and rumpled.

"This room, however," I said, sighing. "It could use some work. You know, if the New York City Police are having trouble with their finances, I could throw a fundraiser. I'm rather good at that sort of thing."

"At planning parties?"

I crossed my legs. The cold metal of the table bit into my kneecap through the thin fabric of my pants. "Exactly. Planning parties and inviting the right people."

"No offense, miss"—he lowered his arms and sat forward on his chair, leaning over until I was grateful for the scuffed-up tabletop between us—"but the city of New York doesn't need your help."

My nose wrinkled. I twisted the pendant of Saint Anthony around my neck. "Are you certain? A judge is dead and you can't even afford to paint this room."

"I can't afford it?" He adjusted his shirtsleeves. "What are you getting at, kid? I'm not in charge of this precinct. I'm the new guy, stuck with Hodgson as a partner."

My blood ran hot again. I felt it thrumming, burning in my ears. What did he mean by *stuck*? "Detective Hodgson is a fine policeman."

He snorted. "Sure. Whatever you say."

"You're a bit young," I said. Men are typically so easy to understand. But this one was different. I suspected it was because he was suspicious of me, so my usual act wasn't lowering his guard. Still, I wanted to understand him as best I could, so I could get out of the interrogation room as fast as possible.

And I was still peeved about the whole thing. Imagine! Me! Murdering a judge with heroin, of all things. If I were ever to murder a judge, it wouldn't be with something so déclassé. Cyanide, at the very least. In his champagne at dinner tonight. Easy yet classy. Like me. "For a detective, I mean."

"Passed the test," he said. "Same as everybody."

The pendant had warmed in my fingers. I dropped it and made sure it rested portrait out on my vest. "You're also better looking than most detectives. Like an actor playing one on television. Starring alongside Joe Friday. *'Just the facts, ma'am.'*"

Detective McJimsey grinned. "Flattery won't help you here, Miss Murphy."

"I'm not trying to flatter you," I said. "I'm stating my opinion."

"You think your opinion matters?"

I pressed my lips together as I thought of an answer. It was obvious he thought me guilty, and while that was the most preposterous thing imaginable, it was the problem at hand. I wanted to get him on my side. That way he would write me off as a suspect and start searching for whoever had killed the judge.

Or, if by some strange and most unlikely turn of events, Judge Baker had left the party moments after his pregnant wife returned home with a doctor in tow; then found a lady of the evening, knocked her unconscious, stuffed her in his trunk, and driven back to the Pinnacle to use illicit materials.

But weren't only valets allowed in the garage? Had the young man waved the judge in the same way he'd done for me and Mac— because Judge Baker was important enough? And wouldn't we have seen him pass us? Mac and I had taken our time in the hallway of the hotel while he convinced me to leave. But how much time had we taken? Enough for the judge to leave and be killed, obviously, but what happened between him leaving and dying so that Mac and I could find his still-warm body without ever having passed him in the garage?

But McJimsey's question weaseled its way inside of my head and drowned out the thoughts I was having about the case. Did I think my opinions mattered? Yes, I did. I thought they mattered a lot because they were mine. But nobody else had ever cared about them before. Not Daddy. Not Hodgson. Not even Mac, who was taking me to his apartment when I wanted to go back to my suite and snuggle my dog. Even if I had known it was in my best interest to get in that car and let him take me to Yonkers.

"Shouldn't it?" I asked. "My opinion. Shouldn't it matter?"

McJimsey nodded and sighed. "In a perfect world. Yeah. But in case you haven't noticed, Miss Murphy, a perfect world is the farthest thing from what we're living in."

The door clicked open. Hodgson stepped inside, hat first. Relief filled me at the sight. "Detective Hodgson," I greeted. "Did you get hold of Mr. Ferretti?"

"Ah," said Hodgson. "No." He opened the door until it knocked against the peeling wall behind it and moved out of the way. Two men followed him inside.

McJimsey was on his feet so fast that I worried I'd missed something. But the two men had been guests at the fundraiser. I stood up and shook their hands.

"Mr. Mayor. Chief Harvey. It is so good to see friendly faces in such an unfriendly place as this. Did you enjoy yourselves tonight? I thought your speech was lovely, sir. I do hope you weren't called away from the fun on my behalf."

The mayor set his hand on my shoulder. "Don't worry, my dear. I had only just walked through the door of my home when the phone rang. Hadn't even taken off my shoes. There's no need to fret. Now, what is all this about?"

"Judge Baker is dead, did you hear? It's terrible." I crossed myself. The mayor and the chief did the same. "Dead in his car in the Pinnacle garage. I discovered the body, and we sent for help. There was some confusion, and I was taken here to answer questions, which I was completely fine with. Always willing to help. You know, I helped solve a murder at the hotel a few weeks ago."

"I remember," Chief Harvey said. "Have a plaque being made for you as we speak."

"Oh." I waved a hand, smiling so big my cheeks hurt. "Isn't that the ginchiest thing? You're such a darling, Chief Harvey. Anyway. I was informed that I was being detained for *two days* because I was a suspect! Daddy always said it's best not to speak to the police alone if you're considered a suspect. So, Detective Hodgson was calling Mr. Ferretti for me."

Chief Harvey's nostrils flared so wide his mustache disappeared up his nose. "You arrested Murphy's daughter?" He wasn't yelling, but he wasn't speaking at a low decibel either. It was with considerable surprise that I realized he was directing his ire at Hodgson.

"Oh," I said. "I don't mean to get anyone in trouble. It's one big misunderstanding."

"Of course, it is, dear. Of course." The mayor pulled a handkerchief out of his inside jacket pocket and dabbed his damp forehead. His tie hung loosely around his neck. *Finally.* I'd been worried his head might pop clear off his body earlier. "No one thinks you hurt the judge. In fact, from the little I've been told, it sounds as if Judge Baker hurt himself. A terrible accident, and one that a doll like yourself doesn't need to get wrapped up in."

I clutched my mother's pendant. While it was a relief to hear I was no longer a suspect, I was still very much wrapped up in the case. I'd discovered Judge Baker. I'd spoken with his pregnant wife at my party. And I knew whoever had killed him had done it to ruin his reputation.

I just didn't know why.

Or how.

Or when.

Most of it was cloudy. But I was determined to get to the bottom of things. It had happened on Pinnacle property, for Pete's sake! Who knew what else the killer might do?

"You don't need to worry anymore about this, Miss Murphy," Chief Harvey said. He put his hand on my back and pushed, urging me out of the interrogation room. "I'll see to it myself that this gets cleared up. You never should've been brought here in the first place." He frowned at the detectives as we turned into the main room of the police station. The paint in this part of the building wasn't green, but instead an off white. It was chipping in odd spots, dents, and scuff marks all along it.

The station needed a major makeover, that was for sure.

"It's no problem," I said. "Please. I don't want anyone to get in trouble. I only want justice for Judge Baker."

The mayor stuffed his damp handkerchief back into his jacket. He reminded me of Burrows, and I thought of the hotel and getting back to my suite and burrowing into my silk bed sheets with my dog and not coming out again for at least twenty-four hours. We'd order room service and drink hot chocolate and maybe watch Gunsmoke. I didn't get the appeal, but Mac loved that show. I was more of a "Dragnet" girl, myself. Detective Joe Friday made me weak in the knees. And I meant what I had said to McJimsey. He had the look of a silver screen detective.

"You are a doll," the mayor said. "Isn't she a doll?" That question was directed to the chief.

Chief Harvey nodded, smiling, and led us to the entrance of the precinct. "Don't spend another minute worrying about this. Okay? You go back to the hotel and rest. That's an order." He opened the front door for me.

"Thank you both ever so." I reached for the chief's hand and gave it a squeeze before doing the same to the mayor's. "You two are the ginchiest!"

They blushed and blustered, and I skipped out of the precinct, feeling lighter than air. The leaves on the trees were yellowing, a few loose and scattered along the sidewalk. The cool breeze stroked my hair and scraped the leaves along the concrete. My Rolls-Royce was waiting for me at the bottom of the steps. Mac, in his party clothes, looking like a rumpled James Dean, leaned against the hood, a bundle of fur in his arms.

"Mac!" I called out. He brightened when he saw me. The busy street quieted, the hubbub of the precinct going silent. There were only Mac and Presley, my two knights in shining armor, coming to save me. I hurried down the steps, arms open, but Mac shook his head. I fell short. "What?" I asked, giggling in confusion. I'd only meant to hug him, and he'd never been shy about public displays before. He slid Presley into my open arms, his face coming close enough for a kiss on the cheek, but he pulled away without making contact.

Presley, however, could not be deterred. He covered my chin with slobbery kisses, and I giggled again, still a little confused, but so relieved to be out of the station that I felt light-headed and lighter than air.

Mac opened the Silver Cloud's door.

A man was sitting back there. An older man wearing a full tux. He was bald, with a rigidly tense jaw, brown eyes, and a perfectly straight nose. He put down the newspaper he was reading and scooted over in the back seat.

I exhaled a shaky breath. The light-headedness disappeared, sending me crashing back down. My legs got so heavy it was a wonder I wasn't falling into the subway below us. I had to be dreaming. Or else I was positively loopy! There was no way, *no way*, he was here, of all places, in the back of my car, picking me up after I'd been arrested for murder.

"Evie," he said, "are you going to stand outside the police station half naked all night, or shall we get back home?"

CHAPTER 6

"Daddy, I'm not half naked." I glanced down to be sure. If this was a dream, it wouldn't be unusual to find myself in exactly that state. But no, I was wearing the same professional outfit I'd had on all evening. "I'm wearing matador pants!"

Daddy patted the seat next to him. Obediently, I sat down, flinching when Mac shut the door.

"I can see your arms, your collarbone, and your belly button. That's naked enough." Daddy shook his head. "Late October, and you're outside the police station, at night, dressed like that."

Mac got into the driver's seat and started the car, the engine rolling over into a fine purr. Presley perched on my knees, staring at Daddy like he wasn't sure who the new man was and whether he needed to bite his ankles.

"Daddy, I didn't know I'd be going to the police station at night. Or ever! I was working at a party at the Pinnacle. You were supposed to be there."

The Rolls pulled into traffic. Daddy held out his hand for Presley, who sniffed his knuckles. Presley sneezed, shook his entire tiny little body, and settled down on my lap. Daddy glared halfheartedly at the dog.

"I was late," Daddy said. "Arrived as everyone was leaving. Excepted it to be calm, but your assistant here was running around like a chicken with his head cut off. Didn't take long to realize it was you who'd caused the ruckus."

"Oh." I fiddled with the pendant around my neck. The silver had cooled since I'd last touched it in the interrogation room. The back was smooth against my thumb, the intricate design of Saint Anthony carved against the pad of my index finger. "I am sorry about that. Judge Baker died in our garage, and I had the misfortune of finding him. I am very good at finding things, you know."

"Finding trouble more like," Daddy said.

"Daddy," I said, laughing, "trouble finds me, not the other way around. I am ever so glad you could make it, even if you are late. Was your flight very long? It's quite a time we're living in, isn't it? A transatlantic jet flight. Why that's the ginchiest thing I've ever heard."

"That's because you've never taken one," Daddy grumbled. "What's this little runt's name, anyway?"

It took me a moment to realize he was talking about my dog and not my boyfriend. I laughed again because I didn't know what else to do. "Presley."

"Presley? After that talentless debaucher?"

I gasped. "Daddy! Elvis is an Army man!"

"She's right, Mr. Murphy," Mac said from the front seat. "He's in Germany now."

"And I was in Germany two weeks ago. What difference does that make?" Daddy scowled at the back of Mac's head. "Your assistant always this talkative, Evie?"

My mouth was frozen open in a smile. I should tell Daddy about my relationship with Mac. I wanted to tell Daddy about my relationship with Mac. I just hadn't planned on it coming up after being released from the police station when I had suspicion of murder hanging over me. "Mr. Cooper is not only my assistant but my . . . my friend, Daddy."

"Your *friend*," he repeated. The muscle in his jaw pulsed. "I see. And what happened to your other friend? That actor?"

"Henry," I said, smiling. Henry and I had a particular arrangement in which we let the press believe that the two of us were in love and that was the reason he never dated when he was in California making movies. We'd ended that arrangement when Mac and I had decided to go steady. Henry was still one of the best friends I'd ever had. "His play opened on Broadway a few weeks ago, to marvelous reviews, by the way. I'm ever so proud of him. But we were never serious and have decided it was in our best interests not to go steady any longer."

Daddy sighed. "How is it possible that you weren't serious, but you were going steady? Also, what a ridiculous phrase. In my day, you were together, or you weren't. You got married and started a family. You kids and your dating around." He shook his head. "You *should* be serious, Evie. You're old enough. Your mother was younger than you when the two of us got married."

"Uh." I floundered around for words, catching Mac's gaze in the rearview mirror. My cheeks warmed. I wanted to be married. But things were still new, and in my experience, men didn't stick around long enough to get a ring on their finger. "Things will happen when they're meant to happen, Daddy. In the meantime, I'm performing well at the job you got for me."

Daddy nodded once. "Mr. Sharpe has said as much. But he's biased."

I pressed my lips together to keep from guffawing. Mr. Sharpe, the manager of the Pinnacle, biased in my favor? Perhaps Henry's influence was the reason for the manager of the hotel to have anything nice to say about me. The two of them had recently grown rather close, and Mac and I were the only ones aware of it.

"From what I saw of the fundraiser, it looked intelligently put together, and the mayor's chief of staff was pleased with the results."

He should be! Those were expensive meals everyone purchased for a chance to rub elbows with Mr. Rockefeller—who didn't even make it!—and those in his orbit.

Daddy tapped his knee. "Now that we have all that out of the way, I'd like you to explain to me, in clear, concise terms, how you ended up discovering a dead judge in our garage."

"Right." I put both my hands on Presley's back, his sleek fur a comfort. "Right. That's easy to explain. I was going to my car."

"And why were you going to your car? At night? Alone?"

I smiled. "I wasn't alone, Daddy. Mr. Cooper was with me."

"Mm-hmm. And Mr. Cooper was with you why?"

My smile faltered. "Yes. He was with me because one of the things that he is . . . assisting me with, in his capacity as my assistant, is that he is teaching me how to drive." I was not the most natural liar, but I did have to give myself a bit of praise for coming up with that one on the fly. But then I caught Mac's look in the mirror again and no longer felt proud of myself.

I should've told the truth, I suppose. That Mac was my steady beau. But then what? Tell Daddy we were sneaking off to Mac's apartment for a snog and a slumber party? That would go over about as well as a lead balloon. Going on dates was one thing, as far as Daddy was concerned. But an overnight visit? That would've resulted in a heart attack for one of us at least.

I'd tell him that Mac was my boyfriend. Tomorrow. Back at the hotel, after a good night's rest. When I could make sure he didn't get the wrong idea.

Or rather, the right idea. But girls had been lying to their fathers about exactly what they were doing with their boyfriends since the dawn of time, I was pretty sure.

"He's teaching you how to drive? I had no idea you wanted to learn how to drive yourself, Evie."

Daddy and I very rarely had long discussions about things I wanted to do, so why he was surprised by not knowing something about me was anyone's guess. I shrugged. "It's good for a girl to be independent, don't you think, Daddy? And this lovely car is in my name, after all—thank you ever so for that. But driving at night is different from driving during the day, so we were fitting in a lesson, and what should we come across but poor dead Judge Baker, slumped over in the front seat of his car, not two parking spaces away from us. We called for the police right away, and there was some confusion, as I said, regarding the needle in which Judge Baker injected the fatal dose, and it was requested of me that I answer some questions at the station. Once we got there and I saw how antagonistic the detectives were being toward me, I did what you have always said to do and asked for legal counsel. By that time, though, it seems you'd gotten wind of the whole fiasco and swept in and saved me. Thank you ever so, Daddy. You've rescued the whole night."

He harrumphed, but the clench of his jaw had eased. "While I can applaud you for learning how to drive yourself, this Rolls-Royce isn't for drivers, Evie. It's for passengers. I'd recommend a different vehicle if you're going to be traipsing around Manhattan."

"Yes, Manhattan," I said because I wasn't about to tell him that I had been planning to go to Yonkers. And then sleep there. In Yonkers. "We can do a bit of car shopping while you're in town, Daddy. You know so much about everything. I know you'd pick the exact right car for me. How long will you be in town?"

He cleared his throat. "A week. Maybe less. We'll see. Busy with work commitments, Evie—I doubt I'll have time to pick out the car myself."

My shoulders sagged. "Of course," I said. I adjusted the necklace my mother had given me. "Next time, then. You'll be in town for Christmas, yes?"

"That's the plan." Daddy said. He jerked his chin forward and I looked up, surprised to find Mac had pulled up outside the Pinnacle. Home already. "Are you hungry? I haven't eaten yet."

A bellhop opened the door and I slid out, settling Presley in the crook of my elbow. "That cannot stand, can it? Come on—I'm sure the girls have your suite ready. I'll make us some dinner."

"You don't have to do that, Evie," Daddy said as the valet closed the door. "We can order something."

"It's no problem at all. I'd love to cook for you." I leaned into the open window. "You'll meet us at Daddy's suite?" I asked Mac. I wasn't about to abandon Mac because Daddy needed food. "Presley needs his walk."

He dropped his attention to his hands on the steering wheel. "Sure thing," he said, "Miss Murphy."

I watched as the Rolls-Royce pulled into traffic and disappeared in the direction of the garage before reaching into my clutch and pulling out a dollar for the valet who held open our door.

Daddy frowned. He touched my elbow, a silent command to start walking, and the two of us strode into the hotel. The employees all greeted him by name, jumping out of his way in either respect or fear or a mixture of both. He looked none of them in the eye. He leaned in close to me and said, "You are far too friendly with the help."

"Mr. Cooper, you mean? He's more than the help, Daddy. I told you. He's my friend."

"I didn't mean him, though the fact that the two of you are friends is something we will have to discuss. I meant tipping that boy a dollar. A dollar, Evelyn, for opening a door? A quarter, at most, will do."

The lift boy opened the elevator doors, and Daddy swept inside. My mouth fell open, staring after him aghast. "But Daddy, I can't carry loose change! I'll *jingle!*"

CHAPTER 7

Daddy's clothes were already unpacked by the time we made it to his suite. The presidential suite was always reserved for Daddy's visits. Two floors, with a grand staircase leading to the master bedroom, and a chef's kitchen on the bottom floor. The fridge was filled with Daddy's favorite things, and after making Presley promise not to piddle on the floor, I got the oven warming and started chopping an onion.

Daddy was a man of infinite sophistication who dined in the very best restaurants all around the world and even owned a few of them himself. But his favorite meal in all the world was tuna noodle casserole. I have no idea why, but Pinnacle staff knows to have all the ingredients on hand when he arrives, either for them to make it in the kitchen or for me to make it up here.

Daddy doesn't make his own food. And I only know how to cook because Nanny thought it important to impart what she referred to as "life skills" on me, whether I saw the point in them at the time or not.

If I was going to tell him about Mac tomorrow, it was best to begin his buttering up as soon as possible. Presley left my side in the kitchen to spin in circles by the front door, so I knew before I heard the knock that the person I was buttering up Daddy for had arrived. I slid the chopped onion into a skillet of melting butter on the stovetop before letting Mac inside. Presley jumped up to Mac's knees, tongue lolling out of his open mouth, demanding to be carried.

He smiled when he saw me, but it didn't reach his eyes.

"What's wrong, lover?" I asked, keeping my voice low. "Are you upset over the arrest?"

He bent down and scooped up my dog. "No," he said. "I mean, I didn't like seeing you get loaded into the back of a copper's car. But I'm fine, Evelyn."

Daddy cleared his throat. I looked over my shoulder and smiled at him. He was at the top of the stairs, having changed out of his tux into slacks and a button-down, collared shirt. The bags under his eyes were puffier than normal, more purple too, and my smile turned into a frown. Daddy needed a trip to the Pinnacle's salon for some spa treatments as soon as possible. A long soak in a seaweed bath, and a manicurist to clean up his hands and feet, and he'd be right as rain again.

"I'll be back with the dog in a bit," Mac said. "Mr. Murphy. Miss Murphy."

"The dog has a name," Daddy said. "Use it when you walk him. And shut the door on your way out."

My body froze. My eyelids stopped blinking, my heart stopped beating, and my lungs stopped breathing. Daddy, who had never once used Presley's name, was barking out orders like my little Pomeranian mix demanded impeccable manners. What a crummy way of putting someone in their place. Especially when that someone was my Mac.

Mac nodded, but his gray eyes met Daddy's dark gaze. "I'll take Mr. Presley out on his walk and be right back."

"Take all the time *he* needs," Daddy said. "That's what we pay you for, after all."

Mac nodded again. He didn't look at me as he shut the door.

My heart started beating again, but at a rapid pace, blood pumping so hard inside my veins it was a wonder steam wasn't pouring out of my ears to relieve the pressure. "That was very rude, Daddy!"

Daddy took a seat at the table and didn't say anything. To him, it didn't matter if he hurt Mac's feelings—or what I thought about it. Those weren't things he cared about, so they weren't worth commenting on.

I stomped back into the kitchen. The onions were translucent and smelled marvelous. I took them off the heat with a long sigh, hoping to expel some of the steam inside my body with it. The water was boiling. In the cupboards, I found a can of cream of mushroom soup, a can of tuna, and a bag of noodles. I salted the boiling water and added the noodles to it. I mixed the soup and the mushrooms with some mayo and sour cream from the fridge, a dash of milk to loosen it up, and some salt and pepper.

"I'll take two fingers of scotch," Daddy said over a ruffle of newspaper. "When you get the chance."

The steam was back inside my body. The noodles needed more time anyway, so I moved to the bar cart and poured Daddy two fingers of scotch, neat, in a heavy crystal glass, the way he liked it.

Everything always had to be the way Daddy liked it.

Or what? What would happen if something wasn't? It's not like he'd be in New York for very long, anyway. He never was.

The noodles were cooked through, so I drained them and added them to the sauce, along with some peas and cheddar cheese. After a good mix, I smoothed the casserole into a baking dish and topped it with fried onions. By the time the dish was in the oven, Mac and Presley were back.

"Just in time!" I chirped, a bit too loudly. I took Presley from Mac's arms and set him down. "Dinner will be ready soon. What can I get you to drink?"

"Oh, I . . ." Mac glanced at my father, who was glaring at us over the top of his paper. "I'm not staying."

"Yes, you are." I smiled. "You're staying for dinner. I'm going to tell him everything."

He smiled back at me, the first real smile I'd seen on his face since before the fiasco in the parking garage at what felt like a lifetime ago at this point. "You don't have to do that, Evelyn."

"Yes. Yes, I do." I turned and walked toward the table. Daddy went back to reading, pretending he hadn't been watching us the whole time, but I could hear the grind of his jaw. "What would you like to drink? It's late, and we all deserve a nightcap, don't you think, Daddy?"

He grunted in response.

"I'll take a beer then, Evelyn. Thanks," said Mac, pulling out the seat across from Daddy.

Daddy kept reading. He hadn't turned a page in a while, so that must've been a doozy of an article.

I went to the fridge and pulled out two cold brown ales, one for Mac and one for me. I was going to need the comforting burn of alcohol to get through this evening with my nerves intact.

After prying open the glass bottles, I made my way to the table, Presley hot on my heels, confused about the change in location and the lack of his regular food bowl. Sitting between the men, I handed Mac his beer and took a sip of mine.

It was awful! I swallowed, but with a grimace on my face, wishing for a glass of anything else to wash the taste away.

Mac laughed, whole chest moving with each guffaw.

I tried to glare at him, but the taste in my mouth was too terrible to make any face other than one of disgust.

"Never had a beer before, eh, Evie?" Mac asked.

I hated when he called me that. That's what Daddy calls me. I licked my teeth and shivered. "Why is it so . . . bready? Ugh!"

Daddy looked at me over the top of his newspaper. "That would be the hops."

"What do bunnies have to do with beer?" I asked.

Daddy's lips pursed like he'd taken a bite of lemon. He and I have vastly different senses of humor.

The egg timer on the stove went off, and I excused myself to get the tuna casserole. "Mac, be a dear and grab some plates, will you? Forks too."

"Don't forget napkins," Daddy said, attention back on the article. His eyes weren't moving, though. Always hiding instead of facing the conversation head-on, that's what Daddy was best at. With me, anyway. With business? You don't get to be the third or fourth richest man in the world—it changed every day, depending on oil profit margins—by hiding from awkward conversations.

First things first, you needed generational wealth. Like, a great-great-grandfather who'd been a pirate and stolen gold from the Spanish Armada. And then subsequent grandfathers who invested that gold and ran for positions of political power to protect that gold and married into powerful, well-connected families to gain more wealth and more power until you didn't have to talk to your daughter about her feelings because you were so rich you could pretend to read yesterday's newspaper for an hour and no one would question you.

I shook my head as if that alone would clear away any lingering anger and annoyance, slipped on oven mitts, and delivered the steaming-hot tuna casserole to the table that Mac was setting. Presley had hopped into the empty seat, his little pink tongue hanging out of his mouth, looking for all the world like the fourth guest at our meal.

I giggled and scratched his head. "Are you hungry, big boy? Mommy can give you a bite."

"Got Mr. Presley a plate too," Mac said with a wink, sliding one in front of the dog.

Daddy sighed. Finally, the paper moved. Onto the table, right in the way of dinner. He was being such an obstinate child, and we hadn't even told him anything yet. Also, he was an adult. Not a child at all!

"You know, Daddy," I said, clearing the paper away with a smile, "I do have some good news to tell you."

"Uh-huh," he said.

I served him the first scoop of dinner, followed by serving Mac, Presley, and then myself. Presley was the first to dig in.

"Mac and I here," I said, "are a steady item."

"I feared as much," Daddy said. He took a big fork full of tuna casserole, chewed it, swallowed, wiped his mouth with his napkin, and took a long sip of his scotch without saying anything else. Mac and I looked at each other, looked at Daddy, looked at Presley when he whined because he'd eaten his entire meal already and wanted seconds. "Evie," Daddy said, "why do you never do what's in your best interest? Why do you seek to sabotage your future?"

"What are you talking about?" No longer hungry, I slid my plate in front of Presley. "Sabotage my future?"

"An employee, Evelyn? Your assistant, at that? As if being photographed with that actor wasn't bad enough, you have to sink even lower."

My mouth fell open. "Daddy! Don't talk about Mac *or* Henry like that! Henry is one of the best friends I've ever had. And Mac is more than an employee. I love him!"

"Love?" Daddy repeated. "What do you know about love, Evelyn? You're still a teenager."

My eyes stung. I blinked to chase the tears away. Sometimes it seemed he went out of his way to wound me so that I might give up the fight before we'd even gotten to the heart of the matter. But he was wrong if he thought he could stop me that easily. "Daddy, I am twenty-one. And a *half*."

Daddy's brow furrowed. "That can't be . . . twenty-one?"

"And a half!"

"You should be married, Evelyn. And not to a worker at the hotel. To your equal."

He'd told me earlier that he and Mom were married when she was younger than me, and now he revealed that he thought I was still in my teens. How old was Mom when he'd swooped in and snatched her up?

Why was this something I didn't already know? How old had she been when she was carting me around from continent to continent, to toy stores late in the evenings? How old had she been when I'd found her dead and still bleeding?

Nanny had never known Mom, so she hadn't been able to fill in the answers to the questions I asked about her. As for Daddy, it was always better not to talk about Mom with him, or he'd get upset or red in the face, or make that terrible jaw-clenching noise he was doing now, and *ugh*, it got on my last nerve.

"Daddy, relax! You'll destroy your teeth. Dentures at your age? Not very ginchy."

"Do not tell me to relax. I am relaxed! We are talking about you. Your choices, your future, and why you are so inept at dealing with either. I paid for private tutors, the best we could find. And for what? Have I raised a spoiled, stupid socialite?"

The stinging in my eyes was back. This time it burned all the way down to the tip of my nose. I sucked in a shuddering breath to respond, but Mac beat me to it.

"Hey, now, that's enough, Mr. Murphy. Evelyn is not stupid."

The horrible teeth-grinding sound was back, interrupted only by Presley's wet licks of his second empty plate.

"You think I don't know my daughter?" asked Daddy.

Mac shrugged. "I think I've worked here close to two years now, and this is only the third time I've seen you. I think I've been steady with your daughter for almost two months, and you've only rung her once in that time."

Daddy took another bite of his food. He and Presley seemed to be the only ones with any appetite at all, as Mac hadn't touched his food either. I wondered if Daddy was that hungry, or if he was trying his best to look unaffected.

"I know you're not stupid, Evelyn, but you sure try hard to act like it. Bunny and hops. Dating the help. Where does it end? When do you make something out of your life?"

My lips trembled, my chin dimpling. This was too much to deal with in one day. I'd been taken into police custody, for goodness sake. What was I thinking, dealing with Daddy straight away? I should've followed my original plan. Not for his sake, but for my own. I should be in bed right now, curled up around Presley, my soft pink sheets over my shoulders. Curlers in my hair. Fuzzy socks on my feet.

I should not have spent my evening being berated by a father who was barely around.

"Mr. Murphy," Mac said, louder this time. "I mean it, mate. That's enough. Evelyn's bloody brilliant, and if you can't see it, that's your problem, right? Not hers."

"You will not speak to me so casually again, Mr. Cooper. Do I make myself clear?"

Mac smiled, half his mouth curving upward. "Sorry, Mr. Murphy. Forget how you posh lot like to pretend you're practically royalty. The way I understand, royalty is all on Evelyn's mum's side, yeah? So, you're just another rich American bloke."

Daddy's jaw clenched so hard it was a wonder teeth hadn't popped out through his cheeks.

I held up my hands. "Boys, please," I said. "It's been a long night. Mac and I discovered a dead body. And Daddy, you are cranky from transatlantic travel."

"I am no such thing!"

"You are! You are cranky!" I stood up and threw my napkin onto the table. "You are cranky, and you need to eat your dinner and drink your scotch and go to sleep! We will talk in the morning!"

Daddy pinched the bridge of his nose. "Would you stop the screeching, Evelyn? You are making this blasted headache a thousand times worse."

All the fight went out of me. "You have a headache?"

He shook his head but said yes. "Been dealing with them on and off the last week or so."

"You need to see a doctor, Daddy."

"I'm fine. It's nothing aspirin can't take care of."

"If it's nothing aspirin can't take care of, then why hasn't it gone yet?"

He glared at me.

"Doctor Smith should be back at the hotel," I said. "I'll give him a call and have him see you."

"Who?" Daddy asked, his glare turning into a squint. He sighed and picked up his fork. "Never mind. Do what you wish. You always do."

"Hardly, Daddy. I took this job planning parties because you told me to."

He looked at Mac. "And you say I don't know my daughter." He turned to me and said, "You never would've thought of it yourself, Evelyn, and look at what a natural talent you are at this. You take after your mother. She traveled around the world to help me with my business because she was good with people and good with details. She could close a sale when I couldn't because she knew how to be a good hostess. And this is what you want out of your life? To hitch your wagon to a boy who can't possibly have gone to college, who has no real future? No, Evelyn. You need to end this now and focus on work. You need to come work for me, the way your mother did. That's what you need."

Planting my fists on my hips, I stared him down. I wanted to know more about Mom and about what things had been like with Daddy, what she had been like. Who she was. But he was not going to use my mother to bully me, of that I was certain. "I am not going to end things with Mac, Daddy. You'll have to accept it. I love him, and that's all there is to it. The business stuff? We can talk about that tomorrow after we've all had a good night's sleep."

Mac nodded and stood, scooping Presley into his arms.

"And will you be going home, Mr. Cooper?" Daddy asked, not bothering to stand. "To whatever hovel you live in? Or do you plan to sully my daughter's virtue?"

I couldn't stop the surprised snort that escaped from me. Out it came, loud and disbelieving—*as if it was Mac who'd originally sullied my virtue; as if my virtue was a thing that could be sullied*—and both Mac and Daddy looked at me.

I flushed.

"I mean," I said, and cleared my throat. "Perhaps it's best not to talk about such things over dinner, Daddy."

He waved his hand. "You both have excused yourself from my table. What does dinner have to do with anything? If that boy goes into your room tonight, Evelyn, or ever again, you will be cut off. Do you hear me? You end this relationship right now, or you are on your own."

I laughed. "Cut me off? You're funny, Daddy. Get some rest. I'll call Dr. Smith for you."

Daddy stood up, his napkin tumbling out of his lap and falling on the floor. Presley squirmed in Mac's arms. My boyfriend kissed the top of the dog's head and whispered something calming to him, and for the first time I was jealous of my pet.

"I am not joking, Evelyn. Stop pretending you're stupid. You are my daughter. And I will not stand for you living this worthless life any longer."

Mac put his hand on my shoulder. "Mr. Murphy, I get it. You don't like me. That's fine. The feeling is mutual. But the way you're talking to Evelyn is not right."

"Don't you dare tell me how to talk to my daughter again!" Daddy yelled.

I stepped back, flinching, bumping into Presley in Mac's arms. I hated when Daddy yelled. Fortunately, he'd never been around enough to do it often.

"You want my money, Evelyn? Then you will live by my rules! I have no problem throwing you out on your ass and forcing you to fend for yourself! Since you're so loose, I'd imagine it won't be hard for you to find a place to shack up."

The tears would not be abated by blinking this time. I turned away from Daddy, tucking my head into Mac's shaking shoulder. "I told you, old man, to knock it off! You can disagree with what she's doing without being such a bloody bastard about it!"

"She ends things with you, or she'll be your full responsibility. And would you even want her then, Mr. Cooper? When she's penniless?"

I wiped my nose with the back of my hand. "You've made your point, Daddy, okay?" I said because I couldn't bear to hear Mac's answer. Why would he want me anymore if I wasn't rich? I was *a lot* to deal with. It was hard for me to leave the hotel; I never knew when the attacks of anxiety would strike. And he was handsome and clever and thoughtful. He could do better than someone like me. "We will finish this conversation in the morning. I promise."

I hopped up on tiptoes and planted a kiss on Daddy's cheek, even though the very act made my stomach churn. "I will call Dr. Smith about your headache. Expect a knock on your door. Have a good night's rest, Daddy."

I didn't say I loved him before I left the Presidential suite.

I don't know why.

CHAPTER 8

"I'll, uh, I'll take Presley out one more time," Mac said. "And then I'll head out."

I unlocked my door and looked at him over my shoulder, both brows raised. "What? No. You'll stay here."

"Your dad said—"

I held up a hand. "I don't care what Daddy said. I will deal with Daddy tomorrow. He's cranky, Mac. He needs to eat his dinner and get a good night's rest, and tomorrow he'll be much easier to talk to."

"It didn't seem like that was because he was cranky, Ev," said Mac, nevertheless following me into my suite.

"That's because you don't know Daddy, lover. He always says no first. Let him throw his fit and be mad and have a drink. When he wakes up tomorrow, he'll listen to reason. He isn't mad about you, after all. He's worried about the picture."

He kept following me out of the living room and into my bathroom. I kicked off my shoes and left them under the sink, my clothes following shortly thereafter. Mac leaned against the door post, Presley half asleep in the crook of his elbow.

"What picture?"

I shrugged on my bathrobe and began the arduous process of removing my makeup. First, the cold cream. "Daddy's concerned with the picture of me he shows his business friends. You know—in a board meeting or at the golf course. He likes to have a current picture of me, so when those old men start talking about their wives or children or grandchildren, Daddy can pull out his picture of me and join in the conversation. But right now, as he sees it, you'll ruin the picture. He can't tell his yacht club friends that his only daughter is shacking up with a bellhop."

"I'm not a bellhop anymore."

"Exactly." I smiled at him and wiped off the cold cream with tissues. "That's all Daddy has to realize. You can say anything you want about a picture."

"I don't get it."

I kissed his cheek and turned on the faucet, ready to wash my face with soap. "You don't have to, lover. I've got it taken care of. Trust me, all right? Speaking of! Let me finish this, and then I have a few phone calls to make."

"At this time of night, Ev?"

"Darling," I said, "justice never sleeps."

The first call I made—after moisturizing thoroughly, of course—was to Dr. Smith. He answered on the second ring, swore when he heard my voice, and grumpily said he'd be up to see Daddy in a few minutes but that Daddy could make an appointment at a doctor's office like any other patient in the future. I did remind him that Daddy was not like any other patient, and Dr. Smith yawned and hung up the phone.

The second call I made was to the police station. I asked the operator for Detective Hodgson, wondering if he'd gone home and if he had, where he lived. But Hodgson answered shortly after the phone rang, and I decided not to worry about where he lived. It was too strange a concept, like when I was a child imagining where Mr. Sharpe lived. He was a part of the hotel, and thinking about him elsewhere was a foreign affair.

Was that odd of me? Should I bring that up with my analyst?

"I'm glad you're still at the precinct, Detective," I said, "though I'm also surprised! It's late, isn't it?"

"I've got a dead judge here, Miss Murphy. Nobody's going home tonight."

I reached for the pendant of Saint Anthony around my neck. "Judge Baker is there? At the precinct?"

"Obviously not," Hodgson said. "I meant it . . . metaphorically. What do you want, Miss Murphy?"

I exhaled in relief, letting go of the silver pendant. "He's at the morgue or something, right?"

"Yes, at the morgue. Miss Murphy. Why did you call me?"

"Any news on the woman found in his trunk? I've been worried about her. She did not look well."

"No, she didn't. And she didn't like the looks of you either."

I put a hand on my hip, even though Hodgson couldn't see. "She must've been in shock. I can see no other reason for her to react that way. Which is why I would like to speak to her. Because I'm so concerned for her well-being, you see."

"Mm-hmm."

"And I'd like to make sure she's taken care of and that there wasn't something I've done to upset her in any way."

"Uh-huh."

"And so, I was wondering, is she at a hospital currently? And if so, which one? And her room number, too, would be wonderful."

Hodgson sighed so loudly that I could almost feel the air in the receiver. "Miss Murphy, please, let this woman rest. She doesn't need you marching into Manhattan General and checking in on her. She might go into shock again at the sight of you, and that's the last thing we want right now."

I held back a giggle. Had he done that on purpose? Tipped me off while acting like he was admonishing me? Or did he not want me to check on her? "Right," I said, deciding that Detective Hodgson was far from stupid and not easily manipulated. He must want me to speak to the girl. "Right. You're right. Thank you, Detective. Have a nice night."

I hung the phone back on the receiver and spun around, finding Mac watching me from the couch, his long legs stretched out on the pink carpet and crossed at the ankles. His feet were bare. He'd changed into pajamas, a blue plaid cotton set I'd gotten for him to keep here. Presley was nowhere to be seen, but I assumed he had made himself comfortable in the bedroom. "Are you up for a little hospital visit first thing in the morning, lover? Manhattan General, to be exact. I'll need you to drive the Rolls."

He shrugged a shoulder before relaxing against the couch, his head so far back on the cushions his chin pointed at the ceiling. But the relaxed posture wasn't fooling me. I could feel the tension rolling off him. "Lover," I said, sticking out my bottom lip as far as it would go, and sitting down on his lap. He "oofed" but brought his feet in so I had a better seat, wrapped one arm around my waist so I wouldn't slip. "You mustn't let Daddy bother you. I promise." I kissed his upturned chin, his stubble tickling my lips. "I'll fix this."

Mac closed his eyes and shook his head, but he said, "Okay."

I kissed his chin again. "Okay. Good! Now. Let's get some sleep. We have a busy day tomorrow. We need to talk to the woman from the trunk, and we need to go speak to Elena Baker."

Mac cracked one eye open. "Why do you want to talk to the judge's wife? She's right pregnant, you know."

"I know," I said. I stood up and motioned for him to follow. "I was the one who sent Dr. Smith home from the party with her. And while it is doubtful that a pregnant woman has the physical strength necessary to load another woman into the trunk of a car, it isn't out of the realm of possibility that she poisoned her husband."

"With heroin," Mac said, following me.

"Right. Heroin. Maybe. We won't know for sure until the lab results come back. I'm not saying she acted alone, lover. Mrs. Baker is a beautiful woman, and as a widow, she'll be filthy rich. Besides, if she is innocent, she knows Judge Baker better than anyone. She can give us an idea of where to look."

"Why are you bothering with this anyway, Evelyn? Last time, I know it was because someone died *inside* the hotel, and that messed with you. But this guy was in the garage. And tonight was your first time in the garage."

Presley was curled up on my pillow, sound asleep. I eased out the covers from underneath and scooted him toward the middle of the mattress. He woke up, but didn't move and went back to sleep the moment he was stationary. "The police think I did it, Mac. Detective McJimsey thinks I'm the guilty party! He took me in for questioning. Besides, if I'm the one who finds a body, I have a moral obligation to be the one who finds the killer."

"Evelyn." He peeled back the crisp white sheets and slid in on the opposite side of Presley. "You're not the police."

"Of course not," I said, reaching for my sleeping mask. "I wouldn't make such a grievous mistake as thinking someone like me was capable of killing anyone."

He huffed a tired but happy sound. "No, of course not. You're gonna question a judge's pregnant wife for the fun of it."

"Lover." I lifted one corner of my pink sleep mask to stare at him. "If I don't ask what I need to know, how will I ever know anything?"

He huffed again, this time closer to a laugh. I flicked off my lamp, sending the room into darkness.

"I love you, Mac. Goodnight."

"Goodnight, Evie."

"Don't call me that."

I settled into my pillow, reaching out to hold on to Presley, his soft fur a balm between my fingers. Mac hadn't said he loved me back. I hadn't told Daddy I loved him when we left the suite. Maybe it didn't mean anything. Or maybe it meant everything. Maybe he didn't want me if I was destitute. Maybe he was only putting up with me because of Daddy's money.

Or maybe he was tired, exhausted. And I shouldn't hold what he didn't say against him. He had stood up for me in a way no one ever had before. He'd told Daddy not to insult me and insisted that Daddy treat with me respect.

Only someone who loved me would do that. Who truly loved me. Like Mom. Or Nanny. No one else would do that. He had to love me.

Right?

He wouldn't leave me if I was penniless. Right?

I lifted my mask, determined to ask him. To talk to him. To get to the bottom of things before I spent the night wracked with nightmares. But he was sound asleep, his mouth cracked open and soft snores leaking out. So I scooped Presley off the pillow—who wiggled his little butt in protest—and wrapped my body around him in a hug. Presley settled in quick enough and gave my chin a lick.

Everything would be all right. I'd get to the bottom of things tomorrow. Daddy's headaches would be dealt with. He'd be rested and restored after his travel. And Mac wouldn't ever again have to worry about me not having money.

Also, I'd talk to the woman found in the trunk and Judge Baker's widow. They were also important too, I suppose. What with the murder and all that.

CHAPTER 9

I slept dreamlessly, a blessing all things considered, and awoke to an empty apartment. Mac must've taken Presley out for his morning constitution. With a shrug and a yawn, I put on my pink chenille robe, slid on matching fuzzy slippers, and padded across the top-floor hall to invite Daddy to breakfast. I was far too sleepy to cook, but Chef Marco's egg-white omelets never disappointed.

Other guests were opening their doors to fetch the morning newspaper delivery. I stepped over mine, preferring to read it with coffee over breakfast. I'd pick up the national papers I had delivered, from the mail desk, after my trip to the hospital. Hopefully, the young woman from Judge Baker's trunk was awake and able to receive visitors. I had a few questions to ask her.

First, I needed to know her age and background and, second, how she might've known the judge. And finally, why was she so terrified of me?

I didn't know her. At least, I was pretty sure I didn't.

That was why talking to her was so important and why I said a quick prayer to Saint Anthony before knocking on Daddy's door. *Help me find this murderer, please, before the police suspect me. Even more than they already do!*

The nerve of that McJimsey. All blond and green-eyed and sus-picious of me. Ridiculous.

"Daddy!" I rapped my knuckles on the door. "Daddy, are you awake?"

His bedroom was on the second floor of the suite. The odds of him hearing me if he was asleep were slim to none, so I didn't think anything of opening his door and strolling inside. It wasn't locked, but that could be because the maids had come by already, to get his coffee ready, or because Dr. Smith forget to lock up after examining Daddy.

He was safe inside the hotel. We all were.

We had to be. Or else, why stay at the Pinnacle at all if it was as dangerous as outside?

"Daddy?" I closed the suite door and cocked my head to the side, straining my hearing to see if the shower was running or if he was responding. The kitchen was dark, last night's half-eaten tuna casserole still on the table. It didn't even smell like coffee, which was odd. The maids knew to get Daddy's coffee brewing at exactly 5:50 AM. "Daddy?"

It was odd for him to still be asleep, already a quarter after six, but he had been irritable and jet-lagged. Perhaps the headaches were worse than he'd let on. I dithered at the foot of the stairs, wondering if I should let him sleep. But I wanted to at least check in with him before I started my day of questioning witnesses.

My slippers padded against the beige carpet of the stairs. I yawned again, wishing the maids weren't tardy. I was looking forward to that coffee. Who drew Daddy's room, anyway? Poppy would've men-tioned it. Florence, then? But she wasn't in my room when I woke up, and it wasn't like her to be late.

"Daddy," I called again, knocking on his bedroom door. It wasn't closed all the way, and I could hear . . . something, from the inside. A thump. A gurgle. Faint. My fingers twitched, and my teeth dug into my bottom lip. Maybe he had a lady friend inside? But then why hadn't he called out, told me to leave?

He was fine. He had to be fine. Everything was fine. I was overreacting. I took a deep breath and forced a smile on my face. "Daddy," I said again, "I'm coming in, so I hope you're decent!"

His bedroom was dark, but not dark enough to disguise the empty, rumpled bed or the twitching body on the floor.

Someone was screaming, and it wasn't until I thought to shout out for help that I realized it was me. My throat burned. Daddy was seizing on the floor. I had no idea what to do, none whatsoever, but standing there and screaming over and over again wasn't working. I ran for the phone next to his bed and hurriedly dialed. The operator answered with, "Good morning, Mr. Murphy."

"It's me!" I shouted. "Daddy is hurt! He's having some sort of fit! Oh God, call for help! Get Dr. Smith! Hurry, please!"

The woman attempted to ask more questions, but I hung up the phone and knelt by Daddy. His eyes were closed, but his mouth was open, drool leaking over the corners of his lips. The veins in his forehead and neck were throbbing, bulging, running down his cheeks and touching each other. I held his hand. It was hot and clammy. "Daddy?" His fit was calming down, his frantic twitching and tensing easing little by little, but not gone. Not yet. What did you do when someone had a seizure? Do I put a pillow under his head? A spoon in his mouth? I clutched his hand tighter and made the sign of the cross. "Daddy, can you hear me? It's going to be okay. Dr. Smith is coming. Help is coming. Please, Daddy."

It had been so long since I'd prayed to any saint but Anthony that I didn't even know who to pray to and ask for healing. Nanny had a saint she called on whenever I got even a hint of the sniffles, but their name was lost to me now. I was unable to do anything but clutch my father's sweating, trembling hand and beg him not to die.

There was something glittering on the floor. Almost under the bed, but not quite. I blinked, unsure. But as my vision cleared there was only one thing it could be: a needle, exactly like the one that had been in Judge Baker's arm.

Daddy's eyes fluttered open. They were bloodshot, more red than white, his pupils blown out so wide the brown that matched my iris was gone. "Gwen." His voice was a hoarse whisper, his Adam's apple bobbing with the effort of speaking.

My mom.

He hadn't said her name in . . .

Golly, I couldn't remember. I almost didn't even remember she had a name to begin with. That she was a person. An individual. For so long she'd lived only inside my memory, like a figment of my imagination.

I shook my head, tears rolling off the tip of my nose. "Sorry, Daddy. It's Evelyn."

"Gwen," he said again. His eyes were still open, but they had lost focus, his hand going slack in mine.

"Daddy?" I lowered my ear over his mouth. If he was breathing, I couldn't hear it. "Daddy? Please, please. You can't leave me. Please, Daddy! Please!"

A heavy hand fell on my shoulder. I gasped and sat back, my eyes too blurry with tears to make out the features of whoever was in the room with me, but the grouchy and yet assertive voice of Dr. Smith answered any questions. "Move," he said. "And direct the police to this room when they arrive."

"But. There—there's a needle, like Judge Baker's! And—"

Dr. Smith pushed me away before taking my place at Daddy's side. I scrambled to my knees, wiping my face with the backs of my hands, not that it mattered. My face was soaked with tears that wouldn't stop.

"Out," he barked, tearing open Daddy's pajamas. "Now!"

I tripped out of the room and raced down the stairs. *Help. Help.* I could get help. Even if I couldn't pray for it, even if I couldn't help him myself. I could scream and cry and beg and get him the help he needed before it was too late. *Please, don't be too late.* The bottom step came sooner than I expected, and I faltered but kept running. I didn't notice anything except for the front door, wide open, and Mac walking inside. Uniformed policeman were behind him.

"Evelyn!" Mac grabbed my arms, and I came to a complete stop, crumpling in his hands.

"Daddy," I gasped. "He's upstairs! He stopped breathing!"

The men hurried away. Mac pulled me against him, holding me tight. I didn't want to be held. I wanted to run and keep running. I wanted to get help. More help. There had to be better help out there somewhere. Someone who could save Daddy. Someone who could wake me up from this nightmare, who could stop this from happening.

This could not be happening. If I could run away, I'd find the truth. I could start over. I could start this entire, horrible day all over.

"Evelyn," Mac said, his hand on my head. He pushed my face against his chest and squeezed his arm around my waist, so tight I could barely breathe. I wasn't breathing. Daddy had stopped breathing. He was dead. He had to be dead. He was dead and I'd found him like that.

I'd found him. He was dead and I'd found him.

My knees went slack. I clung onto Mac's shirt when my balance failed me. He lowered me to the ground until we were both on our knees, his arms still wrapped around me, forcing my face against his neck. I choked in air and let it scratch my throat, desperate to feel the pain, to feel anything that could put me back inside my body again. Because all I wanted to do was run.

"Evelyn," Mac said, rocking back and forth on his knees, his hands pressing hard against me. "He's okay, Evelyn. He's okay. They're taking him out now. He's okay."

"He wasn't breathing!"

"I can see him breathing, Evelyn. I can see him. I can see his chest move. It's okay. Dr. Smith saved him. It's going to be okay, love. It's okay."

CHAPTER 10

Daddy was gone. I don't know how long Mac and I sat there on the floor before Mr. Sharpe arrived and ushered me into a nearby chair.

"You're in shock," he said.

I blinked at him, unsure of what he was talking about. He knelt in front of me and made such direct eye contact that I shivered.

"I'll be fine, Mr. Sharpe."

He put his hand on my forehead. "You need to be seen by the doctor," he said, standing. "He left with your father. Mr. Cooper, will you drive Miss Murphy to Manhattan General, please?"

"Not yet." Detective Hodgson walked in, trailed by Detective McJimsey.

McJimsey put his hands on his belt. "She needs to catch us up on what happened. Then she can leave."

Mac walked up behind me, pushing my hair off my shoulders and giving my arms a gentle squeeze. It was such a sweet gesture of support that my eyes filled with tears. I blinked up at the ceiling because I couldn't start crying again. If I started, I wasn't going to stop anytime soon.

"Hey, Miss Murphy," Hodgson said. He took the seat across from me. "You holding up okay?"

No. Not even close. "Why are you here, Detective?"

"I called the police," Mr. Sharpe said. "We needed help, first of all, to get your father to the hospital quickly. They can clear traffic for the ambulance. Not to mention the look of it. A judge died last night, and Mr. Murphy is now in the hospital? We need the police. Actual police."

It didn't take a detective to figure out that was a shot at me and my penchant for sleuthing.

Detective Hodgson pulled out a small notebook from his jacket pocket. "Why don't you make us some tea, huh?" he asked Mac. "You posh types, that's what you drink, ain't it?"

"Posh," Mac snorted, but he moved around in Daddy's kitchen to find a teapot. "That ain't me, mate."

Hodgson met my eyes. "Tell that to your accent, Mr. Cooper."

I sniffed. Hodgson was trying to calm me down before he questioned me about the murder of my father. *Attempted* murder, I corrected myself. Even if it did seem far-fetched. Judge Baker, dead of an apparent heroin overdose, and not twelve hours later, Daddy having a fit due to a suspected heroin overdose. Maybe they were both secretive drug users. Mac had promised Daddy was breathing when Dr. Smith took him away on a stretcher.

He'd called me my mother's name. At death's doorstep, he'd wanted her. Now the vision of finding him seizing on the floor of his suite would exist side by side with the nightmare of finding Mom, bleeding to death, in an alley behind a dumpster. Trash. Piles and piles of it, stinking, flies swirling. And Mom, beautiful Mom, dying—and dead because I wanted to look at toys days before Christmas.

I'd fought with Daddy last night. Would that be the last conversation we ever had?

Hodgson and McJimsey exchanged a heavy look, and the younger detective sighed. "I'm gonna look at the crime scene."

"I'll take you to the room," Mr. Sharpe announced.

Hodgson nodded and waited until the two men had gone up the stairs, before flipping open his notebook. "I know this is hard, Miss Murphy, but I need you to tell me what happened this morning."

I wiped my face dry on the sleeves of my robe. "Um," I said. I shook my head. I couldn't remember what had happened this morning. All I could think about was the last conversation I had with Daddy. "We fought," I said. "Oh, we had a *big* fight."

"This morning?" Detective Hodgson asked.

I shook my head again. "I'm sorry. Last night. I cooked him dinner and invited Mac to eat with us. He called me names."

"Mac did?"

"No. Daddy." My nose was running, but I wasn't about to wipe that with my robe. Sensing my discomfort, Hodgson reached into his jacket and handed me a handkerchief from an inside pocket. "Sorry," I said again. "He was cranky, you see. He'd gotten off a long flight and was dealing with a headache. I told him to finish his dinner and scotch, and I'd ring up Dr. Smith to check on him, and then he was to sleep until he wasn't cranky anymore. Daddy doesn't like to be bossed around, but Mac and I left all the same. That was . . . one in the morning? Right before I called you."

Hodgson made a note in his book, and I dried my nose. The stitching in his handkerchief was meticulous, his initials engraved in navy blue on the corner. Someone who loved him had made him this, and I'd put snot in it.

I would have it dry-cleaned immediately.

"And then this morning?"

I nodded, tracing my fingers along the "LH" in stitches. "Yes. I woke up around six. Daddy always wakes up at 5:50. I came over here so we could have coffee together and have a chat before we start our day. I don't like it when the two of us are at odds. But he wasn't awake. And the coffee wasn't on, which I thought was strange, because the maids here know his schedule. The coffee should be ready for him when he wakes. A pot of it, all his own, brewed with the beans he likes best. But there wasn't a maid either. I assumed the girl was running late. The shower wasn't running. I yelled for Daddy, but he didn't answer. I thought to wake him up myself, to see if his headache hadn't improved. But when I knocked on the door, there was a noise. A weird, gurgling noise. And when I went inside, Daddy was on the floor."

Mac set a steaming cup of tea in front of me, and I sipped it. There was sugar and milk, but I couldn't taste anything. My tongue was numb. But it was warm all the same, and it heated my belly in a welcoming relief. Mac put his hands on my shoulders, and I closed my eyes and took a deep breath.

"Where on the floor?" Hodgson asked. "Where was your father?"

Another breath. I forced myself to remember. "Right between the bed and the door. The sheets were a mess, like he'd fallen off the mattress. He was on his back. His eyes were closed, but his muscles were tense. The veins in his neck and forehead were bulging. I rang for help and held his hand and tried to talk to him. After a minute, the fit subsided. And he opened his eyes. And he . . . he . . ."

I pressed the dirty linen to my mouth, trying to hold in the sob. Mac rubbed my neck in slow, small circles.

"He what, Miss Murphy?"

"He called me by my mother's name. And then he stopped breathing. I saw the needle next to him, near the underside of the bed. It must've rolled away when he fell. Right after, Dr. Smith arrived and forced me from the room. I don't know what happened next."

"A needle. Hmm." Hodgson finished writing something down. He closed his notebook and sighed. "Dr. Smith was with him when they took him out of here. He was unconscious, Miss Murphy, but Dr. Smith had him breathing again. Which leads me to believe . . . this might be unrelated to the death of the judge last night."

"What? How can that be possible?"

"I said *might*, not *for sure*. But Chief Harvey and the mayor had all hands on deck in the hours after Baker's death. Nothing's been confirmed yet, not one hundred percent, but it looks like Judge Baker was injected with pure heroin. It woulda killed him in minutes. Your father still isn't dead. So, it probably wasn't the same drug."

I nodded and took a sip of tea. He didn't have to tell me that. I was both grateful and anxious. Though I was always anxious, so what was a little more? Two killers? No. That was silly. It had to be one. Didn't it? Why would both victims be injected with different types of drugs? That made no sense, and yet . . . And yet . . .

That was the problem at hand.

"Daddy is stubborn," I said, as much to myself as to the detective. "He's too stubborn to die so shortly after we had a disagreement. He'll want the last word.

Hodgson sat back in his chair, his fingers on his forehead. "Sure," he said. "I get it. This fight you two had last night—was there anything else about it?"

"Like what?"

"Anything you want to tell me? Why did he call you a name? Why did it start in the first place?"

"I told you," I said. "He was cranky. He'd flown from London and was struggling with a headache. He needed dinner and a stiff drink and a nap, and so that's what he had. I don't . . ." My lips trembled. "I don't know what happened when he woke up."

"And you, Mr. Cooper? You were present at the argument, yes?"

"Yes. I was."

"And did you and Mr. Murphy exchange words?"

"No," I said at the same moment that Mac replied, "Yes."

I reached out a hand like that could stop it. "No, it was nothing. Really. Daddy was mad at me. Mac just happened to be in the same room."

Detective Hodgson licked his teeth. "That's not what I heard. Mr. Cooper, what did Mr. Murphy say to you?"

"What did you hear?" I asked.

Hodgson ignored me and tapped his pencil on the notebook cover, waiting on Mac.

Mac sighed.

"He didn't like me and made that clear. I don't like him much either, to tell the truth. Not after seeing the way he was talking to Ev. Might've called him a bastard—can't quite remember the exact wording. Coulda told him to go to hell. I was thinking it. But then Evelyn sent us all off to bed, kissed his cheek, and that was that."

Hodgson flipped his book back open and jotted down a note. "That's all you have to tell me?"

"That's all that happened," I said. "We went to bed, and when I came in here to check on Daddy, there was no coffee being brewed, no shower running. No maid. Which is . . ." I worried my bottom lip. "Which is troubling."

"Why?" Hodgson asked.

"The staff knows better. They know that Daddy expects his coffee to be ready and waiting for him by six AM. That he expects a maid in his room, cleaning up after his night and ready to iron anything he needs to wear for the day. But no one was here."

Hodgson scribbled something else in his notebook, nodding once. "I remember you saying that. I'll follow up with Mr. Sharpe and the head of housekeeping. You're heading to the hospital now?" He stood. "So I know where to find you, if necessary." The last part was said to Mac. Which I found to be rude.

"Mac was with me all night, Detective."

"Mm-hmm. And are you a very heavy sleeper, Miss Murphy?"

I tugged on the edges of my borrowed handkerchief, unsure of how to answer. I had slept through him getting up and getting ready and leaving with Presley for his morning walk. But I was positive, *positive*, I would've woken up if he'd left to finish the argument with Daddy.

Right?

I was saved from answering, however, by terrible news.

Mr. Sharpe came running down the stairs with a hand over his mouth. Detective McJimsey followed, a grimace on his face. "It's not a double, anymore, Hodge," he said. "There's a stiff in the closet."

CHAPTER 11

odgson dashed up the stairs. He and McJimsey disappeared into Daddy's room. My heart raced and forced its way into my throat. I held on to my neck with a cold hand, my pulse vibrating beneath it.

"Mr. Sharpe?"

He clutched his knees and bowed his head. "Poor lass," he said.

Mac approached him. "Who, Mr. Sharpe?"

And I realized I hadn't yet seen his sister, Poppy, this morning.

Mr. Sharpe drew in a deep breath and stood up straight. "Florence," he said. "Florence."

My maid. My day maid for the last decade or more. How treacherous, my heart, to be relieved that the name spoken wasn't Poppy's. And then to be filled with grief at the name of the employee who knew me best. Who always looked out for me. Who kept my secrets close to her vest, who took care of me the best way she knew how. Who never once judged me for finding Mac in my hotel room when he should've been long gone and in his apartment.

Dead. In my father's bedroom closet.

"I have to see her," I said. "I have to know how she died."

"The police will take care of it, Miss Murphy," Mr. Sharpe said. "Trust me. You do not want to see."

But I had seen worse, and I'd been younger when I'd witnessed it. I could do this. Florence was dead, and I owed it to her to find out why. I tightened the belt of my robe and snuck up the stairs. If the police didn't hear me coming, they couldn't stop me from entering. She was hard to see at first glance, with Hodgson kneeling and McJimsey hovering. But there she was—Florence, crumpled in a seated position, her lips blue and discoloration on her neck.

I closed my eyes. Mom was on the inside of my eyelids. Dead and bleeding. I shook my head to chase away the vision and blinked my eyes open. Florence was still there. She was not my mother, but she was my employee. My friend.

McJimsey saw me first. He glared and pointed. "Get out before I have you hauled away."

But I met Hodgson's gaze and stayed put. "Strangled?" I asked. "No drugs this time?"

Hodgson stood up. "We won't know until she's been examined by the coroner," he said. "But there's no evidence of heroin."

"What was she strangled with?"

"What difference does it make to you?" McJimsey grabbed my elbow and pulled me toward the door.

"Was it something he found in the suite, or did he bring it with him? Was Florence an intended target, or was she accidental, because she walked in on what he was doing to Daddy? There was a woman in the judge's trunk for a reason. Florence being in Daddy's closet might be more of the same."

McJimsey's steps hesitated, but nonetheless, he continued ushering me rather rudely away from the crime scene. "Let the police worry about the modus operandi, little girl. Go to the hospital and visit your father before it's too late."

The bedroom door swatted my backside when it closed. I stood there, blinking. Too late? Too late for what? Daddy wasn't going to die. I'd already decided that. He wasn't. No matter how things might look, no matter what that green-eyed detective might think. And *little girl*? He was hardly older than me!

"Mac?" I made for the stairs. "Mac, we need to get to Manhattan General as fast as possible."

"Yes, ma'am." He stood up from the table, alone in the room except for the occasional officer in blue. Mr. Sharpe must've left already. "I'll ring Burrows, get somebody looking out for Presley."

I wanted to bring Presley with us, but Mac was right. The hospital wasn't about to welcome in a dog, no matter how perfect he was.

"Thank you. I'm gonna throw on some clothes and brush my hair. We'll leave in ten."

He arched a judgmental eyebrow.

I sighed. "Twenty."

In the end, it took closer to twenty-five because I stood in the center of my closet, with my jaw slack and my mouth open. What did someone wear to the hospital after finding their father half dead? As it turns out: denim jeans and a black sweater.

Once we made it to the lobby, Mac tugged on my hand and headed to the direction of the front desk. But I shook my head and pulled him to the front door.

"I want to look at the garage again."

Mac made a noise between a sigh and a groan. "'Course you do."

"Need to talk to the valets."

"Yep."

"See which one of them let Judge Baker walk inside."

Mac shook his head. "Nobody would've. The cars get brought out to the guests."

"Every time?"

He shrugged. "Pinnacle rules."

"But they let *us* walk in."

"Yeah. You're the boss's daughter. You go wherever you want. Plus, I worked here."

"But he was a judge, Mac. A well-known one. Hard to tell a man like that no."

"What makes you think he walked in anyway?"

I looked at his profile. The glowing, carved pumpkins in the window of the Pinnacle's sweetshop just behind his head. The sidewalk was busy with people, but we kept close enough together not to be separated. "He was in his car. Inside the garage. He had to either walk in or drive in himself. And how did the woman get in the trunk? When did she get in the trunk? Was she there for the entire party? Was Mrs. Baker aware of the fact that there was a woman in the trunk of her family vehicle?"

The parking garage came into view, a bright red sign twinkling in the morning sun. "More curious, Mac. What do Judge Baker and Florence and the woman in the trunk and Daddy all have in common? Why were they targeted by the same killer?"

"Maybe they weren't," Mac said. "Maybe Baker and your Dad were—or . . ." He didn't finish the sentence, out of politeness or respect for my feelings.

I finished it for him. "Or they both overdosed on heroin within a twelve-hour period. Yes. That is possible. It is possible that Judge Baker stuffed a girl in his trunk with the intention of murdering her before accidentally killing himself. It is possible that Daddy strangled Florence and stuffed her in his closet before sticking a needle in his arm. Those things are all possible, lover. But it still doesn't explain one thing."

"And what's that?"

"How did Judge Baker get in the garage in the first place?"

CHAPTER 12

It was the same young man who had waved us in the night before that stood behind the valet stall now. Cars were coming in and out, and he was in charge of taking the paper ticket from the guest, finding the corresponding key, and handing it over to the other young man in green, who drove the cars out or parked the cars in— whatever the guests needed.

"Good to see you again," I said, though I didn't mean it. Not because of anything he'd done. It wasn't his fault that Florence was dead and my father was ill.

An older woman handed him her car keys, and I watched as he scribbled something down on two pieces of paper, handed her one, and hung the other on the key.

The woman walked away, smelling of Chanel Number 5. I took in a deep breath and said a prayer to Saint Marilyn, which was probably blasphemous, but my father was ill and Jesus forgives. That's kind of his whole thing.

"You too, Miss Murphy," he said. "Mac." He rang the bell on the valet stand, keys in his hand.

Scott. His name was Scott. Mac had called him Scott last night. I had no idea what his last name was, and felt uncomfortable referring to him so casually so soon into our acquaintance, so I didn't call him anything at all and got right down to business. "I assume you've spoken with the police?"

"Yeah," he said. "Pretty cut-and-dry business, if you ask me."

"That's wonderful because I *am* asking you," I said, brighter than I felt. "Specifically, I wanted to know, how was Judge Baker when you saw him last night?"

Scott clicked his tongue. "Dead."

I tilted my head to the side, the smile still on my face. "That was the first time you saw Judge Baker?"

He nodded. "I didn't get the key from him," he said. "His wife drove. I think she dropped him off at the hotel for the party and then brought the car here."

Another valet walked over, and Scott handed him the older woman's keys. Why would Mrs. Baker drop Judge Baker off at the hotel and then bring the car herself to the garage? Many guests leave their cars with the staff at the hotel's entrance.

"One moment," I said to the new valet before he could leave to do his job, aware of the line building up behind me. "Were you working last night?"

"Part of it," he said. "For the party rush. I clocked out by nine thirty, miss."

Scott nodded his agreement. "We have a skeleton crew at night, miss. Budget cuts and all."

"Budget cuts?" I repeated. I hadn't heard of such a thing. Besides, New York never slept. It didn't make sense to cut staff when guests would want to be a part of the nightlife. That was bad business. "Hmm. Did you see Judge Baker then, sir?"

He pointed at himself with a fist full of jangling keys. "Me, miss? I'm Alan. And no, I didn't see him. Saw his wife, though. Big ol' belly, looked about ready to pop. She walked herself back to the hotel. Felt bad for her, in shoes like that. My wife had a baby a few months ago. I notice those things now."

"Congratulations! How is your new family doing?"

"Very well, thank you, miss."

"I wonder, were there any other valets on duty last night?"

"Sure," Scott said. "A few others here, helping park cars. Let's see. There's Lars. Big Tommy. Little Tommy. Chester. And any of the bellhops working the steps can bring cars over for folks."

Mac put his hand on the small of my back and gently pushed. "Thanks, fellas. We'll let you get back to it."

"You need the keys, Mac?" Scott called.

But Mac pulled them out of his pocket. "Never got to take our drive last night! See ya!"

I exhaled hard, frustrated and in desperate need of coffee. "No one saw Judge Baker enter or leave the garage last night!"

"Probably not no one," Mac said, leading the way to the third level, where the Rolls was parked. "But not those two. Somebody must've seen him. Makes sense, if you think about it."

"I *am* thinking about it," I assured him, "and it most definitely does not make sense."

"He's not allowed in the garage in the first place," Mac said. "If one of the valets had seen him, they woulda stopped him. You tie that with the fact he had a girl in his boot? He's sneaking his way in."

For a moment I pictured Judge Baker trying to force a woman into wearing cowboy boots, but now was not the time for delightful wordplay. "Maybe you're right." I wrinkled my nose. "And maybe this is all one big . . . well, it isn't *nothing*. Because there was a woman in his trunk. And one in Daddy's closet. Something is going on here, even if it's only men who are injecting themselves with drugs and being predatory toward the opposite sex."

"Yeah," Mac agreed, opening the passenger's door for me. "Still bad."

"Still very bad," I said. "I need to talk to that girl in the boot."

★ ★ ★

Hospitals give me the heebie-jeebies. I kept close to Mac as we walked up to the receptionist and asked what floor my father might be on, and for the room number if she had it. The receptionist flipped a few papers around before picking up a phone and holding up a finger, indicating that we wait. Several minutes after she hung up, a man in a suit and tie approached, his hand outstretched.

"Miss Murphy," he said, "I am glad to make your acquaintance, though I am sorry for the circumstances. My name is Ed Hindley, I work for the hospital."

I shook his hand, though Mac made a huffing sound.

"As what?"

"Beg pardon?" Mr. Hindley asked, letting go of my hand and offering it to Mac.

Mac shook it and repeated. "You work for the hospital as what? Not a doctor, I don't think."

"Oh. No. No." Mr. Hindley wiped his hands on his jacket, and I wasn't sure if it was because he was nervous or because he regretted touching us. "I'm the CFO."

I wrinkled my nose. "Why is the chief financial officer talking to us about Daddy? I want to see my father, Mr. Hindley, and I want to see him now."

"I'm sorry, Miss Murphy, but that isn't possible. He's with the doctors right now. In excellent hands, I assure you. But we've got a waiting room set up for you, if you two would follow me."

We followed after him, my hand clutching Mac's. He didn't complain and he didn't adjust; he stayed by my side and squeezed back. "Rolling out the red carpet for a hospital visit, eh?"

I frowned. "It's probably because we donate so much money to the hospital every year. Although Dr. Smith works here now. He's very fond of me, you know."

"Dr. Smith ain't fond of anybody, love, but if he was? It'd be you."

Mr. Hindley led us through several doors before pushing open two beige ones that revealed several stiff-looking chairs, a low coffee table, and a stack of magazines strewn about. "Dr. Smith will meet you here as soon as he can," he said. "Is there anything you need?"

"Coffee," I said. "Please. Cream and sugar."

"Ditto," Mac said. "And mate? Where's your toilet?"

Mr. Hindley pointed to the right with his thumb. "Down the hall. Can't miss it. I'll be right back with those coffees."

Mac kissed me on the cheek and headed in the direction of the bathroom, leaving me alone in the stark waiting room. The only things to distract me from my thoughts were months-old issues of *Vogue* that I'd already read. I sat down on the most comfortable looking of the uncomfortable chairs and leaned my head against the wall.

"Too late," McJimsey had said. What did he know that I didn't? Daddy was breathing when Dr. Smith had taken him away. They'd all told me that. Mac had seen him breathing. Daddy was breathing and stubborn, and there was no way he'd die without the last word in an argument.

And what was it that valet had said about budget cuts? Could that have something to do with Daddy threatening to cut me off financially? But no, I was certain he was more worried about keeping up appearances than anything to do with our vast wealth. He wouldn't throw me out, not even if I was desperate to run away. I was his only child, his sole heir, and if I didn't live up to appearances, then the picture would need to be redeveloped. He'd come around to Mac. He wouldn't risk the embarrassment. A fate worse than death, in my father's estimation.

Mac walked into the waiting room only seconds before the CFO, holding the swinging doors open for the man, who held two mugs of coffee. He gave the first one to me, sidestepping Mac as he did so, who could only roll his eyes. If he wasn't used to me being a princess now, he'd never be.

"If there's anything else," Mr. Hindley said, "inform any nurse that you wish to see me."

"And Dr. Smith?" I asked, holding the mug tight. I hadn't realized how cold my fingers were until they were wrapped around the warm ceramic. "He knows we're here?"

Mr. Hindley smiled, though it didn't reach his eyes. "He will be here to brief you as soon as he can, I promise."

The doors swung closed behind him, and Mac took a seat next to me. "Don't like that bloke. Bad feeling about him."

"That's because he's wearing an expensive suit and gave me my coffee before yours."

"He had to walk right by me with full hands! I even had to open the door for him!" Mac gulped his coffee and exhaled with his tongue sticking out of his mouth. "Rich people. I'll never get it."

"But Mac," I said. "I'm rich."

"Yeah, but that's like . . . the least interesting thing about you. These other jerks? The money's the only thing they've got goin' for 'em."

My nose stung and I smiled to keep the tears away. Happy tears this time. This beautiful man, and here he was with me on one of the worst days of my life, and I was gonna marry him, no matter what Daddy said. I was just about to reassure Mac of my feelings when the doors to our private waiting room opened again.

CHAPTER 13

I jumped to my feet, coffee sloshing over the sides of my mug and running down my hands.

Dr. Smith grimaced at the sight of it and plucked a box of tissues off the magazine table.

I handed my mug to Mac, who was now stuck with both cups. "Thank you." I wiped my hands as dry as I could, trying to guess from Dr. Smith's expression if I was about to get good news or bad news. He wasn't wearing his usual suit, but a white coat with a stethoscope around his neck and several pens in his pocket underneath his name stitched in black. I thought of the party that had now been only a few hours ago and wondered if he wore the same outfit.

"He's alive," Dr. Smith said. "Your father. We have him stabilized. But he's not awake. And I don't know when he'll regain consciousness."

My chin quivered. I cleared my throat. "I see. But you did say *when*, yes, Dr. Smith? And not *if*?"

Two deep lines etched between his eyebrows. "I'm sorry, Miss Murphy. I can't say for sure either way."

"But," Mac said, carefully standing up, "in your professional opinion, Doc?"

"My professional opinion is that I'm not able to tell you," Dr. Smith said.

"May we see him?"

Dr. Smith sighed. "Follow me."

Daddy's room was cold. He was lying on a bed in the middle of the white room, the lights off, the scratchy beige blankets pulled up under his armpits. His eyes were closed and his mouth open, and he looked so vulnerable it felt wrong to notice. I pressed the back of my hand to his forehead, relieved to find his skin a regular temperature.

"Daddy?" I whispered. "Can you hear me?"

He didn't respond. Mac and Dr. Smith hovered in the doorway. I sighed and made up my mind. Daddy wasn't going anywhere. But there was something I needed to do. "Dr. Smith? May I speak to you for a moment?"

"You've never asked my permission before," he grumbled.

"Mac, will you wait with Daddy?"

He shrugged, both hands still clutching coffee mugs. "Yeah. Sure. Hey, Mr. M. How's it going, mate?" He set the mugs down on the windowsill and took a seat in one of the two chairs in the room.

I closed the door of the hospital room and looked up and down the hall. "The woman from the trunk," I said. "She's still here?"

"Yes."

Another doctor walked past us, his head buried in a file, his white coat fluttering behind his legs.

I waited until he turned the corner to ask, "Where?"

"Miss Murphy," he complained.

"Dr. Smith," I retorted. "We both know I will badger and badger you until you break down and give me the information I require. Please, Dr. Smith. Daddy was attacked, and this woman might have an answer."

"The police—"

"The police suspect *me*," I said. "Me! Of all people! Please, Dr. Smith. I'll only talk to her for a minute."

He turned on his heel and walked away. I stared after him, dumbstruck, but the doctor looked over his shoulder and said, "Three-eleven. Go down this hallway and take a left after the swinging doors. It's the first turn on your right after that."

I popped into Daddy's room. Mac was still seated, sipping from a single cup of coffee. I stared longingly at my mug left on the windowsill. Daddy was asleep, the rise and fall of his chest a comforting sight, even if he wasn't awake.

Yet.

He would wake up. Us Murphys, we're a stubborn bunch.

"Come, lover," I said. "We have someone else to visit this morning."

Dr. Smith had said to take a left after the swinging doors at the end of the hallway. What he hadn't said was that the hallway went on almost forever. My toes hurt by the time we finally came upon the doors.

Mac blew out a breath that made his lips rattle. "Woulda brought a snack if I knew we were walking to New Jersey."

I pushed the doors opened and hurried to the left. The first right, he'd said. Except. The first right was a janitorial closet. I blinked at it, surprised that it existed.

"This is wrong," I said.

"Gotta keep hospitals clean, Ev."

"No, Mac. Dr. Smith told me to take a left after the swinging doors and then the very first right. But there is nowhere else to turn."

"Maybe he got it mixed up? And it's a right after the swinging doors and then the first left?"

I nodded. "Let's try."

There was a dull, ever incessant pounding behind my eyes that wouldn't go away, no matter how hard I blinked or how long I didn't blink. Coffee would've solved it, I was sure, but I only regretted leaving my mug behind a little. There was a murderer out there, somewhere, in the Pinnacle or elsewhere, and I needed to find him.

Or her. Sometimes the killer is a woman.

But what sort of a woman could've put another person in a trunk? I didn't have the arm strength for that. Unless, like I'd suggested to Mac, she'd been able to convince the woman to get into the trunk herself. But why kill Florence? Why kill Judge Baker? And what did either of them have to do with Daddy? In the Christie novels, the female killers often have a male partner. Could something like that be happening now?

We backtracked and reversed course, taking a right after the swinging doors and the first left after that. Here was another hallway, with patient rooms on either side.

The door to 311 was wide open. Mac and I approached around the corner, on tiptoe, but the nurses were frantic, calling out technical terms to each other. It didn't take a genius to see why. The woman from the trunk was dead on her hospital bed, her lips blue, the pillow on the floor. Nurses were gathered around her, trying to bring her back to life.

Mac swore. I made the sign of the cross. "Too late," I said.

★ ★ ★

Dr. Smith came running down the hall. He gawked at me, but I held up my empty hands. I hadn't even made it into the room! This was not my fault!

"Come on," Mac said, and guided me to nearby seats. We could almost see into the room, and frankly I was grateful we didn't have a direct view. "This is terrible, Evelyn."

I nodded and grasped his hand. "I wanted her to tell us how she ended up in that trunk."

"And also she's dead."

I closed my eyes. "Right, of course." I sighed. "I'm sorry. That's terrible. The poor thing. I'm still all messed up from this morning. Daddy. And Florence. Oh, sweet Florence." My eyes stung, and I squeezed them tighter shut. "I don't even know her last name, Mac. How do I . . . how do I send my condolences to her family? She worked for me for ten years, and I don't know where her family lives, or if she even has one!"

"Hey, hey." He wrapped his arm around my shoulders and pulled me closer, the arm of the chair digging into my hip. The comfort and the pain both distracted me from the ache in my chest. "Breathe, Evie, baby. Breathe in and out. Remember what Dr. Sanders told you to do."

The breathing technique came from Dr. Smith, but I was too focused on my breath to correct Mac. What Dr. Sanders told me to do was find *where* in my body I was feeling things, and then give that thing a name. To talk to it the way I would a child. To soothe it and comfort it and allow it to leave. But I'd only gotten as far as three breaths before Dr. Smith came out, looking at his watch.

I stood up and wiped my cheeks. "What happened?"

He gave the nearest nurse the time and shook his head. "We won't know for sure until an autopsy is done."

"But?" Mac pressed.

Dr. Smith sighed. "Looks like she was suffocated."

My nose wrinkled as my throbbing, tired mind tried to catch up with what he was saying. "Someone snuck in here and killed her before she had a chance to talk?"

Fear crossed the doctor's face.

I turned on my heel and ran.

I ran so fast that my shoes slipped off my feet and slapped my heels with every frantic step. Mac was behind me, calling my name and asking me to slow down. There was no time. What was I thinking? Why would I sit there and wait? Why didn't I realize what was happening earlier?

If someone had gone to finish off Daddy while I was sitting outside the room of the woman from the trunk, feeling sorry for myself, I'd never, ever get over it. My fault. This was all my fault. The killer wasn't only at the Pinnacle. He or she was everywhere all at once. Outside of the toy store a few days before Christmas. In my father's hotel suite. In the parking garage. In the hospital. In Nanny's bed. Parading as nothing but a cold until days turned into weeks. Until there was nothing a doctor could even do.

Death haunted my every step. How long did I have before it caught up to me?

I flung open the door to Daddy's hospital room, my shoes askew, my breath shaking out in rapid pants. Detective Hodgson was sitting in the empty chair, spinning his fedora on his fingertips.

Daddy's chest rose and fell with the steady breath of sleep.

I bent over and grabbed my knees. My heart hurt with every beat. Mac came running up behind me, his hands on my back to keep from running into me.

Hodgson eased the hat back on his head. "Hello. I was hoping to speak with you both."

I struggled to stand up. "Detective Hodgson," I gasped. "The woman. From the trunk!"

"Yes?"

Detective McJimsey cleared his throat. He was standing in the doorway, a mug of coffee in each hand. Awkwardly and still out of breath, Mac and I eased out of his way. "The nurses here are scary," he told Hodgson, handing him a steaming cup. "But they finally caved when I showed them my badge for the third time. I see you found our next interviews."

"No!" I said. "No, you don't understand! We went to talk to the woman who was found in Judge Baker's trunk!"

Hodgson stood up. "Did she tell you something?"

"No!" The tears were back. I snatched his cup out of his hands and took a sip to keep from crying again. Oh, it was hot, and it was bitter, and it burned like heaven down my throat. I offered him the mug back, but he glared at me. "When we got there," I said, "there were nurses. And Dr. Smith came running in, and when he left the room . . . when he left the room, he told us she died. Someone suffocated her."

Hodgson swore and pushed his way past the both of us. "McJimsey," he yelled behind him, "we need to shut down this hospital! Right now!"

McJimsey sighed and offered his mug to Mac. "Right behind you!"

CHAPTER 14

I sat next to Daddy's bed and sipped my stolen coffee while Mac stayed near the door, his ear pressed against the wood.

"Anything new?"

He shook his hand side to side. "More cops," he said, "but they haven't found anything. That suit from earlier—you know, the one who cares about your money?"

Most men in suits did. "The CFO from the waiting room?"

Mac nodded. "He's high-strung. I only hear pieces of everything, but he's not a fan of Hodgson."

I finished off the detective's mug and set it by Daddy's bedside table. He looked peaceful as he slept. At least there was that. At least if this was the end, it wouldn't hurt.

Not him, anyway.

"Detective Hodgson did declare this hospital a murder scene. I can see why someone so image conscious as . . . Hmm. What was his name? Whatever his name is, I can see why he'd be upset, but I can't say I care."

Mac put his hands in his pockets and walked toward me, his attention, however, on Daddy. "No. We gotta get to the bottom of whoever is doing this."

I reached over and squeezed Daddy's wrist. His pulse beat steadily under the pads of my fingers. "Three people are dead, Mac.

What if whoever came back for the woman in the trunk is waiting to get at Daddy?" I shook my head, more to tell myself not to cry than anything else. "I won't let them. I don't care if I have to call in the Chief of Police or the mayor, who are both personal friends. I won't let Daddy be alone for a minute."

"Armed guards," Mac said, nodding. "Someone in the room with him around the clock. You know, Evelyn, if you want to stay too, I bet the nurses will make you up a bed. I can crash in the waiting room. I'm pretty good about sleeping in chairs."

"I'll stay as long as I can," I said. "But I want to check on Presley and speak to Mrs. Baker today. I . . . oh golly, who is telling Florence's family about what happened? What family did Florence even have?" I pushed my palms against my face, my hands cold against my flushed cheeks.

Mac cleared his throat. "I didn't really know her," he said, "but Poppy might've. She'd at least know who to ask."

Poppy. That was a good idea. Somewhere to start, at least. My head was spinning with things to do, people to talk to, and the overwhelming need to lie down and not wake up again.

Not that I wanted to be dead.

But it wouldn't hurt to not be alive for a week or so. Pop back up when things were more normal. When Daddy was okay. When Florence's family was already told, condolences were shared, and bodies were buried.

The door opened. I lifted my head and sighed at the sight of Detective McJimsey walking in with his notebook already out. "Mr. Cooper," he said. "I'm looking to have a word with you."

Mac raked his fingers through his unstyled, floppy brown hair. "Sure."

McJimsey looked at me.

I stared back at him, unblinking. He was not about to bully me away from my father's side.

He rolled his eyes. "Let's go somewhere more private, then. Come on."

Mac put his hand on my shoulder and bent down to kiss the top of my head. "I'll be right back."

I smiled up at him, though there was no happiness in it. "You better. Or I will be phoning the chief of police." I'd said the words to Mac, but they were directed at McJimsey, and both men knew it.

"Come on," McJimsey said, opening the door. "Don't got all day."

Mac tucked a strand of hair behind my ear before following after the detective.

Only a single day ago I'd been watching Poppy and Mac argue over the proper way to wear a wolf head. I'd *been* happy. Stressed, yes; worried, sure; but happy beneath it all.

And now someone had killed three people and injured my father all on Pinnacle property. I'd give anything to go back in time and enjoy normalcy again. To ask Florence about her life, for once. How selfish I'd been the entire time she'd worked for me. She'd changed my sheets and washed my dishes and told me all the gossip she'd overheard from the other maids.

And not once, not a single time, did I think to ask her about her personal life. Her parents, her siblings, her lovers.

I'd never forgive myself. But finding out who had done this to her, to Judge Baker, to the poor woman in the trunk, even to Daddy—that was a good start. A way to seek penance. *Hail Mary, full of grace.*

A quiet groan pulled me out of my self-hatred. Blinking wildly, I looked at Daddy.

His hands were curling into fists, his face tightening.

"Daddy?"

He made a noise of acknowledgment.

"Daddy?" I reached for his hand. "Can you open your eyes?"

He scrunched his eyelids before relaxing, and his brown eyes slowly opened. He searched around the room before looking at me.

"Evie?" His voice was little more than a whisper, a heavy scratch running through it. "Evie, what's going on?"

"You were drugged with something," I said. "The same type of needle they found in Judge Baker's arm was on your floor. Do you remember what happened?"

Daddy blinked, his tongue darting out to wet his lips. "Needle?"

There was a small bowl of water and a stack of hand towels on his bedside table. I soaked the topmost towel in the cool water before ringing it out "Yes." I dabbed his forehead with the damp towel. "A needle. Probably had heroin in it? Though we haven't gotten the full report back from the police on what exactly was in the needle."

"Drugs," Daddy said. "I don't do drugs, Evie."

"I know, Daddy." I smiled at him. "I know. But someone drugged you and tried to kill you. Do remember anything that happened this morning?"

His gaze wandered over my face, a bit lazily but with recognition too. "Evie?" he asked.

I nodded and dabbed his forehead with the towel again. "Yes, Daddy. It's me. You're in the hospital. Do you remember how you got here?"

"In the hospital? Why?"

He wasn't well and wasn't up for being a fountain of information. Still. I had one last question to ask before I fetched the nearest nurse. "Daddy, a maid was found in your closet this morning. She was dead. Do you remember the maid at all?"

"Dead maid," he said. "That was years ago, Evie. Why am I in the hospital?"

My hand stilled above his forehead, fingers twisting in the wet fabric. "A maid died years ago?"

Daddy didn't answer.

I glanced down at him to find he'd fallen back asleep again.

Even if he was groggy and unable to help with the investigation, he'd woken up. He'd spoken. He'd recognized me. I needed to tell a nurse. I'd told Hodgson my father was too stubborn to die after a fight, and what do you know? I was right.

I kissed his wet forehead and left the towel by the bowl. I tiptoed to the door, planning on poking my head out and waving at whoever happened to be manning the nurse's station.

But Detective McJimsey swung the door in, missing me by inches.

Mac was nowhere to be seen.

CHAPTER 15

McJimsey barged into my father's room like he owned the place. He was, concerningly, alone.

"Mac?" I asked. "Where is he? Because if you are taking him to the station, I will have my lawyer meet you there."

The detective shook his head, golden locks catching the light from the open blinds in the hospital window. "Hodgson took over. Sent me in here to talk to you."

"Me? Again?" I groaned. "Fine, but in a minute. Daddy woke up and I need to tell a nurse."

"He woke up?" McJimsey strolled over to Daddy's bed. His arms were limp at his sides, and it seemed a strange, uncomfortable posture to me. He was tall and broad-shouldered, and good-looking, and yet . . . yet he carried himself like he was none of those things. Some sort of tactic to lull me into a false sense of security? I'd had enough grumpy men in my life; I wasn't about to open up a spot for another. McJimsey looked at me over his shoulder, arms still hanging uselessly, not unlike cooked pasta. Hanging noodle-ly. "Did he say anything?"

I frowned. "Not really. He seemed confused and asked several times why he was in the hospital. But he recognized me and seemed himself."

"It's normal for people not to remember traumatic things," McJimsey said. "We see it all the time with victims."

I hummed in agreement, not about to argue with him. I remembered the most traumatic moments in my life, and in vivid detail. Maybe I wasn't victim enough for my brain to help me out. "If you'll excuse me, I'll—"

The door opened again, but this time it was a nurse who entered.

"Speak of the devil," I said. "I was heading out to the nurse's station. Daddy woke up a few minutes ago."

"He woke up?" The nurse rushed to Daddy's side, and I had a very annoying sense of déjà vu. "Did he say anything?"

"He recognized me and asked me several times why he was in the hospital, but wasn't able to answer any questions about what happened to him."

"You were asking him questions?" the nurse snapped. "About his attack? No wonder he's unconscious again. You caused him additional stress! Both of you need to get out, right now."

Offended, I started to protest. But she pointed at the door with her entire right arm and glared so fiercely at us it made me miss Nanny. I flicked my hair off my forehead and stormed out of the hospital room. "I'm not leaving the hall!" I said. "I'm staying right by this door!"

"It's a free country!" the nurse called back.

The door clicked shut. McJimsey grinned. "They got some mean nurses here."

I was so tired. My head hurt. I trusted Hodgson more than McJimsey and was glad he had taken over whatever conversation they were having with Mac, but I was nervous that the police were talking to Mac at all. My chest felt like it was filled with bees with nowhere to hunker down and produce honey, buzzing about inside of me and stinging all the tender parts. What name would I put to that emotion?

I didn't know. I had no idea what I was feeling except that I didn't care for it, and it would be best to do away with feelings altogether. I'd have to call Dr. Sanders today, on top of everything else I needed to do.

"What did you want, Detective?"

"It's suspicious, Miss Murphy. You find the judge, dead in his car. And a few hours later, you find your father, seizing in his room." He leaned against the wall, closer to me than I cared for. But moving away felt like losing something. "What do you think those odds are?"

"Detective," I said, "I've never placed a bet in my life. But if the odds are for or against me finding something? Always bet on me to find it. If you'll check your notes or converse with your partner"— he grimaced when I said *partner*, and I wondered what Hodgson had said about me—"you'll learn that I am very good at finding things. And anyway, *you* were the one who found Florence."

McJimsey shook his head, but it wasn't out of disagreement. He seemed genuinely sad when he said, "Poor girl."

"I need to speak with her family."

"You were close with the maid, Miss Murphy?"

And there it was. He'd won. I took a step away from him and leaned my upper back flat against the wall, pressed my head into the plaster. "She was my maid. I appreciated her very much. She was hardworking, honest, and loyal." Blinking hard, I stared at the nearest light to keep the tears away. "She was a good person. And both the Pinnacle and I will miss her."

"Pinnacle's not a person, Miss Murphy. But I'm sure her parents will be delighted to hear you say it all the same."

His voice was laced in sarcasm, but I would not be deterred.

"You know her parents? Please, will you give me their names? A phone number? Anything. I only want to offer my condolences and see if I can be a help in any way."

"You know what?" McJimsey said, eyeing me up and down. "I almost believe you. But, see, the thing is, if you appreciated your maid as much as you say you did, you'd already know the name of her parents, wouldn't you? Maybe you didn't care that much. Maybe you're trying to make sure her family doesn't sue yours now. And that—that would be a breach of trust if I gave over their phone number and let you and your team of lawyers harass them into silence."

My nose wrinkled. "What are you on about?" I asked. "Team of lawyers? Harassing them into silence? That . . . what?"

"Don't play innocent with me." McJimsey leaned in closer, and as I was pressed against the wall, I couldn't escape the nearness of him. "I know exactly how rich people like you and your father operate."

"Given the state of your clothes, I doubt that."

He pulled away like I'd struck him. Oh, good, a sore spot. Those were nice to know about. He straightened out his jacket and opened his mouth, but Dr. Smith rounded the corner and came barreling toward us.

"Hello," he greeted, not sounding friendly at all. "How's the patient?"

"He woke up," I said.

"He woke up? What did he say?"

Ah, wonderful. I loved having the same conversation multiple times. "He was confused about why he was in the hospital and didn't remember anything about the attack, but recognized me and called me by name. There's a nurse in there with him now. She kicked us out."

"Yeah," McJimsey agreed, "and she wasn't nice about it."

"Why would she have to be nice?" Dr. Smith asked before pushing open the door with his shoulder and strolling away from us.

The door closed, leaving me alone again with the detective I liked least. My stomach rumbled, and I closed my eyes and begged it to be quiet. Now was not the time for breakfast. Even if it was, actually, past the time for breakfast. I had the police to deal with, had to get someone to watch over Daddy, had to go talk to Poppy and Mrs. Baker and check on Presley. I missed him so much. If he was here with me, he'd be tucked in my arms, licking my chin. Comfort in these repeating conversations.

Footsteps squeaked on the linoleum floors. I opened my eyes to see Mac approaching, Detective Hodgson behind him. Mac held what looked a lot like a bagel with cream cheese in his beautiful hands.

He handed me the bagel and kissed my cheek. It was the most romantic gesture I'd ever received. "Hodgson and I went to the deli across the street. Thought you might be hungry."

I smiled up at him, so bright it hurt my face, and if we hadn't been surrounded by detectives who suspected us of foul play, I'd have planted a kiss right on his lips. "Thank you."

He winked at me.

"What's going on with your father?" Hodgson asked.

I swallowed my first bite of food in way too long. "Dr. Smith and a nurse are in there with him now. He woke up."

"He woke up?" Hodgson asked. "What did he say?"

Wow. This was the most annoying thing that had happened to me in a long time. "Not much," I replied, licking cream cheese off the corner of my mouth. "He recognized me and called me by name, but didn't know why he was in the hospital and couldn't recall anything about his attack."

Hodgson nodded. "I'll be back in a minute. I need to speak with him."

"Wait—" both McJimsey and I said, but Hodgson opened the door, and the loud, commanding voices of Dr. Smith and the nurse immediately told him to leave.

He stepped out of the room, cleared his throat, and adjusted his hat. "Well," he said after a moment, "I suppose that's why the two of you were out here in the first place."

"Yep," McJimsey said.

I took another bite of my bagel.

CHAPTER 16

After I'd eaten the last bit of bagel and searched furtively for a place to wipe my fingers clean—Mac pulled out a napkin from his pocket—the chief of police arrived with his hat under his arm.

"Miss Murphy," he greeted, offering me a hand. I shook it with a now clean one. "Detectives," he said. He nodded at Mac but didn't bother introducing himself.

Mac sighed behind me but didn't force a scene.

"How is your father doing?"

The door opened, and Dr. Smith and the nurse walked out. The nurse stared daggers at all of us collectively before walking away to her next patient in need.

I reached for my necklace. "What's the news?"

Dr. Smith cleared his throat. "Yes. Prognosis is good. He roused with some effort and is confused, but he knew the year, his name, and that Eisenhower is president. We will be keeping him under observation for some time."

"Wonderful," I said, clapping my hands. "That's marvelous news! I'm ever so relieved!"

"He's not out of the woods yet, Miss Murphy," Dr. Smith said. "But things are currently headed in the right direction."

"I'll take it. Anything is better than this morning."

"Yes," Dr. Smith agreed. "But I must insist that you gentlemen leave Mr. Murphy alone for the time being. We will call the station when he is healthy enough for questioning."

McJimsey shook his head, but the chief nodded. "Of course, of course. We will not be asking Mr. Murphy any questions until he is recovered."

"Actually," I said. "I was hoping you'd put a security detail on him, sir. After what happened to the poor woman from Judge Baker's trunk."

"Terrible." He grimaced. "Yes. I am glad you asked, Miss Murphy because I came here to insist on it myself. He needs round-the-clock protection until we can determine where this threat is coming from. First Judge Baker, and now your father."

"Also, the girl from the trunk," said Mac. "And the maid from the hotel."

"Yes, yes. Ghastly state of the world, isn't it? I'll have officers assigned to your father's room, Miss Murphy. Round-the-clock protection."

"As long this protection lets him rest," Dr. Smith said. "And I mean it. He is in no state to be interrogated. Not by anyone." That last bit was directed at me.

I smiled apologetically.

"Right." The chief put on his hat. "I know you boys have work to do. A killer to catch?"

Detectives Hodgson and McJimsey backed away from the watchful eyes of the chief, from Daddy's door, and the possibility of getting to talk to their best witness. Once they were gone, the chief turned his attention back to me.

"I'll get that protection squared away, Miss Murphy."

"Thank you ever so," I said. And without thinking about it, I gave the chief a quick hug. "You're the ginchiest, sir."

He grumbled something, his face beet red, and then left in the same direction as the detectives. I sagged against Mac, his arms wrapping around my middle to keep me on my feet.

He set his chin on my shoulder and whispered, "You holdin' up all right, love?"

"Better after food," I said. I stretched my neck to kiss his cheek. He hadn't shaved yet, our morning too frantic, too dramatic, and the stubble felt electric on my lips. "You're a dream of a beau, Malcolm Cooper, I hope you know that."

He rubbed the tip of his nose against mine. "I do."

I giggled. He kissed my laughing mouth.

"You want to go back in, see your old man?"

I sighed and patted his forearms until he let me go. "Yes. I want to sit with him until his guard shows up. And then we have work to do."

★ ★ ★

I settled into the lone seat next to Daddy while Mac opted to stare out the window. We had only seconds of silence before Daddy sniffed.

I looked away from the profile of my beau to the face of my unconscious father. Only, he wasn't unconscious. He opened his groggy eyes and stared at me from under his lashes.

"That mean nurse gone?" he asked, his voice quiet and thick with exhaustion, but way more lucid than he had been before. Whatever that mean nurse had done to him after kicking us out of the room must've been beneficial.

I sat forward and touched his forehead. His skin felt clammy and cool. I looked around for the washcloth I'd used earlier, but she must've cleaned up and taken it away. "Yes, she's gone. How are you feeling?"

"Terrible," Daddy said. "What happened?"

"Seems like a heroin overdose."

He made a face, his tongue between his teeth. "Never in my life."

"I know, Daddy." I took his hand in mine and squeezed his fingers. "Someone drugged you. And then they killed Florence, the maid, and stuffed her in your closet."

He closed his eyes and took a breath so deep his chest pushed the blankets up. "I don't remember."

"That's fine." I rubbed my thumb over his knuckles. "Don't stress yourself. Relax and heal. That's all you need to do right now. Shall I fetch the doctor, tell him you're awake?"

"Heavens no," he said. "That nurse will come back with him."

I hummed, amused. He'd almost died that morning, and he was well enough to hold a grudge against some woman doing her job.

He sniffed again and looked at me, his dark eyes—the same ones that looked back at me in the mirror every morning—glazed and glassy. His pupils dilated, and he stared at something over my head.

"Why is that boy still with you?"

I'd forgotten that Mac was at the window. "Daddy," I said, "I told you last night. I love him."

"And I told you," he said, "that it needs to end. Now."

Mac shuffled on his feet. "I'll, uh, I'll be outside. If you, er, if you need me."

"Mac," I called, but he walked away, Daddy watching his every step out of the room.

"Good." Daddy settled into his pillow, eyes closing once more. "At least one of you has ears. And sense."

I sighed and shook my head. My hair bounced in my eyes, and I blew it away with a loud puff. His hand was cold in my own, but he was alive, and I'd never been more relieved to be rehashing an argument.

"Mac left the room out of respect for you. But I am not leaving him. Not in any sense of the word. I've chosen him. I love him."

"You're too young to understand the meaning of the word," said Daddy.

"Didn't you tell me only yesterday that Mom was younger than me when you married her?"

He cracked his glassy eyes open only to glare at me. "I do not recall."

"Sure," I said, pressing my lips together to keep from smiling.

"This is not a joke, Evelyn Grace."

I sat back in my chair, finally letting go of his hand. "What a relief to hear."

He opened his eyes wider, his glare more intense, offset by the exhaustion in his eyes, the way his pupils didn't expand and constrict as quickly as they should. "The first thing I'm going to do when I get out of this hospital is call my lawyer."

"Oh?" I examined my fingernails. The cuticle on my thumb was getting a bit out of hand. Too bad I didn't have time to visit the salon. With a frown, I pushed it down with my other thumbnail. "Big business meeting you're missing?"

"I am going to have you removed from the will."

I looked up at him, one eyebrow raised. "Is that so?"

"Yes. I'll leave everything to my sister's child. That good-for-nothing loser in Arizona."

"My cousin? The antiwar protestor who grows hemp?"

"The very same. And then my next call will be to hotel security. I will have you removed from the Pinnacle. You will no longer be allowed to live in any building I own."

"Mm-hmm." Thumb cuticle fixed, I looked over the others. "Sure."

"I will."

"Let's say you do. You follow through with these threats." The nail polish on my left pinkie was chipped. At that, I sighed. I couldn't do anything about that right now. I set my hands in my lap and looked back at my father. "That won't happen quietly, Daddy. Think of the scandal. Splashed across newspaper headlines all over the country. 'Heiress Thrown out on Her Rear.' It'll be everywhere. You won't be able to escape the gossip."

Daddy closed his eyes. "I don't care about gossip."

"But you do care about scandal. And what will your business friends think? Hm? When they have their pictures of their perfect families in their wallets? On their desks? And you, alone, because you kicked your only child out in the cold. She married some penniless man, and they have children you have never seen, don't even know their names."

He clenched his jaw.

"Daddy, you're cranky. You were almost killed. Now is not the time for threats. We will discuss this later. When you're feeling better."

"No." He said. "I've made up my mind. The moment I get out of this hospital, Evelyn Grace, you'll be an impoverished orphan. Do you think that boy will still want you when you don't even have two cents to rub together?"

There was a knock on the door before the boy in question stuck his head in. "Hey, Evie? The copper is here to watch the door."

"Perfect. Thank you, lover."

He blushed, glanced at my father, and then closed the door.

"I guess it works out for me you'll be in the hospital for a few more days, huh, Daddy? More time to change your mind." I kissed his forehead. "I love you, Daddy. I'll see you later."

I was halfway to the door when his head raised from the pillow, his eyes snapping open. "Where are you going?"

I spun around, hands on my hips. "I have a murder to solve! Three, actually. Don't worry." I smiled at him. "It won't take me long. Get some rest, Daddy. Toodles!"

And then I left his room without a look back, even as he sputtered my name. He missed me now, did he? How would he feel if he never spoke to me again? Let him think about that, stew on that for a while. Who would care for him when he was old? Who would visit him when all his friends are out with their grandchildren?

I didn't expect him to ever spend large amounts of time with any children I might have. After all, the most I saw him was around the holidays. But he'd want updated pictures to show off how good a family man he was.

That was the point. He didn't have to be a good family man. He simply had to look like one. And how could he do that without me, his only family?

Besides my cousin, of course.

I wondered how Martha was doing. I hadn't spoken to her in years.

A uniformed police officer stood to the right of Daddy's door. He nodded at me in greeting. I returned the nod. "You keep him safe, now," I said, looking around for my bag. Had I not brought a purse with me to the hospital? How was I going to tip him? "He's surly and rude at the best of times, so don't take any foul treatment personally. Mac, do you have a dollar or two? I'll pay you back."

"It's okay, miss," the officer said. "Can't take tips on the job anyway. Looks too much like a bribe."

"Understood," I said. "Good luck, Officer."

"Thank you, miss."

Mac offered me his elbow, and I took it with gratitude. I wasn't wearing heels, but my feet hurt like I'd climbed every step in my hotel wearing stilettos.

"I'm sorry," Mac whispered. "About your dad."

I patted his forearm. "It's awful but he'll survive. My main concern now is for the victims who perished."

"No, I . . ." He made a noise in his throat I didn't quite understand. "That's bad too, yeah. Horrible. But I meant. I meant your Dad, he don't like me. And I'm sorry, love. I really am."

I kissed Mac's scruffy cheek. "He'll come around. I promise. Leave it to me."

Mac nodded but didn't meet my eye the entire walk to my car.

CHAPTER 17

All I wanted to do was rush up to my room and hide away for a while. I missed Presley so much, even if we'd only been apart for a few hours. He was a comfort, and I wished I'd snuck him into the hospital, hygiene rules be damned. He was clean! He had a hairstylist who washed him and blow-dried him once a week! Sometimes she even painted his toenails.

But it wasn't like pulling up to the curb in a Rolls-Royce garnered me zero attention. A bellhop rushed to open my door while another took Mac's keys. And the employees of the Pinnacle all know me, so they greeted me by name and asked me how I was because the news of Daddy and Florence had passed around the staff already.

"Is Mr. Sharpe in his office?" I asked, because he was the best place to start. He or his secretary could get me Mrs. Baker's address.

The bellhop closed my door and shrugged. "I haven't seen him, miss, so I'd assume so."

Mac came around the front of the car and offered me his arm. "You want to meet with Sharpe first, eh?"

"Get it out of the way," I agreed as we ascended the steps. "And then your sister. And my dog."

The doorman held open the door for us and tipped his hat, greeting us both. Good. He recognized Mac. That was important to me. I smiled at the doorman and thanked him ever so politely before moving inside.

Mr. Sharpe's office was toward the back of the lobby, past the shops and the café, past the fish tanks and the concierge stand and the check-in counter, which was all decorated for the upcoming holiday. It was lined in pumpkins and gourds of different sizes and colors, pillar candles burning among the display, a black lace cloth covering the expanse of the counter.

I knocked on the office door twice. No one answered. I looked at Mac, who shrugged and knocked his knuckles against the wood. Once more, the secretary didn't respond.

I grabbed the handle. It was unlocked. The door opened to an empty office, but there was a voice coming from the room behind the secretary's desk.

Mr. Sharpe was arguing with someone in hushed tones, his Scottish accent thick with evident anxiety.

Mac and I both stared at each other, wide-eyed, before shutting the office door and creeping closer, on tiptoes, to Sharpe's office. We pushed our ears to the door and eavesdropped on what was clearly a private conversation.

That's the thing about finding things. Sometimes, you find things were not meant to. But that is a risk you have to be willing to take.

"Aye, I heard ya—ain't deaf. No, you listen to me." Whoever Sharpe was talking to decided not to listen, because it was some time before Sharpe spoke again. "Please dinna dee 'at!"

I mouthed the words to Mac, who shrugged in response.

"Fit's for ye winna ging by ye," Sharpe said, which made my brain fizzle a bit. What in the world was he talking about? "Ah luve ye, ken?"

Sharpe was speaking to someone named Ken? Who was Ken?

"Love," Mac whispered. "He said I love you."

Mr. Sharpe told someone named Ken that he loved him? The last I'd checked, Henry's name was Henry!

"Aye," Sharpe sighed. There was a click, the phone being hung up, and Mac and I sprang as quietly and as quickly away from the door as we could. We reopened the secretary's door and knocked on it again before closing it behind us, never leaving the room.

"Mr. Sharpe?" I called out. "Mr. Sharpe, are you available?"

Mr. Sharpe cleared his throat. "Miss Murphy, is that you?" There was a pushing of furniture, his chair most likely, and then his door opened wide. He looked tired, the silver scruff on his face in desperate need of a shave. He pushed the drooping pompadour of his hair back and beckoned us into his private office. "How are you? How is your father?"

"Dr. Smith says the prognosis is good, though Daddy isn't out of danger yet. He woke up, and he knows his name and my name, but not what happened to him, and he falls asleep after being roused. Also, there was a bit of . . . um . . . hmm."

"Another murder," Mac said, plopping down in one of Sharpe's plush seats. He tossed his leg over the armrest, knee crooking in the air, and kicked the heel of his foot against the side. "The girl in the judge's boot? Somebody snuck into her room and smothered the poor thing before buggering off to lord knows where."

"The chief of police has ordered around-the-clock protection for Daddy," I said, refusing to take a seat. I didn't want to sit with Mr. Sharpe if he had said what I thought he'd said to someone who wasn't Henry.

Although maybe it was a parent? Or a sibling?

I've never . . . asked. I've known Mr. Sharpe for almost two decades, and I never, ever asked.

I sat down in the other seat, a bit heavily, the guilt and the shame making me more uncoordinated than normal. I didn't know Florence's life, and I don't know Mr. Sharpe's. What else didn't I know because I was so focused on my own life? I knew a good majority of the staff, if not by name, then by sight. But I didn't really know them, not in any way that matters.

"Miss Murphy?" Mr. Sharpe asked. "You all right, lass?"

I shook my head and pressed my lips together to keep from blurting out the truth. All this death, all this violence, and my main concern was still about myself. Even if the concern was to be less selfish, there were other things to be focused on at the moment.

"I'll be fine," I said. "I was hoping your secretary would find the address we used for Judge Baker's invitation. And if you have Florence's family details, I'd like to request those too. I need to offer my condolences."

"She went home early today," Mr. Sharpe said. "She was friends with Florence. I can find those for you, though." He stood up and patted his vest. "Give me a moment." He left his office, the door not quite closing behind him.

I waved my hands at Mac, who was sprawled out like a cat and looking like he might fall asleep at any moment.

"What?" he asked.

I put my hand to my mouth and pantomimed shushing because Sharpe would hear it if I actually shushed him. "His appointment book," I mouthed.

Mac's left eye scrunched, his upper lip plumping his cheek.

I opened my hands, pretended to flip through pages, and then pointed at the desk.

Mac pointed at himself.

I nodded.

"For what?" he mouthed.

"Who was he talking to?"

Now his right eye scrunched almost to the point of closing.

I pretended to hold a phone to my ear.

He glanced up at the ceiling as if he were praying, and then rose to his feet, approaching Mr. Sharpe's desk on tiptoes.

"Your secretary was close with Florence?" I asked, outside the not-quite-closed office door. I'd be able to offer Mac some warning for when Sharpe was coming back, or at the very least distract the manager while Mac finished up with his date book. "I must admit, I'm feeling rather guilty that I didn't know her personal life better."

Mr. Sharpe said, "No one expects you to, Miss Murphy."

Honest and to the point. He wasn't trying to be mean, but it hurt me all the same. "Have you spoken with Henry? I haven't had a chance to tell him about Daddy—or Judge Baker. Any of it."

"Not since early this morning," Sharpe replied, closing a desk drawer.

I glanced at Mac, who was shaking his head as he read through Sharpe's book. He looked up at me and shrugged.

"Ken," I whispered. "Look for Ken."

Mac furrowed his brow. He opened his mouth, as if to say something, but popped it closed when Sharpe spoke again from the other room.

"I'll be sure to keep Mr. Fox informed," Sharpe said. "Shall I give him a time in which you're able to meet him?"

Mac closed Sharpe's date book and snuck around the desk, back to his chair. Did he find something? I pointed at the book, but he shook his head and sat down.

"I'm not sure," I said, as Mr. Sharpe opened up his office door and stepped inside with two pieces of paper.

"I've got a full docket today, unfortunately, and I'll head back to the hospital this evening before visiting hours are over. Then he's got a show tonight, doesn't he? It is Saturday."

"Two," Sharpe said. "Afternoon and evening. Perhaps you can meet with him for coffee in the morning."

"That's a good idea." I took the papers with a small smile. "Will you invite him for me? To my room for coffee tomorrow morning?"

"I can do that," he said. "I found the Bakers' address, but all I've got for Florence is one phone number. I don't know who it belongs to."

Chewing on my bottom lip, I looked over his handwriting. A single phone number and no idea whose it was. It seemed like, as her employer, we should've known more about her.

Mr. Sharpe held a hand over my shoulder, as though he meant to touch me. But instead, he adjusted his vest again. "I'm glad that your father is recovering, Miss Murphy. The staff will be sending over a big bouquet later today. Everyone's pitching in."

"That's very sweet," I said because it was. But also, Daddy was their boss, and he didn't even like flowers. It felt weird, the staff all having to pay for a gift that my father would never even appreciate. "Let me cover some of it?"

Mr. Sharpe arched a brow. "You can't expect your father to pay for his own get-well-soon gift, can you, miss?"

Again, honest and to the point. Painful. I made sure my hair was lying correctly around my ears. "I'll use money earned planning parties. Send me a bill, okay? Let me help reduce some of the costs on the staff, Mr. Sharpe. It's the least I can do."

"All right." Mr. Sharpe turned toward his desk. Was it my imagination, or did his critical eye linger on the date book? "Please let me know if there's anything else I can help you with, Miss Murphy. Have a good day. You too, Mr. Cooper."

Mac stood up with a loud groan. "Yeah. You too. See ya, mate."

The two of us left Sharpe's office, each flashing parting smiles on our way out. Once the main door was closed, I whirled on Mac. "Did you find Ken in his date book? Who is it?"

"Evelyn," Mac said, exhaustion and fondness evident in his tone. "*Ken* means 'you know.'"

"Oh." We walked together to the elevator bay. "So, who was Mr. Sharpe talking to? If it wasn't Henry?" And it wasn't. He said he hadn't talked to Henry since earlier that morning, and Henry would now be in full costume and makeup, getting ready for the matinee of his play.

"It's right dodgy, if you ask me," Mac said. "But we got bigger fish to fry right now, Evie."

"You're right," I said, smiling at the lift boy as we stepped inside. "And please don't call me that."

CHAPTER 18

Presley was waiting at the door when we walked inside my suite, his little tail shaking so hard his whole body was rocking back and forth. I picked him up and shoved my face in his fur, breathing in his scent while he licked my shoulder.

"My baby," I cooed. "I'm sorry I left you, my baby. I'll keep you with me the rest of the day. I'm so sorry, my baby. My baby."

Mac made a noise that was something between a sigh and a chuckle. "I'll call the front desk and ask for Poppy to come up here."

I smiled at him, Presley still tucked under my chin. "Thank you, lover. I'm going to wash up and change."

"Change?" He looked me up and down. "Why?"

"Because Presley is coming with us," I said. "My outfit needs to match his purse. Don't be silly, Malcolm."

He made that noise again before kissing my cheek and scratching between Presley's ears. Presley vibrated in my arms, turning to lick Mac's fingers. "I'll take him out while you get ready," he said. "And we should grab something to eat on the way. And coffee. More coffee."

"So much coffee," I agreed.

He goosed me.

I jumped, squealing in surprise.

Mac laughed and walked off to the kitchen. Presley pushed his paws against my arms, so I set him down, watching as the traitor followed his walker. My boys. Plus Daddy, but he . . . he wasn't likely to join the two of them in my kitchen, and not only because he was hospitalized.

Right. I had things to do. Suspects to question. A face to wash and a hairstyle to touch up.

No time to wallow, Evelyn Elizabeth Grace Murphy.

I washed my face with cold cream and soap, spritzed water on my drooping curls to liven them back up. I put on some makeup, though only a little color on my cheeks and lips, leaving my eyes bare in case I cried again.

Smeared, watery mascara was not ginchy.

For my outfit, I put on light brown gaucho pants and a soft yellow twinset. A dress seemed like too much effort. So did heels. I opted for white flats and called it a day. The shoes matched the large bag I had in mind to put Presley in once he returned from his walk.

Alone with myself and uncertain, I picked up the phone and spun the rotary dial. The operator connected me to my analyst's office.

Dr. Sanders's secretary answered right away.

"Is the doctor available?" I asked. "This is Evelyn Murphy. I have had . . . *quite* the morning."

"She's out of the office right now, but I'll let her know you're in need of an emergency session, Miss Murphy. She'll be in touch soon."

Mac opened the door, with Presley in his arms and his sister pushing a room service cart at his heels. She smiled at me, but her eyes were rimmed red.

"Oh, Poppy," I said, my heart going out to her before my feet got moving. I met her halfway to the couch and wrapped my arms around her shoulders. She was shorter than me, though not by much, and she held me around the waist, her forehead on my shoulder. Mac came up and enveloped us both in a hug, and I felt the inhalation of breath shudder through her body.

"Chef Marco wanted you to eat," she said, her voice muffled in my cardigan.

I glanced at the room service cart. My stomach rumbled at the sight of fresh fruit and yogurt, hot cross buns, Monte Cristo sandwiches, raspberry preserves, a carafe of coffee, and all the accoutrements.

"God bless that man and both his bushy eyebrows," Mac said. Presley hopped out of his bag and marched around underfoot, confused about the hugging and sniffing at the arrival of new food.

Poppy sniffed one more time, and we released each other.

"I'm sorry, Evelyn," she said, wiping her face dry. "You're the one with a father in the hospital."

"Daddy is on his way to a full recovery," I replied. "Don't you fret. You were friends with Florence?"

"She trained me," Poppy said. "When I first got hired here. She was kind. Always."

I smiled. "Yes." That was the truth of it. She was always kind. "Eat with us?"

Poppy checked her watch. "Sure. I've got a bit left in my break. Thanks."

Mac shoved his sister's arm. "Gonna be all right," he said. "We're gonna find whoever did this."

Poppy shook her head. "You mean Evelyn's gonna find whoever did this."

"Hey!" He clutched his heart. "I help!"

The two of us laughed, and we settled into something a bit easier, piling our plates with food and filling up mugs with cream and sugar and coffee. So much coffee. Would I ever feel well rested again? Had I ever felt well rested?

Presley made himself comfortable in Poppy's lap. We ate in relative quiet, him chewing on a slice of ham from her fingers.

"I've gotten Florence's information from Mr. Sharpe," I told her. "I'm going to call her family and offer my condolences later. See if there's anything I can do to help."

"That's very nice, Evelyn," Poppy said, "but Florence doesn't have family here. She lives with another maid. They split the cost of a room at a women's-only boarding house."

I took a bite of a hot cross bun. "Where does her family live?"

"She has a brother. In Seattle. But they aren't close. Florence is a bit—*was* a bit, I mean . . . She . . . I'm sorry, Evelyn. It's not my place to say."

Mac and I exchanged a look over the table. I thought of Henry and Mr. Sharpe's particular relationship and wondered if he was thinking of them too.

"She bucked tradition?" I offered. "And her brother didn't approve?"

"Yes," Poppy said. "Exactly that. She wasn't, um, currently seeing anyone. You understand. Romantically. Her last relationship didn't work out and that—that *person* moved out of New York. But Florence was always positive. Always kept her chin up. She was a brilliant friend."

Presley, annoyed that Poppy had stopped giving him pieces of ham, hopped off her lap with a huff and trotted into the kitchen. Moments later, soft splashes could be heard from the direction of his water bowl.

Mac tossed his napkin on the table. "I'll get it. Hey, you little bugger, knock that off."

I watched him leave, with a small smile. "Poppy." I set my hand on top of hers. "I promise not to tell anyone. So don't you worry. Thank you for sharing with me. I am hoping that you'll be able to share one more thing?"

"I'll do all I can to help, Evelyn. What is it?"

"Do you happen to know in what boarding house Florence was currently living?"

She shook her head. "No, not exactly. But I can find out."

"Would you?" I squeezed her wrist. "Thank you ever so."

★　★　★

Filled with good food and bountiful caffeine—and accompanied by my dog in his rightful place in my purse—we took the lift to the lobby. It was busy, as always, though Burrows was not behind the mail desk.

"I'll send one of the boys to fetch the Rolls," Mac said. Then he pointed his chin toward the café. "Somebody's waving at you."

I spun around, only to see Dr. Sanders sitting near the fish tanks, drinking an espresso and trying to flag down my attention.

CHAPTER 19

Mac kissed my cheek, and I went into the little café alone. Dr. Sanders stood and motioned to the empty seat across from her. The tables had been decorated with orange tablecloths, with miniature pumpkins and gourds acting as centerpieces. The only thing that separated us from the hustle and bustle of new arrivals was a row of plants in marble pottery and fish tanks teeming with life.

The table she'd chosen was in the corner and away from other patrons, I noticed with no small amount of chagrin. She always liked to talk about deeply personal things. I did not like to talk about deeply personal things. She always insisted on asking anyway. I tried to limit their effect by scheduling our meetings in public places. She fought back by getting us the most private area in the requested space.

What I wanted was to no longer be subjected to random bouts of panic. It would be nice if that could happen without ever talking about why the panic-stricken feeling occurred in the first place.

"I didn't expect to see you," I said, shaking her hand and taking the indicated seat. "I only called your secretary an hour ago."

"I was in the area, and I heard rumors about your father. Are they true?"

"Yes. He was attacked this morning."

She frowned sympathetically. "And his outlook?"

"It's good," I said. "He was awake and complaining, thank God."

Dr. Sanders smoothed out her skirt before crossing her legs. "How have you been?" She pulled a giant, white, three-ring binder and a fountain pen out from under her seat. It landed on the table with a thump.

I cleared my throat. Really! A binder that big? A bit rude, if you ask me. Where did she even get it? Her secretary said she was out of the office!

"I'm okay, I suppose. This weekend has been very rough, but before that, you know, with Henry's play? It opened a few weeks ago, and I attended. Front row seat and everything. Had to crane my neck the entire time. Should have opted for a box seat, but he was a delight. He'll win a Tony, I'm sure of it."

She smiled. She was an older woman, mid-fifties, her oak-brown hair graying at the roots. But her porcelain skin was fabulous, hardly a wrinkle on her save for smile lines around her hazel eyes.

"I do know all about Henry's play. I am so proud of you for going, Evelyn. And you took your steady boyfriend, correct?"

I nodded. I'd been so proud to have Mac at my side in the suit I'd had tailor-made for him. He looked as handsome—no, *more* handsome—than any celebrity on all Broadway, and he'd kept my hand in his the entire time.

"Presley, unfortunately, wasn't allowed to attend," I said, reaching in to my bag to scratch under his chin. "But I did all right anyway."

"And that was how many weeks ago? Two, three?"

"About three," I said, nodding. "Yes."

"And"—Dr. Sanders took the cap off her pen—"not counting the trip to the hospital today, have you left the hotel since?"

I stared as her pen hovered over the ridiculous-sized binder. Thick, with pages describing who knows what. I sat back in my chair and waved at the nearest waiter. "An espresso, please."

The waiter looked at Dr. Sanders, but she shook her head. When he left, she said, "You know, Evelyn. I've also dealt with bouts of anxiety from time to time. I've noticed that when I consume caffeine, I often feel that anxiety all the more."

I crossed my legs, my pants wrinkling at the knees. "I have had a long night, and I have a long day ahead of me. I'm tired and need the pick-me-up."

"Anxiety itself can cause exhaustion. Cutting out something that might make it worse can only help."

"You're saying that when you drink coffee, you feel more anxious, and that being anxious can make you tired, but if you drink coffee, you'll be anxious again?" I shook my head. "I admire your analytical skills, Dr. Sanders, but that can't possibly be true. We must let the chemists do the chemistry."

The fish tank to our right bubbled. I watched as the wiggly reflection of the guests behind the tanks disappeared into wobbly elevators. The lobby was as busy as usual, with new arrivals checking in, employees slamming their hands down on the countertop bells, and bellhops hurrying to cart luggage across the white marble floors and colorful rugs. Still others sat at the autumnal decorated tables, reading newspapers and having a pumpkin muffin and some coffee, ignoring the general hubbub but passing their time inside of it.

It was like an entire world here in the Pinnacle Hotel. Its own city, its own country. Was it any wonder why I didn't like to leave it if I didn't have to? And yet. Annoyingly. It was good for me to try new things, and I'd been trying my best.

Dr. Sanders tapped her pen on the paper, dripping uneven splotches of ink. "Evelyn, we can always talk about your relationship with your father and your feelings involving—"

"Yes, I have left the Pinnacle." I drummed my fingers on the table between us. "Every day I go for a walk in Central Park with my dog. Most of the time Mac is with us, but once it was just me and Presley. Mac and I went to the pictures last weekend. *The Old Man and the Sea.* With Spencer Tracy? We even took a cab there. Mac wanted to ride the subway, but"—I shuddered—"no. *No, thank you.*"

Her pen scratched over the paper. "What's wrong with the subway?"

I leaned forward against the table and dropped my voice to a whisper. "How do they clean it? Is it after every ride? Once a day? Once a week? Not to mention it's under the ground! I have no intention of being under the ground until I am six feet underground, if you know what I mean."

She pressed her lips together, the corners of her mouth twitching, before she said, "I do get what you mean. And I'm proud of you for going to see a movie. How have you felt lately? Before this weekend?"

I ran my tongue over the sharp ridges of my teeth while reflecting on her question. "I'm quite happy planning parties. I'm good at it too. Shortly after Henry's play opened, I had to put together a quick wedding for a young couple in a bit of a family way. And then we get to this weekend, and I put together a fancy dress party as a political fundraiser. Isn't that so very ginchy? It was our first one, and it was all my idea. Did you know that Mrs. Eisenhower is decorating the White House for Halloween for the first time this year? Great minds and all that."

The waiter delivered my drink. I took a long sip. "And then, Mac talked me into the leaving the party and visiting Yonkers with

him. I went to the garage and found Judge Baker dead in his car."
I sat back in my chair and admired the lipstick print I'd left on my
porcelain cup. "It's all spiraled since then. I got arrested and then
released. My father picked me up from the precinct. I didn't expect
to see him there, and I haven't told him anything yet. That you
diagnosed me with a little bit of agoraphobia—"

Dr. Sanders shook her head. "That isn't how diagnoses work.
You're not a *little bit* something."

"Teensy, weensy bit," I said, holding up my thumb and index
finger close together to show just how barely agoraphobic I was.
"He didn't know about Mac. Or at least, that Mac is both my assistant and steady beau. When I told him, he got angry and yelled at
me! And then he almost died. That's not fair. How do I argue with
a man who almost died?"

She scribbled something down before closing the binder with a
snap. "Why do you think you haven't confided in your father about
your agoraphobia and anxiety?"

The espresso was too hot and too bitter, but I sipped it anyway.
"I suppose it's because Daddy and I don't talk about those types of
things."

"What do you and your father talk about?"

Another sip of hot, bitter coffee. "The markets. The USSR. The
dangers of communism. You know," I said, forcing a laugh because
saying it out loud sounded ridiculous, even to my ears, "the usual."

Dr. Sanders stared at me unblinking for several more sips of
espresso before opening up her binder again and streaking notes
across the page. "The first thing you might consider doing is figur-
ing out what you want to say. I'd recommend writing a letter, one
that he'll never see. Use it to get your thoughts in order. Journal
it. I know we've discussed you keeping a journal. Have you started
one?"

She didn't wear glasses, but if she did, she'd be staring me down over the top of them.

I licked my lips and looked around the lobby. "Yes," I said, and it was only slightly a lie. I'd purchased a one-hundred-page hardback notebook with gold overlays from the Pinnacle's boutique and written my name on the inside cover. But it was such a beautiful notebook, it felt sinful to write anything more in it than Mac's name inside of a heart.

"Once you've got that finished, you can ask your father if he's available to talk. If you decide to do that, use 'I' statements when you speak with him one-on-one. You could say something like, 'I feel anxious when leaving the Pinnacle.' You can talk about your mother's death—"

I choked on my bitter drink. "Oh no. No, no. Definitely not. That's never going to happen, Dr. Sanders. I'm sorry." I put a fist to my mouth and coughed. "This isn't—this is unproductive. Let's not talk about Daddy anymore. Let's talk about visiting Mac's apartment, because that's on my list to do before the end of the year. He lives in Yonkers! *Yonkers.* Can you believe it? "

"Evelyn." Dr. Sanders held up the flat of her hand. "Are you implying that you've never spoken to your father about your mother's murder?"

I shrugged a shoulder and tapped the side of the tiny, half-empty cup. "What's there to talk about? Mother was murdered taking me Christmas shopping, Daddy flew into town for her funeral, hired Nanny, and left the next day." My eyes itched. I smiled as wide as I could until they crinkled and blurred. "Now. How *does* one get to Yonkers?"

*   *   *

Once Dr. Sanders got up to leave, Mac took my arm and led me out of the front doors to the Rolls-Royce waiting for us at the curb.

He didn't ask me about my conversation with my analyst, and for that I was grateful. I was not a good liar.

The same valet that we saw that morning stood by the hood. Alan? The one with the baby.

"Hi, Miss Murphy," he said in greeting, opening the passenger door for me. "You heading back to the hospital?"

I barely knew this man, so I hesitated in telling him the truth. However, there was a possibility he'd seen Judge Baker last night, even if he said he hadn't, and that was something I needed to press on. "Not right now, but I plan on visiting him later."

"When you see him, tell him we're all pulling for him, will you? Our families too. My wife's been a wreck since the news. She thought the garage was a safe spot before." He gave one last pet to Presley's head. "I tell her she doesn't need to worry about me, but she's the type to worry about everything."

I smiled. "It seems your wife and I have that in common. Have a good day."

"You too, Miss Murphy. No racing, Cooper—you won't win."

"Har har," Mac said. He was already seated behind the driver's seat, his hands on the wheel and his elbow on the open window.

I slid into the passenger seat, Presley's purse on my lap. I pulled out a dollar from underneath his fuzzy paws and handed it over. Alan closed the door, tipped his green hat, and hurried off in the direction of the garage.

All right. Nothing too suspicious about that exchange. And yet, I wasn't willing to write him off completely. But what would he have had against my father? What would anyone have against both Judge Baker and my father, enough to kill them in the same way? The woman in the trunk. If only I'd been able to speak to her. She was important, I knew it. And Florence! Why kill Florence unless there was some need to kill innocent women along with them?

"You doing okay, love?" Mac asked, reaching over to put his hand on my knee.

I laced my fingers with his. "Not really," I said, "but at least I have a crime to solve. I like it, you know. Having something to focus on. Does that make me weird?"

"Evie, baby, lots of things make you weird." He grinned at me, gray eyes crinkling. "But that's why I love you."

Chapter 20

The Bakers owned a brownstone on the Upper West Side of Manhattan. Traffic was heavy, and it took a while until we arrived at Mrs. Baker's door. A bit longer to find a parking spot. And longer still to walk to her door and knock.

An unsmiling housekeeper ushered us inside and pointed in the direction of a sitting room. "Don't leave," she said. "Mrs. Baker will be down when she can."

"She *is* pregnant," I replied, smiling bright enough for both of us. "We don't mind waiting."

Presley stuck his head out of his purse, tail wagging so hard it thumped against my side. The housekeeper arched an eyebrow but didn't say anything as she left the three of us alone.

Mac let out a low whistle. "Nice place."

"Very," I agreed, taking a turn about the room. There was an unlit fireplace, bookshelves stacked with original leather works, and a rug between two green, high-backed chairs. The art between the bookcases looked original, though I wasn't sure of the artist. That was more Poppy's area of expertise than mine. In the corner, there was a chess table; a mini grand piano; and on the other side, where the light came in from the window, an extra seating arrangement of a love seat and an armchair, with a pewter crucifix hanging above it all.

"Yep," Mac said, relaxing into the love seat, with his face turned toward the sun, "I could nap here."

"You're turning into a cat." I sat next to him and waited with Presley on my lap. "I do hope we haven't caught her at a bad time. I should've brought a gift."

"What do you bring a pregnant woman whose husband just died?" Mac asked, cracking one eye open. "Not sure flowers fill that void, love."

I crossed my arms over my chest. "No, but it would've been nice." Chocolates are what I should've done. Everyone loves chocolate.

Mrs. Baker walked into the room. Mac and I stood to greet her, though I set Presley's bag on the floor first. Mrs. Baker was in a black, flowing dress, her curly hair hanging long past her shoulders. She wore sensible red flats, black wrist gloves lined with lace on her hands, and a bright red purse on her arm that I recognized.

I blinked and shook my head.

There was no possible way. None. It had to be a knockoff or a look-alike.

She wasn't wearing makeup, but she was wearing bright red glasses. They were enormous but did little to hide her pretty, tear-stained face.

"Thank you for waiting," she said, caressing her swollen stomach. "I need to leave in a few minutes to visit the doctor. A checkup after last night's scare and then . . ." Her bottom lip fluttered. "I didn't get much sleep."

I hurried to take her arm and led her to the open seat. Discreetly, I studied her purse. Because there wasn't any way it could be a real Archambeau. Not when I hadn't been able to snag one.

She lowered herself with a quiet groan.

"You okay, Mrs. Baker?" Mac asked.

She nodded, her curly hair falling into her face. She didn't bother to push it away. "Everything hurts," she said, "but Dr. Smith says that's normal this far into the pregnancy."

"You're due soon?" I asked, sitting on the love seat across from her.

She nodded again, looking at me from under her veil of hair. "A week or two. But hopefully, any day now."

"And you've known Dr. Smith for a while?"

Finally, she moved her hair out of her eyes. "Yes. He gave us advice about a year ago. Some medical advice. I've considered him a friend since. Cliff and I both." Her dark eyes went glassy, and she closed them, long lashes brushing her cheeks. "Sorry."

"Don't apologize," I said. "We've come to call on you at a terrible time. I wanted to express my deepest condolences, Mrs. Baker. And if there is anything I can do, or the Pinnacle can do, please let me know."

"Thank you, Miss Murphy. Cliffy loved your hotel. We honeymooned there." A soft smile toyed on her lips before sadness once more crept over her expression. "Gosh, that was only two years ago."

"How are Judge Baker's boys doing? They're both at Harvard, right?"

She pulled a cotton handkerchief out of her bright red purse, calling my attention to it once more.

It had that same gold clasp that the Archambeau was supposed to have. *Golly, I think it's real!*

"We've been in touch every few hours since last night. Gordon is heading home now, to help me deal with . . ." She stopped herself before having to say the inevitable. To help her plan a funeral. To help her bury her husband. "He's hoping to stay until after the baby is born. He's working as a teacher's assistant now, and the professor that he helps is being so understanding. An old friend of Cliff's, thankfully. Michael is having a harder time getting away, what with it being in the heart of the fall semester. But he'll make it to the funeral—he's sure of it."

I wondered if it was weird for them that their stepmother was hardly older than they were, and that she was about to have a child. A younger sibling, when they were old enough to have kids of their own.

But they'd both been at college last night. At least probably. I wondered how I could get their alibis. Though, even if it was weird for them, why kill their father and not their stepmother? Then you'd get rid of the new child too. The new encroachment on your inheritance.

As it stood now, Mrs. Baker was about to be a very wealthy widow.

"Mrs. Baker," I said, "I hope you don't find me terribly rude. But is that—is that the new Archambeau handbag?"

"Oh, this?" She set it on her knee. "Yes. Cliffy got it for me last month on my birthday."

My smile felt large and fake, but there was nothing for it. "I see. He had marvelous taste."

She laughed a little. "He was always spoiling me with designer things. Dior, Gucci, Balmain."

Ball. Main.

She said, *"Ball main."*

Two words.

Both wrong.

My smile hurt my cheeks. I swallowed, licked my lips. "He loved you," I settled for.

She sniffed, her curls falling in her eyes again. "And I loved him, Miss Murphy. I can't believe he won't be here for the baby."

I set my hand on her shoulder and squeezed, my fake smile turning into something much more genuine. I hadn't missed the crucifix on the wall. And it didn't matter which one of them was Catholic, because even if it had been only him, she might find comfort in his religion now that he was gone. That's how it had been for me when Mom died. "He will. He loved you—he's with you still. Watching out for you from heaven. I promise."

"Thank you for saying so, Miss Murphy. It's all still too raw and real."

I put my hand back in my lap. This was the hard part. Getting to the nitty-gritty without acting like I was getting to the nitty-gritty. But how do you ask someone if she murdered her husband without directly asking her if she murdered her husband? "He was excited for the baby?"

"Oh, very. The nursery is ready to go. Cliffy picked out most of the decorations himself. Even built the crib, if you can believe it. My Cliffy, with a hammer and nails." She wiped her cheeks. "I should've taken a picture."

"You left early last night. I was worried about you. Were able to enjoy any of the party before the contractions started?"

"Some," she said. "Though it feels like a lifetime ago now. I can't believe that's the last party I'll ever go to with Cliff." Mrs. Baker blew her nose. "I wish I could stay and talk more, Miss Murphy, but I'll be late for my checkup."

"Of course." I stood and offered her a helping hand. "The baby is the most important thing. You call the Pinnacle if you need anything at all, all right?"

Once steady on her feet, she squeezed my hand. "Thank you, Miss Murphy."

"You're most welcome."

The housekeeper from earlier appeared in the doorway as if summoned and ushered Presley, Mac, and me out of the house. The door to the brownstone closed with a click, and Mac took my hand, leading the way down the sidewalk and to the Rolls.

"Well," he said, "she seems aboveboard, yeah? Squeaky clean and the like."

"Are you joking? She was holding the newest, hardest-to-get Archambeau, and yet she mispronounced *Balmain*. She said 'ball main,' Mac! It's 'bal-mah'! *Bal-mah!*"

Mac's face twisted up into a mix of pain and good humor. "What's that got to do with anything, Ev?"

"It has everything to do with it! A person who owns the newest Archambeau will *know* how to pronounce Balmain. You don't collect luxury pieces without knowing who the designers are. You just don't! It's *important*. The fashion house matters! And it was the real deal too, lover, not a cheap copy."

"She said Judge Baker bought it for her."

"Exactly!" The Rolls on the corner came into view. I hurried, my heels clacking on the sidewalk. There was a chill in the air, orange and yellow leaves fallen from the trees planted along the sidewalk scattering under our feet in the breeze.

Mac pulled the keys out of his pocket. "You lost me."

"Judge Baker bought it for her. But, lover, Archambeau is notoriously hard to purchase. You have to be invited to buy things. If you don't buy what you're invited to buy, you're blacklisted. And! You have to spend a certain amount every month to even be invited to purchase something!"

"So what?" He held open the door. I put my hand on the window and stared up at him.

"So Judge Baker bought it. But I wasn't invited. Me! I wasn't invited to purchase the new bag. And I know, I *know* that judges are wealthy, lover, I know it. But there is no way, no *feasible* way that Judge Baker has more money than Daddy."

Mac nodded and took a deep breath in through flaring nostrils. "Yeah, okay. I see what you're getting at here. It's right weird."

"Yes."

"But that don't mean it's not feasible. Maybe the salesgirl didn't like you, Evie. That's why you weren't invited. Could be as simple as that."

I wrinkled my nose. "Maybe," I said. "But, no. No, I think it's weird. And it deserves further investigation."

"You just wanna go shopping."

"Mac, I am *distressed*." I slid into the passenger's seat. "And shopping is good for the nerves."

CHAPTER 21

Once more, we arrived outside the steps of the Pinnacle. I felt much more presentable this time, much more capable of rallying the troops, so to speak, and assuring everyone that all would be okay. That if they asked me again how I was doing, I'd be able to answer.

I didn't feel like all would be okay. But I could look like I felt that, and that was almost as good.

Mac handed off the keys to the nearest bellhop. I checked on Presley. He was awake in his purse, his paws on the edge and his perfect little face peeking out at the world around us. He'd need another walk soon. Maybe some cheese from that pretzel vendor he liked in the park.

But first things first.

"I need to see Judy," I told Mac.

Mac said, "For your nerves."

Judy runs the Pinnacle's shop. It sells mostly Pinnacle-branded merchandise, plus various sundries that guests might have forgotten to pack, or realized they wanted once they arrived. She also orders for me anything I want, from any boutique around the world, and schedules my in-person shopping sessions.

I don't like to go out to boutiques if I can help it. A few weeks ago, I might've lied and said it's because I was far too busy with

Pinnacle matters to leave Pinnacle grounds, but the truth is, I am a teensy-weensy bit agoraphobic, and too much time spent away from the hotel wreaks havoc on my emotions.

Already I'd been to the hospital and the Bakers' residence. I'd have to visit Florence's home and go back to the hospital. That was too many places, and as much as I love shopping, I couldn't bring myself to leave the hotel to do it.

"Miss Murphy!" Judy gasped when I walked in. Her face flushed immediately at the sight of me, though I wasn't sure why. She normally saved her blushing for after a compliment. "Miss Murphy, I wasn't expecting to see you today. How are you? How is your father?"

Customers were milling about the shop, trying on hats and holding up monogrammed robes to see if the one-size-fits-all fitted their particular size. I approached the register. Presley hid back down in his purse. Mac stood behind me, greeting Judy with a soft, "Hello."

"I'm all right," I said. "Thank you ever so for asking. Daddy is on his way to a full recovery, thank goodness. It could've been so much worse. Our sweet Florence." I shook my head. "Devastating."

"It is. I didn't know Florence well, but everyone has only nice things to say about her. Even those rude parking garage boys."

"Judy," a man's voice said with a tone of warning.

Mac leaned his elbows on the counter. "You hiding back there, Chuck? Change of pace from you pretending to work at the mail counter."

Burrows was behind Judy, sitting cross-legged on the floor, binders open in front of him. "Not all of us can get paid for trailing behind our girlfriends."

"Mr. Burrows is helping with the restock," Judy said. "Inventory is difficult all by myself. So is reordering. And staffing the cash register. But"—she raised her chin—"this job is my dream, and I am grateful for it. If only everyone who worked here understood what an honor it was."

Mac tilted his head. "Something you want to tell us, Chuck?"

He sighed, closed the binder with a thump, and rose to his feet. "No."

Burrows and Mac stared at each other. More accurately, Mac stared at Burrows, his eyes narrowed, while Burrows stood there and looked everywhere but at Mac. His feet, Judy's elbow, the spot behind my ear.

Annoyed, I broke the silence. "Judy, I need you to please schedule an in-room try-on with an Archambeau sales associate, please. At their earliest convenience. Unless it is today, I cannot do it today. But other than that, my schedule is wide open. Isn't that right, Mac?"

My boyfriend blinked and jerked his head away from the man he was staring at. "What?"

"My schedule?"

"What about it?"

I put my fist on my hip. "Are you my assistant or not? I'm trying to give Judy a window of time to schedule the personal shopper from Archambeau."

"Oh!" Mac's mouth formed a perfect O. "Right. Quite right. Yes. Not today."

"No, not today. I already said that."

"Tomorrow, then," said Mac. He leaned fully against the counter and smiled at her. "Or Monday. Whatever works best."

She ducked her chin to her chest, a soft blush spreading across her cheeks. Burrows shuffled side to side. And I . . . I didn't know what was happening.

"Mr. Burrows?" I asked. "Do you have something to say?"

He shook out his arms like he was trying to detach his hands. "All right, all right," he said. "You've broken me, Miss Murphy. The valets don't like your father. They're talking about how it's sad he's pulling through." Burrows stepped into my personal space without once ever looking me in the face. "They wish he was dead, Miss Murphy, I am sorry to tell you." He grabbed hold of my wrist with his damp hand, and once more I wondered what Poppy saw in him. "I'm so sorry, Miss Murphy. It's not all of us. Most of us respect your father. But the valets got hit hardest with the budget cuts."

"Budget cuts," I repeated. Scott or the other one, what was his name? The one with the wife and new baby. Alan. His name was Alan, and he'd talked about Mrs. Baker looking ready to pop. One of them had mentioned budget cuts to me earlier. "What do you mean, Mr. Burrows?"

A lady trying on hats gasped. I spun around, surprised to find Detective McJimsey barreling toward us. He'd knocked into the woman and hadn't even apologized. An officer behind him was picking a hat off the floor and mumbling an apology.

"Detective," I admonished, "who raised you? Knocking into ladies like that!"

He ignored me in favor of pulling out a pair of handcuffs. "Mr. Cooper. Turn around. I'm placing you under arrest."

Mac barked out a surprised laugh. I exclaimed, "What?" And Presley yipped, his ears flat against his head as he peered at the detective from the safety of his purse. Burrows took a step away from me. More police officers filled the shop, and the customers snaked their way out of the room. Mr. Sharpe hovered in the doorway, his hair a mess, his tie undone.

"What for?" I asked. "What are the charges?"

McJimsey was smiling so big the corners of his eyes crinkled. "Murder," he said. "And attempted murder. Turn around. Hurry up. This is the last time I'll ask nicely."

Mac turned around, hands behind his back.

I was stunned. But not into silence. "Don't say anything," I said. "Not a word. I'll have a lawyer meet you at the station."

"Evie," Mac whispered, "Evie, this is a mistake. I didn't—"

I put my finger on his mouth. "Not a word. You don't even give them your full name—you understand me, lover?"

He nodded, lips pressed together in a thin line.

The cuffs went around his wrists with a clink, the green in McJimsey's eyes catching the light and twinkling.

"Where is Detective Hodgson?" I demanded. "I must speak with Detective Hodgson at once."

"That's gonna be difficult," McJimsey replied with a smile. "Hodgson was relieved of duty about an hour ago." He winked and tugged on Mac's elbow to pull him away from me. "You'll be dealing with me and me alone from here on out, kid."

CHAPTER 22

Sometimes, when the weather is bad, the power goes out, and there's nothing to do but sit in the dark, alone with your thoughts. That's a big reason why I have a dog if I'm being honest. I hate being alone with my thoughts.

And as Mac looked at me, his gray eyes shining with sadness and worry and fear, McJimsey's grin glinting with malice, that's what it felt like. Like the power had gone out, and there was nothing I could do but sit in the dark.

It wasn't until Judy touched my shoulder that the electricity turned on again. "Miss Murphy?" she asked in her soft voice. "Shall I still schedule that shopping appointment?"

"What?" I pressed my palm to my forehead. I was sweating, my heart racing. What was this feeling? I took a shallow breath and tried to hold it in my lungs. *Calm down, calm down. Now is not the time for an attack of anxiety.* "Yes," I said. "Yes, please. Thank you, Judy. Burrows?"

"Yes, miss?"

"Go get Poppy. Right now." I didn't look at him, instead finding Mr. Sharpe in the crowd and hurrying toward him.

"Miss Murphy?" he asked. "You all right, lass?"

"No," I said. "Please. I need you to call Mr. Ferretti's office. I'll pay whatever the retainer is, but I want one of the Ferrettis to hurry to the precinct."

Mr. Sharpe nodded. "Of course, of course. I'll call right now. Will you be meeting them at the precinct?"

"And do what?" My breathing still wasn't right, but at least I had something to focus on besides the fact that the world was ending. "That detective said Hodgson was fired. Fired! That simply cannot be. I have to . . . I don't know. I don't know what to do." I wrung my hands together in front of me. "Call the lawyer—let's request the grandson. He's not much older than me, and he isn't friends with my father, so I can get him on my side."

Mr. Sharpe guided me by the upper arm to a corner of the shop. We were surrounded by slippers with the Pinnacle logo on the toe, while guests and customers and the last few remaining police officers moved in and out of the shop.

"Evelyn?" His voice was low. "What do you mean? 'On your side'?"

"Daddy doesn't want me dating Mac anymore." My brain was moving too fast to think about what I was saying. "There's no way he'll pay for Mac's lawyer fees. I'll have to dip into the trust my mother left me. Are bankers open on Saturdays?" I closed my eyes, swaying on my feet.

Mr. Sharpe wrapped an arm around my shoulders and led me to the fish tanks. He pulled out a seat and helped me into it, ordering a tea from the closest employee. "Miss Murphy," he said. "I will call Mr. Ferretti for you. His office will bill you, and I'm sure you'll cover the cost of the retainer on Monday when the bank opens. This is not a problem. Not for you. I do not know why Detective Hodgson was fired, but if you'd like, I can look for him in the phone book. What is his first name?"

My eyes burned. I couldn't remember. Had he ever told me? I didn't know Florence, I didn't know Hodgson. I didn't know who Mr. Sharpe was talking to on the phone. I'd only ever focused on myself, on my problems.

"Don't worry," Mr. Sharpe said. "Hodgson is not so common a surname. Drink your tea. I'll be back in a moment. Do not leave this table."

I nodded, stupidly, uselessly, and took the cup of tea from the waiter. It was hot and tasted like nothing, but I sipped it nonetheless. Was Mr. Sharpe only being nice to me because I was Henry's friend? Was it from years of knowing me, even if I'd made his professional life difficult? Was it because I was the owner's daughter?

And why did I care about his reasons for being nice to me? There were so many more important things to worry about.

Mac, stuck in the back seat of McJimsey's squad car.

Mac, in the interrogation room, sitting on the uncomfortable chair, alone.

Florence, in my father's closet, her lips blue. Nanny, coughing until she struggled to breathe. My mom, agreeing to take me to the toy store, even though it was late. Even though we were alone. Alone like Mac was right now.

Poppy and Burrows arrived at my table, holding hands. I grimaced, even with the turmoil wreaking havoc in my mind. His palms were always so damp! How could she stand it? Even if he was cute in his sort of blond, pale way. His glasses, his duckbill haircut. His green uniform and black shoes, dingy from work. There were definite parts of him I could understand the attraction to, but those clammy hands would be a deal breaker for me, no two ways about it.

"Evelyn." Poppy sat down next to me, breathless. "What happened? Chuck was light on the details."

Burrows took the other seat, his head hanging. Good. He should be ashamed, leaving me to tell his girlfriend the bad news. The coward.

"Mac was arrested," I said. Not tactful. But I couldn't be tactful currently. I was able to sip tea, wait, and repeat what I'd seen, and not in that order.

"What?" Poppy mouth fell open. "What do you mean?"

"That awful Detective McJimsey," I said. "He—he stormed into the shop and arrested Mac! Said the chargers were murder and attempted murder. And then he left! That was it!"

Poppy held onto her head with both hands. Her eyes were wild, shifting around, not settling on me, her boyfriend, or the scenery. Not looking at anything at all. "Mac? They arrested Mac?"

"Not *they*," I said. "McJimsey. Don't worry. I'm hiring the best firm in the city. They'll clear this up. We'll get him out of there by the end of the day, tomorrow at the latest. Tea?"

Poppy poured herself a cup, her gray eyes, so similar to Mac's, still not quite focusing on anything. Burrows pushed his glasses up his nose with the back of his hand. "Miss Murphy," he said, "what should we do? What . . . what are you going to do?"

"You and Poppy," I said, thinking about it. "You should . . . I still need Florence's address." My tongue felt thick.

"Aren't you going?" Poppy asked. "To Mac? To the lawyer?"

I blinked. My lashes were heavy. I wasn't even wearing falsies. "I should," I said. "And I need to go back to the hospital before visiting hours are over. And I need to talk to a sales associate. And . . ."

And what? And Mr. Sharpe was talking to someone who wasn't Henry on the phone, and that was weird. And Judy and Burrows were being strange in the shop before Mac was arrested. Dr. Smith had given me the wrong directions to the hospital room. Mrs. Baker can't pronounce *Balmain*. And the valets were mad at Daddy because of budget cuts. Daddy hated Mac. Mac was arrested. And Florence was dead.

Mr. Sharpe walked over to the table. He gave Poppy a not unfriendly look before saying, "Don't the two of you have jobs to do?"

Burrows and Poppy hurried off, leaving me alone with the manager and special friend of my special friend. "Mr. Ferretti, the grandson, is on his way now." He slid me a piece of paper with an address and phone number written on it. "There were a few Hodgsons in the phone book, but I called this number, and it was Detective Hodgson on the line, no question."

I stared down at the address. Laurence Hodgson. Queens.

Queens? Really?

I pushed my teacup away. "Thank you, Mr. Sharpe. And now, if you'll excuse me"—I swallowed hard—"I must hail a taxi."

CHAPTER 23

The last time I'd ridden alone in a taxi, I'd had a massive attack of anxiety that left me sprawled out on the sidewalk in front of my hotel.

This time, I told myself, would be different. This time, I knew what to do. I'd done it before, and though it felt like I was dying, I hadn't died. Since then, I'd left the hotel multiple times without ending up short of breath and feeling on the brink of death. Since then, I'd learned how to know when an attack of anxiety was oncoming, and what to do to stop it in its tracks.

More or less.

My father was in the hospital and my boyfriend was in jail, and there was nothing else to do. I had to hail a taxi, whether or not it killed me.

"Miss?" A bellhop asked, lifting his little green hat. "Need anything?"

"Oh." Okay. So, maybe I didn't have to do the hailing, then. That was fine. "I need a taxi. Thank you ever so."

He stuck out his arm and whistled. A yellow taxi pulled up, and the bellhop opened the back-seat door. "Have a good day, miss."

I tipped him a dollar and slid into the back of the dab. With Presley's purse in my lap, I opened the piece of paper with Mr.

Sharpe's handwriting. The bellhop slammed the door shut, and the taxi driver stared at me in his rearview. "Queens," I said, and read off the address.

Daddy would have to wait. So would Florence. So would everything else.

Nothing was as important as solving this murder before the maniac struck again. And I could not do it on my own.

The taxi dropped me off on a corner of Roosevelt Avenue, the address given on my paper, where there was a red brick building with blue signage that said "NORTH CORONA BODEGA." This could not be right. Mr. Sharpe had said he'd heard Hodgson on the line.

I paid the driver and got out of the taxi, too confused to be scared. I'd done it. I'd gone to Queens almost completely on my own. Presley was a huge help. But now where? I could ask the owner of the bodega.

Fixing the buttons on my cardigan, I strolled into the shop. If I kept my chin up, if I kept my breathing even, if I kept a smile on my face, no one would know how torn up I was inside. Maybe not even me. Maybe I could pretend I was fine hard enough that I would be fine.

Ha. Take that, analysts. I'd solve all my problems from here on out, thank you ever so.

A cat was lounging on the counter by the register, and the little grandma who sat on a stool behind it didn't even look up from petting the cat's belly as she told me, "Upstairs," when I asked if she knew Laurence Hodgson.

Upstairs. Sure. Where were the stairs?

Presley stared at the sleeping cat with both ears pricked outward. I don't think he'd ever seen one before—only other dogs, and only at the park on his walks.

She lit a cigarette while still scratching the cat. Quite impressive, when you thought about it. "Back door. Swings open. Can't miss it."

I adjusted Presley's purse higher up on my shoulder and headed for the back, eyes peeled for a swinging door that I couldn't miss. It was tucked between a dairy section and a produce section, and if I hadn't been looking for it, I would have missed it. The same color as the wall, except more dinged up, with nary a handle to turn. I pushed it open and stuck my head in, found the stairs like she'd said. I almost couldn't believe she was telling me the truth.

There were a few apartments up the stairs and even more stairs to more apartments. I checked my paper again and knocked on door number 2. I waited a moment, sticking my hand in my purse to scratch Presley between the ears. He nuzzled my wrist with his cold nose and gave my skin a lick. *Right. Knock again.* That's all there was to this. I'd made it this far.

I knocked, harder this time. And when still no one answered, I kept knocking. This was important, and by golly, I'd see it to the end.

A rumbly male voice said, "Yeah, yeah," and I stopped knocking before Detective Hodgson opened the door. He wasn't wearing a jacket, and that stunned me for a moment. No suit, no hat, no tie. A white, collared shirt with the sleeves rolled up past his elbows, a pair of dark slacks, and argyle socks.

It was a strange thing, seeing a man without shoes on for the first time.

"Why am I not surprised?" Hodgson said, "I thought you were a homebody."

"I am! It was very difficult coming here. Might I come in?"

Laurence Hodgson looked me up and down. He sighed, loudly—so loudly, in fact, that the hair around my face fluttered, and Presley sneezed in his purse. Hodgson took a step back.

"Come on in," he said. "I'll make coffee."

CHAPTER 24

"No coffee for me, thanks. Do you have champagne?"

There was no question that Hodgson's apartment was made for a family. The kitchen was large, with a table in the corner that had seating for three. A new television was perched on the floor of a living area, with a big couch and an armchair in front of it. The carpet was beige. The walls were beige. The curtains, surprisingly, were green. Down the small hallway were a bathroom and two bedrooms. There were pictures too, in black and white, of a younger Hodgson, a woman, and a boy. The woman was pretty, with round cheeks and wide, happy eyes, her bronze skin glowing in the light used to take the picture. The boy was young, a child when the photograph was taken, and he wore a bow tie and smiled without his two front teeth.

But looking around now, it was evident a family did not live here. This was the pad of a bachelor. There was still a bowl and a cup and silverware on the table, but only enough for one person. A box of cereal on the counter. A suit jacket and tie flung over the couch. Last night's dinner piled in the sink.

I took a seat on the armchair, lest I wrinkle his discarded clothes, while Hodgson moved around the kitchen, getting a pot of coffee brewing. There was a bookshelf behind the television, filled with books and more pictures. A shadow box of a flag and medallions from the army. A portrait of a soldier who looked like Hodgson, but different, still. His jaw wasn't as sharp, his chin not as defined. His eyes were rounder, softer. He smiled, and his cheeks were full, and he was as dapper as Hodgson, yes, but he resembled the woman in the family picture too.

Their son was grown. Hodgson didn't wear a ring. Not every man did. His wife could be at work.

But I doubted it.

The aroma of coffee filled the air and I took a deep breath. My throat felt slick with the coffee I'd had with Poppy and Mac, the espresso I'd had with Dr. Sanders, but the smell was heavenly.

Presley put his paws on the top of his purse. I fished him out of the bag and settled him on the floor next to my feet. "Do not pee in here, young man, or I'll never hear the end of it."

Hodgson walked over with two mugs of coffee in his hand. He gave me one while glaring down at my unaffected dog. "You break it, you bought it," he said.

Presley trotted off toward the kitchen table in search of scraps.

"Will your wife be joining us?" I asked, staring into my cup. It was definitely not champagne. Oh well. I took a single sip so as not to be rude. It was good coffee. Strong. I let it burn my tongue for a moment before swallowing.

Hodgson sat down on the couch. "Subtle," he said. "Real subtle, Miss Murphy."

I jiggled my foot up and down, and thought about what to say. "But you are married?"

He nodded once.

"Does she live here?"

"Miss Murphy." Hodgson set his mug down on his messy coffee table, the sports section of the newspaper spread out. "Did you come here to question me about my marital status? Or my job status?"

"Job," I replied. "Sorry. And not question so much as—Detective, that awful McJimsey came into my hotel and arrested Mac. My Mac! On suspicion of murder and attempted murder. Can you believe it? And where were you? Why are you here, and not at the station? What is happening?"

Hodgson crossed his legs, his ankle on his knee. "I got fired."

"Yes," I said. "But why?" I didn't mean to sound like his getting fired was a personal affront to me, but that's what it felt like.

"Somebody—probably whoever murdered Judge Baker and tried to kill your father—snuck into the hospital and killed our only witness. I was on the job." He shrugged a shoulder, his fingertip sliding under the clasp of his sock garter. "I no longer have that job."

Incensed, I stood up. Then, I sat back down again. I set my full mug down, stood up, and marched around the coffee table. "That wasn't your fault! How could you have known the hospital wasn't safe? How completely unfair!"

"Sit down, Miss Murphy," Hodgson said. "Since when has anything ever been fair? It's just a job. I'll get another."

"It's not just a job. You—you're a detective! You need to detect things! Solve crimes!" I did sit down, with a loud *oof*, and Presley came running in from the kitchen to see what all the fuss was about. "I need you to help me, Detective. Please."

"I'm not a detective anymore." Presley hopped up in his lap and panted at him. Hodgson, frowning, scratched his back. "You'll have to let the police work this out for themselves."

"Are you mad? The police think Mac is responsible! Ludicrous. Completely incompetent!"

Hodgson picked up his mug and raised it in a cheers.

"We have to find the truth, Detective. You and me."

"I'm not a detective anymore, Miss Murphy," he said.

I crossed my arms tight over my chest. "Fine, then. *Mr.* Hodgson. I need your help. I don't have anyone else."

He took a big gulp of his coffee, a single finger raised to keep me from talking anymore. He sucked his teeth clean and set the empty mug down on the article detailing the St. Louis Hawks's win over the Boston Celtics. "Let's look at it from McJimsey's point of view. Okay? Your father and your . . . *boyfriend* . . . get in a big, loud fight a few hours before your father is attacked in the same way that Judge Baker was killed. Loud, Miss Murphy, meaning other top-floor guests heard it and told us about it. Even if you softened the details."

"I didn't soften them." I sniffed. "I told you the important parts."

"The important part was that your father threatened to cut you off financially if Mr. Cooper didn't end his relationship with you. That alone is motive enough for Mr. Cooper to go after your father."

I clenched my jaw, my tongue waggling behind my teeth. Heat rose from my belly to my neck, lighting a fire on my skin the whole way. "You are suggesting then, Mr. Hodgson, that Mac is only interested in me because of my father's money. Is there nothing else I have to offer a romantic partner?"

Mr. Hodgson cleared his throat and glanced at the ceiling.

My fingers dug into my arms, the fabric of my cardigan soft beneath the hard digits. "Then perhaps you'd be interested to know that my mother left me a significant inheritance. All mine. My father cannot strip me of it if he does decide to follow through on his baseless threat. Daddy will not kick me out of his life. He won't. I'm all he has. He needs me if he wants his contemporaries to believe he's the family man he portrays himself to be."

"Careful, Miss Murphy," Mr. Hodgson said. "You're giving yourself a motive."

"Fine." I slapped my hands against my knees. It hurt. Too hard. I winced and rubbed my legs. Hodgson hid his smile behind a fist, pretending to cough. "What motive would I have to kill Judge Baker? To kill the girl in his trunk? Florence? What motive would Mac have for any of it?"

"I don't know," Hodgson said. "McJimsey must have a theory, but he didn't share it with me. Maybe he's only bringing Mac in for your dad and the maid. The maid is the murder, and your dad is the attempt. He got a good look at what happened to Baker, got a wild idea in his head, followed through in the morning, and when Florence walked in on him—"he moved his thumb from one side of his throat to another—"he took care of the witness."

"Mac was with me! The entire time! During the party and . . . at night. He was with me until I went to check on Daddy."

Hodgson arched a brow. "You sure about that, Miss Murphy? You willing to stake your, um, stellar reputation on that boy?"

My teenage years, a blur to me now, hadn't been the wisest of my life. I pushed a curl off my forehead. Stellar reputation. A boy can go around dallying with whatever lady he likes. But a girl is a bit too friendly from time to time, and it's her reputation that people have a problem with?

"Are you a light sleeper, Miss Murphy?"

"Not particularly. No."

"And when you woke up? Mac was asleep still?"

My fingers traced my mouth. "No," I said. "He was out walking Presley."

Hodgson sat back in his chair like he'd won an argument.

"That proves nothing. Besides, that's hardly *evidence*. Mr. Ferretti will have him out of there, lickety-split." I snapped my fingers.

"Then what do you want with me?"

Presley hopped off Hodgson's lap and trotted over to me, his tail shaking. I scooped him up. "I told you. I need your help. Someone killed Judge Baker. That same person, I believe, attacked Daddy. For whatever reason, they also went after and murdered two different women. Why? They're connected, I know it. And I need to find who did it before they go after Daddy again. Before this hurts Mac even more than it has already. Before they go after someone else."

Hodgson stood up. He grabbed both our mugs and walked into the kitchen. "Sorry. I got bills to pay. Need to find a job. Can't spend that time babysitting Miss Marples in training."

I hurried to follow after him, Presley landing on the carpet with a squeak. "You need money? I have lots of money! I can pay you. Anything you want!"

The mugs clanged on top of the other dishes in the sink. Hodgson turned on the water. "Uh-huh."

"You're not a detective anymore, but you can be a private investigator, can't you? A private eye. That's a job! And I'll be your first customer. A paying customer. You'll be Poirot and I'll be . . . not Hastings because he's useless. And not Miss Lemon, because I'm paying you, not the other way around." I tapped my lips, thinking about how to make this Agatha Christie example work. "You'll be Poirot and I'll be the character who hires Poirot, but I won't turn out to be the murderer in the end."

Hodgson, rinsing out our coffee mugs, said, "Uh-huh."

I hated discussing money. It was so déclassé. Daddy accused me of not knowing the value of a dollar, and maybe that was true, but I'd yet to meet a person who wasn't swayed by a dollar of a particular value. I rummaged around for the slip of paper with Mr. Hodgson's address on it, then flipped it around and wrote down a figure I thought might interest him. Slapping it on the counter next to the sink, I counted in my head the seconds it took him to read it.

One, two.

His hands stilled on a dirty bowl.

Three. Four.

He set the bowl back down in the sink and turned off the water.

"Are you serious?" he asked, his wet hands hovering in the air, water droplets splashing onto the paper.

I nodded. "Very."

Mr. Hodgson dried his hands on a nearby dishtowel. "All right, Miss Marple," he said. "You got yourself a deal."

I clapped my hands. Presley barked and jumped up on my shins. "That's wonderful, Detect—I mean, *Mr.* Hodgson! Thank you ever so! We'll be the best crime-fighting duo since Tommy and Tuppence."

"Who?"

I waved my hand. "It was a bad example anyway. Let's compare notes. Tell me everything you know, and I'll tell you where you're wrong."

Hodgson leaned against the counter with a sigh. He crossed his arms over his chest. "Miss Murphy, I said we had a deal, not that you were the boss. If this is gonna work, we're doing it my way."

The smile tried to slip off my face, but I kept it there. "I see. And what does your way entail, Mr. Hodgson?"

"Go ahead and tell me everything you know, and I'll tell you where you're wrong."

The smile fell, my whole mouth dropping open.

Hodgson grinned. "We'll talk at your hotel. I'm starving. You're paying for all my meals too, on top of this." He used his chin to point at the damp paper I'd written on. "You dig?"

"Don't say 'you dig'—ugh." I pinched the bridge of my nose between my thumb and forefinger. *You dig* sounded stupid when Mac said it. It sounded even stupider when it came from the former detective. "Yes. That's agreeable. Presley needs a walk, anyway."

Hodgson pointed at himself. "Not on your life will I be walking that fluff ball. Get one of your other lackeys."

I picked up Presley and walked over to my purse waiting on the armchair. "'Other lackeys' implies you know you are one of them," I singsonged. "That's good, Mr. Hodgson. I always knew we'd be friends."

"Miss Murphy, a bit of advice?"

"Yes?"

"Friends aren't people you have to pay to be around you."

I blew out a big breath, my lips rattling. "Then I'd never have anyone around me," I said. "Except for Henry, and he's *terrible* with this snooping business. You'd think, being an actor, he could handle it. And he's great at lying. But snooping? Finding clues? It's embarrassing how bad he is. Are you driving? Or do I also need to pay for a taxi?"

Hodgson grabbed his jacket and tie off the armchair. "I'll drive," he said. "But you're paying for the fuel."

CHAPTER 25

We were seated at a corner booth in the Pinnacle's diner, the best place for cheeseburgers—I'd told him as much when we each ordered the same meal—with Presley by my side, eating his plate of beef.

Hodgson pulled out a notepad and pen from his jacket pocket. "All right, Miss Marple. Tell your story."

"Do I not get to eat my burger first?"

He sighed.

"I'm sure you're hungry too. And look at little Presley."

My dog perked up his ears at the sound of his name but did not pause in licking his plate clean.

"Yeah." He set the notebook down. "Fine. But I want to get one thing straight." He tapped his finger against the shiny tabletop. "I'm in charge here, yeah? But I'm going to need your help if we're gonna get to the bottom of this. I don't belong in this world. And without a badge, it's gonna be hard to get these people to talk to me."

Wincing, I said, "It was probably difficult to get them to talk to you before, even with the badge. What with your personality and all."

Hodgson glared at me, but there was no heat in it.

We ate in silence until the table next to us left, and a waitress came over to clear their booth. A wallet was lying partially open on one of the chairs. I snatched it, but the waitress and the patrons were gone.

"Stealing now, Miss Murphy?"

I slurped at my strawberry shake. "Finding," I replied. "I'll give it to the lost and found when we're done here. Are you ready?"

He nodded and wiped his mouth clean. Hodgson flipped open his notebook and uncapped his pen. "Go ahead."

I recounted, to the best of my ability, everything that had happened since the party. I didn't skate around why Mac and I had been in the parking garage in the first place, didn't lie like I had to my father about our less than stellar intentions. I mentioned the valet because that seemed important, and talked about what it was like finding Judge Baker, about the woman who had sat up out of the trunk and screamed when she saw me.

He knew what had happened at the police station, but I recounted the conversation between McJimsey and myself when he had been out of the room. Hodgson wrote everything down so fast it was a wonder his pen didn't leave smoke behind.

I closed my eyes and tried to remember everything that had happened once I returned from the police station. Daddy had picked me up. I'd cooked for him. He didn't like Mac, and Mac didn't like him. I'd ended the conversation. Rang for Dr. Smith to check on Daddy. Called Hodgson for information about the woman in the trunk. Gone to bed without a kiss goodnight.

Why hadn't Mac kissed me goodnight?

And then, a few hours later, Mac and Presley were gone. Daddy's suite hadn't been like I was expecting. No coffee brewing, no maid cleaning, no early morning shower getting hot. Instead, Daddy had been on the floor of his bedroom, convulsing.

The part after that was harder to remember, even with my eyes closed and my nose wrinkled. I'd cried a lot. Mac had comforted me. Dr. Smith had saved Daddy.

"Dr. Smith," Hodgson said. "That's the second time you mentioned him. He was with Mrs. Baker at the party?"

I blinked my eyes open. "He wasn't *with* her. He came to her aid when she started feeling unwell. He volunteered to take her home and do a more thorough exam there."

"Right," said Hodgson. "And did you see the two of them leave?"

"I saw them leave the party," I said. "But not get into a car, no." I'd been waylaid by Mac.

"And Dr. Smith, he's staying at this hotel, correct?"

"Yes. He's a regular while he's trying to find a place to buy near the hospital. I don't blame him. He works hard. He must be tired by the time he's done for the day. It's hard to cook for yourself after all that, much less go house hunting."

Hodgson wrote something in his notebook and then waved his hand in a circle, telling me to continue.

"Right. Where was I?" I talked about the hospital, even about the man in the suit who brought us coffee. That I'd guilted Dr. Smith into telling me the room number of the girl in the trunk, but I'd been too late, and Dr. Smith had called her time of death.

"He's popping up a lot in your story," Hodgson said.

My milkshake was empty. I ran a limp French fry around the edges of the cup to get any remaining streaks of ice cream. "So what?"

"Interesting, is all. Go on."

"You know," I said, "he gave me directions to the woman's room, and they turned out to be wrong. Told me to turn left when I should've turned right."

Hodgson wrote that down too.

I didn't tell him about the conversation that I'd overheard Mr. Sharpe have with someone who wasn't Henry, because frankly, that wasn't anyone's business and could get both of them in hot water. I did tell him I'd gotten the address for Mrs. Baker, and that Mac and Presley and I had visited, and golly, was that all today? Did all of this happen today?

No wonder my shoulders ached. No wonder there was a building pressure in the center of my forehead.

I lowered my voice and whispered, "She had a brand new, sold-out Archambeau bag, but she mispronounced *Balmain*."

It was Hodgson's turn to say, "So what?"

"Interesting, is all." I twisted my lips in a wry grin, plucked a few dollars out of my pocketbook, and left them on the table as a tip. "She said Judge Baker bought it for her. And I believe it because if you're able to purchase such an exclusive bag, there's no way you'd mispronounce another designer's name. She's obviously not the one interested in luxury items in their relationship.

"Then Mac and I came back, and we weren't here for ten minutes before McJimsey was arresting Mac. We got your address from the phone book, and you know the rest."

Hodgson scribbled something else before closing the notepad with a snap. "I do, and it's late. I'll have to tell you tomorrow all the ways that you're wrong."

I gathered the lost wallet and my sleeping dog to my chest and did my best to smile. "I look forward to it. Have a good night, Detective."

"Not detective anymore."

"Sorry." I slid out of the booth and hid my yawn behind Presley's ears. "Have a good night, Mr. Hodgson."

"Just Hodgson is fine," he said. "Get some rest, Miss Murphy. You look terrible."

I patted his shoulder. "Your kindness in my time of need means the absolute world to me. Thank you ever so." I left the restaurant, motioning to our waitress to send the bill to my room, and headed toward the mail desk. Burrows was there.

He smiled at me. "Miss Murphy. You find something?"

"I sure did." I gave him the wallet. "I'm also looking for something, though. Someone, rather. Where is Poppy?"

Burrows tossed the wallet in the box behind him labeled "L&F."

"I'm not sure. Somewhere around the hotel. Oh, a call came in for you. Here." He reached under the desk and pulled out an envelope. "It's from Mr. Ferretti's office."

"Mac's lawyer," I said. "Thank you, Mr. Burrows." I slid my finger under the seal of the envelope. "I know it's late," I told him, "but I need to talk to you."

I pulled the note out, frowning.

Mr. Ferretti had left a message saying that while he believed completely in Mac's innocence and knew he'd win at trial, Mac wouldn't go before a judge for his bond hearing until at least Monday, and the judge they'd been assigned was good friends with Baker. Mr. Ferretti essentially told me not to hold my breath; my boyfriend would not be released anytime soon.

"Preposterous," I told the note. "He wasn't even arrested for the judge."

"Miss Murphy?" Mr. Burrows asked. "Are you all right? Is there something you needed to talk to me about?"

Budget cuts and valets, but that could keep until morning. The pounding behind my eyes was getting worse. "Tomorrow," I said with a fake smile. "Have a good night, Mr. Burrows."

"You too, Miss Murphy."

★   ★   ★

Someone was crying in my room. It only took a moment of confusion to put the sound to a familiar voice. "Poppy? Poppy, darling, where are you?"

The bathroom door opened, and Poppy walked out, her maid uniform wrinkled and her eyes wet and red. "Sorry, Evelyn. I was doing the turndown service, and I went to check the bathroom trash, and I saw Mac's comb and I–I—"

"Oh, darling." I set Presley down and moved over to her, wrapping her in a hug. I rubbed her back. "Don't worry. Okay? Don't you worry. I've spoken to Mac's lawyer, and he's very positive about the whole thing. He assured me that Mac will be out no later than Monday."

It was a good thing her chin was on my shoulder, or she would've seen the face I made when I was lying. I'd never been good at lying directly. Indirectly, omission—I can do those. Bald-faced lies make my face look strained.

I held her at arm's length. "Do you want to stay over tonight?"

She wiped her face with the back of her hand. "You don't mind?"

"Of course not. Go on. Take a shower—no, a bath. A *bubble* bath! I'll bring you pajamas. Have you eaten? Do you want me to call you some room service?"

"I'm fine."

I pursed my lips.

She sighed. "Okay. A sandwich would be wonderful. Or meatloaf. Is that weird? Meatloaf and mashed potatoes sound so good right now."

"Meatloaf and mashed potatoes it is." I shoved her gently. "Go on. Take a bath. Your food will be here when you're done."

Poppy sniffed. "Thank you, Evelyn."

I pushed her again. "Don't mention it." Once she was behind the bathroom door, I called in her order. I found a yellow silk nightgown and slipped it into the bathroom. Poppy was more or less submerged under bubbles, and she waved. It distracted me long enough for Presley to bully his way inside.

He trotted over to the toilet, jumping on the lid and put his paws on the rim of the clawfoot tub. "He'll make sure you're safe," I said, shutting the door behind me. Finally, I was able to slip off my shoes and hide Mr. Ferretti's message in my bedside table. I didn't need Poppy learning the truth. Not now, anyway.

Besides, I'd think of something. I'd get Mac out of the jail by Monday, or I'd . . .

I sat down on the edge of my bed, burying my pounding head in my cold palms. There wasn't anything I could do. It was unfair of the judge to deny Mac bail because he was upset that Judge Baker had been killed. But it was called the justice system, not the fairness system, and there was nothing I could do about it except keep pouring money into it.

Flopping down on the mattress, I stared up at the ceiling and did my best not to think about what sort of bed Mac was sleeping on that night.

I failed. Miserably.

CHAPTER 26

I woke up and even though I could see the sun coming in through my window, my body protested, and my bleary mind whispered, *It's the middle of the night—go back to sleep.*

Poppy slept where her brother usually rested his head. Presley was tucked under her arm, his head on the pillow, awake and smug about it. Ridiculous. There was a soft knock on the door. That's what had woken me up in the first place, then. I blew Presley a sleepy kiss and staggered out of bed. My toes dragged on the soft carpet. I yawned, stretched my arms over my head, and managed not to fall on my face as I threw my pink chenille robe on over my nightgown.

Henry stood outside the peephole. My brow furrowed, my brain trying to catch up with what it was seeing. Oh, right! I'd told Mr. Sharpe to send Henry my way. I'd completely forgotten.

I unlocked the door and swung it open. Henry's face was contorted into a deep frown. He held out his arms and said, "My darling girl. I'm so sorry."

It was like someone hit me. Knocked the air and the life right out of me. I sagged forward and collapsed against him. Henry held me to his broad chest, his hands smoothing my back. "That's it, darling. I'm here."

The tears burned when they fell, wetted Henry's soft Tiffany-blue sweater. But he patted my back and held me still. "Have you had breakfast, darling? Let's get some food and caffeine in you, and then we can talk about it."

Henry was the best friend I'd ever had. At least until I'd met Mac, and that wasn't a fair comparison. Henry and I had all the same taste in everything, from music, to clothes, to men. But Mac was more than a friend. Mac was the other part of my heart, and now he was in jail, and I was watching a movie star place an order for a breakfast feast from the comfort of my couch.

I grabbed a heart-shaped throw pillow and held it over my face. Everything was bad. I'd had to go to so many places yesterday and talk to so many people! But today was Sunday, there was no chance for Mac to get out until at least tomorrow, and I would be going nowhere and talking to no one who didn't either work or live at the Pinnacle.

Henry sat down at the end of the couch and set my feet in his lap. "Darling," he said, "do you want to talk to me? Or would a foot rub be the best thing?"

I hugged the pillow to my chest. "Both would be nice."

He smiled, his bright white teeth sparkling. Henry had made a career out of his good looks, with his perfect jaw and his bright blue eyes.

He held my feet in his uncalloused hands and dug his knuckle into the arch of my foot. "Whatever you need to talk about," he said, "I'm here to listen. Ha, I should've said I'm here to hear."

At his joke, I nudged him with my toes. "Everything is bad right now. Terrible. This new detective, McJimsey, arrested *Mac* for the attempted murder of my father. Detective Hodgson got fired for some stupid reason. And Daddy doesn't like Mac. He threatened to cut me off financially if I keep seeing him."

Henry rubbed my toes. "That's silly," he said. "You're his only family. He brags to all his business associates about his beautiful daughter. You don't believe that empty threat."

"No! But Mac seems to." I closed my eyes. "I know he didn't do anything. I *know* he didn't. But I don't know how to prove he didn't."

"What about that judge? The one from the garage?"

"Yes, I found his body," I said.

Henry nodded, half his mouth quirked in a grin as if to say, *"Obviously."*

"I don't know what he and my father have in common, darling. Why would someone attack them both? And that's not all of it either. There was a woman killed in connection to Judge Baker, and my maid, Florence, was killed and hidden in Daddy's bedroom closet."

Henry shook his head. "Awful, darling. Simply awful. Why would someone go after all four of those people? What could the connection be?"

"I don't know." I crushed the pillow against my face again in an attempt to keep from crying. This was hopeless, completely hopeless. I was never leaving this room—this seat!—again. "And," I said, pushing the pillow to my forehead, "I spoke to Mrs. Baker yesterday. Darling, she had the newest Archambeau bag."

His hands froze on my heel. "You're kidding? The handbag they only made two dozen of? That you had to be invited to purchase?"

"It gets worse," I said, scrambling into a kneeling position. "She mispronounced *Balmain*. She said *ball main*!"

Henry's mouth fell open. "That's suspicious."

"Right? Thank you!" I groaned. "No one else can see it for how odd it is."

"How did a judge's wife even get the newest Archambeau?"

"Exactly, yes!" Finally, someone who could see how strange this whole thing was. "And sure, maybe I am jealous since I wanted one and wasn't invited, but that doesn't mean—"

"That it's not weird," Henry finished, nodding. "Very weird."

I was so relieved someone understood me that I wrapped my arms around him and pressed my forehead to the crown of his hair. "I love you so much, Henry Fox. Thank you ever so for being the very best friend there ever was."

He laughed and patted my back. "Anytime, darling. Anytime."

I sat back on my heels. "And how are you doing? I didn't even ask—I'm sorry."

He waved me off. "Don't worry about me, Evelyn. You've got enough on your plate."

"Don't worry about you? Did you not hear me a moment ago? You're the very best friend there ever was. It is my honor to worry about you."

He rubbed the back of his neck. "It's nothing."

I wrinkled my nose. "What's nothing?"

"It's only—Silas. He's been . . . odd, lately."

"Mr. Sharpe?" I verified because while I knew his given name was Silas, I'd never actually heard someone speak it before. "Odd, how? We did have a dead judge turn up in our garage, plus Florence and my father and that other woman."

"No." Henry gave a self-deprecating laugh. "That's way more important. I mean, a few days before this all started even. More than a week ago? He's been . . . distant. Harder to spend time with. All of the sudden, he's even busier than I am. He made an effort to come to a showing on Friday evening and then rushed right out. And I know it's because of Judge Baker, but he was acting strange in my dressing room even before the emergency call came in."

I laced our fingers together and squeezed. "Men," I said. "What are we to do with them?"

Shortly thereafter, the breakfast Henry ordered was delivered. I offered the waiter two dollars to walk Presley—but Presley growled and showed his teeth, so I had to give him four—and woke up Poppy, warning her we had a guest for breakfast. Poppy and I had gotten close the last few weeks, but Henry was still a movie star, and it wasn't like he was around me often enough for her to be used to him too. He'd been so busy now that his Broadway play had opened to incredible reviews. At least, I only read the incredible reviews. If anyone had anything critical to say of Henry's acting, singing, or dancing, they were not the sort of person I needed opinions from.

Poppy covered a piece of toast in orange marmalade and took a crunchy bite. "What is the plan for today, Evelyn? Mac will be released tomorrow, right? Is there anything we need to do to get ready?"

"That's . . . yes," I said, pouring cream into my coffee and not looking at her. "Yes, tomorrow. The lawyers will handle all of that. Today, however, I plan to stay right here in this room and talk to no one but the two of you."

Henry reached over to tuck a strand of hair behind my ear. "Good for you," he said, lifting my chin with a knuckle. "You deserve a day off. I wish I could stay with you, but my understudy isn't ready yet."

"Yours are quite the shoes to fill." I winked. "That's fine, Henry. You'd be very bored. I'll call the hospital and check on Daddy, but other than that, I am doing nothing. I am staying in my pajamas, reading a book, and I might put on the telly or the radio. That's it."

There was a knock on the door. "Miss Murphy?" Judy's voice came from the other side. "The Archambeau sales associate is here for you."

I swore.

CHAPTER 27

The salesgirl, with the help of Judy, wheeled in in a clothes rack filled with beautiful designer gowns and dresses. The bottom was lined with shoes and purses. But the bag that Mrs. Baker had was nowhere to be seen.

As Henry had said, they'd made only two dozen of the bags. And just a chosen few had been invited to purchase the red lambskin bag. I had not been one of those few, but for some reason, Judge Baker had. It was important to talk to this girl, even if I was exhausted and wanted to do nothing of the sort.

If only I'd remembered to cancel when I still had a chance.

The salesgirl paled when Henry stood. He had that effect on women. He winked at her before offering me a hand. "Darling, it's been wonderful catching up, but I'll be late." He kissed my cheek. "Have a wonderful, marvelous day, and I'll see you later. Poppy, always a pleasure. Don't be a stranger."

Poppy, her hair unbrushed, wearing borrowed pajamas, and her mouth filled with marmalade toast, giggled so hard crumbs tumbled onto her chin. They'd been eating and talking together, and even she wasn't immune to Henry's charms.

"Take care of my girls, won't you?" he asked the salesgirl before leaving the room with a wave.

Judy excused herself shortly thereafter. It took several heartbeats before the Archambeau seller cleared her throat.

"Miss Murphy," she squeaked. "I thought you and Henry Fox weren't going steady any longer?"

"That's right." I gave a dramatic sigh. "But we'll always be friends. Now. Let's see what you brought me. Miss . . .?"

"Rose, Miss Murphy. My name is Rose."

"Nice to meet you, Miss Rose. Poppy, will you be joining us?"

She looked at me with one eyebrow raised, slumped in her seat, her cup of coffee still steaming in her hands. If I didn't know any better, I'd say she was hungover from a night out partying. But I did know better, and my beau's sister had spent the better part of the night in bed, crying softly, trying not to wake me.

She deserved a new outfit more than anyone I could think of. Even more than myself. And I definitely deserved a new outfit.

"I'm not working today," she said. "But, Evelyn, I couldn't afford—"

I waved my hand. "Don't worry about it, Poppy. Pick out whatever you like. We'll have fun shopping together, won't we?"

Poppy glanced over at the salesgirl—who was glancing at the door like she hoped Henry Fox would wander back in—and smiled. "I'd like that, Evelyn. Thank you."

"Don't thank me. Thank Miss Rose here. Let's see if you brought anything worth buying, darling. Show us what you've got."

★ ★ ★

Miss Rose was near enough to mine and Poppy's age that after thirty minutes or so, her shoulders relaxed and her tongue loosened. Presley's appearance, trotting around and sniffing at her ankles, didn't hurt either. She cooed at him before offering me another choice of shoes. "It's a good thing you and Miss Cooper have the same size feet," she said. "I didn't bring anything over that wouldn't fit you, Miss Murphy."

The clothes were a similar story. I was tall, taller than Poppy, but our measurements were otherwise near enough that anything she wanted from the rack could be altered by a tailor without too much difficulty.

I slipped on a pair of white heels that would be very good for a bride. I didn't currently know any brides, but these shoes weren't such a bad thing to have ready to go in one's closet. Just in case. "You know, I visited Mrs. Baker yesterday, and she had that lambskin leather bag. It was to die for."

Rose nodded. "I sold that one to her husband myself. The only one I'd seen in person. Incredible craftsmanship."

"How sweet of Judge Baker," I said conversationally to Poppy. "Buying his pregnant wife a designer handbag. Not many men are like that, unfortunately."

Poppy ran a silk blouse across her cheek. "I can only imagine."

"Judge Baker is one in a million," Rose agreed. "He's always in our shop, buying something lovely for his wife. He spoils her." She sighed. "I hope I can find a man like that one day."

She didn't yet know the judge was dead. Obviously, Miss Rose wasn't a newspaper reader, as his death had made it on the front page of the paper delivered with our breakfast. I bit my lip and thought about what to say. "Judge Baker likes the finer things, then?"

"He's got an eye for beauty," Rose said. "And the bankroll to back it up. Once he pulled out a wad of cash so large—oh, sorry." She blushed and hid her mouth behind her hands. "It's ever so rude of me to discuss another client like this. I apologize, Miss Murphy."

I smiled. "A bit of gossip never hurt anyone, Miss Rose. And you aren't saying anything untoward. Have you met Mrs. Baker?"

Rose twisted her mouth to the side, casting her glance up and to the ceiling in thought. "I think, once. Truth be told, I got the impression that the gifts are something that the Judge enjoys more than Mrs. Baker herself. He likes dressing her up, I mean. Like a doll. Oh, but in a good way!"

"Of course." I slid off the bridal shoes. "Try these on, Poppy. They'd be excellent for a wedding."

Poppy blushed crimson but tried them on anyway.

"Are you engaged, Miss Cooper?" Rose asked.

"No," said Poppy. "Evelyn's teasing me, is all. I have a boy-friend and he's swell, but—" She shook her head. "I don't know if I'm ready to be a missus quite yet. Evelyn and my brother, though? They'll be betrothed any day now—take my word for it."

I rolled my eyes but smiled anyway, the color rising from my chest up to my face. I wanted Mac to be my husband almost as much as I wanted to solve this triple homicide. Almost.

Poppy set the silk blouse in her lap and reached for the shoes. "Why, a week ago he was writing Gran about—" She pressed her lips together hard, eyes wide. "Never mind," she squeaked. "Nothing. No. I . . . um. Hmm. These *are* lovely shoes! And this blouse! Shall I change into it in the bedroom?" And then she scurried off like a mouse running from a cat.

Mac was writing their grandmother about what? Something to do with weddings?

My nose wrinkled. Was he . . . was he inquiring about marrying me, getting advice from his family? My heart skittered in my chest. That would be the ginchiest thing that had ever happened to me. Hopefully, this kerfuffle with Daddy hadn't put a damper on Mac's plans, because being Mrs. Cooper would be ever so dreamy.

"I'll take the blouse and the shoes for Poppy," I said. "And that pink dress with the matching belt for me. Thank you, Miss Rose."

"No pocketbook today, Miss Murphy?"

There was only one Archambeau bag I was interested in, and it was in the hands of Judge Baker's widow. "Not today. But thank you ever so."

Chapter 28

Once Miss Rose left, I stilled Poppy with a hard look. "You know I need to hear what it was Mac was writing to your grandmother about."

She grimaced. "Please, Evelyn. I was sworn to secrecy. But I promise"—she took my hands in hers—"it's good. Okay?"

I squeezed her fingers. "Okay."

"Now, since you bought me the most expensive shoes and blouse I have ever had the pleasure of owning, I'll take Presley for a walk."

My picky dog put up no fight at all, and I was left alone in my closet, which used to be a second bedroom. I admired myself in my new dress, tightening the belt. The push of it against my girdle felt good, earned, like I needed to be uncomfortable. Mac was in jail, for goodness sakes, and my father in the hospital. I didn't need to be able to empty a breath. I should slip on last year's stilettos that were a little too tight around the toes—the pinch might do me good.

No. It's okay to be nice to myself. With a sigh, I loosened my belt and reached for the pendant of Saint Anthony on my necklace. I prayed I'd be able to find whoever was responsible for the tragedies that had befallen the Pinnacle of late.

A knock on my door roused me from my prayer. I made the sign of the cross and headed toward the door. Through the peephole,

I was surprised to see Detect—*Mr.* Hodgson standing in the hallway, his hands in his pockets, his fedora crooked on his head. Light brown this time, in coordination with his jacket.

Mr. Hodgson was a comely man who was always sharply dressed, but he looked even sharper when he wore darker colors. I unlocked the door and let him in.

"Hello, Mr. Hodgson," I greeted him. "I didn't realize you'd be coming over today."

He stepped into the room, craning his neck to look behind me.

I turned around to see what was so fascinating. It was completely normal, except the nightgown that Poppy had slept in was strewn over the back of the chaise.

"Poppy is walking Presley," I said. "She'll be back in a minute. We went shopping this morning, and I have some interesting news to share with you about Judge and Mrs. Baker."

"News you got while shopping?" Hodgson clarified. "Doubt it's that interesting. But you can tell me about it on the way to the hospital."

My hand went to my heart, fingers reaching for my mother's pendant. "The hospital? Is something wrong?"

He looked at me like he was disappointed. Or, that is to say, he looked at me the way he almost always looked at me. "Your father. He's still there, and the chief hasn't let anyone question him yet."

"I know that Daddy's still in the hospital. I assumed . . ." Clearing my throat, I rolled back my shoulders. "I went to many places yesterday, and I was hoping I could stay here today. At the Pinnacle."

Hodgson sucked his teeth. "Tomorrow will be too late. He's ill now, but he'll be ready to talk to the police Monday. We won't get a chance like this again, Miss Murphy."

While I could see the reason in his argument, I did not like it. Not one bit.

"Fine. Let me leave Poppy a note. But I'm only going to the hospital," I said. "Nowhere else."

He held up empty hands in surrender.

I stomped into the kitchen to write out a note for Poppy. Once that was done, I called down to the front desk and told Burrows the same thing. I was going to the hospital—please pass on that information to his girl—and I'd be back for Presley in an hour or two. I hated the idea of Poppy not knowing where I was and Presley somehow getting the short end of the stick because of it.

"Do you want to drive my car?" I called out from the kitchen. "Or will we be taking your wagon of death again today?"

His car wasn't terrible, but it was dirty. For a man who keeps himself put together, the old cups of coffee and wrappers of half-eaten food were a surprise. *"Stakeouts,"* he'd said when he'd pushed the trash off the seat to make room for me.

He hadn't answered by the time I was done in the kitchen. I grabbed my clutch, leaving Presley's larger purse behind, and raised both eyebrows. "Well?" I asked. "Or do you want to grab a taxi instead?"

"I'll drive your car," he said. "But I'm not . . . I'm a cop, all right? I'm not a fill-in for your normal errand boy."

"No, you're not." I opened the door and left without a look back. "But you aren't exactly a cop anymore either, are you? Besides, there are worse things than having to drive a Rolls-Royce around for half an hour."

The elevator arrived, and Hodgson told the lift boy to take us to the lobby. "Yeah," he said to me, "not having your choice of passenger would be one."

An offended chuckle puffed out of me without my say-so. "I'm a delightful passenger," I said. "*Delightful.* How dare you suggest otherwise."

"I dare because I've met you before," he said. The left side of his mouth was twitching in what I assumed to be the beginning of a smile. He didn't smile much, but it was always a sight to behold when he did, and it made me think of Daddy. Alone, recovering in a hospital bed. And me, not on my way to visit him as I said I would do, but to question him again about the attack, this time with a former detective at my side.

I sighed and resigned myself to what was sure to be another unpleasant encounter with my father. It was a good thing he didn't visit more often if all of them were going to end up like this one.

★ ★ ★

"So," Hodgson prompted once we were in the thick of Manhattan traffic, "what did you want to tell me about shopping and the Bakers?"

I settled my clutch across my knees and dug around for my tube of lipstick. I felt off balance, off-kilter, and when that happened, there was nothing quite like putting on red lipstick. It made me feel more powerful than I was, more put together, more in control. I didn't want to leave the hotel today, I didn't want to talk to Daddy, but if I had no choice, I'd put on my warpaint and attack it head-on.

"The salesgirl only met Mrs. Baker once. She said Judge Baker did all the shopping. He was regular, and he enjoyed dressing up Mrs. Baker like his own personal doll."

Hodgson glanced at me from the corner of his eye. "And . . . so what?"

"And so what!" I said. "Archambeau is expensive, that's what! One of their pocketbooks costs even more than a Chanel."

"Judges make a lot of money." He shrugged. "Who cares how he spends it?"

I closed my lipstick tube with a snap and tossed it back in my clutch. "Mr. Hodgson," I said, "the newest bag she owns? The one that I was denied the opportunity to buy. That alone costs three hundred dollars."

He choked on his tongue, coughing and sputtering, the car swerving in the lanes. A taxi behind us and one to the left of us each honked simultaneously.

"Three hundred dollars?" He yelled when he'd gotten himself together. "For a purse?"

I pointed my finger at his face. "Exactly! And in order to purchase said three-hundred-dollar bag, you had to have spent at least *fifteen hundred* dollars there in the last six months. Now, tell me, Mr. Hodgson. Judges are wealthy, sure, but how many of them do you know can do all that, plus put two sons through Harvard?"

He drummed his fingers against the gleaming red steering wheel. "Okay. You might be on to something. Not quite a smoking gun, mind. But it's not . . . not nothing either."

Delighted by his acquiescence, I ran my fingers through my hair. "I do hope Daddy is feeling up to answering questions. He wasn't quite altogether yesterday."

"No," Hodgson said. "Heroin'll do that to ya. He'll be miserable, but I bet you can get him to talk. He might not remember his attack, and that's a problem. But maybe he'll have some insight into what he has in common with Judge Baker."

"Besides the fact that they're both wealthy, you mean," I said. "Though, it is strange. To go after two wealthy men and two, um, working-class women. At least, I'd assume the woman in the trunk was not as wealthy as Daddy or Judge Baker."

Hodgson snorted.

"Were the police ever able to identify her?"

He clicked his tongue. "Yeah. She was a regular down at the ninth precinct."

"A regular?" I blinked. "Whatever do you mean?"

"She was a member of the oldest profession," Hodgson said. "And as such, spent a lot of nights in jail instead of working."

I pressed my lips together while I thought about what to say. What did a judge, a businessman, a maid, and a prostitute have in common? It sounded like the setup for an unfriendly joke.

"Poor thing," I said. "What was her name?"

"Joan. Joan Wilson."

"I hope we can give her family a reason for her death."

"Sure," Hodgson said. Traffic ambled forward, and my car breezed through one green light before stopping at the next red. "But police? We don't need a reason."

I turned toward him on the seat. "What do you mean?"

"The police, to make an arrest? And the prosecution, to put the bad guys in jail. All we need is means and opportunity. We don't have to answer the why of it. Lawyers like it if we can, though. Makes it easier to sell the story to the jury."

"But we are not police, Mr. Hodgson."

He looked at me as if I'd said something particularly rude.

"I am not. And you aren't anymore either." I almost put my hand on his arm to offer comfort, but thought better of it. Hodgson was not the sort of man who found comfort in the reassuring touches of others. "While it's all well and good for police officers and lawyers to determine guilt with only the how and when of it, you and I will need the why."

Hodgson scratched at his forehead, his khaki fedora bouncing on his knuckles. "Your dad should give us insight there. A project he and Judge Baker worked on. A mutual friend. Something."

I smoothed the fabric of my dress over my knees. "Hopefully, Daddy is up for the task at hand."

"Hopefully you are, you mean."

Buildings sped past the car window, traffic giving way to let us ride. "Means and opportunity," I mused. "The MO."

Hodgson breathed out a chuckle. "No. MO stands for modus operandi. That's the method behind the deaths. Like, three out of four of the Pinnacle victims were dosed with heroine. That's the MO. Even if Wilson survived the first round of attacks."

"Florence being the odd one out," I said, tapping my finger against my lips and immediately regretting it. The red lipstick came off on my skin. I sighed and dug around in my clutch for a spare handkerchief, finding only the very piece of fabric Hodgson had given me. I needed to have it laundered. Shame on me for forgetting. I cleaned my finger. "She must not have been an original target."

"No," Hodgson said. "I don't think so either."

"She surprised the attacker by simply doing her job, and the attacker improvised." I reapplied my lipstick, still mad at myself. "I still haven't called her family yet."

"You've been busy," Hodgson said as we finally pulled into Manhattan General. "You can call them later. Right now, you got your own family to worry about."

CHAPTER 29

The nurse let us in—though she scowled at Hodgson particularly hard—and told us both to keep our voices down, and not to bother Daddy for too long.

"We won't," I assured her. "I'm here only to check on him." The officer guarding the door opened it for us, and I smiled at him. "Thank you ever so."

Daddy's room did not smell as I'd remembered it. The odor of vomit and heavy strength cleaner mixed in a pungent combination. I pinched my nostrils and hurried over to the window. Daddy was lying in the fetal position in his bed, snoring and drooling on his pillow. When I was done with the window, letting in blessed fresh air, I turned to find Hodgson looking over the medical chart at the foot of the bed.

He pointed at Daddy with his chin. "Wake him up. We don't got all day."

I swallowed down the urge to argue with him. As it was Sunday, my boyfriend was in jail, and Hodgson was out of a job, we did in fact have all day. Unless the nurse insisted otherwise. I could always throw a fit at that CFO. If I could remember his name, anyway. Slimy and concerned with donations, I doubted the hospital employed many men matching that description.

At least I hoped not.

"Daddy?" I ran my fingers over his forehead. He was cold and clammy under my skin. "Daddy? It's Evelyn."

He groaned and rolled onto his back with a wince. "Evie?" His voice was quiet, hoarse, but it was clear.

"That's right." I held his cheek while I bent to kiss the top of his head. "How are you feeling?"

"Terrible," he said. "What's worse, they won't let me near a phone. I have business to attend to."

"I know you do, Daddy. But it *is* the Lord's day. Business can keep until tomorrow."

He closed his eyes. "You sound like your mother."

"So you've said." I cleared my throat. "Daddy, there is someone here I want you to meet."

He popped one eye open.

"This is Mr. Hodgson. He's a private investigator I hired to get to the bottom of what happened."

Daddy's single gaze drifted to the end of the bed before he closed it again. "Don't trust the police now that they've arrested your boyfriend, do you, Evelyn Grace?"

I took the seat next to his bed. A giant bouquet of orchids was on his bedside table, and from this close I could smell their floral perfume. A much better scent than whatever was happening to the air in his room currently. "Can't say I've trusted the police since I was a child, Daddy, as they have yet to solve Mom's murder."

He hummed his agreement.

"I need you to tell us what you remember from the night you were attacked."

"It's like I told that detective. What's his name? McJerry or—"

"McJimsey?" Hodgson and I said at the same time.

Daddy opened his eyes and nodded. "I don't remember what happened, but I doubt it was that moron you're enamored with."

"Why do you doubt that, Mr. Murphy?" Hodgson asked.

He shrugged a shoulder. "Maybe saying I don't remember it isn't correct. My memory is fuzzy. I don't remember recognizing the bastard who drugged me." He licked his lips. "His feet. I *saw* his shoes. It was a man. They were men's shoes. They were . . . dull," he said. "Not recently shined."

Hodgson and I exchanged a look. Shoes. Daddy remembered shoes. It was better than nothing.

"The other thing we wanted to talk to you about was Judge Baker, and what the two of you might have in common."

"Cliff Baker?" Daddy asked, his nose wrinkling.

Oh no! It was an inherited trait, but not from my mother. How embarrassing. I glanced at Hodgson to see if he'd noticed, but all his attention was locked on my father.

"We went golfing a few times over the years. His wife sent a Christmas card to my office every year. His first wife. I don't know this new one."

"You ever do any business with Judge Baker?" Hodgson asked.

"No. That's what I just said. We golfed a handful of times. That's all."

"Did he ever represent you in court, back before he was a judge?"

Daddy huffed. "No. He went up against me once. The Pinnacle." He pointed his thumb at me. "But that was years ago. More than a decade. He won too, if memory serves."

I sat on the edge of my seat. "What was the case, Daddy?"

"Some lawsuit or another." Daddy said. "Personal injury or some such nonsense. Every few years there's an employee who tries to get themself set up for life by issuing a baseless lawsuit. Most of the time they lose, and it's never even worth my while. But Cliff Baker? He *did. Not. Lose.* I was glad when he became a judge, to keep him off my"—Daddy coughed—"behind."

That had to be something. Judge Baker was a lawyer who had won a lawsuit against the hotel, and he could afford to buy his wife an unlimited supply of designer goods. There was something there. But what? I didn't realize my nose was wrinkled until Hodgson spoke again.

"Thank you, Mr. Murphy. And if you remember anything else about those shoes, you let Miss Murphy know straight away."

Daddy glowered at the former detective halfheartedly. He hated being told what to do. But it's not like Hodgson was wrong either. "Fine," he said. "Now, let me rest. I'll see you tomorrow, Evelyn."

I kissed his forehead. "Get some sleep, Daddy."

He harrumphed but closed his eyes and relaxed into his pillow. Hodgson held open the door for me, and we nodded our thanks to the officer stationed in the hall.

"That was interesting, right?" I asked.

Hodgson smiled. "That's what we in the police business would call a *clue.*"

CHAPTER 30

We returned to the Pinnacle, Hodgson parking at the steps. A bellhop rushed to open the door, but Hodgson held up a finger to tell him to wait.

"I read your father's chart," he said. "You want to know another clue?"

"Obviously."

"His blood work results were in his chart. It wasn't just heroin they found. It was heroin—street-level heroin, not pure like what got Judge Baker—but it was mixed with something called phencyclidine."

My nose wrinkled. "What's that?"

"I got no idea. But I'm gonna find out." He waved at the bellhop who popped open my door.

"Oh. Well. Goodbye then, Mr. Hodgson."

He flicked his fingers at me in response.

I huffed. The nerve of some people. I climbed out of the car, tipped the bellhop, and watched Hodgson take my Rolls-Royce in the direction of the garage without throwing so much as a *"Have a good day"* over his shoulder. I huffed again but started walking.

A glint on the bottom step caught my eye. I snatched it up as I walked. A watch. A man's watch. Sensible, sterling silver, something probably bought from Sears. There was a man at the top of the steps who was studying the ground with a curious expression on his face. The bellhops were giving him a wide berth as they pushed golden carts stacked with luggage into the hotel.

I tapped his shoulder. My nail polish was chipped. "Did you drop this?"

"Oh!" He blinked at me. "Oh, *way out*! That watch was a birthday present from my wife. I couldn't go home without it. This sure is swell of you, miss. Thanks."

I handed it over with a smile. "You are most welcome. Have a great day."

An interaction with a strange man on the sidewalk, and I'd handled it politely. I'd even initiated it. *Good work, Dr. Sanders.* As soon as Mac was out of jail, I'd surprise him with a visit to his apartment. I was basically unstoppable now.

I needed a bath and a nap and an entire twenty-four hours locked in my bedroom as soon as possible, but once those things were done—unstoppable!

And a manicure. I needed a manicure. My roots were coming in too. I needed a day at the salon plus a day in my suite, and they needed to happen concurrently. Consecutively? What word meant one before the other?

"Afternoon, Miss Murphy," the doorman greeted me.

"Good afternoon to you," I said. "Does concurrently mean one before the other?"

"Uh." He held the door open. "No, ma'am. It means at the same time."

"Oh. Yes. I need it consecutively, then."

An unsure smile twitched on his face. "Need what, Miss Murphy?"

"A visit to the salon. Look at my nails! No, wait—don't look at them. I'll see you later. Have a marvelous day!"

Mac would go before a judge sometime tomorrow, and I wanted to look perfect for him. Mr. Ferretti was one of the best defense attorneys in the state. I was sure he'd be able to get Mac bail, even if the attorney himself was doubtful. There was almost no evidence to hold him.

Or there was more than I was aware of.

But Daddy was sure it wasn't Mac who attacked him. And more than that, I knew it wasn't Mac. I know his heart. He'd never do something like this. Especially not to someone so important to me. Even if Daddy wasn't the best father, he was the only parent I had left, and I treasured that connection. No matter what.

Modus operandi. The method of the killing. Could the how of it all explain the why of it all? Whoever had killed Judge Baker, the woman in the trunk, and Florence had also used heroin three out of four times to overdose their victim. Florence had been strangled, and probably because she'd surprised the killer. She hadn't been the intended target. The woman in the trunk, as well—once she'd survived the overdose—had been suffocated with a pillow in her hospital bed. And Judge Baker had been injected with pure heroin, unlike Daddy, who'd gotten dosed with regular heroin mixed with some other drug. Phen-something or other. Was the heroin that important, then? Or was it a means to an end? And what did Judge Baker and Daddy have in common besides one lawsuit over a decade ago and a few rounds of golf?

What was the killer trying to say?

It had been obvious to me, days ago, that whoever had killed Judge Baker had been out to ruin his life. After Daddy's attack, that intuition faded a bit. But now it was back, gnawing at my insides.

Maybe they were trying to ruin Daddy's life too. Maybe that was the modus operandi of it all.

"Miss Murphy?"

The lift boy was looking at me. He was younger than me, but not by much—an elder teen—but he'd been working at the Pinnacle for a while now. He was polite and easy on the eyes, with his dark hair and warm brown skin, a hint of a tattoo peeking out under his uniform sleeve. I blinked. We were already on the top floor. I didn't even remember getting in the elevator.

"Sorry, Mr. Castillo," I said. "I . . . I was thinking too hard, I suppose."

"Happens to the best of us?" he said though it sounded more like a question. "Do you need anything, Miss Murphy?"

"No," I said, "but thank you ever so. Have a good day."

My nails might still be chipped and my hair might be browning on top, but at least I'd get in a good snuggle session with the world's best dog.

"Evelyn, is that you?" Poppy asked from the vicinity of my kitchen.

Presley trotted down the hallway toward me, his tail wagging so hard his butt shook with every little step. I scooped him up and kissed the top of his fluffy head. "Yes," I replied. "Just me."

She came out of the kitchen with a piece of paper in her hand. "I was writing you a note. A few of us are getting together at Florence's place. Do you want to come?"

My shoulders sagged. Behind her, I could see my beautiful, comfortable couch, where only a few scant hours ago I'd had a movie star rubbing my feet. My nails were chipped. My roots were coming in. I'd left the hotel so many times! I'd talked to a stranger when I gave him back his watch!

And now there was something else?

"Okay," I said, frowning. "But I'm taking Presley."

CHAPTER 31

Florence lived in a women's-only boarding house that, from the outside, appeared to once have been a decent hotel, but time had chipped away at it until *shabby* was the best word to describe it. The building was loud. Or rather, the occupants were. I could hear voices on every floor. Women talking and laughing. Someone was playing an Eddie Fisher album and singing along in a high-pitched harmony that rattled my eardrums.

Poppy knocked on the door, and another young woman answered. The two of them hugged, and then Poppy introduced me.

"I know who she is," the woman said. "Hi, Miss Murphy. I'm Jennifer. I clean on the third floor. Won't you come in?"

I offered her my hand, and she shook it before I stepped inside the apartment of the woman who had cleaned up my messes for the better part of a decade. There were several other employees from the hotel scattered about the small living area. They were talking, drinks in hand, and while the atmosphere didn't feel quite celebratory, it was nice to see that a few people had gathered together in Florence's honor.

The room, small but cozy, was decorated with a mishmash of dark-colored furniture and teal and aqua paintings. The sea. On every wall, a painting of the sea.

"I'm from Florida," Jennifer said when she noticed me taking in the art. "I like to paint."

"Jenny and I go to the same art classes," Poppy explained. "It's where we became friends."

"They're lovely." I meant it too. "I can almost *feel* the saltwater on my skin."

Poppy rolled her eyes, but Jennifer's grin lit up her entire face. "Thank you, Miss Murphy. That means the world to me. And is this the famous Mr. Presley?" She gestured at my tote bag, and I moved it more toward the front of my body so Presley could poke out his head between the handles.

"He's *so* cute," Jennifer cooed. "But keep him in your bag, if you don't mind? Florence's cat is loose."

I scratched Presley's ear. "Not a problem. We're guests here, after all." I smiled. "Thank you for having us."

Jennifer held open her arms. "I didn't know what else to do. Her brother doesn't care, and I've got to come up with her half of the rent by the first, and . . ." She blinked, her eyes going wet. "She was my best friend. Who am I going to talk to after work now?"

Nanny used to say that any problem money could solve wasn't a problem at all. I didn't know how to fix the hole in her life that no longer having her best friend had created, but I could cover Florence's half of the rent without a second thought.

I mentioned it to Poppy when Jennifer went off toward the kitchen table, falling into the arms of a friend. The young woman stared at us over Jennifer's head, and it wasn't friendliness in her eyes. Suspicion. Anger. I looked away first.

"That's nice of you, Evelyn," Poppy said. "I'll ask and get the amount for you. You gotta be careful, you know. Don't want anybody to take advantage."

"Advantage of what?" I asked.

"It's just that . . ." Poppy stuck her hand into my bag to pet Presley. "You and money. You have so much of it, and you're . . . you give it away to whoever all the time."

Oh dear. Now she sounded like Nanny talking about an entirely different topic.

"It's only money. It's not like it lasts forever."

Poppy gave me such a Mac look—like I was insane but adorable at the same time—that it made my chest ache. I swallowed, surprised to find a solid lump had formed in the middle of my throat. "Do you happen to know where the ladies' room is, Poppy?"

She directed me across the hall, and I hurried into the small space, resting against the door after locking it closed.

I couldn't do this. I couldn't do this! Mac was in jail, arrested for the murder of Florence, and here I was, in Florence's apartment with his sister. These Pinnacle employees, Florence's friends, did they believe Mac was innocent? Or were they angry with Poppy and me for showing our faces? Why hadn't I thought about what they would think before I even stepped in here?

When had I become so self-centered? Had I always been like this, all my life, thinking only of myself and my comfort until thrust into the harsh truth that other people existed outside of my own circle, that other people mattered as much as I did?

All Florence had done was her job. And she'd gotten killed for it. Now, I was standing in her bathroom, the girlfriend of the man blamed for the homicide.

My legs shook. I slid against the door, coming down hard on the tile. My breathing was little more than shallow puffs. My hands were numb. My chest was filled with bees.

Those stupid bees. Where was that feeling coming from? What did it even mean?

Breathe in. I took a deep breath through my mouth. *Hold it, you idiot.* I held it and counted backward from three. *Breathe out.* I exhaled hard, emptying my lungs until it hurt. I repeated the process, reaching into my tote bag to hold Presley. He sat on my lap and allowed himself to be petted while I breathed in and out, in and out.

What was I feeling right now? I closed my eyes and focused on the buzzing in my chest and the heaviness in my stomach. Shame. Fear.

I was terrified, and I was ashamed of what people thought of me, what I thought of myself.

Pinching my eyes closed as tight as possible, I forced myself to imagine little Evelyn. She was playing with her too many bunnies, because the two female bunnies she'd managed to convince Nanny to get for her were, in fact, a boy and a girl bunny. But then, all those bunnies had been given away, leaving a very lonely, angry girl, who sought revenge by haunting room 13 on the thirteenth floor.

I shook my head and tried to recall the girl with the bunnies, no different from who I was now, with a dog in my lap. She'd been afraid because she'd been told the bunnies had to go to a new home. To a farm or whatever other lie Nanny had come up with.

What would I say to her?

"You'll miss the bunnies, Evelyn, but look at them! Look at the mess they're making already. They're so many of them, and you're barely sleeping because they're so loud. Nanny might be lying about the farm, but I'm not lying to you. You will survive this. You will get through this loss and make it to better times. I know this because I am you. Because I've done it. We've done it. We're still here, still kicking, even after burying Mom. We'll still be here, even after giving away the baby bunnies. We've survived."

And if I've done it once, I can do it again.

Presley yipped and licked my fingers.

I took one last steadying breath before opening my eyes.

A cat sat on the edge of the bathtub, its black tail flicking. It meowed.

CHAPTER 32

"Oh, hello," I greeted my host. The little back and orange cat blinked its green eyes at me and did not respond. Slowly I set Presley back in his bag, so as not to start a war for territory in the bathroom. "I didn't know anyone else was in here."

The cat hopped off the tub. It slinked toward me, stopping at my feet and smelling my shoes. I smiled.

"My, you're a pretty kitty," I cooed. "It's lovely to meet you. My name is Evelyn, and this is Presley."

Presley's paws were on the edge of the bag. He watched the cat with unabashed interest, his head tilting to the side, his tongue lolling out of his mouth. I giggled and scratched his chin.

The cat hopped into my lap. Surprised, I raised my hands in the air so as not to hinder its exploration. It sniffed at my elbows, before leaning toward Presley, chin out.

The two animals smelled each other. Presley sneezed and hid in his bag.

I understood the feeling.

"You're very friendly." I ran my fingers over the cat's back. It arched under my touch, tail going straight in the air. Its purr buzzed in the quiet of the bathroom. I giggled. "Are you hiding too?"

Someone knocked.

"Evelyn?"

The cat made no move to get off my lap, so I scooped it up into my arms and stood. After getting Presley's bag settled on my shoulder, I opened the bathroom door.

Poppy and Jennifer were standing outside.

"You all right?" Poppy asked.

"I'm not feeling so great. I think I'm going to head home. But, Jennifer, if there's anything at all I can do, please let me know."

She was staring at the cat in my arms. "Miss Murphy," she said, "you know what? There sure is."

★ ★ ★

The taxi dropped me off in front of the Pinnacle steps, alone. Poppy had opted to spend the night at Jennifer's. The bellhop opened the yellow cab door and did a double take when I stepped out. I didn't blame him. It's not every day the daughter of the owner is clutching a dog in one hand, an empty cat box in the other, and a meowing tote bag tucked under her arm.

The doorman also looked at me with the same level of confusion as the bellhop.

"It's Florence's cat," I explained. "Or was, rather. Her roommate isn't able to care for it anymore and so, yes, I have a cat now. Thank you. Good day."

Mr. Burrows waved me over to the mail desk. Resignedly, I approached. "Things okay, Miss Murphy?" he asked, handing me an envelope.

I had no way to take the envelope. "Just swell, Mr. Burrows. Can you open it and tell me what's inside, please?"

"Ah. Yeah. You got your hands full, don't you?"

I smiled because it was a better alternative than screaming. "I do."

He ripped open the envelope and unfurled the letter. "It's an invoice." His eyes went so wide from behind his massive glasses that he looked a bit like a microscope. "From Mr. Ferretti's office."

"Of course it is. And on a Sunday afternoon, no less. You know what they say, Mr. Burrows?"

"What, Miss Murphy?"

"The devil works hard, but debt collectors work harder. Please have it delivered to my room. I will also need a bag of kitty litter and some Friskies."

"Oh." His microscope eyes blinked. "Sure. Right away, Miss Murphy. I'll see to that myself."

"Thank you ever so, Mr. Burrows. Have a nice evening."

I rang for a lift and smiled at a familiar face.

"Miss Murphy, Mr. Presley," Mr. Castillo greeted us, nodding his head at both of us in turn.

"I've got a cat now too," I told him.

The cat meowed.

He took a step back. "I'm allergic to cats."

"Then I would advise you not to put your face in my purse."

He laughed, surprised. "Yes, Miss Murphy. I'll try to avoid that."

I did my best to get Florence's cat comfortable, though, truth be told, the cat seemed comfortable enough all on its own. It strolled through my suite, as if it was judging my taste in furniture, before hopping onto my pink chaise lounge and having itself a bit of a doze.

Presley watched, entranced, from the door of my bedroom.

I set up the cat's litter box in a corner of my bathroom and placed food and water bowls for it on top of my kitchen counter, so Presley wouldn't be tempted. Then I took a nice, long, hot soak; ordered room service; ate turkey tetrazzini until my stomach hurt; and went to bed, clutching the pillow that Mac usually slept on.

One more day, and he'd be free.

Hopefully. Probably.

That would have to be enough for tonight. There wasn't anything more I could do. I'd left the hotel so many times this weekend! I'd spoken to strangers and hired a personal detective—a private investigator. I'd talked to Daddy, even though I didn't want to. He'd said he didn't think it was Mac who'd attacked him, so there was at least that.

I buried my face in Mac's pillow and took a deep breath. The mixture of citrus and smoke that clung to the pillowcase soothed the buzzing inside of me.

Daddy had even given us a clue. Judge Baker had been the lawyer who'd won a lawsuit against the Pinnacle Hotel. I wondered who he'd represented, what had happened. My nose wrinkled. Daddy had said something the other day too, hadn't he? When he'd been half out of his mind from the drugs. He'd said the maid had died years ago. Maybe those two things were related? Maybe the family of the maid who died had sued the hotel? So how had she died? And who had won the money?

With a groan, I reached for the pad of paper and the pen I kept by the side of the bed. I jotted down my questions to ask Hodgson and then made a separate list of all the things I needed to do Monday.

1. Nails
2. Hair
3. Ask Mr. Sharpe if he's being unfaithful
4. Ask Mr. Sharpe about any dead maids from years ago
5. Hopefully Pick up Mac from the courthouse

I crossed out hopefully. I *would* be picking up Mac tomorrow. And I'd have excellent hair and nails when I did so. I'd also be able to assure Henry that Mr. Sharpe was not being unfaithful, even though I had no actual idea if that was true. With a sigh, I set the pad of paper and pen down and pulled the covers up to my chin. I had a plan. I had a direction. There were murders to be solved, I didn't have time to be sorry for myself.

And what did it say about me that I was at ease solving murders? That I was able to leave the hotel, talk to strangers, and calm myself down from an anxiety attack, when all those things were taxing?

What sort of weirdo did that make me?

Florence's cat hopped up on the bed. It walked along my body before making itself comfortable on my chest, immediately purring as it pinned me down.

"I don't even know your name." Jennifer hadn't told me. She hadn't seemed to like the cat, which was a surprise to me, as it was probably the world's friendliest cat. It continued to purr. "Normally, I'd make you take me dancing in the Silver Room first before letting you sleep on me."

The cat closed its eyes.

"Are you a girl or a boy?" I yawned. "You need a name. A proper name. I certainly can't call you Omelet or something."

There was no way I was going to call my new cat Omelet. I'd think of a better name tomorrow, and I'd remember, even if it wasn't on my list.

CHAPTER 33

Getting dressed felt like a chore. An unfamiliar feeling, as getting dressed was one of my favorite things. I put on high-waisted jeans and an oversized black and white checkered button-down shirt, tying the extra fabric in a loop at my belly button. My shoes were black mules, simple and comfortable. Even putting my makeup on didn't bring me joy. I washed my face with cold cream and soap and almost left it at that, but I looked like I'd barely slept a wink, and that wouldn't do. Mascara, pink rouge, and pink lipstick were all I could manage.

And then I swiped a bit of Vaseline on my eyelids and the center of my bottom lip too, because I was tired and could use a bit of shine.

"Okay, kitty." I hadn't thought of a name yet and was refusing to call it after a breakfast food. "I'll be back later. You hold down the fort. Presley, honey, want to get breakfast with Mommy in the café?"

He hurried over to me. The cat, from its spot on the floor near my balcony doors, bathed in sunlight, did little more than raise its hind legs and clean itself. Picking Presley up and placing him in his purse, I waved goodbye at my disinterested cat and headed to the lobby.

The café was one of my favorite places to lounge. I liked watching the guests and new arrivals filter in and loiter. I found an empty table near the fish tanks and ordered an espresso and a croissant for me and a plate of scrambled eggs for Presley, and waited for Mr. Burrows to notice me. He came over shortly after I got my coffee, with a newspaper under his arm.

"Good morning, Miss Murphy. Haven't heard from Mr. Ferretti's office yet. Poppy asked first thing this morning. She's real worried."

I sipped my coffee. "Mr. Ferretti has it all in hand." I fumbled open the Monday paper, not quite reading anything. Mr. Ferretti was the best I could do for Mac, and I could only hope it was enough. "Thank you again for the kitty litter and the Friskies, Mr. Burrows. My new pet appreciated them both."

He pushed his glasses up his nose with the back of his hand. "Nice of you to take in Florence's cat," he said. "What's its name, again?"

"I have no idea."

"Is it a boy or a girl?"

"With a cat? How can you tell?" I tore off a bite of my croissant. "Perhaps I'll name it Joe Friday."

"Joe Friday?"

I shrugged a shoulder, the flaky, buttery croissant melting in my mouth. "A better name for a cat than Omelet."

Mr. Burrows pushed his glasses up his nose again, his hand lingering near his face. "I better get back to work, Miss Murphy."

"Have a good day, Mr. Burrows."

Daddy's attack was front-page fodder. I should've been expecting that, as Judge Baker's death had been all over the weekend papers. It was below the fold, with a mention of Judge Baker just beneath it. But the two women were not included at all, much less named. Malcolm Cooper, former Pinnacle employee, was listed as the suspect arrested. *Former employee? They missed that he was my current beau? That was a much better angle. The editor should be ashamed of the reporter's shoddy investigative work.*

The fact that it left out Florence's murder boiled my blood. Ridiculous that Daddy being attacked and surviving was more of a story than Florence losing her life! None of the articles had, as of yet, even mentioned the woman found in Judge Baker's trunk. Another injustice to add to my growing list.

Mr. Sharpe walked in the front door, his tie undone around his neck. I watched him cross the lobby. His eyes were shifty, flitting back and forth, though he greeted anyone who said hello to him. He had a briefcase clutched in one hand, his jacket hanging from the other. I sighed and took another sip of coffee.

Mr. Sharpe was guilty of *something*. I didn't think I had the energy to deal with the consequences of his choices, but there wasn't any way out of it. Henry was one of my best friends. He deserved the truth if I could find it.

★   ★   ★

I finished my beverage, collected my dog, and sauntered past the check-in counters, toward Mr. Sharpe's office, giving him enough time to settle, but not enough to be in the middle of a work-related project.

His secretary wasn't in yet. All the better for me. I knocked on his door and waited for him to acknowledge a visitor. When nothing happened, I knocked again. Still no response. My heart skipped a beat and picked back up again at a furious pace. Oh no. Was I too late? Had Mr. Sharpe been attacked, same as Daddy? Was the bad guy still in there? Should I run for help?

I held on tight to Presley's bag and swung open the door. There was no time for dilly-dallying. If Mr. Sharpe was in trouble, I'd save him or die trying.

But he was slumped over at his desk, his head in his hands, all lights off except for one pitiful lamp shining on his elbows.

Panting, I glanced around the room. There was no one else. Just the two of us. I cleared my throat. Mr. Sharpe peeked at me between his fingers and groaned. "Yes, Miss Murphy. How may I be of assistance?"

"Mr. Sharpe." My voice was shriller than I meant it to be. I took a calming breath. "What is wrong with you?"

He set his arms down on his desk, palms flat against paperwork. "I'm sorry. I slept poorly. I'll be my usual self in no time."

"That is not what I mean." I stomped over to his desk, hand on my hip. "Henry says you're distant all of a sudden. And I—what I mean is . . . hmm." As loathe as I was to admit to eavesdropping, there wasn't a way around it. I made my hand a fist against my hip-bone. "I heard you speaking on the phone with someone who is not Henry, and you said you loved them. And now you come into work disheveled and exhausted, and something is wrong, and I would like to know what it is, because if you hurt Henry—*my Henry*—I swear, Mr. Sharpe, I will make your life a living hell."

"Worse than you do now, you mean?" Mr. Sharpe asked. "Hard to believe that, lass."

I narrowed my eyes. "And here I thought the two of us were on good terms."

"You overheard a private conversation."

"Yes. But you were having it . . ." I wanted to say he had been speaking loudly, but that wasn't the truth. He had been whispering. Mac and I had had to put our ears to the door to listen. "Around me," I settled on.

"With my *son*."

Very rarely in my life have I been at a loss for words. But there I was, standing in front of a man I'd known most of my life—in both an adversarial and friendly way—with my tongue a useless muscle in my mouth. My fist slid off my hip as all air left my lungs.

"Huh," I said.

"Yes." Mr. Sharpe leaned back in his chair.

"I did not know you had a son."

"Very few people do. Henry doesn't. Not yet. I'm asking you, Miss Murphy, please do not tell him."

"That is fair enough as long as you do plan on telling him at some point."

Mr. Sharpe scratched the deep lines on his forehead. "What choice will I have? My son, a few weeks ago, moved from Chicago to Brooklyn. And now he wants me to get him a job here. At the Pinnacle."

I nodded. "A bit of nepotism never hurt anyone."

"You *would* say that. But I do not know my son well. I do not know what kind of man he is. And I do not know what he will think of Henry."

I pressed my lips together to keep from smiling. What a silly man, so worried over something so easily fixed. "Is that all?"

"What do you mean, *is that all*? That's—"

I waved a hand, interrupting him. "Mr. Sharpe, please. Offer him a job on a trial basis, and I will feel him out for you. Personally. Give Henry a heads-up. But he's an actor. He'll be fine around your son. No issues there."

He stared up at me, mouth open under his silvering mustache.

A smile happened despite my best efforts, and I giggled, reaching across the desk to pat his hand. "And you were so worried. Silly man. If anything, you should be way more stressed about the bad press the Pinnacle is getting right now. Have you read the paper? Not good, not good at all. Do let me know when you expect your son. I'll be sure to fit him into my schedule. But until then, I have work to do and I must be off. Toodles!"

I sauntered out of the room, Mr. Sharpe spluttering somewhere behind me. If only all solutions were as easy to find as that one.

CHAPTER 34

I went back up into my room, feeling more energized than when I'd woken up. Thank God for solving the problems of silly men and a hearty helping of caffeine. Dr. Sanders needed to reevaluate her opinion on coffee. My phone was ringing, so I hurriedly shut the door, set Presley's purse down, and picked up the nearest receiver.

"Evelyn Murphy speaking."

The man on the other end of the phone call introduced himself as my banker. "I've got the payment for Mr. Ferretti's retainer all squared away, Miss Murphy, except I can't send it out without your father's approval."

"Oh no," I said. "Don't worry about that. I wanted to pay Mr. Ferretti out of my trust. You know, the one from my mother? That she left me as an inheritance?"

"Yes, ma'am," he said. "That's what I've done. But you still can't draw on it without your father's approval."

I smiled, even though he couldn't see it, because the alternative was to throw the receiver against the humming refrigerator. "But it's *my* money. It isn't Daddy's money. That's the point."

"Yes," he said again, and he sounded like he was smiling because the only alternative was to throw *his* phone. "And until you are married, you cannot draw on that account without your father's approval. Once you're married, you'll need your husband's."

"Of all the barbaric nonsense! You cannot be serious."

"I assure you, ma'am, I am not one to joke."

"Well! Thank you very much, you have been *ever* so helpful. Daddy will talk to you soon, I am sure!"

I slammed the receiver down to hang up the call, picked it up, and knocked it back down a few more times for good measure, the rotary dial shaking with every impact.

My money and I couldn't spend it? I admit I didn't have the best handle on banks, bank accounts, and what to do with the money inside of them. Daddy was always talking to me about the markets when we did talk, but our conversations were few and far between. Money was always there. Or rather, I wanted something, I indicated I wanted it, and then it was mine. The transaction that made it belong to me was always rather out of my hand.

Stupid! It wasn't Daddy's money, and it certainly wasn't my future husband's. It was my mother's, an inheritance from her father, and that made it mine by birthright. Mr. Ferretti's retainer had to be paid one way or another, so Daddy would . . . he would just . . .

He'd have to agree to it! I'd make him agree. I'd throw a fit, is what I'd do, until I was blue in the face, and he was desperate for quiet. Fine. So be it.

Plan settled, I clicked my tongue and wandered my apartment. My new cat was nowhere to be seen, but the litter box had been freshly used. The cat must not have appreciated the noise I made hanging up the phone.

I sank into the nearest chair and hid my face in my hands. Everything was terrible. Absolutely terrible. And I was stuck, unable to help, unable to even afford to help. And affording things was the one thing I'd always been able to do! Always! If I was nothing else, I was rich. My sweet, wonderful Mac was stuck in jail, and I couldn't even get access to the one thing I had in abundance.

"I'm a failure," I said out loud, my fingers muffling my voice. "A failure." Presley licked my ankle. "Don't bother trying to cheer me up. There's nothing to it. Daddy and Mr. Hodgson both say Mac only wants me for my money, and it turns out I can't even spend it as I want, so what's the point? Florence's murderer is walking around outside somewhere, Mac is stuck inside somewhere else, and I've failed."

There wasn't another lick. I opened my eyes, but Presley had wandered off. I huffed. Rude. All the men in my life: rude.

But not Mac. I sat up and rubbed my chest. It hurt like a rib was cracked open. A broken, empty thing inside of me. I needed to help him and I couldn't.

Except that wasn't true now, was it? I could go to his bond hearing and offer support. I could hit the pavement and figure out who the real killer was. Both of those things were in my realm of ability, and both of those things would be as helpful to Mac as paying for the best defense attorney in Manhattan. More or less.

I glanced down at myself. None of this would do. This mopey, sad, depressed thing wouldn't solve a crime, and it wouldn't help in a courtroom. This was war, and I needed to dress for it.

★　★　★

First, I changed into a bullet bra and a roll-on girdle. They were both a simple white. I slid on new stockings, clipped them onto the bottom of the girdle, and washed off the little bit of makeup I'd put on that morning. I'd need full coverage to face this day. Yet another spent outside of the hotel, and this one in a courtroom, with the man I loved being defended by the man that I could not pay.

Next, I put on a Chanel suit—a dark pink tweed jacket and coordinating pencil skirt, lined in a solid pink color, with a coordinating blouse. The buttons closing the jacket were gold, clashing with my pendant of Saint Anthony, but I didn't dare take off the necklace. I slid it under my blouse and put a pair of simple gold studs in my ears.

Makeup came next, and I didn't skip a step, covering my face in a dewy foundation before tapping Vaseline onto my upper cheekbones and swiping it along my eyelids. Blush and setting powder came next, and then I did my eyes in a sparkling white eyeshadow, lined the waterline with a white pencil, and curled my lashes before applying mascara.

I lined my lips in red before filling them in with the brightest red lipstick I owned, and a dab of Vaseline in the bottom center of my lip to make it shine. I'd read about Marilyn Monroe's makeup routine in a magazine some time ago, and it used to be the guideline I followed religiously. For the past month or so, I'd been choosing more matte, pink looks than the dewy ones my idol preferred, but not today. Today I needed her.

Marilyn, give me strength.

The accessories came next. I wore dark pink heels and pinned on a whimsy. A pink bow, with a delicate lattice of pink lace, hung over my eyes. It covered my browning roots too. The salon would wait for me until after Mac was free.

As I stood in front of the full-length mirror in the middle of my closet in a second bedroom, Florence's cat wound its way between my legs.

"Hello, darling," I cooed. "Did I scare you earlier? I am ever so sorry about that. What do you think? Am I ready for court?" I clasped my hands under my chin and gave the mirror a watery, beseeching look. "Please, Judge, release my lover to me. I'll be good to him, I pinkie promise."

The cat sat on my shoe, its purring vibrating up my leg. "I'd pick you up, but you'll get fur on my outfit, and we can't have that, now can we?"

The cat did not move. It stared up at me with its big green eyes.

"Fine." I picked it up and held it under my chin, enjoying the vibration against my throat. "You still need a name."

There was a knock on the door, and Presley barked.

"Who is it?" I called from the closet.

The cat didn't like me raising my voice and wiggled in my arms. I let it jump down. A voice answered, but I couldn't make out the words. It didn't matter, though. I recognized it all the same. "Come on in, Poppy!"

Presley followed Poppy into my closet, his tail wagging so hard his entire body shook from side to side. Poppy's eyes were rimmed red, but she smiled at me.

"You look lovely, Evelyn."

I ducked my head. "Thank you ever so."

"Have you heard from Mac's lawyer?"

"Not yet," I said. "But soon enough. I'm going to the courthouse for his bond hearing. Would you like to go with me?"

She gestured at her maid's uniform. "I'm working today."

I shrugged. "Take the day off."

"I need the money, Evelyn."

"I'll pay you."

She made a doubtful face. I hooked my arm through hers and brought her deeper into the closet. "I'll tell Mr. Sharpe I need you to take over Mac's assistant duties temporarily, and I'll pay you the same wage I pay him. Hm? What do you say?"

She was still frowning.

"I do need your help, Poppy. I need assistance. I've got three murders to solve, after all."

"I thought you hired that grumpy detective?"

"Yes. But there's only so much one man can do, you know. Please, Poppy? It would be a massive favor."

She sighed, giving in.

I grinned. "Wonderful! Now, go on! Pick out whatever you want to wear."

Poppy looked at me with her wide gray eyes. "Really? I can wear whatever I want from your closet?"

"Absolutely anything! But do hurry. I want to get to the court-house as soon as possible."

CHAPTER 35

The grumpy detective I hired put a stop to that, however. He seemed to materialize in the hall outside my door, fist raised in a knock the moment I swung it open to leave, Poppy trailing behind me.

We both squealed in surprise.

Hodgson only arched an eyebrow. "Morning."

I locked the door and placed the key in my Chanel 2.55 handbag, glaring at my visitor the entire time. "Don't you know it's rude to go over to a lady's home without calling first?"

He stuck his hands in the pockets of his slacks. Hodgson wasn't wearing a hat today, and it threw me for a second. His suit was navy blue, with thin white pinstripes, and it looked much better on him than that tan affair from yesterday. "Glad you're ready to go. We need to speak with Elena Baker this morning."

"Oh, *we* do, do we?" I crossed my arms over my chest, tweed sleeves going tight at my shoulders. "For your information, Poppy and I are on our way to the courthouse. We want to be there for Mac for his bond hearing. I intend to pay his bond the moment it is set."

This would prove to be tricky, as apparently I could not access my money without Daddy's approval, and Daddy was not very approving of Mac, to say the least. I was hopeful an idea would come to me while we were waiting for Mac to be brought before the judge.

Hodgson checked his watch. "Yeah. You got a few hours. He won't go before the judge until afternoon."

"You had time to call and find out the time of Mac's bond hearing, but not time to call me and let me know you were coming over?" I sighed. "Typical man. Still, I do not wish to speak with Elena Baker again. I was at her house only Saturday." I didn't think I could do more than one big thing today, and that thing had to be rescuing Mac. Supporting Mac.

And then calling Dr. Sanders, because my bones were starting to feel too big for my skin, like my skeleton might burst out of me at any moment.

"Yeah," said Hodgson, "but *I* didn't get to talk to her. I want to talk to her and Dr. Smith, match up their alibis."

"Go talk to them, then. I'm going to the courthouse."

"Miss Murphy, we spoke about this. Remember? In the diner? I need your help talking to these people. These people are in your circle, and I don't have a badge anymore."

I fiddled with the flap of my pocketbook. "Take Poppy with you. Poppy, you go with Mr. Hodgson. Tell Mrs. Baker and Dr. Smith you're my assistant, and then help Mr. Hodgson in his questioning."

Poppy put her hand on my arm. She didn't speak until I finally stopped messing with my bag and looked at her. "He's right, you know. Of the three of us, you're the only one in their league. Mrs. Baker won't talk to me as your assistant. I'd be . . . beneath her. And Dr. Smith won't either. I've cleaned his room before. He's very dismissive of me."

I slid the gold chain over my shoulder. "Then what is the point of paying either of you if you can't do your jobs? Hmm?"

Poppy's attention fell to her shoes, and I immediately regretted my words.

But Hodgson spoke before I had a chance to apologize. "Because I found out about that lawsuit. All about it. Got the file in my car. You can take a look at it on the drive over to the Bakers' brownstone. That is, if you're still interested."

"Fine. But I need to stop at the boutique first."

Hodgson looked me up and down in a rather judgmental way that I did not appreciate. "Why?"

"I cannot show up empty-handed at Mrs. Baker's home. Not when I was there two days ago. I'll have a gift for the baby wrapped, and then we will be on our way. Mr. Hodgson, you'll drive us?"

He nodded.

"Poppy," I said, and wound my arm through hers. "Please forgive me. That was terrible of me, and I'm not proud of it."

She met my eyes, the corner of her lips twitching upward. "I understand, Evelyn. It's been a hard weekend for all of us. Let's go speak with Mrs. Baker, and then we'll meet my no-good brother at the courthouse. He'll be with us before the end of the day, won't he?"

I smiled. Why did people keep asking me questions that I couldn't answer truthfully? "Yes," I lied. "No question."

★   ★   ★

Poppy and Mr. Hodgson waited outside the shop doors after I promised I'd be "Just a sec!" The baby section was small and toward the back, and I hadn't spent much time in it considering I didn't spend much time around babies and I didn't have friends. Friends that had babies, I mean! I had friends. Plenty of friends. Like Henry. And Mac. And Poppy. And the only one who was in danger of having a child anytime soon was Poppy. I found the display with minimal difficulty and grabbed an infant's gown and a bib.

Judy wasn't behind the counter. Odd. She hadn't greeted me when I'd entered either. Even odder.

I stood in front of the counter, craning my neck to look behind, wondering if she was sitting on the floor and going through her inventory again. But no one was there.

"Judy?" I asked the air.

The air didn't respond.

I fidgeted on my feet. We didn't have time for this. I needed to help Mr. Hodgson conduct his interview and get to the courthouse before it was too late.

"What's the holdup?" Mr. Hodgson asked, walking into the shop. We were the only two in the boutique.

I shrugged. "I don't know where Judy is."

He checked his watch. "Look. Stealing is wrong, right? But you own this whole joint, don't you? Can't you just take what you need and leave?"

Sighing, I said, "Mr. Hodgson. I can't hand the pregnant woman an unwrapped present. Can you even imagine doing something like that? Well, I'm sure *you* could, as you don't even decline a very thoughtful party invitation. I'll pop in the back and grab a box, and we will be on our way in no time."

"Yeah? Looking forward to that."

I sashayed around the corner to show him that I was not in a hurry and opened the door into the back room.

The first thing I saw was the moon.

Then I realized the moon had a crack in it. And it was moving.

Judy's eyes opened wide and Burrows turned to look at me over his shoulder. It was his moon that I was witnessing.

I screamed.

Judy screamed.

Burrows screamed.

"Miss Murphy?" Mr. Hodgson jogged over to me. "Miss Murphy, what's the—Oh, for the love of—Put your pants on, boy!"

Burrows grabbed at his pants. I had seen more than the moon. I had seen all of space and I wished very much to be back on Earth.

"How could you?" I shouted. "How could you?" I meant it too! Poppy was stunningly beautiful. And Judy, lovely in her own right. And this pale man with coke-bottle glasses and clammy hands had managed to snag them both? *How?*

Burrows, now that his pants were in their correct location, held up his hands. "I can explain!"

Judy fixed her dress and her hair, all while tears streamed down her face. "Please, Miss Murphy! I'm so sorry!"

Poppy ran into the shop. "Evelyn! Evelyn, are you okay?"

She stopped short of the register, her mouth falling open.

"Poppy," Burrows gasped. "Please. It isn't what it looks like."

"Yes, *now*!" I yelled. "Because they've put their clothes back on! Poppy! They were engaged in physical activity of a most sensitive nature—and I can't believe you didn't lock the door!" I smacked Burrows's arm as hard as I could. "Why wouldn't you lock the door? You stupid man! Judy! I need a box for this!"

She was holding on to her throat with both hands. "What?"

I waved the onesie and bib in her face. "I need a box for this. Now, if you please!"

Poppy's mouth had yet to close, but there were tears in her eyes. Mr. Hodgson approached her slowly, the way a trapper might approach a cornered animal, and set a hand on the top of her shoulder. "There, there," he said, patting it.

Judy made a noise of understanding and took my purchases from me. With a flutter, she had them wrapped in a shiny, white box and in my arms in moments.

"Miss Murphy," she begged, "you *must* let me explain!"

"I do not have the time. I have a bond hearing to go to." I glared at both of them. "Honestly. The door *unlocked*. What if I'd been a guest?"

"Chuck," Poppy all but growled, "this is unforgivable. You know that."

"Poppy." He tried to move toward her, but Mr. Hodgson stepped between them.

"I'm sorry about this," he said, not sounding sorry at all, "but we don't have time for this kind of conversation. You figure it out this afternoon, yeah? Come on, Murphy. We need to go."

I tucked the box under my arm and took Poppy by the hand. "Please. Lead the way."

Chapter 36

"Ugh, Mr. Hodgson." My lips twisted into a deep grimace. "Are there no trash cans in Queens?"

A sniffling Poppy and I slid into the back seat of his vehicle, empty Styrofoam cups clinking against our ankles. He climbed into the front seat with nary an apology. "The files are there on your right. You're welcome, by the way."

"I paid you for this, by the way." There was an untidy manila folder on top of a stack of newspapers. I pulled it on my lap and slid it open, immediately gathering the papers up and rustling them straight.

"Not yet," Mr. Hodgson replied. "Still waiting."

"I'll have my banker pay your banker."

"I am my banker." We left the Pinnacle garage and pulled into traffic. "You pay me. Cash or check—I'm not picky."

Poppy tapped the papers in my lap with her fingertip. "Evelyn. Mr. Hodgson. My brother is in trouble, remember?"

I bristled at the accusation. As if I could forget that Mac was stuck in jail, or that Mr. Ferretti feared he wouldn't be able to secure a bond from the biased judge, or that my banker wasn't letting me use my own money. I took a deep breath, held it in my lungs, and let it out through my nose.

Poppy was staring at me with her lips pressed together and her gray eyes glassy. Her complexion had gone a bit green. Her fingers were not steady on the folders.

This wasn't Poppy's fault. She was as stressed as I was, if not more so. After all, it was her boyfriend we'd caught in the boutique storage room with Judy.

That wasn't an image I was likely to forget anytime soon. Ick. So pale. So very pale.

Shaking myself, I read the information Mr. Hodgson had found regarding the lawsuit. The Pinnacle Hotel was implicated to be at fault in the death of a maid. A window in the laundry room had been broken for weeks. Staff had complained. No one had fixed it. And then one day, Mary Carter had tripped over a dirty tangle of linens, her shoulder crashing against the broken window. It had immediately opened, swinging outward on its cracked hinges, and the maid had fallen three stories, landing on her head.

She'd died on impact.

Mary Carter's husband had sued the hotel. He'd been left a single father of a teenage son, with no recourse. He had been injured in the war and couldn't work. Without Mary's income, they were destitute.

Cliff Baker had acted as their lawyer and sued the hotel, winning for the Carters a grand total of twenty-seven thousand dollars.

Poppy licked her lips. "Whoa. How did they come to that number?"

I arched an eyebrow but didn't respond. It seemed such a small number to me, hardly equal to the life of a wife and a mother. The family should've gotten more. A lot more.

"They factor in distress, lawyer fees—things like that," Hodgson said. "The hotel paid the amount in full, so it's not like they didn't have it."

I wrinkled my nose and stared up at the top of his sedan. "We paid?"

"Yes."

"And Cliff Baker secured the money for the Carters."

"Right."

I shook my head. "So it probably isn't Mr. Carter."

"He's dead, anyway," Mr. Hodgson said. "If you kept going through his files, you'd see he died not long after the settlement. Their kid got the money."

I flipped through the pages, sure enough coming upon a photocopied death certificate of one Mr. Michael Carter. "Manner of death," I read, "natural. Heart failure."

"Mm-hmm."

There was no other information. I chewed my bottom lip, nose still wrinkled. Was this anything? Mr. Carter going after Daddy, that I could see, as it was his hotel where Mr. Carter's wife died. But going after the lawyer turned judge who won you a wrongful death suit? That made no sense whatsoever. "And the son? What happened to him?"

"He was a minor when all this happened," Mr. Hodgson replied. "I couldn't find anything about him. Except he was Michael Carter Jr."

"There goes that clue, then," I said. "Judge Baker and Daddy are back to having nothing in common."

Poppy pointed at the stack of newspapers. "What's with those? More trash you haven't cleaned up, Mr. Hodgson?"

"From the library," Mr. Hodgson said. "I pulled information on Judge Baker's most recent cases. To see if there was some crossover there with your father that he forgot about."

I slid the bottom half of the stack to Poppy and took the top half for myself. They weren't full newspapers, only the relevant pages from the issues in question. Poppy and I read them in relative silence as Mr. Hodgson drove on to the Bakers' brownstone, occasionally honking at other drivers with whom he disagreed. I read about a murder case Judge Baker had presided over, assault and battery, and child endangerment. Nothing led back to Daddy.

"Here," Poppy said. "Look at this, Evelyn." I took her article and skimmed it over. Judge Baker had ruled in favor of a manufacturing company, dealing a blow to a union that had tried to organize the factory workers. The ruling hadn't dismantled the union, but the company had been able to hire replacement workers without any repercussions, which is essentially the same thing.

"What does this have to do with Daddy?"

Poppy wrinkled her brow. "I thought you knew?"

"Knew what?"

"The valets, a few months ago? They started talking about forming a union. Not only for the Pinnacle valets but for a bunch of them in the hotels here in Manhattan. Rumor is your dad got wind of it, and that's why he slashed the valet staff in half and cut their wages."

That's what Burrows had wanted to talk to me about the other day. I had been too busy with my new cat to follow up on it. And then he'd been rather busy with Judy. I shuddered again. The paleness of his "moon" filled my memory. I'd never understand it. Poppy and Judy? What did they see in such a sweaty-palmed man?

Mr. Hodgson parallel parked the car.

I forced my mind to focus on the issue at hand. Mac was in trouble. *He* needed me to focus. His hands were beautiful and warm and tan. I made a promise to myself to pay special attention to his hands the moment I got him out of that jail. "Both Daddy and Judge Baker are anti-union. Maybe a valet took it upon himself to right that wrong. But why inject them with drugs? Why go after a lady of the evening and Florence?"

Poppy shrugged.

"I'm not opening the door for you ladies," Mr. Hodgson said, pulling his keys out of the ignition. "I'm a cop, not a chauffeur. Let's go."

Poppy opened the door with a roll of her eyes and held it open while I climbed out. I clutched the wrapped baby gift to my chest and smiled at Mr. Hodgson. "While it's true that you are not a real chauffeur, you must pretend to be one now. Mrs. Baker wouldn't appreciate me bringing a cop to her sitting room. She might refuse to speak to me on principle."

He sighed but shut both doors with a flourish, as if to prove he was willing to play along.

Poppy dug out a tissue from her pocket and dabbed at the corner of her eyes. She blinked up at the sky and took a deep breath. I admired how well and how quickly she'd pulled herself together.

"I'll hold the package, Evelyn," she said. "Shall I knock on the door too? I don't know what all is expected of me as your assistant."

I handed her the package. "Good instincts. Your brother fetches things for me when I need them. He makes sure Presley is taken care of. And he is the one who picks the loc—" I cleared my throat, glancing out of the corner of my eye at Mr. Hodgson, who'd put his hands on his waist, his elbows sticking out in a wide V—"picks the dinner. Orders it. From the . . . room service." I coughed.

Poppy's giggle turned into a laugh that she tried to muffle behind her arm.

"Not a cop," I said to Mr. Hodgson. "Don't forget."

He crossed his heart with his index finger.

CHAPTER 37

Poppy knocked on the brownstone door. I stood a few steps back, forcing a smile on my face for whoever checked the peephole to see. Mr. Hodgson loitered behind both of us on the sidewalk. The same maid from the other day opened the door. She sighed when she saw me but stepped back and let us in.

"This is my assistant, Poppy," I said, "and my chauffeur, Mr. Hastings."

Mr. Hodgson sucked in a breath.

"I have a gift for Mrs. Baker. Is she available for a visit?"

"You shoulda phoned," the woman said. "But I'll go ask if she's up to see you again. Where's the other one? The good-looking one?"

"Mac?" I gathered. "He's, um, busy today."

She shot me a pinched expression, distrusting, but shut the door and left the lot of us standing there while she went to fetch Mrs. Baker.

"I'm good-looking," Mr. Hodgson said. "At least, that's what my grandma always told me."

Poppy held the package over her face as she giggled. I was glad to see her laughing. I wasn't sure how she would take her recent breakup, but truly, she could do better. She was so beautiful and talented. And for a man like Burrows to go behind her back, sneak around with a fellow employee when he could've ended things with Poppy first? Disgraceful behavior. How could I even trust him with my mail again? I'd seen where he put his sweaty hands, after all.

Mrs. Baker descended the stairs into the entryway with a man at her side. He held her elbow, his other hand on the small of her back.

My tongue pressed against the roof of my mouth. *Interesting.*

"Miss Murphy," Mrs. Baker called in greeting when she stood on the landing. "Back again so soon? It's so kind of you to be keeping me in your thoughts and your schedule."

I took the package from Poppy and handed it over. "I wanted to bring the baby a gift and make sure you're holding up all right." I did not mention the man at her side, although I was dying to.

She took the package with a smile. "Thank you, Miss Murphy. Gordon, would you put this in the baby's nursery, please? Oh, Miss Murphy, this is my stepson, Gordon. Gordon, this is Evelyn Murphy."

He held out his hand and I shook it. "We've met," he said. "At the hotel, some years ago."

That was probably true. I'd definitely been introduced to both Baker boys at some point, though I had zero recollection of what they looked like or the circumstances of the meetings. "It's good to see you again. How is Harvard treating you, Mr. Baker?"

"Swell," he said. "I'll be graduating soon. My professors are giving me a bit of leeway to see to Dad's funeral—and the baby's birth." He squeezed his stepmom's shoulder, his fingers resting a bit too close to her collarbone for a bit too long. "But then I'll be back in Massachusetts until winter break."

"You must come see me at the Pinnacle sometime," I said. "I'd be delighted to treat you to coffee or tea. I'd love to hear all about Harvard. I've always wanted to visit." That was partly true. A massive college crawling with young men and no female students had held a certain appeal back when I was single.

He smiled but it did not reach his eyes. "I'd like that. I'll be right back. Do you need help getting to the chair, Elena?"

She waved him off. "I'll be fine. Come, Miss Murphy. Frannie will bring us tea. My ankles are sore, and I need to sit."

"Poppy, will you help Frannie make the tea?" Behind their back, I opened and closed my fingers in an imitation of a puppet talking. Maybe the maid had seen something useful.

Poppy nodded once before skipping over to Frannie's side.

"Thank you ever so. Mr. Hastings, make sure Mrs. Baker makes it to her favorite chair, please."

Poppy and the maid went off in the direction of the kitchen, but Mr. Hodgson stood there dumbly for three heartbeats before realizing what it was I'd directed him to do. Hard to invite a chauffeur into the drawing room for tea with two women of a particular social circle. He hurried into action, offering Mrs. Baker his arm. She took it with a smile and a shake of her head.

"Thank you," she said. "I'm so ready to have this baby. Walking is supposed to bring on labor—not that I've found it particularly helpful."

My mouth fell open. I snapped it closed. "I did hear from the valets that you brought your car to the garage yourself and then walked to the party."

She sighed, shook her head. "I really thought that night I'd finally managed to go into labor. I walked from the garage to the party on purpose to make something happen. I'm desperate to have this baby, Miss Murphy. I'm uncomfortable all the time, you understand. But Dr. Smith took one look at me once we were home and said it was only the practice contractions, not the real thing."

Mr. Hodgson and I shared a look. Nothing suspicious about how the car got dropped off after all, at least on the face of it.

We entered the drawing room that only days ago had hosted Mac and me. I took my same seat, feeling the loss of both him and my dog.

Mr. Hodgson helped Elena lower herself into her preferred armchair and then stood back, out of her sight but not mine. He clasped his hands behind his back and I stopped looking at him, hoping that if I didn't pay him attention, neither would my host.

"I do worry about you," I said to Mrs. Baker. "I'm on edge, I must admit, especially with Daddy's attack coming so soon after the horrible tragedy that befell your husband."

She sighed and rubbed her large belly with both hands. "I saw they arrested someone for what happened to your father."

"The wrong person," I said. "My boyfriend, unfortunately. I'm his alibi, though, so I suspect he'll be released today at his bond hearing. If only Judge Baker were still on the bench, he'd see how ridiculous this entire thing is."

"The young man who was here with you on Saturday? *That's* who they arrested?"

"Unfortunately."

She shook her head. "The police here, I swear! Manhattan police are incompetent. Cliffy always used to say so. Always looking to pin the blame on the easiest suspect instead of doing their jobs and finding the real criminal."

Mr. Hodgson puckered his lips.

I pretended not to notice.

"That is so true. Did you know a few weeks ago there was a murder at the hotel, and a detective blamed *me*? I had to find the real killer myself!"

She guffawed.

Mr. Hodgson jutted out his chin.

I hid a smile behind my hand. "The chief is a real sweetheart, though."

"Oh, he sure is," Mrs. Baker agreed. "He came by himself to check on me. I do appreciate the visits from dear friends."

Steps thundered down the stairs, and Gordon Baker appeared, pushing his foppish hair off his face. "I see I haven't missed the tea yet." He took the seat closest to Elena, his back to Mr. Hodgson. Good. They hadn't noticed his presence enough to dismiss him.

Actually, not good. In fact, it was downright rude. But it was to be expected. He was my employee, so it was my job to dismiss him, and if I wasn't paying him attention, they wouldn't either.

"Are you studying law like your father, Mr. Baker?"

"Gordon is fine, Miss Murphy. And yes, I am. I intend to follow in his footsteps all the way."

"You must call me Evelyn then, Gordon."

He inclined his head, and I had a flash of a memory of Judge Baker at the party, making the same motion.

"You and your father hold similar beliefs then?" I asked.

Poppy and Frannie arrived with tea service. Frannie served Elena first and then Gordon, which left Poppy to serve me. She did so, adding a bit too much cream and not enough sugar, before the two of them collected the silver trays and walked away. She gave me a glance and an even quicker smile, and I determined to buy her another dress as soon as possible. She'd earned it, having to serve me hand and foot.

Gordon took a big sip of his tea and exhaled in relaxed delight.

A strange state for a man to be in who'd lost his father in a most disturbing way. But then again, my father had almost been killed in the same way, the love of my life sitting in jail for the offense, and I was sitting in a tastefully decorated sitting room, drinking tea his sister had made for me.

"Yes," he said. "Father and I talked about everything. Shared everything. I agreed with him on every verdict he ever rendered, every case he ever took on. I can only hope to be as good of a man as he was."

"What a lovely tribute to your father. I hope to be like mine as well. He's been talking to me about business at the hotel lately." I took a sip of tea to swallow away the aftertaste of my words. "I wonder what is your take on unions? I admit I'm undereducated on the subject. There were several valets in our hotel and the neighboring garages talking about forming a union. Daddy put a stop to that, but I don't know what all the fuss is about."

He shook his head. "A man works all his life for his money, and then these unions form, a group of jealous, lazy individuals, bent on robbing him blind of all he's earned."

I smiled, showing all my teeth. This was always an intricate balance, asking the right questions in the right way to get information. Something I've had to practice in my time spent gossiping at the Pinnacle, especially given that my face has a hard time lying. "It's a good thing Daddy and I have men like you and your late father to protect us."

He returned my smile. "Miss Murphy, it is my honor. I know Dad felt the same."

"Union bosses didn't like your dad very much," Mr. Hodgson said. I'd quite forgotten he was there, and if the startled jump the Bakers gave in unison was anything to go by, so had they. "Neither did the workers who tried to form one. It's a good cover."

Gordon blinked. First at me and then at Mr. Hodgson. "A good cover for what?"

Mr. Hodgson shrugged one shoulder. "Unions don't like your dad, don't like Mr. Murphy. Maybe it throws suspicion on someone else when both are attacked. Maybe people don't look too closely at where the threat usually lies."

"And where does the threat usually lie?"

"With the family."

Gordon Baker's mouth fell open. He stared at me, agape. "Is your driver accusing me of murder?"

"Of course not!" I laughed, feeling awkward. "Of course not. That would be foolish. You aren't doing that, are you, Mr. Hastings?"

"No," Mr. Hodgson said. "Just making conversation. Pointing out the obvious. Your dad has got money, he's got a pretty wife, he's got a nice house. With him out of the picture, maybe you get all those things yourself."

Mrs. Baker shriveled in her seat. She wrapped both arms around her stomach, her face screwing up in a wince behind her large glasses. Gordon immediately moved to her side.

"Elena, darling? What's wrong?"

"Hurts," she whispered. "Like at the party, but worse. Please. Gordon. Will you call Dr. Smith for me?"

"Right away, right away." Gordon straightened up. "You'll please excuse us, Miss Murphy."

I stood up, still smiling, though my teeth were now hidden under my lips. "Yes. Certainly. Good luck, Mrs. Baker. I'll be thinking of you."

She nodded.

I glared at Mr. Hodgson and marched toward the door. "Poppy, it's time to go!"

CHAPTER 38

Poppy ducked out of the kitchen in time to hold the door open for me. I couldn't even smile at her, my shoulders tight against my ears. I stormed down the sidewalk, my hands clenched into fists, my heels clunking hard against the cracked pavement.

"Honestly, Mr. Hodgson!" I said, wrenching open the rear Rolls-Royce door. "You cannot simply accuse people of murder all *abruptly* like that!"

Mr. Hodgson made a noise in his throat. "You want me to casually accuse people of murder. Is that it, Miss Murphy?"

"No! Except yes!" I sat down on my seat and slammed the door. I was alone with only my shallow breath until Mr. Hodgson took the driver's seat and Poppy slid into the space next to me. "You have to ease into it. Guide people there with your questions. You, as an investigator, should know better."

He met my eyes in the rearview mirror. "I wanted to see what his reaction was. Had to accuse him to get a reaction."

I picked up the stack of newspapers about Judge Baker, set them on my lap, put them back down on the seat, then on my lap again. Hodgson chuckled and rolled the car into traffic.

Finally, I blew a big gust of air out of my puffed cheeks. "And what reaction were you looking for, Mr. Hodgson?"

"When you accuse an innocent person of murder, you know what they do? They get *mad*. But that guy? That man who couldn't keep his hands to himself? He didn't get angry, did he? He only got confused."

"Lack of proper emotional reaction is hardly a reason to suspect someone of murder."

Mr. Hodgson shrugged. "I can suspect whoever I want. He's only one person of interest. I'm not closing the case. At least not with what we have now."

"We have, roughly, nothing," I said. "Except for some rumblings from upset valet drivers."

"Evelyn," Poppy said, her voice gentle, "it isn't only the valet drivers who are upset with your father."

My brow had been furrowed so hard and for so long I began to worry about fine lines and wrinkles. I massaged the pads of my fingers against my forehead. "No? Who else?"

She pulled the corner of her mouth down in a half grimace. "Matter of fact, it's most of us. We're required to have two uniforms, yeah? But now we have to buy them ourselves. And, if we're gonna wash them on Pinnacle property, which is what is encouraged, we have to pay a nickel. Each time. If one goes missing in the wash? That's on us. Why, Chuck," she swallowed, "he lost one a few days ago, had to pay out of pocket for a new one. It ate into his paycheck pretty good. That's why he's been doing so much overtime. At least, that's what he told me. Heh."

The memory of Burrows and Judy came rushing back into my memory, and I shook my head to rid myself of it. "An employee who is mad at both the judge for siding with corporations over unions and at my father for being anti-union attempts to kill them both. But what about the woman in Judge Baker's trunk? Florence, I can see. She's an innocent bystander, a witness who must be taken care of. But why the woman in the trunk?"

Mr. Hodgson cleared his throat. "Been thinking about that. When a judge, a lawyer, or a detective gets caught in a crime, their cases can get reopened and reexamined. A judge doing heroin, running around with prostitutes? A lot of angry people sitting in jail because of Baker's rulings are gonna make a fuss."

"So it could be someone with a vendetta against Baker as a judge. And Daddy?"

"I'm sure McJimsey is going with the copycat route," Mr. Hodgson said. "But I'd bet it's the same person. And I like that arrogant son for it. He gets his father's money, his father's house, and his father's wife. He ruins his father's reputation while he's at it. And he goes after your father in an attempt to hide his tracks. Get us all looking outside the Baker family. Get us onto this pro-union track."

Poppy crossed her legs. "I might not know as much about this sort of stuff as you two, but that sounds rather serpentine to me, Mr. Hodgson. Too complicated."

"Nah," he replied. "Family member did it? That's the least complicated plot there is. Even still, can't rule out the doctor."

"This again?" I said. "Dr. Smith is a teddy bear. A crotchety teddy bear, sure."

"He was with Mrs. Baker moments before her husband was murdered. And he was the first on the scene after your father's attack. Whether you like it or not, that is suspicious. Besides that, remember how I told you your dad's results came back as heroin mixed with something else?"

"Yes."

"Turns out that something else is used in hospitals as an anesthetic."

I tapped my foot. "Okay. You have me there. But if a killer can sneak into a hospital and kill a patient, couldn't he also sneak into a hospital and steal a drug?"

"Yeah. Sure. But he also told you to turn left instead of right, thereby buying himself time."

"Theoretically. Half a minute, maybe. But there were nurses in Mrs. Wilson's room tending to her before Mac and I arrived. How would Dr. Smith race down there, kill her, and then get out again without being seen, and circle back just as Mac and I arrived thirty seconds later?"

Poppy hummed. "I'm with Ev on this one, Mr. Hodgson. I don't like Dr. Smith and dread the days I have to clean on his floor. I talked to Frannie, and she said Gordon Baker arrived last night, so when would he have had time to kill his father?"

Mr. Hodgson said, "You think he'd announce himself as being in the area when the murder was committed? No. He'd go out of his way to have an alibi set up in Boston."

"Mr. Hodgson," I said, "you think everyone's guilty."

"Holding contradictory points of view at the same time is a sign of genius, Miss Murphy. You should know a good detective looks at all suspects and all angles and follows all the clues, not just the ones he likes best."

I cleared my throat. "Or she." But then, my nose wrinkled. "Mr. Hodgson? Remember when we talked to Daddy? He was so sure it was a man wearing sensible shoes, not recently shined. Dr. Smith's choices in shoes are almost as atrocious as his ties. And speaking of valet uniforms, I noticed all of their shoes tend to be on the dirty side as well."

"So, does that leave out Mrs. Baker, then?" Poppy asked. "I doubt a man like her stepson would wear shoes that weren't perfectly acceptable?"

"He'd have been traveling," Mr. Hodgson said. "Maybe didn't have enough time to find a boy to shine 'em before he offed his own father."

I crossed my arms over my chest. "You both are forgetting the most suspicious thing of all. Mrs. Baker owns the hardest-to-get Archambeau bag and yet cannot pronounce *Balmain* correctly."

Both Poppy and Mr. Hodgson groaned in unison.

Traffic bogged down closer to the courthouse. My heart thumped up into my throat, so hard it felt like it might tumble onto my tongue. There were so many vehicles near the steps. I placed my hand over my mouth and told myself to *breathe. In. Hold. Out. In. Hold. Out.*

"Are those press vans?" I managed after my third round.

Hodgson clicked his tongue. "Looks like."

"I'm . . . I'm going to have to go in front of the press?"

Poppy put her hand on my wrist. "You look lovely, Evelyn. Keep your chin up. Let them get their picture. We'll be walking out with Mac soon enough."

Once again, Hodgson met my eyes in the rearview. Did he know what Mr. Ferretti suspected? What I feared? That the judge presiding over the bond hearing wasn't favorable to Mac's cause?

I closed my eyes and focused on my breathing. I'd get to see him. I'd get to see him and speak to him and his lawyer, and I would make this all okay. Even if it meant selling off my closet to get the money. I'd take care of this, of him, the way he'd always taken care of me.

★ ★ ★

Mr. Hodgson cut hard into an alley, the front of the car knocking over a trash can and driving over the rumbling contents. Poppy and I both made sounds of discomfort and alarm. But he didn't apologize. "We'll park at a neighboring building, go in a back way."

"There's a back way into a courthouse?" Poppy asked.

I sat up straighter and relaxed my shoulders away from my ears. The back way was infinitely preferable to going in front of the press. I loved getting my picture taken and put in the paper when I was on the arm of a movie star. *Not* when my boyfriend was going before a judge for allegedly attempting to murder my father and strangling a maid to death in my hotel. That type of press was terrible.

"Thank you, Mr. Hodgson."

He grunted in acknowledgment. When we parked at the neighboring building, I had to open up my door. My chipped nails glinted on the silver handle. Fine. It was fine. That was fine. I didn't have to look perfect for things to go perfectly. And anyway, my outfit was darling. That would have to be enough for now.

Though my roots were growing in.

The buzzing bees were back in my chest. I was so far away from home. And Daddy had almost died. Florence was dead, and I had her cat in my suite. Mac had spent two nights in jail. Two whole nights in who knows what sort of surroundings. The bank wouldn't let me have my own money to free him. My mother's money.

My mother, in an alley. Blood pooling in her mouth.

Nanny, coughing up blood. So sick she couldn't breathe.

My mother. In an alley. Blood pooling in her mouth.

I couldn't breathe. There was blood in my mouth. Filling my lungs. I was sure of it. I could taste it. Copper. Bitter. Sour bile.

Air hit me in the chest like a punch to the heart. It rocked me backward until I almost collapsed inside the car. My feet were on the pavement, my butt was on the seat, and all I wanted to do was stand up. Stand up. Walk inside. Free Mac. With my mother's money.

My mother. Blood in her mouth.

But my knees knocked together, and my fingers with their chipped polish trembled. I held on to my shaking thighs and sucked in a shallow breath. Poppy squeezed my shoulder.

"Evelyn? Are you okay?"

I shook my head. No. Definitely not. But I couldn't speak. My heart was thundering at a million miles a minute. It was going to explode and fill my mouth with blood, and then they'd all find me in this alleyway like they'd found my mother. I was dying. I was dying right here, in this messy car, while the love of my life waited for me to rescue him.

"Head between your knees," Mr. Hodgson ordered. "Now."

The edge of my vision yellowed. I followed the order, putting my head between my knees, the hem of my skirt tickling my chest. *Breathe in. Hold it. Hold it. You can do it. You idiot, hold your breath. Now, let it out. Do it again. In. Hold. And out.*

The buzzing feeling in my chest was anxiety. No, it was beyond that. It was fear. I was afraid. I was *terrified*. I closed my eyes and tried to picture little Evelyn, terrified too. She would've been in that alleyway, crying for help. She would've been older, waiting on news about Nanny's surgery.

What would I have said to her then? What had I wanted to hear then?

"The only way out of this is through it. Life will go back to normal. To a new normal. It always has before. It will still. Pretend like you're okay, and you will be. You do not have any other choice."

That was terrible advice, but it was all I had to offer myself. Doctors hadn't been able to make Nanny well again. The police hadn't been able to answer the lingering question of *why* Mom had been killed. But *I* could do something. Right now, I could make a difference in Mac's life.

I did another round of my breathing exercise and sat up. The color of my vision had returned to normal. My heartbeat was decelerating. I sniffled and reached for my purse. With a compact and a tissue, I did what I could with my tear-stained makeup. My arms felt heavy, filled with lead, and exhaustion threatened to end my day right there.

But I said a quick prayer and checked the mirror once more.

Snapping it closed, I shoved it back in my clutch and stood. My legs trembled, but not so badly that I couldn't stand.

"Sorry about that." I forced a smile. "I'm ready now."

Mr. Hodgson sighed. He offered me his arm.

I thought about refusing it, but my knees *had* turned into jelly. I was so tired. I wanted to sleep for days and not come out of my room for weeks.

"Mac mentioned you suffered from attacks of anxiety," Poppy said at my other side, rubbing a soft circle between my shoulder blades. "I hadn't realized how . . ."

"Dramatic they were?" My smile turned genuine. "Mr. Hodgson, please lead the way."

CHAPTER 39

The Supreme Courthouse was massive inside, with its black and white marble floors and intricately carved stone pillars holding up a painted, vaulted ceiling with a massive circular skylight in the center. There were more people than I'd anticipated, and the design of the room made even the quietest of noises sound like a ruckus. We'd used a guarded side entrance to sneak past the press, but there were still a few reporters milling about with their press passes and notepads. Beyond them were a lot of ruffled-looking people, disheveled and exhausted, waiting in a line, with chains on their wrists. The weekend's arrests, waiting to go before a judge for the first time.

I let go of Mr. Hodgson's arm on the steps. I couldn't afford to be seen leaning on someone else right now. Technically, I could afford nothing, since the bank was being ridiculous. But that was neither here nor there.

"Miss Murphy," a man's voice called out, followed by a whistle. The sort of short, commanding whistle you'd expect a dog trainer to use.

Frowning, I turned in the direction of the voice, unsurprised to find Detective McJimsey leaning against the space of wall between two water fountains. A line had formed behind each fountain—a short one for white people only, a longer one for everyone else. McJimsey crossed his arms over his chest and grinned at me.

"Care for a chat?"

There was no way to get to him without cutting through a line. I raised an eyebrow in disgust before turning away.

"Got some info that you might be interested in," he called out. "About Cooper."

I froze midstep.

Mr. Hodgson shook his head. "Whatever he's got won't be any good. You know that."

Obviously. I knew that. But nothing about my life had been good lately, so what did one more piece of terrible news matter? Besides, going forward at this point *not* knowing something seemed a worse idea.

"You shouldn't be alone with him," Poppy whispered rather loudly, ruining her attempts to keep it quiet.

"It's a very public building," I said with a roll of my eyes. "What's one more rumor for my stellar reputation anyway?"

"Let me be alone with him. I'll punch him. Right in his attractive face," she replied.

Mr. Hodgson adjusted his hat. "You think he's attractive?"

She blinked a few times, owlishly. "Oh. Um. No?"

I said, "I'll be right back."

I felt the pierce of their twin gazes on my back as I walked toward McJimsey. He bent his head to indicate the hallway across from the fountains and moved away from the wall. With an exaggerated exhale, I followed behind him. He could've started from the hallway in the first place, but no, he had to be all *dramatic* about everything.

The detective was as bad as my attacks of anxiety, and that was saying something.

He reached into his pocket and pulled out a small square of paper. A business card. He handed it to me with a crooked grin, a dimple popping on his clean-shaven cheek. "My number," he said. "Because you'll want to call me."

I didn't take his card. "Why on earth would I ever want to do that?"

"Because." He kept the smile on his face as he leaned in closer to me, his dimple inches from my ear. "You're gonna wanna thank me for saving you from a very bad man."

"What? What are you talking about?"

"Mr. Cooper? Miss Murphy, I can see by the confusion in your eyes that you're innocent of all this. I knew it from the moment we connected in the interrogation room. You're too sweet, too naive to see how dangerous Mr. Cooper is. I wanted to soften the blow before you go into that courtroom."

Was this . . . was this man calling me stupid? To my face? I tapped my foot against the tile of the hallway. "Get to the point, Detective. Please."

He held up his hands in surrender, his business card sticking between the ring and middle fingers of his left hand. "I wanted to tell you myself that a fingerprint was found on the heroin needle."

"Yes," I said. "Mine. As I said, I picked it up off the garage floor when it fell out of the judge's arm."

"No, not that needle. The needle in your father's room. And it's unfortunate that the fingerprint lifted from the needle matches that of one Malcolm Cooper."

My chest heaved. I panted for breath. "Liar."

"No. Not lying, Miss Murphy. That fingerprint got us a warrant into Mr. Cooper's apartment where a large amount of drug para-phernalia, specifically related to the consumption and the selling of heroin, was found."

"That isn't true."

He held his arms open wide. "All of it was taken into evidence."

I shook my head so hard my whimsy came loose. "No, that's not true. I don't believe it."

"Miss Murphy, were you at Mr. Cooper's apartment recently?"

"No."

"Have you ever been to Mr. Cooper's apartment?"

I repinned my whimsy. "No."

"What grounds then do you have to say it isn't true?"

"What grounds? I . . . I know him! Those are the grounds I stand on! I love him. He's incapable of something like this. He's good. To the bone, he is a good man! He wouldn't hurt or kill anyone."

His arms dropped to his sides, and his smile slid off his face. In its place was something sad, something that could've been pity. "Miss Murphy. You are young. And young love is fleeting. Please, take my card. I'll be here for you when you need me."

He placed his card in my hands, his fingers folding over mine. Warm and long and somewhat clammy. Clammy enough I thought of Burrows. Clammy enough I came back into my body. Clammy enough I jerked my hand out from other his. "Rest assured, Detective. I will *never* need you."

McJimsey chuckled. "Whatever you say, kid."

The card fluttered to the ground. I turned on my heel and stormed away.

★   ★   ★

Hodgson held the door open. I walked in first, my head on a swivel, trying to catch sight of Mac's hair. Would he be allowed his clothes for this, or would they put him in a prison outfit? What had he been wearing when he was arrested? The mahogany and maroon room was packed, standing room only toward the back. A row of men in black and white stripes sat in the front of the room, one by one being brought before the judge. I saw the back of Mac's head in the middle of the row.

Poppy said my name, but I hurried down the aisle, aware that people were staring at me.

"Mac," I called.

A police officer stood in front of me, his hands on his belt. He was taller than me—quite a feat indeed, no pun intended—and much more muscled. An impenetrable wall.

Mac looked at me over his shoulder, and my heart stuttered. He waved, a small smile tugging up the corners of his lips.

"Mac," I breathed.

But the police officer would not budge.

"No touching," he said.

"I'm not here to touch," I lied. "I wanted to speak to him."

The officer jerked his chin in the direction of the seats to our immediate right. "Try the lawyer."

My neck, suddenly stiff, ached when I turned in the opposite direction. Mr. Ferretti, a short, dark-haired man in an expensive suit with diamond cufflinks and an Italian briefcase, waggled his fingers at me in the same wave Mac had only a minute ago. Funny how it didn't tug on my heartstrings the same way.

Legs heavy, I dragged my feet toward him, crouching at his aisle. The judge was talking to another prisoner and his court-appointed attorney, but the large gathering of people was otherwise silent.

"Hello," I whispered. "You're getting him out of here today, yes?"

He chuckled humorlessly. "We were handed a stack of evidence moments ago, Miss Murphy. It's going to take my office a lot of overtime to get all this in order."

Money. Always money. "Good news then." I smiled. "I spoke to my banker only this morning." That was not a lie, and I looked him right in the eye as I said it. "I want him out of here today. I will pay any price. Do we understand each other, Mr. Ferretti?"

"It's up to the judge," Mr. Ferretti whispered. "But I'll do everything I can, Miss Murphy. That I can promise you."

I held out my pinkie.

Mr. Ferretti stared at it.

"Well? Are you going to pinkie promise me or not?"

Swallowing so hard his throat clicked, the very expensive lawyer I'd hired and yet had not secured payment for, wrapped his pinkie around mine. "You are . . ." He took out his pocket square and dabbed his forehead. "You are as your father describes you."

I stood to my full height, my chin up. "Dramatic?"

He smiled, and it was a surprise to me when two spots of pink colored his cheekbones. "Enthralling."

That my father might say anything positive about me to strangers came as even more of a surprise. I worried about him for the first time that day. Was he all right? Was he waiting for me? How would I convince him to allow me access to my own money?

The judge called out, "Mr. Cooper."

Mr. Ferretti hurried to stand. I looked around and caught sight of a feminine hand waving in the back of the room. I hurried toward Poppy, looping my arm through hers. Mr. Hodgson stood a few feet away in a corner. He nodded at me. I nodded back and held Poppy tighter.

Mac hobbled towards the judge's bench with a chain between his ankles and a shorter one between his wrists.

I fished the pendant of Saint Anthony from under my blouse and held it tight. *Please,* I prayed, not sure to whom. Anyone who would listen. *Please. Let McJimsey be lying. Let Mac be innocent.*

The judge exchanged words with both a prosecutor and Mr. Ferretti. My pulse was so loud inside my ears I couldn't understand what they were saying. The buzzing bees were back, and I squeezed Poppy, hoping the terror I'd felt in the parking lot wouldn't return. *Do not have an attack of anxiety in front of all these people. Do not do it.*

Sweat pooled at the base of my neck and dripped down my spine under my jacket. My mouth was dry, my tongue stuck to my teeth. My feet shook in my shoes. The scratch of the pencil on a pad caught my attention. A member of the press was staring at me as he scribbled away.

I exhaled and rolled my shoulders back. Now was not the time to be afraid.

There'd be plenty of time for that later. When Mac was back and a killer was still on the loose.

"Your honor!" Mr. Ferretti said, exasperated.

But the judge looked at him over the top of his bifocals. "Given the amount of evidence against your client, the fact that he has an international passport, and has managed to somehow secure *your* representation with his stated employment, I have no choice but to deny bond at this time." He banged his gavel on his tall desk. "Next."

Poppy gasped.

"Your honor," Mr. Ferretti said, exasperated. Police officers appeared from the shadows of the room and moved toward Mac. He spun around and looked me in the eyes. He mouthed something, but I couldn't make out what.

"Mac." I moved down the aisle. "Mac!"

They were pulling him away from me, out of the room, and it didn't matter how fast I walked, I couldn't catch up. Someone was calling my name, the press in the room was shouting for me, and the judge banged his gavel again.

"I said next! And if you, ma'am, can't be quiet, then get out of my courtroom."

He was talking about me. I froze, my watery gaze watching as Mac was guided away. He mouthed something else, and it might've been *"Sorry,"* but for what? What was he sorry for? He'd done nothing wrong. It was me. I'd failed him. I hadn't figured out who was framing him, because someone was.

Someone had to be.

Mac would never, ever hurt my father. Probably. But he definitely wouldn't hurt Florence. Florence, who's name wasn't even worth the ink to the newspapers.

Or Joan, the woman from Judge Baker's trunk, another woman no one was talking about.

Mr. Hodgson took my elbow. He pulled me down the aisle, and I let him. Poppy joined us, and silence descended as the massive doors to the courtroom closed.

CHAPTER 40

Poppy swore. Viciously. She stamped her foot on the shining marble floor. Swore again.

"What evidence?" Mr. Hodgson asked.

I stared at him. He'd spoken to me, I was sure of it, but I didn't know what he'd said.

He moved closer to me. "*What evidence? The judge said—*"

I held up my hand. "McJimsey claims they found Mac's fingerprint on the needle used on my father and that there was drug paraphernalia in Mac's apartment."

"What?" Poppy shrilled. "There's no—I live there too! We do not do drugs! On our pay? We can't afford it!"

"Someone's framing him," Mr. Hodgson said. "Or . . ."

"Or he did it?" I snapped. "Mr. Hodgson!"

He stepped away from us, his eyes on the painted, vaulted ceiling. "McJimsey says they've got the evidence. The judge says they've got the evidence. Sometimes the right answer is the simplest one."

The simplest answer! Of all the most ridiculous things. "And what of Judge Baker? Hmm? The woman in his trunk? There are two different attacks here, Mr. Hodgson, and Mac is not responsible for *either* of them. I am paying you to help me find out who is!"

"Am I not doing my job, Miss Murphy? You're not paying me to have blind faith in your criminal boyfriend."

"Hey!" Poppy's cheeks and forehead flushed. "He was a thief back home, sure. But petty thievery. Nothing like this! Not murder!"

"Everybody's gotta start somewhere."

I stormed away, realized the only exit was out the front door and through the press, and stomped back toward Mr. Hodgson. This was madness. Everything in my life was spinning out of control, a hurricane in the middle of Manhattan, and the least he could do—because I was paying him to do it—was to be on my side. "Hodgson. Please. I cannot have my father, the police, and you all against me. I cannot. I'll never get to the bottom of things. I'll never figure out who killed Florence, who wanted my father dead. *Please.*"

Hodgson hummed. He put his hands in his pockets and rocked back on his heels. "Fine. But I'm keeping an open mind."

Poppy raked her fingers through her hair and held on to the ends. "This is terrible, Evelyn. What are we going to do? They're . . . the police! They're fixated on putting an innocent man in jail."

Hodgson made a noise.

Poppy let go of her hair. "Innocent of this, anyway."

I stared at the entrance, my bottom lip between my teeth. I'd bitten off my lipstick, I was sure. There was only one thing I could do right now, and it was the thing I wanted to do least. There was a killer on the loose. A killer who had come back to cover his tracks. Who had murdered a woman in a hospital. Who had strangled Florence and left her in a closet.

A killer who was sure to be watching the news of this trial, and the patsy he'd planted in his wake. I should've known that McJimsey was a cop who wouldn't like to do police work. I thought of Gordon Baker sitting in his father's beautiful home with his father's beautiful wife. I thought of the valets making comments about my reputation and letting us into a crime scene. Of Dr. Smith and his attentive manner toward Mrs. Baker, the way he'd sent us in the wrong direction for the woman's room in the hospital. How he'd been the first one at the scene when Daddy lay dying. How the drug in Daddy's needle was something found in hospitals. Of Mrs. Baker herself, falling into distress and pain the moment her stepson was accused of hurting her husband. Carrying around designer pieces without knowing anything about designers.

"Miss Murphy?" Hodgson asked. "What are you doing?"

I popped open my handbag and fished out my compact and my lipstick. "Are you religious, Hodgson?"

"No, I'm not. My wife, she's Baptist. We . . . we raised our son in that church."

I covered my lips in red. My mascara and blush were as they should be, though the shine of the Vaseline had worn off. Nothing to do about that now.

"You don't know the story of Judith, then. She's a Catholic saint. A widow, in the old testament. Beautiful and rich, she enchanted a general of an enemy's army and then cut off his head." I snapped my compact closed and tossed it and the lipstick in my handbag.

"What's your point?"

I shook out my curls and tucked the pendant of Saint Anthony under my blouse. It wasn't his prayer I needed now.

Oh, Lord, heed me, a miserable thing. Put your words in my mouth and reinforce the plan in my heart.

It was a terrible, stupid plan. But it was the only one I had. I made the sign of the cross and smiled at my companions.

"Want to watch me make a killer angry?"

★ ★ ★

I pushed open the doors with both hands. The wind caught my hair and the hem of my skirt, and I grinned and waved as the bulbs from the press's massive cameras started to flash. People in press hats and wearing tan jackets called out my name and rushed up the grand stairs of the courthouse. I descended to meet them halfway, wondering when they'd decided on matching uniforms.

"Good afternoon, gentlemen," I purred. "Were you waiting for little old me?"

They had notepads and pens. A few had voice recorders, the microphones attached to large, silver cases by twisting, winding cords. Another flashbulb went off, and I knew they'd gotten a good picture of me surrounded by them, my mouth only inches away from one such microphone.

Questions were shouted rapid fire, and I had trouble discerning one from another. Someone close to me asked how my father was.

"Daddy is recovering swiftly, thank you ever so. His main concern is the lack of a dedicated business phone line in his hospital room."

That got a few laughs.

"What are your thoughts on today's bond hearing?"

"My thoughts?" I moved closer to the microphones. "How kind of you for asking. What we witnessed today was a mockery of our justice system. An innocent man was held without bond for a crime that he didn't commit, that—might I add—none of you have accurately reported on."

A murmur, growing louder, rippled through the press.

"Daddy was attacked, yes. But a maid was killed. She was strangled because she witnessed the attack. Her name was Florence. Not one of your papers has printed her name."

"Aren't you worried that the death of a maid will impact your hotel's business?"

I couldn't see who had asked me that question, so I made eye contact with the journalist in front of me. "This is Manhattan, darling. I dare you to find a grand hotel without its share of scandal and tragedy. My concern is not for the Pinnacle—it is for Malcolm Cooper. My assistant was accused of this heinous crime because of his proximity to myself. Whoever did this, whoever really did this, is still out there. He's a madman, and I'd warn all of New York to stay vigilant. A lunatic is on the loose. We must band together to keep each other safe."

"A lunatic?" someone asked. "Care to elaborate?"

"Disorganized. Sloppy. *Stupid*." I overpronounced the last word, meaning every stretched-out syllable. "You'd have to be to attack so blindly the way he has! Judge Baker? My father? *Florence?*" I didn't mention the woman in the trunk because I didn't know if that had been released to the press yet. "Without cause, without reason. Is that not the definition of lunacy?"

"Miss Murphy," a young man to my left asked, "a few weeks ago, you were credited with solving a murder. Do you intend to solve these as well?"

Brilliant. Absolutely brilliant. I couldn't have paid him to ask a better question. "I do indeed."

I blew a kiss at a cameraman, waited for the bulb to flash before I lowered my hand and unpuckered my lips. And then I turned around and walked up the stairs, reporters still calling out questions, cameras still flashing.

Poppy's jaw hung slack.

Hodgson put his hand over his eyes. "That'll do it."

CHAPTER 41

We neared the Pinnacle, its familiar green roof coming into view, and I asked Hodgson to drop us off at the stairs.

He grunted in answer. I had no idea if that meant he would oblige me or not, and decided that the worst thing that would happen is I'd have a chance to talk to those valets again.

"Poppy," I said, taking her hand, "you don't have to come back here if you don't want. But if you do want, you can stay in my suite again."

She frowned, her chin dimpling. "The alternative is my place. My lonely flat. That the police have *rooted* through. I don't want to deal with it by myself."

I squeezed her fingers. "Tomorrow, then. We'll deal with it together. Today let's go inside and relax. Order room service, play with Presley, try to name that cat because I will not call it Omelet, Poppy, I *won't*."

Poppy stared at me before breaking out in a laugh. "All right. Works for me."

The car stopped in front of the Pinnacle's stairs, and a bellhop in a green uniform opened the door. I smiled at Hodgson in the rearview mirror. "Thank you, Hodgson."

He grunted again.

I moved to slide out from the back seat, but he twisted around to look at the both of us. "Murphy, you've likely made a dangerous person angry. I want the two of you to stick together, and keep your door locked. Don't open it for anybody you don't recognize."

"Making the dangerous person angry was the point, Hodgson."

He scowled at me. "Yeah. I get that. Stick together. You hear me?"

I brushed my hair out of my face. "You're rather bossy for being one of my employees. But I have heard you, and I will take the necessary precautions. Have a good evening."

"I'll be here in the morning. Have coffee waiting."

I rolled my eyes at Poppy, and the two of us left the vehicle. She wound her arm through mine, her chin tucked against her chest. A Pinnacle employee waved, and the doorman tipped his hat. I smiled back at everyone, but my eyes had trouble sticking to their faces.

Any one of them could've gone after Daddy. Any one of them could've framed Mac. Although getting a fingerprint on the needle seemed dastardly for a valet or a bellboy. But perhaps not a doctor. He'd been the first one in the room, and he'd shooed me out the moment he saw the device on the ground.

And why had he sent me to the wrong room in the hospital? And why had he been so nice to Mrs. Baker? He'd always huffed and puffed whenever I'd dared to ask for so much as an aspirin, yet he'd abandoned drink and conversation to take the pregnant woman home.

The pregnant woman whose husband shortly thereafter died.

A woman of means with the most expensive, hardest-to-get handbag on the planet, who couldn't even pronounce *Balmain* correctly.

Poppy said, "Please warn me if you see either one of them."

It took me a moment to realize what she was talking about. We were almost to the elevators, and she hadn't lifted her head once on our trek across the lobby. I swallowed, glanced around, but Burrows and Judy were nowhere to be seen.

"Worry not, darling. The coast is clear."

We stepped into an open elevator, and I told Mr. Castillo to take us to the top floor.

"Right away, Miss Murphy." He smiled. "Good to see you again." He might've said my name, but it was Poppy he was staring at.

I dug my elbow into her side.

She peeked her head up.

"Hi, Russell," she greeted. "Having a good day?"

"It's all right. Better now with you two here. Will you be taking Mr. Presley out for a walk this evening?"

"Why?" I asked. "Are you looking to make an extra buck? Because, as it so happens, I require a dog walker."

"I can do it, Evelyn," Poppy whispered.

"Nonsense. It's getting late and you've had a very trying day. Russell, was it? Presley is finicky when it comes to his walkers, but I can pay you five dollars a day to take him to the Park and let him attend to his business to the best of your abilities."

His dark eyes bugged out of his head. "Five dollars? A *day*?"

I held out my hand. "We have a deal then."

He shook it. "Boy, do we ever!"

The elevator came to a stop, and he cranked and opened the door for us. "I'll see you soon, Miss Murphy. Miss Cooper."

Poppy waved in reply, her chin ducked down again. I led the both of us to my suite, fishing my keys out of my handbag. "He's cute," I said. "Have you been friends with him long?"

"He lives in our building," she said. "Mine and Mac's, I mean. He's nice enough, I suppose."

We stepped inside my suite, and Presley immediately trotted over to us, his tail in the air and his tongue hanging out of his mouth. I scooped him up and kissed his perfect little head, losing myself in the greeting. He was so small and light in my arms, but solid and warm too.

"Are there other Pinnacle employees in your building?" I asked. "I know that Florence lived in that women's-only building with a surprising number of Pinnacle maids. But are there other employees all the way out in Yonkers?"

She laughed and slid off her shoes. "Sure. There's a couple of bellboys and valets there. One of them had a baby not too long ago. Lives right under our apartment so I get to experience the sleepless nights with them."

I knew that valet! Alan. He'd been the one who told me about Mrs. Baker walking to the party on her own. He'd also asked me a question when opening the door for me on my way to visit Mrs. Baker. He hadn't seemed suspicious, but living directly underneath Mac's apartment would make it easy to plant evidence for the police to find. Although, how could he gave gotten Mac's fingerprints on the needle that went into Daddy's arm?

I'd need to consult my Poirot novels.

She sat down on the carpet in front of my couch and clicked her tongue. Florence's cat crawled out from underneath the sofa and slinked toward her outstretched fingers. The cat ducked its head under Poppy's hand and let her scratch down its back and to its tail.

"You know your new cat is a girl, right?" Poppy asked.

Stunned, I set Presley down. He trotted off toward the kitchen. "How can you tell with a cat?"

She smiled at me. "I mean, look under her tail?"

I did. It was not a pretty sight.

"Poppy, why on *earth* do you want me to look at its bum?"

"No, not the—" The phone rang on the end table next to the couch, and Poppy answered it without being asked. "Evelyn

Murphy's residence, how may I help you?" She grimaced and held out the phone, the cord wrapping around her shoulders. "It's Mr. Sharpe," she said. "Your father—"

I snatched the phone so quickly out of her hand the cord snapped up to her neck. Poppy gurgled and slid down to her back to free herself of the attempted ligature strangulation. The cat—the female cat—plopped itself on Poppy's belly.

Offering Poppy an apologetic smile, I said into the phone, "Mr. Sharpe? What is it? What's the matter with Daddy?"

"Er, nothing's the matter. It's only that, he's . . . He's *here*."

CHAPTER 42

I dropped the receiver and ran out the door. There was a *thunk*, and Poppy swore before calling out my name and scrambling after me.

"At least shut the door, Evelyn! Presley almost got out."

I called for an elevator, but Russell the operator was already opening a door. And there stood my father, Dr. Smith at his side. His skin tone was alarmingly gray. His shirtsleeves were rolled up to his elbows, his tie loose around his neck. There was a fine sheen of sweat on his forehead and upper lip, and his eyes were glassy.

"Daddy!" I rushed inside the elevator and wrapped an arm around his waist. "Daddy, you should've told me you were leaving the hospital. I would've sent a car!"

He begrudgingly put his arm around my shoulders. We were of almost equal height, my father squeaking out an additional inch over me. Dr. Smith would've been better support for him, but the doctor kept his hands behind his back and a grimace on his face.

Grouchy man.

Possible murderer too.

I glowered at him. Somehow this was his fault. I knew it.

"I'm fine, Evelyn." But he was proved to be a liar when he swayed as he stepped out of the elevator. I held him tighter and glowered even harder at Dr. Smith.

"He insisted!" Dr. Smith said. "He said he could recover at home."

"I refuse to spend another night in the hospital," Daddy said.

Russell waved and closed the elevator door.

Poppy was in the middle of the hallway, holding my dog in her arms. "Mr. Murphy," she greeted. "Hello. I'm Poppy, Mac's sister."

"Who?" Daddy asked. "Doesn't matter. Let me talk to my daughter in peace, please."

Poppy nodded and scurried away into my apartment.

"Daddy," I said. "That was rude. You know Mac is my boyfriend. That's his sister and one of my dearest friends."

He took a shuffling step toward the door of the Presidential Suite. "So you've moved her into your home?" He sighed. "*Evelyn Grace.* Those sorts of people are always taking advantage of your naivety and big heart."

"She's staying the night. Good thing too. She can take care of Presley while I'm watching after you. Or do you intend to stay the night, Dr. Smith?"

"I am here to make sure your father is comfortable. He is at no risk of dying. There is no reason for me to be at his bedside twenty-four/seven."

"I can be sick on my own," Daddy said. "Don't need a nursemaid for that."

"If you'd only given me time, Daddy, I could've had someone here waiting for you. I could've had your room set up for you. Are you feeling up for a shower? Would you like me to make you some dinner?"

"I'm fine, Evie. All I need is a newspaper and a telephone, and I'll be back to my old self in no time."

I knew almost nothing about what it meant to recover from an overdose, but seeing as how drugs often held people in their grip until they succumbed on a regular basis, it sure seemed to me like Daddy would need more than one night with a phone and a newspaper.

"I'll have a boy bring a paper," I said. "And you've got a phone by your bed. But you're mistaken if you think I'll let you be alone right now. Dr. Smith, I'm disappointed in you. I have half a mind to put a call into what's-his-face. That slimy man who brought me coffee."

Daddy pulled a key out of his pocket and opened the door to the Presidential Suite.

Dr. Smith followed us in, his cheeks and neck burning red. "Call whomever you wish. All I am doing is what is best for my patient."

Daddy swayed on his feet, and if I hadn't been holding him, he would've collapsed. I gasped. "Here, Daddy, sit. Sit on the couch."

Dr. Smith had to jump in to get my father to the couch in question. Daddy closed his eyes, put his hands on his head, and took a shuddering breath. More sweat had gathered above his eyebrows.

"Thank you ever so, Dr. Smith—you've obviously done what is best for your patient," I snapped.

Dr. Smith frowned so deeply it looked like his lips might touch his jaw.

I hurried over to the kitchen and grabbed a towel, cranked on the sink, and ran it under the cool water. Ringing out any excess liquid, I brought it over to Daddy and pressed it against his forehead.

"I'm fine," he said, though he let me continue wiping the sweat off his brow. "It was a longer walk than I anticipated from the lobby to the room. That's all."

"And yet, you did it," I said. "How wonderful."

He glared at me.

I put the washcloth in his hands and kissed his cheek. "Let me get you something to drink. Dr. Smith, do you have a minute?"

The doctor made no move to follow me. I waved both my arms in exaggerated circles.

"You better get it over with," Daddy advised. "She's not likely to let it go once she's got it in that head of hers." He put the washcloth over his face and reclined on the sofa.

Dr. Smith thumped into the kitchen, his every step rattling my teeth. Hodgson's suspicion of him had become my suspicion. Was that why he was here, alone with my father? If Mr. Sharpe hadn't phoned me, would Dr. Smith be delivering another fatal dose of a drug into my father's overtaxed system right now?

I slammed open a cabinet and snatched a glass.

"You are extremely angry," Dr. Smith said. "I'd advise you to calm down before you work yourself into another anxiety attack."

"I'm extremely angry? I'm the right amount of angry, thank you ever so! You brought my father out of the hospital *alone*!"

"Everyone leaves the hospital alone, Miss Murphy. That's how it works. The hospital staff doesn't leave with you. The fact that I am here shows how highly the hospital regards your father."

"Is that right?" I twisted the sink handle and shoved the glass underneath the cool water. What was it Hodgson had said? If someone is accused of something they didn't do, they get angry. "Or did you come here to finish him off?"

Dr. Smith took a step back. "I beg your pardon?"

"You arrived incredibly quickly to help me when I found him," I said. "Faster than anyone else. And then you kicked me out of the room. I don't know what you did in there, alone with him."

"I saved his life."

My nose wrinkled. "Or did you plant a fingerprint on the needle?" If Dr. Smith was the killer, he would've had time to plant evidence or finish the job. Not both. But Daddy had been brought to Dr. Smith's hospital. If Chief Harvey hadn't put security in Daddy's room, Dr. Smith would've had all the time in the world.

His head tilted to the side. "What are you talking about? Miss Murphy, have you lost your mind?"

The glass was overfull, the water running over my fingers. I dropped it in the sink and turned the faucet off. "I'm saying you poisoned my father. After poisoning the judge."

Now he stepped toward me. I was taller than him, so he had to lift his chin to look me in the eye. "You *have* lost your mind. I didn't hurt your father—I saved his life. And I didn't hurt Judge Baker. I was busy attending to his wife."

"Attending, hmm? And what does that mean?"

Dr. Smith snatched the overflowing glass out of the sink. He dumped off the top quarter and stormed toward my father. "I will not stand for being questioned in this way. You"—he forced the cup into Daddy's hands—"stay hydrated and sleep often. You"—he pierced me a withering look—"I hope to never see you again."

Anger. Okay. I could see his anger. I wished Hodgson were here to explain whether his anger was enough for us to no longer suspect him. But if Hodgson were here, I wouldn't listen to what he had to say anyway. I was still suspicious of Dr. Smith, and I was not done talking to him.

"Wait a minute!"

But Dr. Smith didn't wait. He threw open the door and continued stomping to the elevator.

I hesitated in the hallway, unwilling to leave Daddy, but in desperate need to get to the bottom of things with the doctor. "Don't you even think about calling that lift!"

He ignored me.

"Don't you step into that elevator!"

He did, in fact, step into the elevator.

Growling, I knocked on my door. "Poppy!" I yelled. "Poppy, hurry! I have to play the elevator game!"

CHAPTER 43

Poppy was in the hallway in seconds, stepping into her shoes. "Tell me what to do, Evelyn!"

"Stay with Daddy!" I was halfway to the stairs. "I'll be right back!"

The elevator game was something a young friend taught me when she'd been visiting with her parents. I'd be playing a more condensed version of it, as I was trying to get access to the same elevator as Dr. Smith before it reached the lobby, and not, as Amelia had played it, stopping the elevator every few floors and meeting it again a few floors later. Up and down she'd go, calling the same elevator back and forth, to what she was sure was the delight of the operators.

I jumped over steps, my tight skirt riding over my knees. Three at a time, my ankles burning with each landing. Two floors down, I hurried into the hallway, calling on the middle elevator, with sweat gathering in my hairline and my breathing harsh and shallow.

Russell blinked in surprise when he saw me.

Dr. Smith only scowled.

"Mr. Castillo, hurry!" I barreled into the small space. "Close the door and keep the lift from moving!"

Dr. Smith threw up his arms. "You have got to be kidding me. Young man, you will not hold me hostage in this elevator! Or anywhere! I will not be taken hostage ever—I have patients to see!"

Russell licked his lips and his eyes darted from me to the doctor and back again.

I planted my fists on my hips. "Stop the elevator, and I'll get you a date with Poppy."

"I thought she was dating Chuck."

I shuddered. "Not as of this morning. I do not want to talk about it. Stop the elevator and lock the doors."

"I can't lock the doors, but—"

"Just do it!"

Russell yanked a lever that jerked the elevator still.

Dr. Smith swore. "Unbelievable. I'll tell your boss about this."

"I've heard about it," I said. "I'm not concerned."

He squinted his eyes at me, his gray brows almost touching above his nose, like wiggling, furry caterpillars. "*You* are not his boss."

"Wanna bet?"

Dr. Smith tried to wedge his fingers in the door but it wouldn't budge. "Unbelievable. Let me out now, or I'll call the police!"

"Oh, please. Like the police are so helpful. Besides, I'm dear friends with Chief Harvey. Whose side do you think he'd take?"

"I have an eyewitness!"

"Mr. Castillo," I smiled at him. "Do you want a date with Poppy?"

"Very much."

"And do you like having me as your employer?"

"Yes, ma'am."

I turned my smile on Dr. Smith. "Still sure about that eyewitness?"

He tugged on today's ugly tie, a red triangle pattern that looked like eyeballs suffering from hay fever. "What is it you want from me, Miss Murphy?"

"Let's start with the truth, shall we? Why were you so attentive to Mrs. Baker? How did you even know her and the judge? She said you were friends! And then how did you get to Daddy's hotel room so quickly after his attack? Why did you kick me out of the room? Why did you bring him back here before he was ready? Why did you send me the wrong way to the hospital room of that unfortunate woman who was found in the trunk?"

"Uh," said Russell. "Um. Hmm."

"Mr. Castillo! Close your ears!"

"How . . . how do I do that, Miss Murphy?"

I glared at him, the smug smile from earlier gone. "Put your fingers in your ears and hum 'Happy Birthday'!"

Russell immediately complied, the bright hum filling the small space.

Dr. Smith said, "I refuse to answer any of your questions on the grounds that you have no right to ask them!"

I checked my chipping nail polish. Still chipping. "And yet, if you don't answer them, I'll complain to that sleazy man who cares deeply about the Murphy donations to the hospital that you put my father in danger. I'll tell him that we cannot continue supporting an organization that employs such an irresponsible doctor."

"You would cost me my job to learn confidential information?"

"Yes," I answered. "And then I'd go to the front desk and inform them that you are no longer to stay with us at the Pinnacle and to please call the police to escort you out immediately."

Dr. Smith's mouth was pulled open in a grimace, his yellowing teeth on display. "You," he seethed, "are a spoiled, entitled brat of a woman. Nosy. Selfish! It is no wonder you have no social life."

Russell's humming grew louder. I wondered how much of that he'd heard, how much of it he agreed with. No matter. I blinked away the sting in my eyes and adjusted my Chanel jacket. "Are you going to answer me, or am I going to have to ruin your life?"

He closed his eyes, exhaled slow and loud. When he looked at me again, his eyes still held that fire of anger but the flames had cooled off with obvious resignation. "A few years ago, before meeting his second wife, Judge Baker had a procedure done that would keep him from having any more children. Very new procedure, you understand, but safe and effective. Not long after, he met Elena and fell in love. She wanted a child of her own more than anything, and that man doted on her, showered gifts on her. And the one thing she wanted most of all he couldn't give her. They came to me and consulted on what could be done. If his procedure could be reversed."

"So, you reversed his procedure, and they were able to become pregnant?"

He snarled at me. "Will you let *me* tell this story? You're costing me my job either way!"

"Puh-lease. I'm not going to tell anyone what you're telling me. Your job is safe as long as you answer my questions. Your lodging too. I'll even give you a week free!"

"As I was saying!" He untied his tie. It slipped out from under his collar with a soft puff. "There was no way to reverse the procedure. But there was something else I could do to help Mrs. Baker fall pregnant."

I gasped. "Are you the father of the baby?"

Russell's humming grew even louder, more desperate. He clamped his eyes shut and bent over at the waist.

"Miss Murphy, for heaven's sake! If you keep interrupting me, I'll quit my job and move out on my own!"

I pressed my lips together.

"What we settled on," he said. "What we went with. And no, I am not the father. We procured a donation. From a donor who had, who was . . . *who is* . . . in the same family tree as Judge Baker."

My hand smacked over my sealed mouth.

He nodded. "Yes. Gordon Baker is the biological father. However, he was not even in the room when the child was conceived. I can assure you, Miss Murphy, that Elena and Cliff loved each other and that they were not unfaithful to each other. Is that enough from me? Can you let me go?"

I nodded. Then stopped. "Not until you tell me about Daddy and why you let him leave before he was ready."

"Have you met your father, Miss Murphy? He's like you, isn't he." That was a statement, not a question. "Rich people always get their way, and they don't care who they have to step on to do it."

"Then why did you give me the wrong directions to the hospital room? I missed the killer by *moments* because of you!"

His shoulders sagged. "I'm new. I didn't know the way as well as I thought. Please. Let me leave now. I have patients to see."

I tapped Russell on the shoulder. "You can take us to the lobby now, thank you."

Blessedly, the humming stopped. He pulled the lever and the lift began descending.

"Dr. Smith," I said. "One more question, if you'd be so kind. Has Mrs. Baker had her baby yet?"

He shook his head. "Not yet. But she's due any day now."

The elevator stopped, and the doctor walked out without a look back. I refused to examine the new feeling that settled heavily in my gut and shifted around a lot like guilt does. I owed him that free week at the Pinnacle. And quite possibly an apology.

Gordon Baker was the father of Elena's unborn child. Elena had faked going into labor when Mr. Hodgson had started accusing the young man of murdering his father. She had dropped her husband off at the party and walked from the garage to "encourage labor" but had yet to go into labor. That wasn't a crime, but it was strange. And I would never forgive her pronunciation of an important French designer.

I owed Dr. Smith.

"The top floor," I told Russell. "If you'd be so kind."

He closed the lift before anyone else could enter and took me back to my floor.

CHAPTER 44

Shame settled around me like a fog. I knew I wasn't the best person—I hadn't even known my day maid's last name or living situation until she was murdered, for Pete's sake—and was aware of the fact that people viewed me as nosy and spoiled and entitled. Nosy, yes. Spoiled, sure. I had a father who parented me with his wallet. It was either open or closed, depending on how little trouble I caused him. And because he was never around, it was almost always open.

But entitled? I'd gone out of my way to threaten both Dr. Smith's livelihood and living situation for information that wasn't any of my business. Was it worth it? Would it make the case?

Did that matter? If it made the case, would it legitimize my behavior?

I'd been so sure of myself when I told Hodgson you couldn't accuse someone of murder, that you had to ask leading questions, talk around it. And then I'd cornered the doctor in an elevator and demanded the truth or I'd ruin his life. I'd been so angry when he brought Daddy home from the hospital. Furious that he'd jeopardize my only living parent's health like that. Concerned he was the murderer, intent on killing off his final witness.

Gordon Baker. The father of his stepmother's child. What better motive than that to kill the judge? What motive at all to go after my father? And why put the woman in the trunk of his father's car, if not to ruin his reputation and embarrass his wife?

That poor woman.

Daddy snored himself awake on the couch. He sniffed, blinked, and sat up. "What? Where . . .? Evie?"

"Hi, Daddy." I was wearing a pink and white striped pajama set and sitting next to him on the couch, with my slippered feet on his coffee table. My face was cleansed and ready for bed, but I hadn't bothered putting curlers in my hair. Too much work after the exhausting day I'd suffered through. "I ordered us some ice cream. It should be here in a minute."

"Were you sitting here in the dark staring at me?"

"I was sort of staring around you. But yes. I'll turn on a light. I can turn on the TV? Catch the latest *Lassie*? Or the record player? I'll turn you into an Elvis fan yet, Daddy."

"I doubt it."

It wasn't a no, so I hopped up and turned on the nearest lamp. Daddy stretched his arms above his head and yawned before resting his feet on the coffee table too. "How long have you been here?"

"Not long," I assured him, placing the vinyl record in the player. Elvis's "King Creole" started playing. It was a bit upbeat for the mood I was in. Maybe it would help my spirits. "But I am going to stay here until you are healthy enough to be alone. A murderer is on the loose, Daddy. We can't be too careful."

There was a knock on the door, followed by a call of "Room service!"

"Oh, goody! That's our ice cream!"

Daddy mumbled something that might've been a comment on my lack of carefulness concerning dessert, but I chose to ignore it. It was a waiter on the other side of the door, pushing a cart with two banana splits. I tipped him a dollar and settled myself on the couch with my dessert.

Daddy stared at his treat. "A dollar? I told you, nickels and dimes for this sort of thing."

"And I told *you*, I don't carry around money that jingles! I'd sound silly."

He mumbled something else before putting a spoonful of vanilla ice cream in his mouth.

I slid a bite of cold, chocolate-covered banana on my tongue. Swallowing, I turned toward Daddy on the couch. "I don't understand. Are we bankrupt?"

"What? No! Why would you ask that?"

"You don't want me tipping well."

"You tip too well."

"They work hard. And I live here. I want them to like me."

"That's part of the problem, isn't it? You want everyone to like you."

"Not all of us have your natural charm and charisma, Daddy."

His spoon clanked around the side of his bowl.

I sucked a bite of ice cream off mine and let it sit until it hurt my teeth. "You fired off most of the valets and cut the pay of the ones who remained."

"They were trying to unionize! Can you believe it? I'm an honest man, and I pay them fairly. Not to mention they get tips. And they wanted more? That's something you need to learn, Evie. The poor are always looking for a handout."

I used the side of my spoon to cut up what remained of my banana and gave Presley a bite. He slurped it down, banana mushing into the fur under his chin. The ice cream was melting into the chocolate syrup, a swirl of white and black coming together in the bottom of the porcelain bowl. Elvis crooned out "As Long as I Have You," drowning out the clinking sound of my spoon stirring what was left of my dessert. "You jumped to cutting me off financially if I keep seeing Mac, who is someone I love."

"That young man is the worst one you've been infatuated with, Evelyn Grace, and you know it. What about that baseball player?"

"He was unfaithful to me. That is to say, he was unfaithful to his wife, whom I didn't know about."

He sighed. "The musician?"

I nodded. "Yes. He moved to Los Angeles. And then to London. And I think he might be in Miami now?"

"The novelist?"

"*Always* drunk."

"The movie star?"

"Henry?" I perked up. "He's wonderful. But I fell in love with Mac."

Daddy finished off the last of his banana split, his spoon scratching the sides of the bowl. He handed it to me instead of setting it on the table himself. "You'll find someone else. You've found enough eligible men already for one lifetime."

"There's no reason to be nasty with me. I'm here taking care of you. I'm your only family."

"That's not true. My niece—"

"The antiwar activist who grows hemp."

"She's my family."

"And is she here? No. And you know what else? She would never attend to you. She'd never sit at your side. Daddy—she does not like you. If you gave her all your money, she'd give it away. To the anarchists, Daddy. To the *communists*."

"That's—" He smacked his lips together. "Yes. I see your point."

"Daddy, listen." I took his hands in mine. "I love you. You know that. And you love me. I know that. But Mac is important to me. So I need him to be important to you. I have to pay for Mr. Ferretti to continue representing him, especially with this ridiculous witch hunt the police have going on."

Daddy didn't take his hands away, but he shook his head. "You chose the most expensive lawyer in Manhattan for your little side project. That's a bill you will have to cover on your own."

"Fine. I have the money I inherited from Mom. I will use that. But the bank said I needed your approval."

He shook his head again.

"Or my husband's. If you do not allow me access to the money, I will marry Mac tomorrow."

He laughed. "How? He's in jail!"

"The chief of police turns into a blushing, love-struck fool when I so much as shake his hand. I think I can convince him of a private visit. And I know I have enough cash in different handbags to bribe a justice of the peace for an hour of his time. I will do this, Daddy. You know I will."

Presley jumped up on the couch and trotted onto my lap. He sniffed at our joined hands before pushing his cold, wet nose on my knuckles.

A muscle clenched in Daddy's jaw. His nostrils flared, but then he closed his eyes and exhaled. "Right. I know you will. Let's compromise."

"I'm open to negotiations."

"I will pay Mr. Ferretti's bill on my own. And you never see that boy again."

"Nope. Not good enough."

"Fine. I will allow you access to your mother's trust to pay this bill, and you promise not to marry him. Not now, not ever."

The song switched to "Hard-Headed Woman" and it was impossible not to giggle. "Closer." I let go of his hand to hold up a pinkie. "You allow me full access to the money Mom left me, to spend however I wish, whenever I wish, and I won't marry Mac without your approval."

"Full access? Evie. Be reasonable."

"I'm twenty-one. It's my money."

"Yes, and you should be saving it. Like your mother did. You know, I bought her this hotel. Like my father bought your grand-mother that emerald-mine in South Africa. Your future husband should buy you something similar. You should not be spending your money on something so fleeting as a criminal love interest."

"He isn't the one who attacked you."

"I know that. You think I don't know that!" Daddy leaned farther into the corner of the couch. "I know it wasn't him. But that doesn't mean he's not a criminal. Final offer. I will allow you partial access to your mother's money if you promise not to marry him without my express written consent. I must also be willing to be present at the ceremony, and any such ceremony, should it ever be agreed upon, must take place in a Catholic church, conducted by a priest of my choosing."

I set my empty bowl on the coffee table next to his. Presley snuffled and hopped off my lap. I smiled and once more held out my pinkie. "You've got a deal."

"Fine then. We have a deal."

"Daddy, we have to do a pinkie promise."

"I . . . a *what* promise?"

"Wrap your pinkie around mine."

"That's ridiculous."

"All right, tomorrow morning I'll go to the clerk of the courts, and I'll bribe the—"

He wrapped his pinkie around mine. *"Fine."*

CHAPTER 45

Hodgson hadn't been joking when he'd said bright and early. It was only sunrise when Poppy knocked on the door, the former detective standing behind her.

"You're joking," I yawned. I held up my finger to finish yawning. "Is the sun even up yet?"

He put his hands in his pockets and grunted. "You didn't stick together."

I rolled my eyes. "She was across the hall with a lock on the door."

"It was fine, Mr. Hodgson. Trust me." Poppy whispered, "It was better this way. Mr. Murphy's scary."

"Go downstairs and have breakfast. I'll cover it," I said.

He grunted again and walked to the elevator.

I shook my head but stopped with a wince. My neck hurt from sleeping on the couch all night. How had Mac done it all those times before we were together? Thinking about him made my chest ache. I rubbed the spot over my heart like that could do anything to relieve the pressure.

"You okay, Evelyn?"

I smiled. "Quite all right, thank you. How are you? How did you sleep?"

"Fine, thank you. I used your yellow pajamas again. Is this dress okay for me to borrow?"

It was a blue, floral Balmain dress, and seeing it reminded me of Elena Baker. That was better than thinking of Mac. Oh, my poor Mac, stuck in jail. My chest hurt something terrible.

"You look lovely. It's yours to keep. I need to get ready. Would you stay here and wait for Mr. Castillo to walk Presley, and keep an eye on Daddy while I'm out with Mr. Hodgson?"

She blanched so thoroughly she was almost green.

"Daddy's not so bad, Poppy. Maybe you can convince Mr. Castillo to sit with you while I'm gone?" I leaned in close to whisper. "He's sweet on you, you know."

She ducked her chin to her chest. "It's too soon, Evelyn. I did care for Chuck."

"I know." I rubbed her arm. "I'm so sorry he turned out to be such a scoundrel. Shall I fire him? I can, you know. Him and Judy too. That home-wrecker."

"No." She laughed a little. "No. It's . . . I thought when he was being secretive that he was planning on proposing to me. And it frightened me a little. Especially when I compared my feelings to his—what I thought was—imminent proposal to the way you and my brother spoke of getting engaged. It . . . made me realize I didn't ever want to marry Chuck. I cared for him. I still do. But I don't love him. I'm not in love with him. And I don't want to be his wife. He should've ended things with me before carrying on with Judy, but we were never going to be together forever. I'd have ended things with him sooner or later."

I squeezed her shoulder. "You're very sure you're all right?"

"Yes." She smiled. "I'm sure."

"Wonderful. Because I did promise Mr. Castillo a date with you. I'm off to get dressed. Do phone the desk if you need me! Toodle-oo!" I hurried out the door before she could reply.

A spoiled, entitled brat, yes. But also a coward too.

· ★   ★   ★

Hodgson was finishing up his breakfast in the café next to the fish tanks. I pulled out a seat, intent on ordering myself a croissant and an espresso, and reading the newspaper to see if my little scene on the steps of the courthouse had paid off. But Hodgson wiped his mouth with a napkin and tossed it on his empty plate.

"I already squared it away with Unfaithful Glasses that you're covering my meals when we're working this case. Come on. Don't wanna be late."

"Late for what?"

Hodgson stood up and started walking. I hurried after him, glancing forlornly at the table. "Hodgson, please! I haven't had coffee yet, and I wanted to see if I made the papers!"

He pulled a newspaper out of his coat and handed it to me over his shoulder without looking back or slowing down.

A photo of me, all done up in Chanel, blowing a kiss at the camera made the front page. Above the fold. I tried to read the article while walking and not running into anyone.

HEIRESS CALLS KILLER A COWARD

Socialite Evelyn Murphy, heir to the Murphy fortune, is an amateur sleuth making a promise to catch another killer. Over the weekend, a judge was murdered in the Pinnacle Hotel's garage. The next day, Evelyn's father, Mark Murphy, one of the wealthiest men in the world, and a maid called Florence were both attacked in a similar fashion. Only Mr. Murphy survives. Charming and beautiful, Evelyn stood on the courthouse steps and called out the killer, saying the man the police have in custody is "the most convenient" suspect,

but not the right one. She promises to find the "madman" who is "a
disordered, sloppy, stupid . . . lunatic on the loose." She warns all
of New York City to be on the lookout.

I tucked the newspaper under my arm. "It takes them a few lines
to get to the point I made about Florence, but there she is, in black
and white." *Charming and beautiful* felt much nicer than entitled and
spoiled.

Maybe all four of those adjectives could be true at once. I'd have
to talk to Dr. Sanders about it.

"You must be so proud." Hodgson said. We were outside and
walking toward the garage. "This is important, Murphy. We need
to catch these valets off guard."

"Oh, so we can accuse them and see if they get angry?" I fell
into step beside him now that I wasn't trying to read. "I tried that
last night on Dr. Smith."

Hodgson came to an abrupt halt. "You did what?"

"Yes, I cornered him in an elevator and demanded he answer
me or I would get him fired and have him thrown out of the hotel."

Hodgson covered his nose and mouth with both hands, a little
tent for his face. Then he dropped them to his sides, lifted them back
up, and pressed the pads of his thumbs against his forehead.

"Murphy."

"Yes?"

"You cornered a man, a grown man, alone, in an elevator, and
accused him of murder while threatening his livelihood and his
place of residence?"

I sniffed. "I wasn't alone. The lift boy was there. He had his
fingers in his ears, and he was humming 'Happy Birthday,' but—"

Hodgson closed his eyes. "What did he say?"

"The lift boy?"

"No!" His dark eyes flew open. "Dr. Smith."

"Oh! Right. It's rather scandalous, if you ask me, though Dr. Smith assures me it was all very clinical. Judge Baker, some years ago, had a procedure done to render him infertile. Then he marries a young wife he adores and dotes on, and she wants a baby. He is willing to give her whatever she wants so he employs his oldest son to, er, donate the necessary . . . fluids. Dr. Smith oversaw the whole thing. He says Gordon Baker and Elena Baker weren't even in the same room when it happened."

"You're joking."

I crossed my heart. "And hope to die."

"Huh."

I nodded. "Very."

"Okay. Okay. Thank you for finding that out, Murphy. Good work. But next time? Call me first. Don't go question someone alone. It's dangerous."

Waving a hand, I made a pfft sound with my tongue and lips. "It's the Pinnacle. Don't worry so much. Now, you want to question the valets? Following up on the union angle?"

"Though the information you got about Gordon Baker makes it less and less likely, yes, it's best to follow all the clues, not only the ones we want to follow." He gave me a pointed look before starting to walk again.

I hastened to his side. "Was that about Mac? Unfair of you."

"Mr. Cooper had a plethora of drug paraphernalia stashed in a secret floorboard in his room. Whether or not he was responsible for the attacks, he was up to no good."

How could that be? No, I'd never been to his apartment before. But Mac was always sober around me, and we were around each other a lot. Poppy swore there were no drugs in her apartment, and I believed her.

"We must agree to disagree. I'll have you know that one of the valets I spoke to is the downstairs neighbor of Mac and Poppy."

Hodgson puckered his mouth. "You don't say."

"I do say. And what's more, I'd like to lead the conversation with the valets if it pleases you."

"It does not."

"Sorry, if last night taught me anything, it's that you can't ask someone if they're a murderer. You have to skirt around the issue. Delicately."

"Delicately doesn't solve cases."

"Is it illegal to lie to the police?"

"No."

"Are you still a detective?"

He glared at me from the corner of his narrowed eyes. "No."

"And can you, as a private citizen, force someone to answer your questions truthfully, or even at all?"

Hodgson grunted in response.

"Wonderful. Delicately it is. Skirt around it. Come on, I see Scott working the booth now."

CHAPTER 46

Scott was behind the valet stand in the standard uniform the male employees wore. I'd never seen him anywhere else and wondered how he handled the summer months. There weren't other valet uniforms as far as I knew. It must get hot, standing outside the garage all day in a dark green uniform, even if he did have a jaunty umbrella for shade.

The dress I had chosen for the day coordinated with the bellhop uniforms, funnily enough. An emerald-green dress with a full skirt and long sleeves, and a brown sailor-tie neckline that kept me quite bundled up for the fall weather. A matching brown belt, heels, and wrist gloves, and a thick pair of tights. I was comfortable now, but if it were June, I'd be miserable.

"Miss Murphy," Scott called out. "Do you need the Rolls? Alan went to park a car—he'll be back in a jiffy."

"No, thank you. I was hoping I could speak to you for a minute. If you don't mind?"

"'Course not, Miss Murphy. Saw you in the paper this morning. Was a great shot, if you ask me."

"Thank you ever so. I thought so too." I winked at him and he grinned. "I wanted to see if you remembered anything from that night that Judge Baker was killed. I know the last time we talked you said you didn't see anything."

He shrugged. "It was me and two other guys working after the party rush. Cutbacks and so, means less hands on deck after nine thirty. I run the stand, the other two drive the cars. I didn't see anything unusual, Miss Murphy."

"Do you ever leave this stand while you're working?"

He shook his head. "Not without backup. Somebody will always be at this stand."

"I've spoken to one of them, haven't I? The man who had a baby recently?"

"Yeah. That's Alan. He's solid, Miss Murphy."

"And the others?"

"Chester? He's all right." Scott shrugged. "Woulda said something if the judge drove himself into the garage at least."

Hodgson touched my elbow. "Murphy? A word?"

"Please excuse me, Scott."

He nodded.

Hodgson and I stepped away from the stand and out of the shade of the umbrella. I shielded my eyes from the sun with my hand and waited for the former detective to speak. He was squinting too, his mouth tugged down in a deep frown.

"Delicately isn't working."

"It's working fine. Already I've found out the names of other gentlemen we should question again."

He pulled his hand out of his pocket to wave it around in my face. "Not working. This is what we're going to do. You're gonna continue being delicate. I'm going to be the opposite."

I'd leaned back, away from his wobbling fingers. It took me a second to hear what he was saying, and when I did process it, I didn't understand it. "Rough?"

"Fine." He shoved his hand back into his pocket. "Fine. Rough. It's called Mutt and Jeff."

This time I didn't have the excuse of being poked in the eye for my trouble following along. "What?"

"The technique I'm teaching you."

He was teaching me something? Starting when? "You're teaching me how to be a dog named Jeff?"

Hodgson exhaled, harsh and loud, through flared nostrils. "Just, just keep doing whatever it is you're doing. I'll back you up."

I was too confused to argue. "Okay." Another valet had jogged up to the stand, and I realized it was the young father. I waved at him and decided to continue doing what I was doing and let Hodgson worry about himself. "Hello, Alan. How is the baby today?"

"Doing good, thank you, miss." He grinned. "Not sleeping a wink yet."

"Costs a lot of money," Hodgson declared from behind me.

I forced a smile and refused to turn around and glare at him. What was he doing? Why was he doing it?

"What?" Alan asked.

"Don't mind him," I hurried to add. "This is Detective Hodgson, he's helping—"

"I'm trying to solve a murder." Hodgson got right into Alan's face. "And it costs a lot of money, doesn't it? Raising a kid in the city."

"I"—he swallowed—"I live in Yonkers."

"Still. Expensive. You could use the money, couldn't you? Got real mad when the union you were trying to form got busted up. Who could blame you? You saw an opportunity you couldn't refuse. That anti-union, fat cat of a judge strolled up in here, and you thought—"

Alan turned and ran away.

"What?" I reached for the pendant around my neck, the pad of my thumb tracing over the familiar ridges of Saint Anthony. "What is happening?"

"Guilty," was all Hodgson said before he broke out in a run.

I looked at Scott. Scott looked at me. I looked at Hodgson chasing Alan into the garage. I wrinkled my nose. "Scott, I think I have to run."

"Yeah. Looks like."

"Will you watch my shoes?" I toed off my heels until I was barefoot on the asphalt. This was not smart, as the dark, compacted gravel was growing hot in the morning sun.

He nodded. "Sure thing, Miss Murphy."

"Thank you ever so!" I jogged off toward the lower level of the parking garage, squinting as I went from the bright sunlight to the shaded area of the car park. I couldn't see much but shadows and shapes of what I knew to be cars.

Hodgson was shouting up and to the right. I cut through parked cars to get closer as fast as I could, small pebbles biting into the soft undersides of my arches.

"Don't get in that car!" Hodgson yelled. "Don't!"

But an engine rumbled.

"Hodgson!" I screamed. "Don't get run over!"

Tires squealed. A crash. A crunch. Glass shattered.

"If you're dead, I'll kill you, Hodgson!"

There was more yelling, a loud thud on the pavement. When I finally made it to the scene of the action, Hodgson was kneeling on Alan's back next to the hanging door of a shining silver Chevy Bel Air. It had crashed into the back of a canary-yellow Ford Thunderbird, both cars crinkled and smoking.

"I'm sorry!" Alan cried. "I'm sorry! I didn't mean for anything to happen! I didn't know!"

I bent over to grab my knees, gasping for air. "Didn't know a car was parked in your escape route?"

He shook his head, his chin wobbling on the pavement. "That was because I didn't want to hit your friend. He jumped in front of me. I'm so sorry, Miss Murphy. Please don't fire me. That man, he offered me twenty dollars to sneak him a valet uniform and keep my mouth shut. I never saw him again. I'd never seen him before! I thought he had a girl he was trying to impress or—I don't know. I didn't think about it. I saw the money and I took it. I've got a baby, and he needs diapers and clothes and . . ." There were tears on his cheeks. "I'm sorry. Please don't fire me."

I swallowed and tried to catch my breath. That was a lot of information in a short amount of time. I looked at Hodgson for clarification but got annoyed instead. "You jumped in front of a speeding car?"

He shrugged. His knee was still pushing against the center of Alan's back. "Worked, didn't it?"

"Alan," I said. "I understand you. A stranger gave you twenty dollars, and you nicked a uniform out of the Pinnacle's laundry."

"Right. Yeah. Can I sit up?"

"You gonna run at me with a car again?"

"No. Promise."

Hodgson stood, letting Alan go. He sat on the concrete floor, his head in his hands. He was filthy and scratched up along the forearms and the underside of his jaw.

"You'll need to see the doctor," I said. "You'll need stitches, at least."

"I don't think I can afford it, Miss Murphy."

"Don't worry about that right now. Because I am sure the police are on their way because I am sure that Scott has made a phone call." I was not sure at all. He would've had to leave his station for that and run back to the hotel. Would he have known to do that without being explicitly told? All I'd said was to watch my shoes. I wondered what was happening to my shoes. No, Scott would've heard the crash, and he would've called for help. "Right now, I want you to tell me everything you can remember about the man who wanted the valet uniform."

Alan wiped his nose with the back of his hand. "He was wearing a hat and sunglasses. His collar was turned up. I couldn't see much more than his jaw and his nose and his mouth. I don't know what to tell you, Miss Murphy. He was tall, but not too tall. He was white. But not pale. Tan, sort of."

"You didn't recognize him?" Hodgson asked. "By his walk or his voice? Did he talk like he was from around here?"

Alan shook his head. "He didn't have much in the way of an accent. He coulda been faking it, though."

I said, "His clothes."

"What?"

"His clothes. What was he wearing?"

"Dark slacks? With a beige trench coat. Collar popped up. A hat. Sunglasses. Kept his hands in his pockets, his head down. Wanted a valet uniform and my silence. That was it. I didn't think anything of it."

"His shoes?" I tried again. "What shoes was he wearing?"

Alan shrugged, helpless. "I don't remember. I didn't look at his feet, Miss Murphy. I'm so sorry. Please don't fire me."

I couldn't see how he wouldn't lose his job. He'd let a killer use our garage as a murder scene, or at least stage one in it. He'd allowed an injured woman and a dead judge to be snuck onto our property.

But he was in desperate straits because of my father.

"You didn't tell the police?" Hodgson asked. "Didn't they question you?"

"I was scared, man." Alan cried. "I can't lose this job. I've got a wife and a baby, and they need to eat. Please, Miss Murphy."

Sirens were approaching.

"I'll put in a good word with Mr. Sharpe," I said.

CHAPTER 47

We reached the steps of the entrance as Poppy was descending them, holding Presley in her arms and walking side by side with Russell.

Something sharp pulled tight in my chest. The three of them together was not unlike something I might've been doing a week ago, with Poppy's brother holding my hand.

"Poppy," I called out. She stopped walking, waved, and hurried toward me. Presley shook in her arms, little tongue lolling out his perfect mouth. I scratched between his ears. "Is Daddy all right?"

"I'm so sorry, Evelyn," Poppy said. "But he insisted I leave him alone. And he's terrifying! When Russell showed up to walk Presley, I took the opportunity to give your father a bit of privacy, but I'll be right back there to make sure his breakfast gets cleaned up."

"He ate, then?"

"Yeah. An omelet and some toast with jam. Two cups of coffee. He read the paper too and commented on your . . . um. Your article."

I laughed at her wording. "Not impressed, was he?"

"Oh, quite the contrary, Ev. He was proud of you."

That would be a first. I dropped a kiss on Presley's cold nose. "Enjoy your walk and take your time. I'll go sit with Daddy for a while."

Poppy, Presley, and Russell made their way to the Park. Hodgson said, "I need to talk to your father again. One last time. See if there's anything besides shoes he remembers from when he was attacked."

We walked back into the lobby of the Pinnacle. It was as busy as ever, business not having taken a hit with the recent murders in the press. Even if I'd been flippant with the reporter about it, I was worried. There had been an unusual amount of crime in the hotel as of late, and while I wouldn't mind having fewer guests per se, my home not being safe wreaked havoc with my ability to relax.

"I better make good on my word and drop a note to Mr. Sharpe," I said.

"I'm sure he'll be out in the garage dealing with the accident," Hodgson said. "Surprised we didn't pass him on the way here."

"He's been getting in later and later lately." I leaned closer to him to whisper, "Family troubles."

"Sharpe has a family?"

"A son, though I only learned about his existence recently. He should be taking a job here soon." I cleared my throat and steered us to Mr. Sharpe's office. "You know, if *your* son ever needs a job, I'd be happy to offer a good word on his behalf to the owner of the Pinnacle."

The side of Hodgson's mouth quirked up. "Nice try, Murphy."

I snapped my fingers. "One day, Hodgson. One day, you'll tell me."

"Is that a threat?"

I knocked on the office door. The secretary called me in immediately, smiling at me over her glasses. "Good morning, Miss
Murphy. I expect you're coming in from the garage?"

I nodded.

"You just missed Mr. Sharpe. He's on his way to deal with the
accident now."

"Surprised we didn't pass him on our way here," I said, stealing
Hodgson's words.

Hodgson noticed. He leaned against the open doorframe, one
foot crossed in front of the other.

"He took the back way," the secretary said. "Through the
kitchen to steal a pastry. His usual route on way to trouble. Is there
anything I can do for you?"

"I need to leave Mr. Sharpe a note, if that's okay."

"Yes, miss." She grabbed a pen and a yellow pad of paper and
slid them across her desk. "I ordered the flowers you requested for
Florence's funeral."

"Thank you." I picked up the supplies and wrote Mr. Sharpe's
name across the top of the page. "Do you happen to know the time
and location of the service?"

"I can get it for you," she said. "I don't think Florence's brother
will make it, but between you and me and your friend, Miss Murphy,
it's no big loss."

"That's what I've gathered." I tapped the pen against my lips and
thought about what to say. *Desperate people do desperate things. Please
don't fire him for being stupid. Also, please do remind Judy and Burrows to
lock the stockroom door. XO, EEGM.*

"There." I ripped the paper off the pad and folded it in half.
"Will you give him this, please? Thank you ever so. You know, I did
learn, during all this, that another maid died about a decade ago.
Were you here for that? I must confess, I don't remember it."

"You were a wee thing at the time, Miss Murphy. Eleven or so. I doubt the details were shared with you." The secretary took Mr. Sharpe's note and put it on a stack of others. "She was a nice lady, Mary was. Worked so hard. That no-good husband of hers." She shivered. "I shouldn't speak ill of the dead. But Mary was the sole provider. Her husband wasted every penny she earned, and I'm sure he didn't put the money from the lawsuit to good use."

I wrinkled my nose. "How . . . if you don't mind me asking . . . how did he waste it? The usual vices? Gambling, women, drink?"

She shook her head. "If only the usual vices would've been enough for him. He was a drug user, Miss Murphy. And not just any drugs." She lowered her voice to whisper. "Heroin. In a needle." She shivered again. "Being around him always made me uneasy. Mary loved him anyway. But their son. Not too much older than you. He suffered for it. I wonder what happened to him."

My heart pounded in my chest. I opened my mouth to speak, but only a shallow breath escaped. My nose, God bless it, was still wrinkled. "The son was not much older than me?"

"That's right, Miss Murphy. Fifteen or sixteen at the time. I remember he looked more like Mary than his father, and a good thing too. Blond hair and these green eyes like you wouldn't believe. She was a looker, Mary was. She deserved so much more than the hand she was dealt."

I swayed on my feet. All the blood left my face and ran to my knees, my legs shaking and knocking into each other. I grabbed onto the side of her desk to keep from falling over. I'd thought the woman from the trunk screamed when she was looking at me, but she was looking at the person who stood in front of me. And then, at the hospital, after Dr. Smith gave me the room number. A doctor in a hurry walked by us with his face hidden in a file. I'd seen only the back of his head. The exact same back of the head. *Stupid, stupid Evelyn!*

"Oh no! Oh no! Mr. Hodgson!"

"Yep."

"Daddy's all alone up there!"

"Ma'am," Hodgson said, stepping away from the door. "You need to call the police."

"The police are already here," she said. "In the garage."

"We need them here and we need them now. Mr. Murphy is in danger."

"Mr. Murphy! Why?"

I sucked down a deep breath and forced my legs to be still. It was time to run and my body would have to figure itself out. "Because Detective McJimsey is the killer!"

★ ★ ★

I ran to the elevator bay, Hodgson hot on my heels. Literally. The toes of my high heels pinched with every hurried step, and I thought about going barefoot. Again.

"Murphy, I don't have a gun," he said.

I stared at him, wide-eyed, as we barreled into an elevator. "Top floor!" I shouted at the lift boy. "Why not?"

"Had to turn it in," he said, short of breath. "Remember? I got fired? They wanted my badge and my gun."

"I can't leave Daddy alone in there. I *can't*!"

Hodgson nodded. "Look, we figured it out. Your father is alone in there. We'll barricade the door until the calvary arrives. There's no point in worrying right now."

"Shall I worry later, then? Would that be better for you?"

"Yeah, actually. It'd help a lot."

I stared icily at him until the operator opened the lift doors for us. "Thank you ever so, Hodgson. I'll call my analyst right away. No need for our meetings anymore, Dr. Sanders, I've chosen to simply not worry until later."

He nodded again. "Yep."

"Fantastic. Wonderful. How lucky for me I decided to employ you."

"Glad I could be of service."

I knocked on Daddy's door so hard my knuckles ached. "Daddy! Are you decent?"

"Why wouldn't he be decent? Didn't he have breakfast with your friend?"

"Fair enough." I tried the handle, and it was unlocked. The lights inside were off.

Hodgson grabbed my elbow, put his finger to his lips. "Call out his name again," he whispered.

I didn't understand what he meant at first. But Hodgson didn't let go of my arm, and his words sunk in. Maybe my father wasn't as alone as we thought. "Daddy?"

There was a muffled reply, like someone trying to speak with their mouth full of water. Was he in the midst of another attack? Were we too late? Had McJimsey come in and delivered the fatal blow while I was writing a note to save the job of a man who'd let this happen?

Hodgson tugged on my elbow again until he had my attention. "Stay here," he mouthed. Then, he pointed at his feet. "Fire escape."

I nodded, even though I only sort of understood what he was trying to tell me. He crept down the hall on his tiptoes, leaving me alone outside my father's open door.

Hodgson had ordered me to stay put. But since when did I listen to him, anyway? I should go in. Shouldn't I? Or should I do what he said, and stay there?

Did I wait for more help to arrive? Did I go in anyway? What if he needed me? What if he was having a fit?

But what if he wasn't alone?

I shook my head. "Daddy. I'm coming in."

CHAPTER 48

I've done a lot of not very smart things in my life, mostly in attempts to find things. To find the truth or the meaning of life or what have you.

I haven't found that yet. I'll keep doing stupid things until I do. One day. A priest might be able to help, but the one my mother would often visit for confession and communion was at least one hundred and fifty years old at the time and would fall asleep with his hands in the wafers—*the literal body of Christ*—so I doubt it. He was probably dead now. Like Mom. Like Nanny.

Daddy was here. He was here and he needed me, and I was doing something stupid in order to find out how to save him.

I made the sign of the cross and waited for my eyes to adjust to the darkness. The room smelled like coffee and bacon. The stillness was eerie, dust particles floating in the little scraps of light between the closed curtains. The Park was out there. Presley and Poppy too.

And here I was, being stupid. Oh well. Lots of people think I'm stupid. It's better that way, I've found, if people think you're stupider than you really are. It's easier to find things they don't want you to find.

"Daddy?" I said again. "Daddy, are you here?"

That strangled, gurgling noise startled me almost out of my shoes. I swallowed hard and stepped toward the couch.

The lamp clicked on. I held up a hand to protect myself from the sudden light or from the scene in front of me—who could be sure. But there they were, plain as day, sitting side by side on the couch. Daddy had handcuffs on his wrists and balled-up socks in his mouth. Detective McJimsey, meanwhile, held a silver revolver in his hands.

"Good morning, Miss Murphy," McJimsey greeted me. "I saw your article in the paper. I was wondering if you'd care to have a little chat about it?"

"It's hardly *my* article, as I'm not much of a writer, and I'd rather wear last season's shoes than be a journalist, but I'm always open for a chat. Did you not like what I had to say about you?"

"Not particularly." He smiled, and it caught me off guard, how such a comely man could look so ghastly. Ashen beneath his scruffy, day-old beard. His teeth a little too yellow, a little too crooked. I glanced at his shoes. Sensible, and not recently shined. Daddy's feet were bare. I hoped those weren't his used socks in his mouth right now, but what else could it be?

I didn't dare look at his face, though. Not when McJimsey lifted his gun and moved it from his left hand to his right.

"Disorganized, Miss Murphy? That . . . that *wounds* me. To pull off what I've done, I had to be organized. Couldn't overlook even the slightest detail. And sloppy? I'm many things, but sloppy isn't one of them."

It was my turn to smile. I glided into the closest seat and crossed my legs. "Funny, then. Because for Judge Baker and my father, you used heroin. Or versions of heroin, anyway. Your modus operandi. But for the woman in the trunk? A pillow over the face. And Florence? A belt. Isn't that right?" I shook my head. "Florence was a maid like your mother. How could you do such a thing?"

McJimsey's green eyes were deep with sorrow. "What choice did I have? She walked in on me. She saw the whole thing. She opened her mouth to scream and tried to run away for help. I did what I had to do to see justice served. Tried just to keep her mouth covered, but she fought so hard I had to use my own belt." He sighed. "Figures a spoiled child like your father would demand a housekeeper wake him up and run his shower and brew his coffee."

I nodded and gave Daddy the briefest of glances. McJimsey had him there. Daddy was staring at me, his eyes, so similar to mine, wide and unblinking. There was nothing I could do to make him feel better. All I could do was keep him alive.

He wasn't going to like it at all.

"He's always been like that," I said with a sigh. "Spoiled child is right. Entitled, you know. My mother died when I was six—she was *murdered*, mind you—and what does he do? He flies in for the funeral, hires Nanny, and leaves the day after my mother is in the ground. I was six! He left me here in this hotel with a stranger and took off to who knows where!"

McJimsey shook his head. "I'm not surprised. He didn't give a rat's ass when my mom died. She died on *his* property. The maids, they'd asked for that window to be fixed for weeks and kept getting brushed off. My mother tripped on the laundry she was washing. She took a wet sheet to the ringer and fell to her death still holding it. He didn't call. He didn't send a letter. He didn't send flowers. He didn't attend her funeral. Nothing. Like it never even happened."

"Like it never even happened," I repeated. "Exactly. And we were children, you and me, when we lost the most important people in the world to us. Does he care? No. Not even a little."

"Not even a little," McJimsey agreed. "Not even a little. It was like . . . when Baker came to Dad. It was like an angel arrived from heaven. He won us all this money, so much money. I was going to be able to go to college. We were looking at houses to buy, nice houses in good neighborhoods. But the money, the money never came. Not really. A little bit, here and there. A few drips and drops. Enough to keep my father's addiction supplied. But the big dough never came. Baker swore he was investing it for us, taking care of it for us, that it would be there whenever we found the house of our dreams or I got accepted into a university. But he never delivered it."

"He was embezzling it," I said, nose wrinkling. "He stole your money. And used it on himself."

That would explain how he'd been able to finance his lavish lifestyle while putting two sons through Harvard and keeping the brownstone on the Upper West Side.

"Baker blamed my dad. He tried to lie to me about it. That Dad got all the money, but he'd killed himself with it. Spent every last penny on heroin. Like I was an *idiot*. Like I'd believe him. Like we were the only people he'd done this to."

"He embezzled money from most of his clients," I said. "Didn't he? But he was a well-connected attorney and then a well-connected judge. And it's not like there's justice to be done then, is there?"

"Exactly!" He hit his knee with his revolver, and I clenched my toes in my shoes to keep from jumping. Daddy breathed heavily through his nose and closed his eyes. I didn't blame him. "Exactly. See, Evelyn. I can call you Evelyn, can't I?"

"Of course."

"I knew that you and I, that we'd see things eye to eye. I knew it. When we first met, at the garage, I thought you'd be like your old man. But you're not. You're not at all. You can see the truth, can't you? I had to kill Judge Baker. And I had to ruin his reputation when I did it. Because then—"

"All his old cases can get reexamined. And if we follow the money—"

"They'll see that none of the victims he represented got what they were due. He spent and spent and spent, and none of it was his money. Couldn't put it in a bank, could he? So he bought luxury goods in cash. Make his widow sell some of her jewelry, some of her bags. She only has them because my mom fell out of a window washing other people's sheets. Where's the fairness in that?"

I shook my head. "There's no fairness in that. None at all. I don't blame you, Detective. I don't blame you at all." I clucked my tongue like Hodgson often did. "Though, I don't understand why you're here with a gun now. Goes against the MO, doesn't it? Killing them with what killed your father?"

He shrugged a shoulder.

"Ah," I said. "I see. You used all you had framing Mac, is that it?"

When he met my gaze, he looked almost shy, and there were two spots of color appearing high on his cheekbones. "I am sorry about that, Evelyn. I know you're fond of him. But it's better this way. He's no good for you."

Mac was the best thing that had ever happened to me besides Presley, but I wasn't about to argue that point with the man holding a gun on my father.

"The woman from the trunk? The regular at the precinct." I reached for the pendant around my neck and said a silent prayer for her. "You picked her up in your police vehicle, didn't you? She didn't put up a fight, she was used to it by then. But she wasn't expecting the heroin you shot into her system. You expected it to kill her?"

He nodded. "Yeah. Would've been a painless death. Soft and easy, she'd drift away in the trunk. Better dead than the life she was living, I'm sure you'd agree."

I hardly thought being dead was better than being alive, but again I wasn't about to argue. I wanted to understand the mind of this killer who had run amok in my hotel.

"You chose heroin because it was your father's drug of choice. Why did you use different types?"

He shrugged like it didn't matter. "Could only get that little bit of the pure stuff. The rest I bought off the street. The Phencyclidine I mixed with your father's dose? That's easy enough to get if you date a girl working in the hospital pharmacy. See, I didn't just want to kill your dad." He slapped Daddy's shoulder. "I wanted him to suffer."

"Understandable." I swallowed. I suppose it was, if you hated someone, blamed them for the death of your mother, that you'd want their death to be as painful as possible. "Did you become a detective to track down Judge Baker?"

He shook his head. "No. I wanted to help people. Figured, you know, I'd spent my life helpless. Hated it. How alone I felt. Thought if I could be a police officer, I could help other people. That would be good for me. Police help people. Or so I thought. And then I became one, and you know who we help? Only the wealthy." He laughed. "Ain't that something? Here to help the likes of the Bakers and the Murphys. The reason my life was destroyed. And my captain treats me like I'm a joke. Gives me Hodgson for a partner. Me? Can you believe that? I'm the best detective Manhattan has ever seen, and he tries to put me in my place by giving me that *man* as a partner. More like a weight around my neck."

I exhaled slowly, quietly through barely parted lips. First of all, the best detective Manhattan had ever seen? Hardly! Being able to plant evidence in an innocent man's apartment didn't quite equal hero status. Second, Hodgson was a fine detective and a good man. McJimsey had no right disparaging his character.

No right. But he had a gun. So, I moved on.

"How did you get Mac's fingerprint on the needle in Daddy's bedroom?"

He quirked up the side of his mouth, a single dimple popping. "You know, it's funny. I've earned quite the reputation during my time as a detective. See, I have a knack for always getting just the right clue at just the right time. But a professional such as myself has to keep his secrets, you understand, Miss Murphy."

Ah. Wonderful. He admitted to planting evidence all the time across many cases. If I survived this, that meant not just Judge Baker's cases would be opened, but McJimsey's as well.

I made the executive decision to allow him his feelings of superiority and changed the subject.

"The one thing I can't figure out," I said, "and I've been stuck on it this entire time. is how did you get Judge Baker in his car? In the garage?"

He leaned back on the couch, the picture of ease, an ankle crossed to his knee and his shining revolver resting on his calf. Sweat beaded on Daddy's hairline and dripped down his nose. I ignored it, ignored him. Now was not the time for sympathy or—wouldn't Hodgson be proud—even panic. I would simply have to be afraid later.

"Bought a valet uniform off one of your workers," he said. "Wasn't hard to do too, by the way—you should look into that. Sat in my car about a block away. Backed up to an alley, one that doesn't get a lot of foot traffic. Had to be an alley. Police car, plain clothes." He gestured to himself. "Judge pulls out of the party, he's had a few drinks. Doesn't blink about getting pulled over. I walk right up to him, ask him how he's doing and put the needle in his arm when he opens the window. He's pliable then. I get him in the back of his car. It's dark. Sure, there are people around, but I've got the alley for cover. Move the woman from my trunk to his, pull the uniform over my clothes, and leave my jacket in my car. Then I drive right up and park the car. He's still breathing, a little conscious, so I can move him into the front seat with his help. He sits there and lets me put one more injection in his arm. The good stuff this time. Pure. I didn't wait. I walked out of the garage and back to my car. Got rid of the uniform and swung by the station to grab a cup of coffee. When the call came in, Hodgson and I were the first ones out the door."

The pendant of Saint Anthony was warm in my fingers. I set it down, portrait side out, and did my absolute best to look at my lap, to look at McJimsey, to look at the gun in his hands, and not at the shadows on the walls behind him.

"Simple," I said. "And yet brilliant. I must commend you, Detective. I don't think I would've ever figured that out."

He smiled. It was soft and slow, and it made my stomach flip until I was grateful I'd been too busy for breakfast, or it all might've ended up on the carpet.

"I hope you know, Evelyn, I don't have any hard feelings about this. But I mean, you called me out in the press. And now you're here, as a witness. I'm glad we had a chance to talk about this, clear the air. But I am going to have to shoot you."

Daddy made a loud noise—almost like he was yelling no—and turned to face McJimsey dead on. McJimsey patted his shoulder.

"Don't worry. I'll shoot you first. Painless, yeah? Right through the temple. I'll have to stage it like a murder-suicide. I am sorry about that, Evelyn, but it makes more sense for you to be the one to kill your father. You're mad because he's the reason your drug-dealing boyfriend is getting put away for life. Et cetera. Now." He sighed, pulled the hammer on his gun. "As promised—"

Hodgson shattered a vase over the top of McJimsey's head. Flowers, dirty water, and shards of glass rained down over the couch, soaking Daddy and myself, digging small cuts into our forearms and ankles.

And McJimsey fell face first into the coffee table.

CHAPTER 49

With McJimsey, aka Michael Carter Jr, arrested and his motivations for all three murders plus two attacks on Daddy's life and one on mine made clear, Mac was released quickly and quietly. Chief Harvey was a blushing, mumbling mess as he shook my hand and apologized for the mix-up.

Quite a mix-up.

McJimsey had been his mother's maiden name, and when he'd moved in with her sister after the death of his father, he'd taken it. When he'd applied to the police academy, he'd done it with forged documents that said his aunt was his mother.

He might've told me that he became a cop to help people, but that act of subterfuge alone told me he'd been building to this for years.

The newspapers had run wild covering the whole thing. It was gratifying seeing Joan's name finally make it into the story. The police had held that detail back while they were trying to investigate the apparent suicide of the judge, to keep his reputation from becoming less than stellar, but now that we knew the judge hadn't done anything wrong, they'd given all the details to the public.

That is to say, he hadn't been doing heroin and putting women in his trunk. He'd been doing lots of other wrong things.

Elena Baker had her baby. Finally. A little girl. Only a little girl would cause her mother that much trouble. Gordon made a statement to the paper, praising the quick work of the Manhattan Police Department and asking for privacy as his stepmother and sister recuperated during this difficult time. There was no mention that his sister was also his daughter. Or that, as the grapevine would have it, there were talks of a spring wedding. I didn't always believe the grapevine, but it did explain why she was so quick to chase Hodgson and me away with fake labor pains. She was protecting a new love. I could respect that, even if the entire thing gave me the heebie-jeebies.

Mac hadn't been to the hotel yet, which was understandable. I wouldn't want to visit the Pinnacle if I'd recently been arrested inside of it either. So, bravely, boldly, and wearing a pink, cashmere sweater and a high-waisted, black swing skirt, I tucked Presley in my purse, kissed the cat goodbye, and made to leave on my own.

She meowed at me, her green eyes blinking.

"I can't take you, darling. You wouldn't have a litter box. But I'll send Mac your love. Which reminds me? What shall we name you?"

She slunk away, jumped on the back of my couch, and stretched herself out in the sun.

I laughed. "You're a Monroe if there ever was one, aren't you, you lovely thing? I'll be back soon."

A bellhop offered to hail me a taxi, but I stuck out my hand and whistled. I winked at the boy in green and climbed into the back seat all on my own. Well, with Presley. He put his paws on the edge of his purse and licked my chin when I told the driver the Yonkers address.

I'd used the inheritance from my mother to cover Mac's lawyer fees, and had asked Mr. Ferretti to have Mac call me immediately upon release, but that call hadn't taken place yet.

He'd only been out for a few hours. Maybe he hadn't come to a pay phone yet. Or he wasn't back at his apartment yet. There was a lot of paperwork to fill out when you'd been accused of a crime. I couldn't wait to see him. For him to see me, in his apartment! The one thing he'd been trying to get me to do when we'd found Judge Baker dead in his car.

It had taken quite a turn, hadn't it? But it had worked out in the end. Sort of. Not for Judge Baker or Joan, the woman in his trunk, or Florence.

Poor Florence.

She hadn't deserved death. None of them had. Even Judge Baker, the no-good, rotten thief. Stealing the money from actual victims. He'd had to hide his embezzled cash by purchasing the latest, hardest-to-get handbags for his wife under the pretense of loving to spoil her. Along with artwork, real estate, risky investments, college tuitions. Maybe even a few laundromats. All the usual ways criminals legitimized their illegitimate gains. I was certain if I had five minutes in his brownstone, I'd find stacks of green bills hidden inside.

Judge Baker had deserved justice, yes. But to make yourself the executioner, the way McJimsey had, didn't sit right with me. I pitied him, though. I knew what it was like to lose your mother and to never have a father, or at least one who cared about you more than himself. But I'd had money, more money than sense, more money than anything else, and that at least had, as of yet, kept me from a life of revenge.

Daddy and I hadn't spoken since the kerfuffle. Dr. Smith insisted he be taken back to the hospital, and neither of us had argued the point. I hadn't visited and he hadn't called.

But he was all right. He was stubborn that way.

Mac's building was an updated dumbbell tenement, with large windows that gleamed in the morning light, and bright red fire escapes covered in drying laundry. As I walked into the building and up the stairs, children raced past me, an orange ball thrown over my head and back again.

A harried mother ran down behind them, flashing me a small smile. "Need help?"

"Cooper?"

"Almost there. First door on the right. Richard! Richard, don't throw that at your sister's face!"

I chuckled and hurried up the last few stairs. Breathless, I knocked on the door. This was it. I'd done it. I'd made it to Yonkers to visit my boyfriend. And his building wasn't even that bad. There were a lot of people here, yes, but there were a lot of people at the hotel. While there were scuff marks on the walls at about knee height, I could hardly begrudge a building for that. It was old, by the looks of it, and pushed into the modern age so as to shake off any vestige of the word *slum*.

The door opened. Mac was there, disheveled, a fine beard growing on his square jaw. His gray eyes widened. I'd forgotten how much I loved that color.

"Evelyn?"

I threw myself at him. Gracefully, of course. Dignified. Wrapped my arms around his neck and kissed his neck.

Mac pulled me into a hug. "I can't believe you're here."

"I know." I leaned back far enough to smile at him. "I know, I hailed a taxi all on my own and everything."

Presley barked. "Oops." I realized he'd been pressed between us in our greeting. "May we come in?"

Mac stood back far enough to let us walk inside. The apartment was small, but it was clean except for the piece of plywood haphazardly thrown over what had to be a hole in the floor next to the small table with four dining chairs. On the table was a small suitcase, clothes piled up so high inside of it they spilled out onto the table itself.

"Your bathtub is right here by your stove," I said brilliantly.

Mac grinned. "Yeah."

I set Presley's purse on the tiled floor, and he hopped out, eager to sniff around and explore the place. There was a bed pushed against the back window, and another on the floor beside it. A small radio sat on the kitchen counter, next to a phone, the only one in the place, the one I assumed he used for our late-night conversations.

It barely smelled of wet pants at all.

"It's lovely." Not much space for privacy, but then Poppy might be up for spending another night in my suite. "I'm so happy I finally made it! How are you?" I hugged him again and kissed his scruffy cheek. "I have missed you. Was it so awful, in the prison? I couldn't believe it when that judge wouldn't give you bail, not that I could've paid for it right then. I have had the worst time getting the bank to allow me access to my own money, of all the inane things." I smiled. "Are you hungry? Shall I make you something to eat?"

He rubbed his neck with his hand, his bicep flexing under the hem of his white T-shirt. My attention snagged on the muscle, and I had to force myself to blink and look away when he said my name.

"I was, uh, I wasn't expecting you," he said again. "I don't know how . . ." He dropped his arm to his side and stared at the floor. "I was going to write you a letter."

I kept smiling. "A love letter? How very dear. I can't wait to read it, lover. But we have plenty of time." I took his hands and squeezed his fingers. "There's a bodega not far from here. Let's walk over and pick out some food. I'll cook you whatever you want." After all, he'd gotten out of jail. His sister had been living with me since the arrest. He didn't have any food in the kitchen. That was hardly his fault, and I always traveled with enough cash to get by. I'd get him anything he needed.

"No, I . . . uh . . ." He closed his eyes. His chest expanded when he took a deep breath. He squeezed my hands and then let them go. "Evelyn, I've got a boat to catch."

I blinked, my nose wrinkling. "Like a ferry? Where are you going? Can I go? I had thought we'd spend the day together at your apartment, but in for a penny and all that."

"No." Mac licked his lips. He opened his eyes only to stare up at the ceiling. He blinked rapidly before looking at me again, and his eyes were shining. "Evelyn, I'm going home."

I tried, valiantly, to digest this information. I reached for the pendant around my neck and nodded. "I see. I'm sure your grandmother has been worried about you. It'll do you all some good to spend time together. When do you think you'll be back?"

"I'm not coming back."

The chain that held my pendant dug into the back of my neck and bit into my skin. "But Mac, I can't—I can't leave the Pinnacle. I can't *move*. I'd love to visit your family, one day, but I can't leave New York right now."

He shook his head. "I'm not asking you to come with me."

Pinpricks of tears clouded my vision. I clutched Saint Anthony. "You're leaving," I said. "You're leaving me."

He nodded.

Everyone always did. I'd thought—I'd hoped, I'd *prayed*—he was different. I believed it. Maybe there was still a way out of this. I could convince him to stay. I could apologize and cry and convince and bribe. *Anything.* Anything at all.

"I'm sorry that the judge denied your bail, Mac. You didn't deserve those extra nights in jail—or any of them—and I can always sue the police." It was a wild idea that crashed into me, but I grabbed onto it. Anything. I'd do anything. "I can sue them!"

"That's not . . ." He wiped a hand down his face. His lips were pulled low in a deep frown. "Evelyn, that's not why I'm leaving."

I searched my recollection for a sign, for something that might've inspired this, but panic and fear were muddling it all up. "Daddy?" I guessed. "Is this about that fight with Daddy?"

"Yeah. Part of it. It's complicated. I could've written a letter and explained it."

"But Mac! I got Daddy to agree not to cut me off financially as long as I promised not to marry you without his express written permission."

Mac leaned against the kitchen counter, his heels coming close to his bathtub. He opened his mouth, closed it, and opened it again. "How is that any better?"

"It's loads better!" I assured. "I told you, lover. Daddy only cares about the picture. He's halfway to walking me down the aisle now. Don't you see? That is, unless you don't want to marry me?" The thought gripped at my heart and tugged on its strings until it was skipping beats. "Then why are you so worried? We can go steady, and I can have all the money I want. All the money *you* want."

"I don't want you for your money."

"It seems like you don't want me at all."

He closed his eyes again, his head bowed. "Your father doesn't like me, Evelyn. That's never going away. And now, after all this? I was arrested for murder. My name was in the paper. How am I gonna get a job after this? How am I going to work anywhere?"

"You will keep working for me."

"Yeah, right up until your dad throws you out because you're with me. How will I provide for you? You want to live here, Evelyn? With me and my sister and the bathtub in the kitchen?"

I looked around his home. Wallpaper and plaster were peeling in the corners, but the window was large and let in a lot of light. The sink was empty, but there was a gas stove with a tea kettle on the corner. Children were playing outside, and the noise vibrated the walls. "It's humble," I said, "but I could do it."

He laughed. Guffawed. "Please. It would destroy you, Evelyn. And you'd hate me. You'd hate me for being the reason."

"I could never hate you!" I reached for him, my hands on his chest. "Mac," I begged, "I don't care about money. I thought you did."

"You're talking like someone who's never had to worry about money. You don't know what it's like to go to bed hungry. Sometimes for days on end. Sometimes without a bed. I'm not putting you through that, Evelyn. I'm not. I'm sorry." He held my hands in his. His thumb traced my wrist bone. "But one of us has to do the rational thing here. One of us has to make the right call." He pulled my hands away from him and let go.

I watched him, dumbfounded, as he stuffed his clothes in the suitcase and zipped it up.

Mac slung the strap over his shoulder.

"So, that's it then?" I swallowed hard and tried to find words. My tongue felt too big for my mouth. Tears were cold on my face and stung my lips. "I love you, Mac. I love you. More than anyone. Please."

He walked past me. He didn't spare a glance in my direction.

"*Please*. Please don't leave me."

But he opened the door and closed it behind him with a soft click and nothing else.

My nose was running. I pushed my hand against it, trying to hold back the deluge, failing to help myself. I sank to my knees on the floor of his dumbbell tenement, holding my palm over my mouth so I wouldn't wail. Kids were playing nearby. I didn't want them to be afraid.

Presley pawed at my lap. He pushed his way onto my thighs, his little head pushing against my belly. I held him tight, tears soaking his fur.

"I don't know how to get home."

Presley licked my chin.

CHAPTER 50

Daddy picked me up in my Rolls-Royce. The driver, someone I didn't know, opened the back door for me and Presley. My eyes were swollen and puffy. I dug out a pair of sunglasses from Presley's purse and put them on before sliding into the car.

"It's a good thing you called when you did," Daddy said as the door closed. "I'm on my way to the airport, but I have enough time to drop you back off at home."

"Oh. I didn't realize you were leaving so soon."

The corners of his lips twitched. "I've had quite enough excitement in New York. I need to get back to work."

"I understand."

I set Presley in my lap. Daddy reached over and scratched him between the ears. My dog gave him a look of complete disdain and buried his face under my arm.

Daddy hummed. "Thought he'd be used to me by now."

Why he'd think that, when he'd spent the majority of his visit in the hospital, was anyone's guess.

"This is hard for you, now, Evie," he said with a sigh, "but that boy made the right choice. I'm glad one of you had some sense."

There is a version of me, hidden somewhere deep inside, that's brave enough to rip off my sunglasses and scream at him: *I hate you. I hate you. You left me here alone. You left me here alone, and I will never, ever forgive you. My mother was dead, and you left the day after she was buried, and I hate you.*

But I am not that version. It's not like it would matter anyway. It's not like he would hear me.

"Besides," he said, "you have a talent for dealing with . . . hmm . . . mysteries, let's say. Suspects. Things that would be wasted if you were tied down with the help. I never regretted how much I spent on tutors for you over the years. The investment was worth it. You're clever. And that's a good thing for a girl to be, in this day and age."

Wonderful. I'd saved his life and solved three more murders, and he makes it about him. About what *he* did to make that happen.

"I wanted to let you know that I've spoken with the bank. Your mother's money is now completely your own. You can draw on it without my permission whenever you wish. You still have access to the family accounts. But I thought you'd wish to invest it. As I said, you're clever. You'll think of something to do with it. Buy that second car we talked about."

"Thank you," I said.

He nodded. Then he picked up the newspaper and hid behind it. We rode in silence the rest of the way to the hotel until the green roof of the Pinnacle came into view. With a deep breath, I gathered what little empathy I had left inside of me. Because I know, like there's a braver version of me, there's one of him too. Somewhere locked inside that stubborn head of his. A version that would tell me he loves me, that he's proud of me, that my achievement is something to be celebrated as my own. But even so, all I ever needed to do to make him proud was simply exist.

It's for those versions of us that I kiss his cheek. "Have a safe flight, Daddy. I'll see you at Christmas?"

The muscle in his jaw flickered. "That's the plan."

The driver put the car in park, and one of the Pinnacle bellhops opened the door.

"See you at Christmas, then."

CHAPTER 51

It was already half past noon, and I was starving.

"*Honestly*, Poppy, my meeting is starting any minute."

"One second!" She was standing behind an easel, a paint-covered apron over her clothes, a painter's pallet in her hand. She surveyed the scene in front of her with her left eye closed. "Open the curtain a bit more, Evelyn. An inch or two to let the light in."

Presley and Monroe were sleeping on my couch, and she was trying to paint them for her art class. I didn't blame her one bit. My two cuties made for quite the subject.

I stood on tiptoes, pinning a bit more of the curtain out of the way.

"Perfect," Poppy exhaled. "Nobody move."

There was a knock on the door. I jumped, but neither my cat nor my dog reacted to the noise. I snuck around from behind the couch and to the entrance.

Mr. Hodgson was standing outside my door, his hands in his pockets. His navy blue suit with white pinstripe and coordinating blue fedora is my favorite outfit of his. I nodded. "Much better than the khaki," I said.

He said, "What?"

I waved a hand. "You look smarter in darker colors. Come on in." I stood back and welcomed him in. "Oh, quietly, please. And into the kitchen?"

He stepped inside, his eyes going wide when he realized what was happening in my living room. "Yeah. Makes sense."

I'd had sandwiches delivered for the three of us, though Poppy had begged off eating hers until her work was done. "Take your pick," I said, and opened up one of the wall cabinets. I'd stashed his laundered handkerchief here so I wouldn't forget it.

Hodgson said, "Um, Murphy?"

"Yes?" I picked up the borrowed fabric and handed it back to him with a smile.

"Why do you have books in your kitchen?"

I glanced back at the cabinet. It was filled with detective novels, mostly—all the Poirot and Marples ones, in release order, and the Chesterton stories featuring Father Brown. A Catholic who solves crimes? What wasn't there to love? But there were also a few romances in the mix, like *Pride and Prejudice* and *Emma*. A rich girl who thinks she can solve everyone's problems? What wasn't there to love?

"Storage is storage," I said.

"But it's the kitchen."

"Right. But it isn't like I need to cook for a big family. Just for me and sometimes a guest, and only ever once in a while. And there's a lot of storage in here. Seems silly to let it go to waste." I closed the cabinet. "Are you hungry? I'd like the turkey, myself, but there's an egg salad and a ham as well."

I motioned for Hodgson to help himself, and the two of us ate in silence for a minute, standing in my kitchen.

"You only call me over here for lunch?" Hodgson asked. "Because I do have an actual life outside of this hotel."

Ouch. I don't know if he meant to hurt me with that comment, but hurt it did. I took a bite of turkey and cheddar cheese and didn't speak until I'd swallowed it down with a cold glass of ice water. "Did the police offer you your job back?"

"Yeah."

"Did you accept it?"

He shrugged a shoulder. "Not much else I'm qualified for."

I put what remained of my sandwich on my plate, the Pinnacle logo in the center of the porcelain. "I'd like to offer you a job."

"There's been another death in this place already? It's been what, a week since the last one?"

"No. There's been nothing of that sort here. This job would be regarding a much older murder."

Hodgson set his sandwich down too. "Ah."

"Yes." I worried my bottom lip and stared at our half-eaten meals. My stomach felt upside down and inside out. I took a moment to sort out why. What was the name of the emotion I was feeling?

Shame, I thought. Because I'd never been able to find the truth for myself, but I'd also never tried. Too scared of what the answers to my questions might be. And now, here I was. Doing it anyway.

I blew out a harsh breath. "My mother died when I was six years old. I do not know who killed her. I have nothing from that day, no clues, no newspapers. Nothing. I should've done more on my own by now. I should—"

"Murphy," Hodgson interrupted, "you were six. No one expects a six-year-old to solve her mother's murder. No one expects a twenty-year-old to do it either."

"Twenty-one," I corrected. "If you're interested, I can pay you. I've finally been allowed access to money that has been mine since my mother's death. And I'd like to it use to hire you to find out who killed her. Let's say . . . triple what I paid for your recent help. Plus expenses, obviously. I'll have Mr. Sharpe open up a tab for you at the diner and the café."

He cleared his throat. "Triple?"

"We could do hourly if that would be better."

Hodgson drained an entire glass of ice water. "That's . . ." He set the glass down hard. "That'll be fine." He held out his hand.

I smiled and held out my pinkie finger.

With a quiet laugh, Hodgson interlocked our pinkie fingers for a brief moment. "You know," he said when he let go, "it gets easier."

"What does?"

"Being the one left behind."

I tore off a piece of bread from my sandwich. "Not in my experience."

He leaned against the refrigerator, his hands in his pockets. "You asked me about my son, Tim. He was a soldier. His mom and I, we were so proud of him. He'd always been a good kid. Good grades. Never got in trouble. Looked good in that uniform too. He was deployed to Korea." Hodgson sucked his teeth. "And he never came back."

He leaned his head closer to the fridge until his fedora sat uneven on his brow. "Missing in action. That's what they told us. Means we don't get a burial. Means we never stop hoping that it's him knocking on the door. My wife, Stella." He smiled, easy and slow, his mouth wrapping around her name reverently. "Love of my life. Since I was sixteen. But when Tim didn't come back, I don't know. It's my fault. Our marriage. Kinda . . . drifted away. Until one day she left to visit her sister and didn't come home. She still calls me on holidays and on my birthday. Tim's birthday." Hodgson's gaze was on the middle distance, and good thing too, as I quickly wiped tears away with my knuckle.

He stood up straight. "Who knows, Murphy?" Hodgson pulled his hands out of his pockets and straightened his hat. "Maybe you're right. Maybe I just got old. Set in my ways."

My lips trembling, chin dimpling. "You should call her." I knuckled my eyes again. "I bet she'd like that."

I knew if Mac called me right now, I'd answer. I might not like whatever he had to say, but I'd listen.

Hodgson nodded. "I'll leave you to your, uh"—he pointed his chin toward the living room—"your important work. Actually." He patted his jacket before pulling out his notepad and pen. "Your mom? What was her name?"

"Gwen," I said. "Gwendolyn Grace Murphy née Byron. And she was beautiful. And brave. And charming. I miss her every day. It was a few days before Christmas ,and I wanted to go to the toy store and make sure I got Santa the most up-to-date list possible. And it's all my fault. It's my fault because I should've been happy with what I had, and she never would've ended up . . ."

He tucked the notebook away. "Hey. None of this. Okay? We've got a murder to solve. Don't we?"

I sniffled and wiped my face dry with the nearest dish towel, the Pinnacle logo scratching my cheek.

Hodgson held out his hand. I blinked at it, unsure, but put mine in his and let him shake it.

"We'll get to the bottom of this, Murphy. We're gonna find your mom's killer."

ACKNOWLEDGMENTS

I'd like to offer my heartfelt appreciation to everyone who had a hand in the making and publication of this book.

To Faith Black Ross, my editor, for her knowledge and skill in making Evelyn the best she can be.

To Madelyn Burt, my agent, for her support and guidance.

To the team at Crooked Lane for bringing Evelyn to life and getting her into the hands of readers: Rebecca Nelson, Dulce Botello, Madeline Rathle, Thai Fantauzzi Perez, and Matthew Martz.

To Kashmira Sarode, for once again knocking it out of the park with the cover art. To Jerry Todd, for bringing it home with the typography.

To Amara Jasper, for doing such an incredible job narrating the first book that my husband listened to it twice. Back to back, even.

To Jill Pellarin, for copy editing.

To Leira, because I said I would.

To Sisters in Crime, Citrus Crime Writers, and the Mystery Writers of America, because writing can be a lonely endeavor without your people.

To the readers who enjoyed Evelyn enough to pick up her second mystery.

To the authors who read and blurbed and recommended the first one.

To Jordan, for always being a single text away, for all the help when I've hit a wall, and for translating Mr. Sharpe.

To Mom and Dad, for being proud, even when it didn't matter. Because that's when it mattered most.

To Doug, for buying multiple copies and not reading a single one.

To my children, the reason I pursue my dreams in the first place.

To my husband, Paul, for everything.